The Only Good Secretary
The Man with the Cane

Two Novels by
Jean Potts

Introduction by Bill Kelly

Stark House Press • Eureka California

THE ONLY GOOD SECRETARY

When Louise gets to magazine office on Monday morning, she discovers that someone has murdered Fern Villard, the only good secretary that editor High Dudgeon has ever had. High on the list of suspects is Max Sutter. He and Fern were seeing each other and had argued that Friday night before he left the office. But, then, W. J. Robinson had reasons to be jealous of Fern as well because she was angling to replace him as editor of the Questions and Answers Department. And then there's sullen Donna Hirsch, who clearly has a personal interest in Max. Could she have decided to remove the competition? Certainly Archie O'Brien must know more than he's telling—he stayed late in the building that night at a party on another floor. Someone in the office had wanted Fern dead, but who wanted her dead enough to kill her?

THE MAN WITH THE CANE

When Val discovers the body of the murdered man lying on the church steps, the first thing he notices is how much he resembles the man with the cane that his young daughter had described earlier that day. But how could she have known this anonymous man? She's just a little girl, living with her mother and her step father, blocks away from here. It's too much of a coincidence—yet Val is convinced that this man must somehow be known to them. So Val sets out on a bit of detecting, querying the family members about what they know. First, there's Maudie, Val's giddy ex-mother-in-law; his argumentative ex-wife, Doris, and her perfect husband, Monroe. And Doris's affable brother, Clyde, formerly married to the beautiful, sensitive Barbara. Clyde wasn't even in town at the time... or was he? Each one seems to harbor a closely-held secret, but which secret will unlock the motive behind the murder of the man with the cane?

Just Folks in Search of a Solution: Two Mysteries by Jean Potts
By Bill Kelly

Jean Potts (1910-1999) wrote fourteen mysteries between 1954 and 1975, all for one publisher, Scribner. She created no series character and while I am sure her work could be binned in some sub-genre category, like "domestic malice", the twelve novels I have read leave me with the impression that Potts was an author who, if she dreaded anything, dreaded repeating herself. All her books do bear "Pottsian" traits: superb characterizations; sympathy for humanity, noble and fallen alike; intolerance for pretense and pomposity and an ironic, detached humor that never crosses over into satire, although one senses the author was tempted. Unlike many of her contemporaries however, Potts eschewed the idea of authority figures (including that literary authority figure, the "main protagonist") stepping in to solve problems for those who are the victims of a crime. The victim list, in Potts' case, consists of those who are emotionally involved in the crime and its solution.

The two novels offered in this third Stark House Press two-fer of Jean Potts' work, THE ONLY GOOD SECRETARY and THE MAN WITH THE CANE, show Potts allowing those with an emotional stake in the crime to figure out the whole mess for themselves, not as "gifted amateurs", but as people seeking to set their world upright again. Good people and bad people are virtually meaningless terms in Potts' universe, as much of the suspense and tension of her work derives from the fact the villain is usually not very much different from those in pursuit of justice. This world view of humanity also makes it very difficult for the reader to figure out "whodunit": Potts' novels are undeniably fair play, but her mystery making skill provides a number of viable candidates with credible motives who are usually very slow to eliminate themselves as the culprit. Both novels are examples of how

Potts avoided repeating herself: if the characters are different the stories must be different. Potts avoided the well-worn path and the difficult task faced by writers using series characters: providing a story where the reader is not tempted to skip passages because once again the writer is describing how the protagonist reacts to authoritarian figures or any of the other stock baggage that is an invariable and unavoidable component of serial tale telling.

In THE ONLY GOOD SECRETARY (Scribner, 1965) employees of a small New York City based magazine, *The Compleat Angler*, find murdered office secretary Fern Villard on an outside window ledge, impaled by a pair of scissors belonging to a man who is to become the key suspect for the police, graphic artist Max Sutter. The magazine is helmed by Harry Dudgeon, "High" to his employees, a nickname that accurately captures his imperious and mercurial nature. The glue and "tranquilizing agent" holding the firm together is stalwart Louise Clarke, who casts the first doubts on the assumption that Max is the actual killer. Max however, proceeds to do everything to incriminate himself and gets a helping hand from several of his co-workers, who supply an ever-increasing avalanche of damaging testimony. High, despite bemoaning the most important aspect of the crime to him—the death of "the only good secretary" he ever had—possesses a sense of justice and his loyalty to his employees kicks in, and he and Louise are off to find out if Max is actually the real killer. The police are satisfied they have the right man and virtually disappear from the story. As in much of Potts' work, policemen are marginal figures whom the characters have little faith in or reliance upon. In this work, they don't even get proper names. The policeman with the greatest on-stage presence is merely referred to as "the detective". Sorting it all out is left in the hands of two less-than-gifted amateurs whose lack of investigative skill is offset by High's enthusiasm and inspiration, effectively channeled by Louise's common sense.

A recurring element in Potts' work is the emergence of a catalyst character, someone whose words and actions bring them to the forefront of the story and who serves to drive others to make decisions and take actions that prevent them from becoming stalled in their pursuit of the killer by a lack of clues or direct evidence; characters that in a police procedural, for instance, would normally guide the detective(s) toward a resolution of the mystery. Louise and High want to get police suspect Max off the hook, but interviews with their co-workers lead nowhere and they are stymied until they meet the murdered woman's ex-husband George, her roommate Beulah and Beulah's son Michael, a troubled lad who has been shunted from school to school, but now at the school where

George is a teacher—George having done a favor for Beulah and falsified records that enabled Michael to gain admission. Michael, however, despises George, and launches a mock murder investigation that no one takes seriously—until it emerges that Michael may be much more involved in Fern's murder (and other crimes)—none of which either Michael or his mother Beulah want exposed to the light. Michael becomes a catalyst: his words and actions come to dominate the story and influence the behavior of the other characters. Although Michael's behavior and personality remain unchanged and everyone else seeks to discount what he says and does, it becomes increasingly apparent that this "crazy mixed-up kid" is much more deeply involved than anyone at first suspected. The suspicions of Louise and High seesaw between George (as encouraged by Michael) and Michael (as encouraged by George) as suspects. The most complex character in the novel is Michael: harmless imaginative prankster?—malicious and vindictive character assassin?—devoted son?—murderer? Louise and High remain rank amateurs as they careen through clues and red herrings like a binary pin-ball bouncing from bumper to bumper, but they eventually get the job done.

Potts' work often comes very close to standing the genre on its ear by discarding or giving short shrift to such commonplace devices as the aforementioned police involvement in a murder inquiry, or such genre staples as the 'art of detection'; or easily recognized heroes and villains and such shopworn ploys as the McGuffin. Throughout the course of the book, High's briefcase becomes a McGuffin that the reader is led to believe is crucial to the solution of the mystery, but for most of the book this briefcase is given comic treatment: no one realizes it may contain a key document; Louise is supposed to get it repaired, but either mislays it or forgets about it; somebody burgles the office unsuccessfully to steal it; another character removes it from High's apartment, mistaking it for his own, etc.

The murder victims in Potts' mysteries are often less sympathetic than their murderers, although neither group could be described as truly innocent or evil people. They are just folks—as are those who bring the murderer to justice and avenge the victim. Murdered Fern Villard in THE ONLY GOOD SECRETARY is not a particularly likeable person, but she was decent person who was murdered to prevent her from performing a benevolent act that would remove the guilt from another wrongly accused person. We never meet Fern, but gradually her story is unfolded through the memories of other characters. Not a sweetheart and not a creep and but her murder knocks askew the stable universe of those who knew her.

Potts often paints her characters using counterpoint. Pompous W. J. Robinson, barely hanging on to his job at the magazine, assassinates the characters of his co-workers, dishes gossip and will bore you to tears with his self-importance. He is hopelessly self-deluded and equally at sea in office or home. Potts pulls no punches in lampooning characters that deserve it, but she invariably reveals traits or actions taken by the character that prevent them from becoming types; we see that even Robinson has "rare flashes of perception" and he would be a better person if he could get out of his own way. Another character, "High" Dudgeon is a selfish, bullying martinet that Louise nevertheless likes and admires for some of his other qualities. Usually: "Yes, she was fond of him. Especially when he wasn't there". High is a load, but he also loyal to his accused employee Max and is relentless in his pursuit of the real killer. Potts invariably does well by all her characters, but she possesses the talented artist's instinct to focus on the nuances of their personalities, particularly on those whose personalities lie in complex convolution below a surface mask.

It could be argued that Potts' main strength as a writer lies in her character portrayals, but her stories also move along smartly with ever-shifting plot points contributing as much to the suspense and tension as her characterizations. When she does the rare action or chase scene, you may find yourself gearing up into speed reading mode. Potts does take murder seriously, but she of course knew that her writing of murder and murderers cannot be deadly to the reader. In addition to the gently satirical treatment given the most foolish of her characters, we see her inject some wry humor into a brutal assault on Louise and High that results in their taking a vicious pounding. But as soon as Louise regains consciousness, she asks High, "Did he kill you?" And late in the story, to ensure that the other characters maintain the correct perspective on the murder of Fern Villard, High reminds them (for about the fourth time): "Only good secretary I ever had."

THE MAN WITH THE CANE (Scribner, 1957) finds Doris and J. Monroe Ward leading successful professional lives in 1950's New York City, but their marriage faces implosion due to mutual distrust and the murder of a threatening and mysterious figure who may or may not have had contact with their imaginative and precocious six-year-old daughter Annabelle. What does the man with the cane know and what will he do? Val Bryant, divorced from Doris, is Annabelle's natural father and remains close at hand, seeking to cement a relationship with Annabelle while braving Doris' acid tongue and imperious manner. Living with the Wards is Doris' mother Maudie (a "harmless, perfectly sweet nitwit"), who like Doris, has a secret. Maudie is already dealing with a blackmailer (the man with the cane?), while Monroe is receiving mysterious letters from someone who tells Monroe that he is "a friend of yours". Monroe lives in mortal fear of this man who may be peddling dirt on Doris, whom Monroe cannot bear to live with. We also soon meet Barbara, "the girl everyone feels sorry for", the former sister-in-law to Doris, who is fleeing her own stalker. Val falls for Barbara, a seemingly benevolent soul, who although fearful and flighty, possesses a strong inner core.

The man with the cane first appears via a story related by Annabelle to Val. The story is among several fantastically whimsical tales of her recent adventures in California. Val suspects the story is a total fantasy, but repeats it at a family gathering and is shocked by the fearful and evasive reactions he receives from other family members. With love on his mind however, Val forgets all about it until a man fitting Annabelle's description turns up murdered on a porch near Val's Greenwich Village apartment. The murder victim is identified as John Custer, a magazine writer. The skimpy facts available from the police investigation fail to enlighten Val as to what role or roles the man with the cane may have played in Annabelle's life or in the lives of other members of the Ward family. An additional family member, Clyde—son of Maudie, brother of Doris, ex-husband of Barbara—appears, and the mystery deepens. Questions accumulate to the point that Val says, "I never realized before how little I know about the people I know".

Of the dozen Jean Potts' mysteries I have had the pleasure of reading, THE MAN WITH THE CANE contains her most complex plot. Members of the Ward extended family (including exes by marriage) possess more than their share of guilt, fears and insecurities, all brought to a boil by external forces that no one in the family seems capable of dealing with individually, much less as a group already hopelessly fractured by past conflicts. Outwardly, Doris and J. Monroe Ward seem to "have it together", but Doris' mastery of her life proves brittle; her brassiness and need to dominate every situation drive everyone away except her mother Maudie, whom Doris has nicknamed "Mud". Mr. Ward is a powerhouse business exec on the outside, but with a jelly core on the inside, hopelessly indecisive under pressure and an "emotional incompetent". Maudie, a candidate to pay off any psychiatrist's mortgage, copes with past and present terrors by "keeping busy". There is plenty of backstory detail here, but Potts skillfully reveals it gradually through succeeding plot points, rather than through prolonged exposition.

Once again, as in THE ONLY GOOD SECRETARY, we see only those emotionally affected by the murder proving relevant to the mystery's solution. Police appear, but are nameless and faceless; none are given even a token name like "detective" here. As Monroe says, "We none of us want the police". Police inquiries may, of course, reveal dark secrets of the past and unresolved threats in the present that, until resolved, the family members wish to keep to themselves, so this dysfunctional extended family is left to fail or succeed on their own, with success seeming a highly dubious outcome.

Despite the rather complex relationships between a fairly large number of characters, Potts manages to present a clear, relatively straight-line path toward solving the murder, although the principal pursuers never feel anything but lost. Several characters may have motives for wanting to silence the man with the cane, but the motives remain unclear to the reader and hopelessly opaque to the characters. Several people continue to chip away, however, seeking answers to the questions, until their persistence applies enough pressure to make the murderer crack. In this story, it also seems entirely possible that the murderer may be a member of the group in pursuit and only appearing to be seeking the solution. A testimony to Potts' skill is she ensures that all the characters who emerge along the way as possible suspects remain viable candidates until the last possible moment, when the murderer is finally revealed at the climax of another Potts thriller-like chase scene.

Once again, we see Potts initially present a character as a "type" and then gradually add additional personality traits, thereby greatly increasing the reader's interest in both the character and the story. Clyde—son of Maudie, brother of Doris and ex-husband of Barbara (by way of reminder)—initially appears as a hail-fellow-well-met type fully equipped with the expected breezy patter and cornball jokes, but soon emerges as a potentially sinister figure who is smack dab in the center of the mystery and may (or may not) hold the solution to the puzzle. We learn that he was a friend to John Custer, the man with the cane, but it turns out that others knew Custer as well, so …

As in THE ONLY GOOD SECRETARY, we see a group of characters functioning as an ensemble cast to unravel all the knots. Neither they, nor the reader, are led to the solution along a cleverly constructed path by a knowing protagonist. Throw in a few authorities/experts—police, lawyers, doctors for seasoning—but they are not going to be much help. If you would like to ride along with "ordinary" folks who possess an immediate heartfelt personal stake in the solution and watch them figure it all out in spite of themselves, Jean Potts has a mystery for you.

THE ONLY GOOD SECRETARY and THE MAN WITH THE

CANE is the third two-fer edition of Jean Potts work offered by Stark House Press. The first includes Potts' first novel, GO LOVELY ROSE, a book regarded by many as her masterpiece. This edition also includes THE EVIL WISH.

The second two-fer Stark House volume includes HOME IS THE PRISONER and THE LITTLE LIE.

Both books are available in paper and e-book formats.

—April 2021
Mesa, AZ

The Only Good Secretary

by Jean Potts

1

As usual on Monday mornings the office smelled stale; Louise's first act was strictly forbidden by the air conditioning crew and therefore peculiarly pleasurable to her. She opened the window. Only in her little cubicle could this misdemeanor be committed without the aid of two strong men and a crowbar—thus putting her one up on everybody else on the staff of *The Compleat Angler* and making her feel superior as well as lawless. She glanced out briefly at the wide parapet that jutted from the building up here at the twelfth-story level. The cement and asphalt of its outer, chest-high wall glistened with dampness from last night's rain, and the sunken spots of its brick paving still held a few shining puddles. There was a fresh little breeze, quite spring-like.

On her desk Friday's debris waited for her, undisturbed by the cleaning lady, each compost heap intact. Louise faced it philosophically: it often looked worse than it was. Besides, her years as editorial assistant to Mr. Dudgeon had developed in her a psychic, trance-like gift for locating whatever obscure item he might want at any given moment. It was all that saved her from being swept under by the flood of details that were dumped on her daily—the overflow of Mr. Dudgeon's busily rattling brain. He never ran out of ideas. He never got tired. Or expected anybody else to.

It all came of his being a self-made man; he had started out as Harry Dudgeon, messenger boy for Peerless Fishing Supplies, and had worked his way up to High Dudgeon—the nickname was inevitable, especially in view of his temperament—originator and editor of *The Compleat Angler.* The same force that had propelled him onward and upward from his humble beginnings had sparked the growth of *The Compleat Angler* from idea to actuality. What to others was a modestly successful little specialty magazine was to Mr. Dudgeon his miracle child, his dream come true, the tangible product of his boundless enthusiasm and energy. For give him credit, he drove himself as hard as he did his staff, and behind the surface disorganization—not to say chaos—there operated an intelligence as purposeful as it was lively. He was an exasperating man to work for (Louise had resigned several times, had once even walked out) but also rewarding (he had taught her all she knew, which was plenty, about getting out a magazine, and in his helter-skelter way he was her dearest and closest friend). The gaps in his own background gave him a curious innocence: he was constantly discovering people like Thoreau, he could be taken in by almost anyone with a college degree, and at social affairs he was often paralyzed by shyness.

Yes, she was fond of him. Especially when he was not there. As he probably was not at the moment, to judge by the prevailing atmosphere of tranquility.

Was everybody else late too? Not Gladys Popejoy; Louise spotted her memo, prominently displayed against the telephone. It was meticulously dated and timed: 8:54 A.M. "Couldn't get a seat on the subway this morning," it read, "you know what *that* means!" Indeed Louise did: twenty minutes of intensive glove-and-hand-scouring in the ladies' room to exterminate the last lurking subway-strap germ. Gladys knew of a woman who had contracted A Disease that way. "Tell him not to worry, I will make up the time at noon hour." She would, too, every inch the martyr, and they would never hear the end of it. Gladys had worked for Mr. Dudgeon for seventeen years and five months—first as file clerk at Peerless, now as proofreader at *The Compleat Angler*, and she could account for every single minute ...

The buzzer erupted, urgent and incoherent; in moments of stress Mr. Dudgeon was likely to forget the intricate signal system he had once worked out. He also lifted up his voice in a tranquility-shattering "Hey!" Well, Louise had known it was too good to last. She rose and made her way (not too hurriedly, no need to spoil him) down the corridor and past the intervening cubicles to his office.

"Did you yell, sir?" she inquired.

He still had his hat on, and was struggling to get out of his topcoat without releasing his grip on the Horn & Hardart shopping bag full of homework and newspaper clippings he collected over every week end. He was stubby and dishevelled-looking, full of uncoordinated energy.

"There you are, Weesie," he said, and as she relieved him of the shopping bag his face broke into the disarming, happy-child smile that, often as she had seen it, could still take her by surprise. "Have a nice week end? You got a new dress on? Makes you look kind of lanky. Where the hell is everybody? Where's Fern?"

"Thanks. Gladys couldn't get a seat on the subway. Patty just came in. I don't know where Fern is. She's your secretary, not mine. Thank God."

"Well, for Pete's sake, it's twenty past nine! Half the morning gone, and the place is like a tomb. What kind of a half-baked staff am I saddled with? She's never been late before. What's her number? Call her up, tell her to get in here. I can't run this place single-handed, I've got to get the work out." He hurled hat and coat on the couch and started scrabbling through his clippings. "Listen, Weesie, you see that piece in the *Times* yesterday? Terrific. Gave me a terrific idea. Wait till I tell you, see how it strikes you. Here it is—No, that's something else, a new stencilling gadget, order one for Max, will you? Anything good in the mail?"

She brought it in from the annex to his office which served as Fern's headquarters; maybe it would keep him occupied until Fern herself showed up. But he tore through it like a cyclone. "Junk ... That phone bill can't be right, check it, will you? Here, you can take care of this. And this ... I can't understand it, Weesie. How long have I had her, five, six months, and she's always been here, right on the button. Damn it, I thought I'd finally found a secretary I could depend on, and about time, too, after all I've had to put up with. They were lulus, some of them, you've got to admit."

"I admit." Before Fern, they had come and they had gone, in a seemingly endless procession—the willing but stupid, the bright but lazy, the beauties with bad dispositions or over-active social lives, the homely ones who went to pieces at the first little crisis. Naturally, in such a multitude, some of them would have to be lulus. "Maybe she's eloped with Max," Louise offered. "He was driving her out to Long Island for the week end."

"He was? No kidding! How come they didn't tell me?"

"If I remember correctly, you and Max weren't speaking to each other last week. About anything. And it could be that Fern figured it wasn't any of your business."

Brushing aside this fantastic notion, Mr. Dudgeon reached for the phone and dialed Max's extension. "Where's Fern?" he demanded.

The answer clicked back, perfectly audible to Louise. "How should I know?"

"Now look here, Max. I understand you took her out to Long Island, and—"

"I did not," Max crackled, and hung up.

"How about that," said Mr. Dudgeon mildly. "Says he didn't. You heard him, Weesie? And he sounded ..."

"He sounded to me as if he's still mad because you wouldn't advance him his salary. Maybe that's why he wanted it, to spend on Fern this week end."

"Well, why didn't he say so? I thought he was just going to buy some more red paint." He gestured toward the blood-colored abstraction on the wall behind his desk; it had come into his possession as a result of past advances on Max's salary. "I didn't know I was spoiling his week end! Nobody ever tells me anything around here. Who does he think he is, anyway, hanging up on me? I'm supposed to be the boss around here! I ought to fire him, nothing but a smart-alecky ... Yes, and her too, kiting off to Long Island when she ought to be here earning her salary. We've got to get the *work* out! Call her up, tell her to get a move on. Meantime, where's little Whats-her-name, Patty? I can get her started with some of this stuff. Not that she knows up from down."

"All right. Only listen, High—" In the presence of other people, Louise tried to remember to address him as Mr. Dudgeon, but when they were alone she lapsed into the informality of calling him by his nickname. "—go easy on Patty, will you? The poor kid's scared of you."

"She is?" He blinked, in pleased surprise. "Why on earth should she be scared of me? I'm not going to bite her."

"Well. Just don't holler at her."

"I never holler at anybody," said Mr. Dudgeon with conviction. "How many buzzes is she?"

"Three longs, two shorts," said Louise, and waited uneasily while Mr. Dudgeon's blunt forefinger executed this pattern once, twice, three times, with growing impatience. At last, after a timid tap at the door, the sacrificial lamb trotted breathlessly in.

Patty really was rather like a lamb—a plump, mindless little creature in a fuzzy blue sweater and a shamelessly tight skirt that did not quite cover her round knees. Her current hair color was Champagne Blonde, and the front of it was still done up in the pink plastic curlers that were part of her travelling-to-work costume. This fact obviously worried her, along with everything else; Mr. Dudgeon was busy rummaging in his shopping bag and had not noticed. Yet.

"Morning, Patty. Think you can pinch-hit for Fern this morning? She's let me down, and—What in the name of God have you got on your head? Oh. Curlers. Stepping out with your boy friend tonight, I suppose. That right?" But already Patty was beyond the aid of pleasantries; she could only blush and gulp. Mr. Dudgeon tried harder. "Now you mustn't be nervous, Patty. Just relax. That way you won't make so many mistakes. I'm not going to bite you or holler at you or anything, no reason for you to be scared of me. Okay? Now what I want first—Where the hell? Maybe it's on the window sill, a big brown envelope ... No, no, not that one. At the other end. What? What's the matter with the kid, Weesie? What's she doing?"

True enough, Patty was behaving oddly. Having moved obediently to the other end of the window sill, she now stood facing the window, and while her feet in their shiny patent pumps remained rooted in one spot, she seemed at the same time to be vibrating violently. The fuzzy sweater shimmered, the short skirt jounced and quivered. And as she vibrated she squeaked, not loudly but shrilly, the nerve-racking sound of chalk skidding on a blackboard.

"Patty!" hollered Mr. Dudgeon. "Stop that noise!"

She turned on him a face as green as her eye shadow, and as he leapt, tripping over the phone cord, to her side—Louise was already there— she flapped an arm toward the window.

Their heads swivelled to the parapet and froze.

"Fern?" Mr. Dudgeon cleared his throat. "Fern. What's she doing out there?"

"Don't," whispered Louise, for he seemed on the point of rapping on the window and ordering Fern Villard back to her desk where she belonged. "She's not—"

She was propped in the corner against the parapet wall, one elegant leg stretched out in front of her, the other folded under, her bronze chrysanthemum head drooping against that noteworthy bosom of hers. Her hands lay half-flexed, as if loosely cradling the red pool that filled her lap.

After the first stunned moment, Mr. Dudgeon plunged at once into a sweating, swearing battle with the window, which would not open. He was about to heave the paperweight through it when Louise stopped him. "Wait. My office. My window." Brushing past Patty, they broke for the door—just as it opened to admit the stately figure of W. J. Robinson, editor of *The Compleat Angler*'s Question and Answer Department.

"Good morning," declaimed W. J. (as he liked to be called) in ringing tones. He blocked the doorway, imposing, impervious, immovable, beaming at them. "Well, well. Glad to see everybody busy and bright-eyed on this lovely spring morning. May I have your thinking on a couple of ..."

"Out of the way," panted Mr. Dudgeon. "Fern—"

"Miss Villard? Ah, I had a feeling something was missing. Where is your charming amanuensis this morning?"

"She's out on the parapet, you thick-headed bastard, don't you know a crisis when you see one? Get out of the way before I clobber you." With a cross between a butt and a swing—W. J. was taller by half a head— Mr. Dudgeon managed to dislodge him and streaked down the hall. Louise caught up with him as he was clambering through the window of her office. Together they pounded down the parapet to the corner where Fern slumped, forever unaware.

"She can't be, she can't be dead," Mr. Dudgeon stammered, on his knees beside her. He lifted one of her hands, and instantly dropped it. "Get the doctor, Weesie. An ambulance. She can't be—What's that? There, in her chest?"

"Scissors," said Louise, in a voice so matter-of-fact that it appalled her. "She's been stabbed. Don't touch her. Don't touch anything. She is dead, High. She must have been out here all night in the rain. Look how wet her suit is."

"Yes. Wet ... Stabbed ... Come on, help me. We've got to get her inside."

"No, we mustn't." She grabbed his arm and hung on. "Don't touch anything, I said! We have to call the police!"

"I've already called them," said a voice behind them. It was Archie O'Brien, complete with his usual Monday morning hangover, yet somehow authoritative, still capable of dominating a situation. Especially one involving Mr. Dudgeon, whose naive reverence for Archie's background ("A Harvard man," he would say, in a hushed voice) persisted in spite of all the evidence—including Archie's own rueful admission—that however brilliant his beginnings, he was now on the skids. At the moment his eyes, though bloodshot, were keen; his once-handsome face, with its customary hard flush, looked composed and decisive. Apparently he had just come in: he was still wearing his beat-up all-weather coat. "Weesie's right, High, you mustn't touch anything."

"You mean just leave her here? Like this?" Mr. Dudgeon looked up, scandalized. Then, reluctant but obedient, he rose from his knees. "It seems so—I don't know—doesn't seem right."

"Makes no difference to her, poor girl," said Archie. "There's nothing anybody can do for her. Except try to find out who murdered her."

The very quietness of his voice made the word more shocking. Through the little group outside Louise's window—for by this time they were all huddled there—there ran a collective gasp, like a gust of desolate wind. And somebody gave a shriek.

"Murdered," whispered Mr. Dudgeon. The sweat broke out on his forehead.

"I don't think she was the suicide type," said Archie. "Do you?"

"Well, but why would anybody want to—Damn it, the only good secretary I ever had, and somebody has to murder her! Where's the police? Why don't they get here and arrest somebody?"

"One of us, you mean?" Archie turned a speculative eye on the staff of *The Compleat Angler*, who shrank even closer together, in a tight, silent knot.

"Certainly not!" yelled Mr. Dudgeon. "One of my team a murderer? You're out of your mind to suggest such a thing!"

"Sorry, I thought you were suggesting it." Into Archie's face came the expression he often turned on his employer, a mixture of slyness, curiosity, and amusement, as if he were drawing out a child.

Mr. Dudgeon, who seldom disappointed him, was cut off in mid-explosion this time by the arrival of the police. Hard on the heels of the first two ordinary cops came what seemed to Louise a swarm of officials, some in uniform, some not, snapping out orders and questions and cryptic exchanges with each other. She found herself, along with the rest of *The Compleat Angler* staff, being herded back through the window and into Mr. Dudgeon's office, where they were to be sorted out for questioning by the detectives. Her state of mind was mostly a confused blur, with now and then some trifling impression leaping into abnormal sharpness. Donna Hirsch, for instance—Donna was Max's assistant in the art department—slouching down the hall ahead of her, with her mane of straight brown hair straggling almost to her waist and her black stockings and olive green suede flats and her pallid, sullen profile. Patty fumbling with her pink curlers, while the tears ran down her plump cheeks. Gladys Popejoy scuttling along, chittering like a distracted squirrel. Archie, trembly-handed as always, lighting one cigarette from another. W. J. Robinson tirelessly booming out inanities, and Mr. Dudgeon snarling at him to shut up. And—

But one of them was missing. Had Max Sutter actually been out there on the parapet with the others? Or had she only taken his presence for granted? Certainly he had been in the office earlier; she had heard his voice crackling over the telephone at Mr. Dudgeon. And just as certainly he was missing now. She took another unobtrusive, nose-counting check of the room, realizing as she did so that several other people were doing the same thing.

Mr. Dudgeon, naturally, was the one who blurted it out. "Where's Max?"

A hush descended, oppressive and ominous as fog. Then one of the officials stepped forward with the inevitable "Max Who?"—and while everybody knew the answer to that one, it seemed that nobody had so much as a shred of definite information about where Max might have gone. Or when. Or why.

2

"Friday night?" repeated W. J. Robinson. As if to show the detective how much at ease he felt, he leaned back in his chair and clasped his hands behind his white-haired, long-jawed head. As usual, he spoke loudly and deliberately; his voice had an amplified quality, like that of a man addressing a multitude through a microphone. "Yes, if I remember correctly, I worked late Friday night. It must have been at least seven thirty before I left the office. Yes. Because the cleaning women had already been here, and I had to sign out in the lobby downstairs —that's not required before seven thirty. And I was late for a dinner appointment my wife had made with some friends. She was quite annoyed. But these things happen, you know. These crises have a way of arising at the most inconvenient times. Mr. Dudgeon insisted on an entire rewrite—Well, no matter. I was here till seven thirty Friday night."

"Did anyone else work late?"

"Yes indeed. The rewrite involved new art work, so that meant Max Sutter had to stay. Mr. Dudgeon himself was here until seven. And Miss Villard. Though in her case I don't think it was so much a question of work. There had been some arrangement between her and Max to drive out to the Island, or so I gathered from what I overheard, and—"

"From what you overheard?"

"Not intentionally, let me assure you. Whatever else I may be, I am not an eavesdropper. But Max's office, as you may or may not know, adjoins mine, and the soundproofing of these walls leaves something to be desired. I had no choice in the matter, especially since there was no attempt on their part to keep their voices down. They were—Well, not to put too fine a point on it, they seemed to be engaged in a fairly heated conversation."

"A quarrel?"

W. J. swivelled gently in his chair, considering. "Difficult to say. One man's quarrel may be another man's ordinary discussion, you know. It depends on temperament. I'm a peaceable type myself ... Even so, I'm inclined to think quarrel might not be too strong a word. Certainly a disagreement. Apparently Miss Villard was disappointed with the week end plans and had decided to cancel the whole arrangement. Over Max's violent objections. He was still bent on going, even though he had had to abandon his original idea of renting a car. Reference was made to other adjustments, too, in the interests of economy."

"He was short of money, then?"

"Right. Mr. Dudgeon refused to give him another advance on his salary, and what irritated Fern—Miss Villard—particularly was that Max had neglected to inform her of this until the last minute. She accused him of misleading her, and he accused her of having no interest in him beyond a purely mercenary one. Or words to that effect. I can't give you a verbatim report, I'm afraid, but that was the general trend. As I say, fairly heated. At one point I even thought of rapping on the wall and asking them to quiet down—I was having difficulty concentrating— but I didn't like to embarrass them."

"What about Mr. Dudgeon? Did he hear this argument too?"

"Oh, no. They waited till after he was gone. I doubt if he knew anything about their projected trip, or he would have given Max the advance. He's not an ungenerous man," W. J. explained meticulously. "In fact, he'll move heaven and earth to help anybody on his staff who goes to him with a problem. Personal, financial, any kind of a problem. But I doubt if Max told him the details. Probably just asked for the advance, without bothering to explain why he needed it. Of course Mr. Dudgeon knew Max was—interested in Miss Villard. We all knew, in a general way. Bound to, in an office as small as this."

"How seriously was he interested?"

"He didn't confide in me," said W. J. primly. "But judging from the tenor of his conversation Friday evening, I would say quite seriously. Certainly much more so than Miss Villard. That was his principal complaint, that she did not reciprocate his feeling for her. He repeated several times that she was—uh—driving him out of his mind, that she knew it, and that she enjoyed making him suffer. He reproached her bitterly for encouraging him when she had no intention of making the relationship as permanent or as exclusive as he wished it to be."

"Did you hear anything in the nature of a threat?"

"A threat," mused W. J. He removed his hands from behind his head and, leaning his elbows on the chair arms, began bouncing one set of fingertips against the other, gently, pensively. "No, not an actual threat. She needn't think she could drop him like this and get away with it, there was a limit to how much he would take, even from her, and so forth and so on. Just the usual vague, blustering statements anyone might make under the circumstances. I do recall that at one point she told him to let go of her, take his hands off her, something like that."

"You didn't feel called upon to go to Miss Villard's assistance?"

"Definitely not. The idea never even crossed my mind. I wasn't going to intrude on what sounded to me like a routine lovers' quarrel. Besides which, Miss Villard was an extremely self-reliant young woman. I couldn't imagine her being in the position of needing anybody to defend her."

"And yet, Mr. Robinson, she was killed."

"Granted. But I can assure you that when I left here at seven thirty Friday evening she was very much alive and, as far as I could judge, in no danger whatever. Naturally I have no way of knowing what happened after I left."

"Naturally not. Were you and Max Sutter on friendly terms?"

"I wouldn't say friendly. Or unfriendly either, when it comes to that. We have very little in common. One point I would like to emphasize." His voice grew even more declamatory; he fixed his chilly blue eyes on the detective. "If Max were a close friend of mine—even if he were my own son—I would still feel duty-bound to report as accurately as possible the conversation I overheard between him and Miss Villard. I would make the same effort at accuracy if we happened to be deadly enemies. It's a simple matter of justice. Personal considerations have nothing to do with it."

"Yes. Exactly. Now about this morning. Did you see Mr. Sutter or talk to him here in the office this morning?"

"No. But I heard him come in shortly after I got here, about a quarter past nine. He always slams his office door. A couple of minutes later his phone rang, and I heard him answer it. There were several matters I wanted to take up with Mr. Dudgeon, so about nine thirty I went into his office. Louise Clarke was there, and Patty. I didn't realize it at first, but they had just discovered Miss Villard on the parapet. There was a certain amount of confusion, but to the best of my recollection I didn't see Max after that. Not that I was looking for him, you understand. I didn't notice he was missing until the police had arrived and we were all assembled in Mr. Dudgeon's office. May I ask if he has been located?"

"We'll find him," said the detective. "One other question, Mr. Robinson. What was your impression of Miss Villard as a person?"

"She was an excellent secretary." W. J.'s eyes were chillier than ever. "Very efficient. Far superior to any of her predecessors. Everyone agreed that Mr. Dudgeon was lucky to have found a satisfactory secretary at last. As for my personal impression of her, all I can say is that she struck me as an attractive, intelligent young woman who handled a difficult job extremely well. My contacts with her were limited to the ordinary traffic that goes on in any office between the executive and the secretarial level. Naturally I can tell you nothing about her private life."

"Naturally. Thank you, Mr. Robinson. You've been very cooperative."

"She was super," quavered Patty Bailey. "I don't care what Mr. Robinson or anybody else says. He was just scared she might take over his job. He makes such a big production of his Questions and Answers bit, but she could have done it with both hands tied behind her. All she needed was a chance to show Mr. Dudgeon, to prove she could do it better and quicker than that old W. J. Everybody knows what a stuffed shirt he is, always making speeches. Why, I can even keep up with him when he dictates!"

"But Mr. Dudgeon wouldn't be very likely to give her a chance at an editorial job, would he? He wouldn't want to lose her as a secretary."

"He likes to promote people," said Patty. "Look at how he kept after me to go to night school so he could promote me from the mail room to stenography. We used to have a ball, back there in the mail room ... Of course like he said, where was it going to get me, you have to think ahead, and Mr. O'Brien's just super to work for, he don't expect you to be perfect. It's Mr. Dudgeon that gets me so nervous, hollering at me. Every time the buzzer goes and it's for me I jump a foot. Like this morning, and then when I looked out—" Once more overcome, she produced another wad of kleenex and swabbed at the fresh flood of tears. "Oh, I can't believe it! Who would do such a thing!"

"Everybody liked her, then? Aside from Mr. Robinson?"

"Oh, but he wouldn't *kill* her! I never said that, I didn't mean it that way!"

"Of course you didn't. Neither did I. But it's my job to check into everything that might give us a lead on who did kill Miss Villard. I'm sure I can count on your help, especially since you were such a good friend of hers."

"I don't know about good friend exactly. You know? We didn't go to lunch together or anything like that. After all, the boss's secretary, and not only that, but I wasn't in her class any other way, either. You know what I mean. She was like a movie star or something. A glamour girl. Not only that, but brains. She graduated from college, and she'd been to Europe and Paris and all those countries. I've never been any farther than New Jersey. And then she'd been married and divorced and everything. Older than me. So it was more—well, like she'd ask me to help out when she got behind with the filing, or sometimes I'd do errands for her. Like that. She gave me a charm for my bracelet for Christmas. A little typewriter. Adorable. And then clothes. This skirt I'm wearing, it used to be hers."

"She gave it to you?"

"Well. Sold it to me. For practically nothing, and it came from Bonwit's, it's still got the label. She only wore it a few times."

"I see. Now then, to get back to the rest of the staff. Max Sutter, for instance—"

"Oh, he was madly in love with her. Always making scenes. Like if she even went out for a drink with Mr. O'Brien, he'd blow his top. I mean, why shouldn't she? Just because she dated Max, he don't need to think he owns her. She told him so once. I heard her."

"Did she often go out for a drink with Mr. O'Brien?"

"I don't know about often. He was always asking her. It depended on if she had another date or not. In a way I think she liked Mr. O'Brien better than Max. He's more, you know, smoother. Max is kind of a kook. He paints these kooky pictures. Mr. O'Brien's very cultured. He's a Harvard man. Of course she wasn't serious about him, either."

"No? Why not?"

"Well, for one thing, he's so old. In his forties. And then—I don't know, he's not serious himself. I mean, *about* himself. You know? When he comes in in the morning, he'll say something like 'Enter the Great Has-Been.' Or 'Patty-Pet'—that's what he calls me—'Patty Pet, is there an aspirin in the house? I seem to have more than the usual number of heads this morning.' He's a riot."

"How about the other women on the staff? Did they like Miss Villard?"

"Miss Popejoy didn't. But then she's kind of cranky. Not to me. She's real nice to me. But she thought Fern was stuck-up, and then they had this thing about the thermostat. Miss Popejoy's always turning it up to about ninety-five, and then Fern turns it down, I mean she used to—" Patty swabbed again, and went on bravely. "Then Louise—Mrs. Clarke—would get Miss Popejoy smoothed down till the next time. She's very good at smoothing people down. She's got a wonderful disposition, otherwise she'd go out of her mind, what with Mr. Dudgeon and all. She said Fern was a lifesaver, after all those other secretaries Mr. Dudgeon had, a good one at last. Not that they were chummy exactly ... That's everybody. Oh. Donna Hirsch. Do I know who she likes or doesn't like? She never speaks to me or anybody else if she can help it. Not even Good morning, Good night, Have a nice week end. Talk about anti-social!"

"Let's see, Donna Hirsch is in the art department, isn't she? Mr. Sutter's assistant. Did you see him this morning?"

"Not to talk to or anything. I was in a rush, see, because when Mr. Dudgeon buzzed I was in the Ladies—I was fixing my hair, and when he buzzes you're supposed to drop everything, so I came tearing down the hall, and Max was just getting off the elevator. After that I don't know if he was there or not, I don't even know what I was doing myself. Do you think Max—" Patty swallowed. "It looks so funny, him disappearing like that. Don't it?"

"We're checking," said the detective smoothly. "Thank you, Miss Bailey. I think that's about it for now."

"I wouldn't know." Donna Hirsch was getting a lot of good hard wear out of those three words. Delivered in a tone of flat indifference that clearly conveyed her contempt for question and questioner, they served as her response to any inquiry not involving such vital statistics as her name, address, and whereabouts on Friday evening. Which turned out to be Queens; she had gone to her parents' home for dinner and had stayed overnight. Her own apartment—one room; she lived alone—was downtown, in one of the less desirable sections of the Village.

"You wouldn't know whether or not Max Sutter was in the office this morning? Come now, Miss Hirsch. You work in the same room. You must have seen him if, as you say, you got here a little after nine. Miss

Bailey saw him get off the elevator, and Mr. Dudgeon talked to him on the phone."

Donna shrugged. "So I must have seen him. What of it?"

"I'm trying to find out when he left the office, where he went, and why. That's what of it. Did you see him go?"

"No."

"Was he still here when you heard about Miss Villard?"

"I wouldn't know."

"How did you hear it? Who told you?"

"Nobody in particular. I heard this racket in the corridor, and then I saw them outside on the parapet, going past the window. Dudgeon and Louise Clarke."

"What about Max Sutter? Did he hear the racket and look out the window too?"

"I wouldn't know."

There was a brief silence; possibly the detective was praying for patience and fortitude. "I suppose you wouldn't know anything about the scissors Miss Villard was stabbed with, either, would you?"

Donna inspected her hands; they were well-shaped but grimy, and the nails were bitten to the quick. Her face—pasty-skinned, with straight black brows and sullen, colorless mouth—remained unchanged, as impassive as ever. "No," she said.

"They're Max Sutter's. There's an adhesive tape label on them, printed with his name."

"So? Other people were always borrowing them and forgetting to return them. That's why he put the label on." She tossed her head, perhaps in defiance, perhaps only to shake her hair out of her eyes. "Villard borrowed them, just last Friday."

"Miss Villard? Did she return them?"

"If she did it would be the first time."

"How late did you stay in the office Friday night?"

She hesitated, almost imperceptibly. "Till about five thirty."

"So Mr. Sutter and Miss Villard were still here when you left. Did you know about the trip they were planning for this week end?"

"Why should I?"

"I thought Mr. Sutter might have mentioned it to you. You're on friendly terms with him, aren't you?"

Donna hooked her hair back of her ears and slid farther down in her chair. "Not particularly."

"But you've known him for some time, haven't you? I understand he recommended you for your job here."

"So? Just because he gets me a lousy job I'm supposed to know all his personal business? I couldn't care less."

"You never see him outside of the office?"

"Why should I?"

The detective sighed. "I'm asking the questions, Miss Hirsch. Incidentally, if you don't give me the answers I'll get them from someone else. So there's really not much point in stalling, is there?"

After a moment of glowering silence Donna said, "All right, if it makes you happy. Once in a while we go to an art show together. Or if we happen to run into each other—we live in the same neighborhood—we'll have a cup of coffee or he'll ask me to his place to show me what he's working on. It's your business if you want to get off on the romantic pitch, but you're wasting your time. I'm not his type."

"And was Miss Villard?"

"I wouldn't know." Then, unexpectedly and briefly, Donna's face flickered into life—a momentary gleam like a fierce little flame leaping up from supposedly dead coals. "If you ask me, she was anybody's type that could pick up the tab."

"Then why would she be interested in Mr. Sutter? As I understand it, he wasn't exactly well heeled."

"She probably thought he was a mad genius or something."

"Do you think he's a genius?"

"No. I don't think he's mad, either. If you're through asking questions—"

"One more, please. Did you by any chance see Mr. Sutter over the week end?"

Her face was once more heavy and impassive. And again she hesitated. "Okay. Saturday. He called me, and I went over to his place for a while Saturday night."

"What time was this? How long did you stay?"

"I wouldn't know. Ten thirty or so. I wasn't watching the time."

"Did he mention Miss Villard?"

"I don't remember."

"He just wanted to show you what he was working on?"

For some reason this seemed to amuse Donna. She laughed abruptly. "Yeah. He just wanted to show me what he was working on."

"What was his state of mind when you saw him?"

"I wouldn't know."

"Well, did he seem in good spirits? Or nervous? Upset?"

"I wouldn't know."

The detective closed his eyes and gritted his teeth. "You didn't get any inkling of what kind of a humor he was in?"

"Sorry. I guess I'm not very observant. Are you through asking me questions?"

"I wouldn't know," said the detective bitterly. He pushed the buzzer on Mr. Dudgeon's desk twice. "I'll get back to you later. You can wait outside. Maybe next time around you'll change the record."

"I felt sorry for her," said Archie O'Brien. His voice was light and pleasant, a voice well suited to conviviality and impromptu harmonizing. "Strange, isn't it, considering what a good-looking girl Fern was. Bright, too. The kind that makes it to the top and stays there. She certainly didn't want pity, or even sympathy, from anybody. Very self-sufficient. It was just a feeling I had about her—that she was never going to be contented, no matter how much money she made, or how important a job she landed, or how many guys she had jumping through the hoop. She'd always find something else to push for. More money. A different kind of success. Some other guy. She didn't know how to be happy."

"You knew her very well, then. A close friend of hers."

"Not really close. She never took down her hair with me. In any sense of the word. More's the pity. So this is sheer guesswork on my part. I could be clear off the beam. I often am, especially when it comes to women."

"You're a married man, Mr. O'Brien?"

"I am." Archie licked his lips. "I have a charming wife who understands me all too well, and two charming teen-aged daughters who expect me to put them through college, ha ha, and a charming house in Connecticut that I can't meet the payments on. Who could ask for anything more?"

"Was your wife a friend of Miss Villard's too?"

"As far as I know they never met, but if they had I doubt very much that they would have been friends. Now don't get off on the triangle tangent. Please. Not that I wasn't perfectly willing, you understand. But Fern wasn't about to waste her time and talents on the likes of me. As my wife would have been the first to appreciate. And point out. She's not only charming, she's sensible."

"Yet you and Miss Villard did see something of each other outside the office. Or so I understand."

"Sure. She'd go out for a couple of drinks with me after work whenever she didn't have a better offer. That was as far as it went. All very casual and innocent as hell. Thanks to Fern. She was an expert at keeping you in your place."

"These better offers you mentioned. Max Sutter, for instance?"

"Yes and no. This is guesswork again—as I say, she didn't discuss her personal affairs with me—but I think she'd about had it with Max. Once the novelty wore off, he was more of a nuisance than anything else. For one thing, he couldn't afford her. He doesn't even make as much as I do, poor devil. And then he made the mistake of letting her see how crazy he was about her. The only way to win with a girl like Fern is to keep her guessing. As soon as she knows she's got you she doesn't want you anymore." Archie's ravaged face crinkled into a rueful smile. "I'm afraid her principal purpose in going out with me was to make Max suffer. As he certainly did. There's nothing more painful than jealousy."

"You're not making her sound like a very sympathetic person."

"Oh, I don't know. There's a streak of the bully in all of us. It's just a matter of circumstance. Opportunity. Max is young. He'll get over it—unless, of course, he turns out to be the one who did her in. I keep forgetting how it must look to you, his skipping out this morning."

"How does it look to you?"

"Not good. But it's about what I'd expect of Max. He has a talent for making the worst of whatever happens to him. Can't seem to resist doing himself in the eye. After all, there must be other suspects. Other men in Fern's life. Some of them might have been as jealous as Max."

"Did she ever mention anybody else to you?"

"I told you before. We weren't on heart-to-heart terms. But it stands to reason ... She shared an apartment with a woman named Beulah Hannaford. She can probably fill you in."

"Yes. Probably. You've met Mrs. Hannaford?"

"Not really met her. I saw her one night when she stopped in at the bar to pick Fern up. They were going shopping for a rug or something. She didn't come all the way in, just looked in at the door. To tell you the truth, I wouldn't recognize her if she walked in the door right now. I'd had one or two that night, as I recall it, and wasn't my usual bright-eyed self." He licked his lips again, perhaps in reminiscence, perhaps in anticipation.

"I see. Now about Friday night, Mr. O'Brien. What time did you leave the office?"

"Out of here on the stroke of five. I always am. Thanks to High's—Mr. Dudgeon's—conviction that it would be sacrilege to ask a Harvard man to work overtime. He'll wise up one of these days. Meanwhile I'm the white-haired boy, and making the most of it while it lasts. Let poor old Robinson sweat it out. It's what he deserves for going to Columbia. And for letting High know he's hungry for a job ... Another case of bullying. Even a softie like High will do it, given the opportunity. When it comes to that, Max got in his licks, too. On Donna."

"Donna Hirsch?"

"The same. As dismal a specimen as I ever saw, but nevertheless female and susceptible to the opposite sex. Namely Max. So there it is, neat as an algebra equation. Fern gives him the treatment, he passes it on to Donna. Nothing's ever wasted, especially kicks in the teeth." He shrugged, and shakily lit a fresh cigarette. "So much for O'Brien's philosophy of life. Where were we?"

"Friday night. You left the office at five. Where did you go? Home?"

"I hardly think so. Friday, Friday. Let me see. Oh yes, the Publix party. I popped in for old time's sake—used to work there myself, when I was on the way up instead of down. Some of the old crowd are still around. I had every intention of catching the 5:47 home, or at least the 6:21. But what with one thing and another … I did make the last train. Only I rode past my station, so my wife had to come and get me. She was not amused. It lent a certain quality of constraint to the week end." He closed his eyes briefly, then opened them very wide. Bloodshot, faded-blue eyes that still retained a flash of wit and youthful charm. "But I'm digressing again. The only point about the Publix party of any interest to you is that it took place here in this building."

"Oh?"

"Right on this floor, in fact. The Publix suite is at the other end of the hall, at the rear of the building. Which puts me more or less on the scene—assuming, of course, that Fern was killed Friday night. I can narrow it down even more. Friday night between nine and nine thirty. That's when the Publix liquor gave out and we passed on to more fertile fields. I know because at that stage I was still time-conscious. I remember thinking when we got down to the street that with luck I could make the 9:36. Could and should. But didn't. And from there on in dismissed the whole damn business from my mind. Clocks. Schedules. Trains. Who needs them?"

"So you were on the scene, as you say, from five to—well, make it nine fifteen. In the Publix suite. You didn't by any chance come back here to your own office for any reason?"

"Not me. Where the bourbon flows, there O'Brien takes his stand. You can check with the Publix crowd. They weren't as stoned as I was. Nobody ever is. I can give you their names."

"If you will, please." He wrote them down carefully. "I understand it was you who called the police this morning, Mr. O'Brien?"

"That's right. As soon as I got in, I heard this hullabaloo out on the parapet, and when I looked out the window and saw High and Louise and—and Fern. I figured somebody'd better call the cops before High bollixed everything up beyond repair. Without meaning to, of course. Just because he's a busybody."

"You knew Miss Villard had been murdered?"

"I knew she was dead. And not from a heart attack. I've seen a couple of corpses in my time, back in my reporting days. Certainly I knew it was a case for the police. So I called them." He grinned. "Want to make something of it?"

The detective grinned back. "Not at the moment. If you think of anything else, anything Miss Villard might have said, any names she might have mentioned—"

"Sure thing. I'll come running." Archie stood up with alacrity and made for the door. Brisk confidence, that was the ticket. Through Fern's office, where the others were waiting their turn in various stages of jitters, past the officers charged with keeping an eye on them, down the hall to his own little cubicle. Sanctuary. He took a good substantial pull from the bottle in the bottom drawer of his desk, shuddered, and leaned back cautiously. Bourbon, bourbon, burning bright.

"I needed that," Archie told himself. "Oh brother. I really needed that."

With Donna Hirsch, the problem had been one of coaxing forth even a tiny trickle of information; Gladys Popejoy, on the other hand, was like a fire hydrant left wide open, and no tools to turn it off with. She perched on the edge of her chair, her little chipmunk face quivering with excitement, round bead eyes trained on her audience, hairnet slightly askew. One hand made little poking gestures; the other marched up and down the front of her gray cardigan sweater, ceaselessly buttoning and unbuttoning. While Gladys talked. And talked. And talked.

Far be it from her to speak ill of the dead—*de mortuis nil nisi bonum*, that was the Latin, or was it bonus, no *bonum*, imagine remembering after all these years, but Gladys had always been like that, once she got something fixed in her mind it was there to stay. *De mortuis nil nisi bonum*. Fern Villard was a paragon of a secretary, no question about that, so maybe she was entitled to lord it over everybody else in the office, Gladys didn't mind taking orders, though it did seem as if seniority ought to count for something. Seventeen years and five months she'd put in with Mr. Dudgeon, he was in Sales when she started, and *The Compleat Angler* was just a little house organ for Peerless Fishing Supplies, he'd built it up into a real magazine with subscriptions and advertisements and Gladys had stuck it out through thick and thin. It wasn't always so easy, either, but she had never before been subjected to such working conditions, practically sub-zero temperatures, why should everybody else have to freeze just because one person ... And another thing, she didn't appreciate other people using her phone whenever they happened to feel like it, surest way in the world of spreading germs, and always just after she got through spraying the mouthpiece, all to do over again, no consideration whatsoever.

Furthermore, it was her own business if she chose to wash her apple with soap and water before she ate it, nothing funny about it, it was a well-known scientific fact that Diseases were spread that way. All very well for Mr. Dudgeon to say don't bother him with petty details, he wasn't being made fun of. And anyway, he was like all men, taken in by all those curves and expensive clothes, put every cent she made on her back. It was different with a young fellow like Max Sutter—though those pictures of his, disgusting, like raw liver, if that was art, well, excuse Gladys—but it did seem as if a man of Mr. Dudgeon's age would show a little judgment.

Not to mention Mr. O'Brien, with his background, and married too, far be it from Gladys to tell tales, but she was practically certain he kept a bottle in his desk, she couldn't help wondering if there wasn't more between him and Fern Villard than met the eye. Maybe Max had a right to be jealous, oh, she'd heard him and Fern, going at it hammer and tongs ... No, not Friday, for once she'd gotten out on time on Friday, before Mr. Dudgeon kicked up all the ruckus. Other times. More than once.

One thing about Mr. Robinson, he saw through Fern, well, of course she was after his job, never missed a chance to give him a dig behind his back, and don't think it wasn't working, if she told Mr. Dudgeon black was white he'd believe her ... She must have led her husband a merry chase. While she had him. Divorced several months ago, so Gladys understood—not from what Fern herself had said, but from Mrs. Hannaford, the woman she shared an apartment with. Such a nice-appearing woman, she'd stopped in one noon hour and Gladys had chatted with her while Fern was taking dictation. Worked for an insurance company. A widow. Lost her husband in a car accident not two years after they'd been married, so sad, it couldn't have been easy for her, having to raise her son alone, he was in prep school now, that was probably why she'd doubled up with Fern, to keep expenses down, the tuition those schools charged was a caution, and for what, youngsters nowadays weren't even taught the rudiments of grammar, they didn't even know how to spell. Look at Patty Bailey here in the office, poor child couldn't parse a sentence if her life depended on it, and what her mother could be thinking of, letting her dye her hair, it would all fall out by the time she was thirty ... At least she washed it. More than could be said for Donna Hirsch, whatever that girl spent her salary on it wasn't soap, you couldn't pay Gladys to touch her with a ten-foot pole, why, she must be crawling with germs ...

Surreptitiously, the detective buzzed for help. Gladys was still talking when they eased her out the door.

"He didn't do it," High Dudgeon insisted. "I don't care if he did fight with her Friday night and skip out of here this morning. I know damn well Max didn't kill her. A murderer on my staff? You must be out of your mind!"

"Now look, Mr. Dudgeon. It seems safe to assume that she never left here Friday night, that she was killed some time Friday evening. Doesn't that suggest to you that a member of your staff might have had something to do with her death? It does to me. She and Max Sutter had just had a row. They were still at it when Mr. Robinson finished work and left them here together. Doesn't that—"

"It could have been somebody off the street. A mugger. Happens all the time, all over town. They're not all that careful, the guys downstairs, about who gets past them."

"Miss Villard's purse was right out on her desk. Fifty-odd dollars in it. She was wearing a diamond ring, and a string of real pearls."

"Somebody scared him off, then. He beat it without stealing anything."

"Taking time to shut and lock the window of Mrs. Clarke's office behind him?"

There was a brief, tense silence. "Well, but—Just because they had a dust-up. Max fights with everybody. Including me. Blew his top only the other day because I wouldn't give him another advance on his salary. Artistic temperament. He's an artist, you know. That's one of his, on the wall there. Don't ask me what it's supposed to be. Weesie calls it The Bucket of Bl—" He choked it off, belatedly.

"Yes," said the detective. "She's got a point there. How do you explain Mr. Sutter's disappearance this morning?"

"Very simple. He was nuts about her, don't forget. So when he saw her out there on the parapet he simply blew up, lost his head, went to pieces. The shock. My God, it shook me up, and I wasn't in love with her. He's probably wandering around somewhere in a dazed condition. Distracted by grief." Mr. Dudgeon inspected the detective's face uneasily. "If you think I'm going to stand by and see that boy railroaded—"

"Nobody's railroading him. Naturally we want to talk to him. As one of the last people to see her alive, he may be able to give us a lead on who killed her and why. Believe me, Mr. Dudgeon, that's all we're trying to do, find out who killed her. But you must see that we can't clear Max Sutter until we've talked to him."

"All right. But he's not the only one ... Hey!" Mr. Dudgeon sat bolt upright, suddenly galvanized. "How about those anonymous phone calls she was getting from her ex-husband? There's your lead for you!

Why hasn't he been hauled in for questioning? Call him up—what the hell's his name?—get him over here, find out what he was doing Friday night. He's got as much to explain as Max. If you ask me, more. A guy that makes anonymous phone calls is capable of anything."

"Phone calls? Her ex-husband's name, by the way, is George Villard. If they were anonymous, how do you know he made them?"

"Who else would do a thing like that? Call her up and tell her to watch her step? Words to that effect. Yeah. George Villard. He's the guy. He called her once here at the office—that's how she happened to tell me about it—and of course what she should have done was get the police on it. I told her so. But she wouldn't do it. Wouldn't let me do it, either. Still protecting him. That's a woman for you, every time."

"Let me get this straight. Did Miss Villard herself connect the calls with her ex-husband? Or was it your idea?"

"Mine," said Mr. Dudgeon after a moment. "She said it didn't sound like him, but naturally he'd disguise his voice. Stands to reason. It had happened before, two or three times, but at home, so she just thought it was one of those nuts. When he called her here, though, that proved he really knew her, knew where she worked."

"And he threatened her?"

"I didn't hear him myself, you understand. But the call came through when she was in here, in my office, and I could tell from her face something was wrong. She kept saying, 'Who is this, who is this?' So then she hung up, and I finally got it out of her—she wasn't the kind to broadcast her troubles, too independent for her own good. Lemme see if I can remember ... He had a regular routine, she said. 'Watch your step, Villard,' he'd say. 'Take my word for it, you're going to be sorry if you don't.' And that was about it. 'Who is this?' she'd ask, and he wouldn't answer, just breathe at her for a minute and then hang up."

"What made you think of her ex-husband? Do you know him?"

Mr. Dudgeon shook his head. "All I know about him is that he's some kind of a school teacher, and the divorce was her idea, not his. So he's probably still got a thing about her, sore because she was going around with Max ... It figures. For my money, it all figures."

"But not for Miss Villard's."

"No, she wouldn't buy it. Or wouldn't admit it if she did. But she couldn't come up with anybody else, either. When I wanted to call the police, she said don't be silly, it wasn't that important, they wouldn't do anything about it, anyway. She was sort of jaundiced on the police, see, because her apartment was broken into a month or so ago and—"

"It was? What was stolen?"

"The usual stuff. Radio. Portable typewriter. Liquor and cigarettes.

Jewelry. Never got any of it back, of course. At least she had insurance. Mrs. Hannaford lost quite a chunk of cash. But it burned Fern up to think of somebody ransacking her place and getting away with it. Can't blame her."

"No. To get back to the phone call, how long ago was this?"

"Lemme see. Last week? Yeah. Wednesday. I remember because I was in a sweat to get out of here and meet my ex-wife for dinner."

"You're divorced?"

"I'll say. The only way to live. Last Wednesday, four thirty or so in the afternoon. Why the hell didn't I *do* something? I might have saved her life!"

"I wouldn't be too sure. There may be no connection between the calls and her death. Not that we won't investigate them, of course, but—"

"Well, for my money there's a connection! Track down the guy that was making those calls and you've got your murderer. One thing sure, it wasn't Max. He was in my office too, the day she got the one here. You're wasting your time worrying about him. Haul that ex-husband of hers in here and give him the works. Boy, would I like to get my hands on him! The only good secretary I ever had, and he's got to murder her!"

"Aren't you leaping to quite a few conclusions, Mr. Dudgeon?"

"What if I am? They're perfectly logical. Nothing wrong with leaping to conclusions as long as you keep both feet on the ground."

So much for the preliminary facts. Louise failed to see what they could possibly have to do with Fern Villard's death, but anyway, so much for them. She was thirty-six years old; married (more or less, there was always the possibility that this time he wouldn't come back) to Russell Clarke, Chief Engineer on a freighter; childless; resided in a two-and-a-half-room apartment in the East Thirties; and had joined the staff of *The Compleat Angler* five years ago, well before it graduated from house organ to specialty magazine. The detective could see the rest for himself: she was tall and thin, with a headlong gait and a delicate, big-eyed face that was somehow both funny and sad. And indeed Louise was often not sure herself whether she felt more like laughing or crying.

"No, I wasn't particularly friendly with Fern," she said. "We had lunch together once, and that was enough for both of us. It was when she first started here, about six months ago, and I got the feeling she was reconnoitering, deciding whether I was worth cultivating or not ... I'm sorry, but that's the way she struck me, as somebody who didn't bother with other people unless she could figure out some way of using them. Like little Patty. The kid thought Fern was doing her a favor, selling her her old clothes, letting her trot around on errands. I know how I sound.

Jealous. And of course that's part of it. She had this stunning figure ..." Louise glanced down disconsolately at her own flat chest: those things never had grown on her. "... and she made the most of it. There wasn't anything too wrong with her face, either, though personally I've never cared for the combination of auburn hair and brown eyes. There. I'm doing it even now, when the poor girl's been murdered." She gave a helpless shrug. "Anyway, after that one lunch when we got the pitch on each other we went our separate ways. Strictly business from then on. No more socializing. Her personal life is something I know nothing about."

"Not even about her and Max Sutter?"

"Oh well, that." She paused and added—rather craftily, in her own private opinion, "Everybody always knows about Max's romantic crises. He's not one to suffer in silence. Fern isn't the first girl to play him for a sucker. I only hope she won't be the last."

"You think she was using him too, as you put it?"

"It was fairly obvious. I suppose she'd hit a dead spot in her love life and figured she might as well string him along just to keep her hand in, so she wouldn't get rusty while she waited for some real talent to show up. Max wasn't really in her class, but he was available, and more than willing. It's always flattering to know you've got somebody eating his heart out over you."

"Did you hear them quarrelling Friday night?"

"No. I left when High did, about six thirty. Robinson was still here, plugging away at his rewrite, with Max breathing down his neck so he could finish the make-up and get out. He and Fern were planning to drive out to the Island—she'd brought her bag in with her in the morning, so she was still here too, waiting for him. What about her bag? Is it—"

"We found it. In the ladies' lounge. Tell me, Mrs. Clarke, did you hear anything from Max, or see him, over the week end?"

"Who, me? No, of course not. Why should I?"

"I thought he might have called you. It seems he went on quite a binge."

"Max? Why, he hardly drinks at all! Except at the Christmas party, something like that."

"He did Friday night. According to the report I have on the state of his apartment, he must have holed up with a bottle for most of the week end. The fellow in the apartment next to his heard him out in the hall late Friday night—or rather, early Saturday morning—and helped him up the stairs. He was too drunk to manage by himself. Never happened before, the neighbor says, and he was concerned enough to check up on Max Sunday afternoon. By that time he'd pulled himself together and sobered up. His assistant—" The detective consulted his notes. "—Miss Hirsch saw him Saturday night and has now recalled, on second thought, that he had been drinking heavily. Incidentally, have you any idea where he might be now?"

She shook her head. So they hadn't found him yet. Was that good or bad? And for whom? Why, for Max. But he might be guilty! She swallowed, and said carefully, "I don't know him all that well. I never see him outside of the office. He doesn't drink ordinarily, but if he'd just had a big bust-up with Fern, he might very well rush out and get a load on. After all, it's part of the unrequited love tradition. Drowning your sorrows." No need to mention the fact that he might have had more to drown than simple sorrow; it was clear that this possibility had already occurred to the detective—had, in fact, changed from possibility to probability for him.

He was off on another tack. "When you came in this morning, did you notice anything out of order in your office?"

She smiled wanly. "It's never in order. Why? Oh yes, I'd forgotten. It's the only way to get out on to the parapet. Through my window."

"Right."

"I didn't notice anything out of the way. Of course I wasn't looking for anything. I'd have to check."

"Yes, I want you to. The window was shut and locked, the way you left it Friday night?"

"It was shut and locked, all right. But that wasn't the way I left it. It gets awfully stale in here, especially when they turn off the air conditioning—they turn it off about five thirty or six—so if I'm not the last one out, I leave the window open. The others were still here Friday night, so I asked them to be sure and close it before they left. Because we're not supposed to open it, you see, it's against the rules."

"You asked 'them' to close it. Who?"

"Well. Fern and Max. His office is right next to mine, and Fern was in there with him. I called in and reminded them as I went past the door." Was that bad or good? She couldn't tell from the detective's face.

"Did you know about the party on this floor Friday night? The Publix party?"

"We heard them whooping it up while we were waiting for the elevator. And Archie O'Brien had mentioned it. He used to work for Publix, so he was invited."

"Yes, he told me about it. I understand he and Miss Villard occasionally had a drink together after work. I'd be interested in your views on how she might have been using Mr. O'Brien."

She felt her face reddening angrily. "All right then, I think she was picking his brains. They're worth picking, you know, Archie's not stupid. He knows the magazine business inside out, and everybody in it. Not to mention public relations and advertising. He can still pull a few strings—maybe not for himself anymore, but for somebody else. Fern was determined to get ahead, and I don't mean just here at *The Compleat Angler*. This was only a starting point as far as she was concerned. She was on the look-out for leads, and Archie was the boy who could give them to her."

And Louise herself was a spiteful jealous woman. Or so the detective must be thinking.

He preserved a gentlemanly silence.

After that they checked her office, and found—as might have been expected, since it was a favorite gathering spot for the staff—something for everyone. Robinson's spectacle case. A crumpled half-empty pack of cigarettes that might be either Max's or Archie's; they smoked the same brand. Gladys' extra pair of rubbers; High's electric razor; a bottle of nail polish belonging to Patty; the remains of one of the candy bars Donna Hirsch was forever eating.

There was nothing that could not be explained, simply and innocently. Nothing to indicate the presence of an outsider or to suggest the violence that must have started here. Yes, here, right here in this cluttered little room that was as familiar to Louise as her own two hands.

It ought to look different, but it didn't. She tried to imagine Fern Villard—trapped, no doubt, in the act of closing the window—scrambling out on to the parapet in mortal terror, fleeing from someone with scissors in his hand and murder in his heart ...

"All right, Mrs. Clarke," said the detective. "I won't keep you any longer."

3

They had all been interviewed, not only the editorial staff but those less closely associated with Fern as well—the receptionist, the mail room clerks, the production and circulation and advertising employees. Presumably they had all been eliminated as suspects. And the reporters had been dealt with.

In a short, subdued speech (a far cry from his customary rousing pep talks) Mr. Dudgeon announced the temporary closing down of *The Compleat Angler*. Till further notice. Probably for the rest of the week.

He made his speech in the mail room, for his own office was still in official use; the detective was questioning Fern's apartment-mate, Mrs. Beulah Hannaford, who had been summoned from the insurance office where she worked. His audience was also uncommonly subdued. They were all acutely conscious that two of their number were missing; the atmosphere was funereal. It went without saying, said Mr. Dudgeon, that this thing, this terrible thing … Meantime, he knew he could count on each and every one of them to cooperate fully with the police … The best thing for all of them to do now was to go quietly home and leave the matter in the hands of the authorities, who could no doubt clear it up promptly …

When the others had straggled out, he and Louise faced each other in glassy silence. It was ended by a sigh heaved up from the depths of High's soul. "What the Peerless guys are going to say about this—" He shuddered. "It doesn't bear thinking about."

"Now look, High, they can't blame you." They would, though. *The Compleat Angler* was no longer a house organ, but Peerless still kept a firm grip on its purse strings—and, as far as this was possible, on its editor. The Peerless Board of Trustees regarded High Dudgeon with mingled admiration and alarm. He was a go-getter, no doubt about that: not only had he worked his own way up from messenger boy, he had conceived the idea of *The Compleat Angler* and nursed it through its spindly infancy to its present promising state. But there was such a thing as being too energetic, too enthusiastic, too impetuous. Give a fellow like that his head, and he might gallop off in all directions at once, no telling where he might end up, and Peerless with him. Louise could see all too clearly the raised eyebrows, tightened mouths, and what-did-I-tell-you expressions with which the Peerless Board would receive this morning's news. "It's not your fault!" she cried.

"No, but it's my secretary. Murdered," said High, with melancholy relish, "practically under my nose. And as if that wasn't bad enough, by one of my team—according to the police. Of course they're out of their mind, but that's what they think, that's who they've picked. They're going to arrest Max on sight. The damn fool, why did he have to sneak out this morning? Worst thing he could have done."

"He was on the spot, no matter what he did. Let's face it, High, he had motive and opportunity. And another thing, he went out and got drunk Friday night—"

"How do you know? Nobody ever tells me anything! I don't believe it!"

She recounted the episode of the helpful neighbor. "So you see what I mean about his being on the spot. But if he did kill her—now calm down, I didn't say he did, I said if—I simply can't believe that he'd come in at all this morning. Not Max. He hasn't got that kind of nerve. It would take nerve, you know, to come in, knowing she was out there on the parapet and that sooner or later somebody was going to find her and start asking questions."

"Of course it would! Of course he wouldn't! He'd—"

"He'd panic right away, Friday night. He wouldn't wait till this morning to start running."

"Come on. Let's tell the detective!" In his excitement and zeal High grabbed her arm and just missed crashing them both into the Xerox machine. "This proves it, proves he's innocent, I said so right from the start ..."

They caught the detective as he was emerging, with Mrs. Hannaford, from High's office. He listened with chilling politeness. Then he looked at his watch, excused himself, and strode off purposefully.

Crestfallen, High watched him go. "I guess he didn't buy it," he murmured. But then his eye fell on Mrs. Hannaford, weeping in the background, and at once he bounced back into action. A lady in distress. Comfort must be dispensed. "Now, now, mustn't give way. Weesie, get her to stop crying. Come on, let's go out and have a cup of coffee. Sure. Do us all good. Cup of coffee and a bite to eat. How about it?"

"Nothing to eat, thank you," said Mrs. Hannaford in a drowned voice. "But I would like a cup of coffee. I'm sorry, I'll be all right in a minute. It's just the shock ..."

She was a nice-looking woman, in an unobtrusive way: regular features, on the worn side, and at the moment tear-stained; dark hair threaded with gray; a neat figure in "classically simple" tweed suit and white blouse. If she was not the type to set heads turning, neither was she the hopeless frump one might have expected Fern Villard to pick as an apartment-mate—by way of pointing up her own spectacular good looks.

"Actually, it was more a business arrangement than a matter of friendship," Mrs. Hannaford confided over the coffee-shop table. She was no longer crying, but she still sounded as if she were talking under water. The odd, engulfed voice must be permanent. "I don't mean we weren't friends. But we weren't intimate friends. Fern led her own life, I led mine. That was how we both preferred it. As a general rule we didn't even have dinner together. Fern went out so much more than I. She was ideal to share an apartment with—if you have to share at all, and I do, I couldn't afford this place by myself, and I'm stuck with a lease. She didn't drink too much or throw noisy parties or leave her stuff all over the place or monopolize the bathroom—you know, the little things that can get you down—and of course she was meticulous about money matters. When

I think of how dubious we both were about doubling up—"

"How did you happen to do it, then?" asked Louise.

"Happenstance, really. My sister and I took the apartment together originally, only six months ago she was transferred to Chicago, so I was left with a year's lease on a place I couldn't afford. I was getting pretty desperate about it when one day I happened to mention it to George Villard, Fern's ex-husband …"

High was on it like a terrier. "Oh, so you know George Villard, do you?"

"Why yes, I know George. We grew up in the same town in New Jersey, and my son goes to the private school where he teaches. So when I told him about the fix I was in, he said Fern was looking for a place—they'd been divorced a couple of months before—and she might be interested in moving in with me. I had only met her once, barely knew her, so as I say I was very dubious. But I figured I had nothing to lose by calling her. Well, the upshot of it was that we decided to try it for a month, and it worked out so well that she's been with me ever since."

"Does George Villard know what's happened to her?"

"Oh yes. From what the detective said, he's on his way in from Jersey now. I doubt if he knows anything that will help, but naturally they want to talk to him."

"I should hope so. Those spooky phone calls she was getting, for instance. They better ask George Villard about them."

"What?" She blinked. (So did Louise.) "You don't think George had anything to do with those! Do you know him? No, you can't, or you wouldn't suggest such a thing. Why, it's ridiculous! Fern couldn't possibly have thought it was George." But she sounded a little tentative to Louise, as if she weren't entirely sure what Fern might have thought. Or pretended to think.

"No, no, my idea," said High, and added plaintively, "What's so ridiculous about it? Maybe he was still in love with her and it burned him up to think of her going out with other guys. How do I know he's not some kind of a nut, a psycho?"

"Because I say so." Mrs. Hannaford's smile was disarming. "I know him and you don't, and George Villard is a thoroughly normal young man who married the wrong girl and realizes it. After I got acquainted with Fern, it seemed surprising to me that they stayed together as long as they did—or that she ever married him in the first place."

"Why not, if he's such a world-beater?"

"That's just it, he isn't. He's a nice, easy-going boy who's never going to get much farther than he is right now." She paused for a sip of coffee. "You know how ambitious Fern was."

"And then she took up with Max," Louise said. "He's never going to set the world on fire, either. Though I guess you wouldn't call him a nice, easy-going—"

"He's high-strung," High put in firmly. "An artist."

"I know. I met him a couple of times when he brought Fern home. A very different type from George. Of course I don't know how serious she was about this Max."

"Serious enough to plan a week end trip with him," Louise pointed out.

"I know. That is, I knew she was going away for the week end. She didn't say who with. Just that she'd probably stay over till Monday morning. So I didn't expect her back, you see. And all the time—" Her voice threatened to submerge to an even greater depth. "It does seem strange, for him to disappear like this."

"People do strange things when they're in a state of shock," Louise intervened hastily, before High could boil over. "Things that don't make any sense at all. So it doesn't necessarily mean—"

"Doesn't mean a thing," High burst out. "That boy's as innocent as the driven snow, and if you think I'm going to stand idly by while they railroad him, well, all I can say is you don't know me. Or Max, either. It's like you and George Villard. I know him and you don't, and take my word for it, Max is no murderer."

"Fair enough," murmured Mrs. Hannaford. She did not look convinced—but then neither had High, when she rose to George Villard's defense. "Murder's so—so hard to believe, isn't it?" she added helplessly.

She left shortly afterwards; the police were due at the apartment, to go through Fern's personal belongings in search of possible clues. And Fern's mother and stepfather would have to be notified. They lived out on the west coast, Washington or Oregon, Mrs. Hannaford wasn't sure which. George Villard would probably know. She didn't think Fern had kept in very close touch with them, even though she was an only child. But then she hadn't been a family sort of person ...

When she was gone, High said moodily, "I don't know what it was about that woman, but she put me off, somehow."

"I can tell you what it was. She disagreed with you. That's against the rules. Nobody's allowed to disagree with Our Leader."

"Oh, shut up. If I'm such a bastard why don't you quit and get another job?"

"I'm a masochist. Why don't you fire me?"

"Someday I will." Hurrying to keep up with her—for she had taken off down the street at her usual lunging gait—he added, "Hey, where you going? Weesie?"

"I don't know. Home, I guess."

"But it's only two thirty!"

She couldn't believe he was right; it seemed an endless stretch of time since they had knelt on the parapet beside Fern Villard. Only two thirty. They waited at the curb for the light to change, oppressively aware of the queer, empty afternoon ahead. Solitude. Nothing to do. They were rare commodities in Louise's life. Ordinarily she would have regarded them as a special treat. Not today, she discovered. Not today.

"Lunch!" High's face lit up with the inspiration. "We haven't even had lunch yet. That's what's wrong with us. We're hungry."

They ate Chinese food and drank more tea than they wanted and speculated about Max's whereabouts. The message in High's fortune cookie said, "Procrastination is the thief of time." Louise's warned her against false friends.

It was still only three thirty.

Again inspiration visited High: they could go to his apartment and Get some of the Work Out. After all, *The Compleat Angler* must appear on schedule, no matter who died or how. He had his briefcase with him; God knew what was in it, but the police had okayed his taking it—and God alone knew when the police would clear out of the office and turn it back to its rightful occupants. Louise acquiesced; she was too demoralized at the prospect of being by herself to do anything else.

They took a cab to High's Stuyvesant Town apartment. On the way they read, in the afternoon paper High had picked up, about the attractive secretary who had been found brutally stabbed on an office parapet, and her mysteriously missing boy friend who was being sought for questioning. Fern's face looked out at them, disdainful and serene under the bizarre headline. There was also a shot of the office building, its facade marked with an ominous X. Reduced to its crude outlines, the story seemed to Louise both banal and fantastic: it couldn't possibly have happened to anyone she knew. High's expression, as he read, was one of blank absorption. From time to time he sighed deeply. Thinking about the Peerless guys, no doubt.

He surprised her, for once, by confiding, with a shame-faced air, "I didn't really like her either, you know. I mean, she was a whiz, and all that, and naturally, being so good-looking—Sets you up, you know, makes you think you're a big shot. But I never felt like she was really with me, the way you are, honey ..." He patted her hand; ah, she thought, these tender moments; and the next instant darted off at another tangent. "If anybody knows where he is, it's Donna Hirsch. I can't get anything out of her, but I bet you could, Weesie. You're good with weirdies. That's what we'll do, call her up from my place, she'll talk to you if you handle her right. She could even be hiding him out down there in that dump of hers. Hey, that's an idea. We could go down there right now and—"

"Whoa," said Louise, just as he was leaning forward to switch instructions to the cab driver. "That's not going to get us anywhere, barging in on her. What makes you think she'd even let us in? She certainly wouldn't, if by any chance you're right and he is there."

"But we're on his side too! She must realize that, weirdie or not. All we want to do is help him."

"How?" asked Louise as they got out of the cab. It was a good question, she thought, but there was an even better one: Are we on his side too, even if he's guilty? But he isn't, High would answer, and that would be that. Life was so much simpler for him than it was for her.

"I haven't figured out how yet," he said impatiently when he had paid off the driver. "All I know is he's in one hell of a mess and somebody's got to get him out of it. He's in no shape to do it himself, that's for sure. And once the police nab him and start working him over—You know how he is, Weesie. Even when he's in his right mind he's apt to say the wrong things. If we could get hold of him first, we could at least try to talk some sense into him."

"Maybe. But I still say it's no good going down to Donna's. To begin with, the police must have already checked there. They know she's a friend of Max's—she's admitted she saw him Saturday night—so that's one of the first places they'd look. Okay, she could still know where he is, even if she's not hiding him herself. But she's not going to tell us just because we ask her. She doesn't trust us any more than she does the police. They're authority. We're conformity. Those are dirty words to Donna."

"I suppose you're right." They moved slowly up the walk between the tidy rows of shrubbery. Beyond—in an unvarying pattern repeated over and over—lay stretches of young grass, concrete play areas, fountains, benches, tree-lined ovals, with the utilitarian brick buildings jutting over all. The essence of conformity. How Donna would hate this place! Well, Louise didn't like it much herself. High probably didn't even see it anymore. Besides, he was still engrossed in the details of his campaign, to save Max. "So the first thing we have to do is get through to Donna. In case she does know where he is, I mean. Convince her we're in there pitching for him. And that's just the beginning. If you ask me, Max is going to be just as tough to convince as she is. Damn it, why can't they use a little ordinary common sense! Why do they have to ..."

He continued to fume as they entered the empty lobby and moved down it toward High's ground floor apartment. There was something disheartening to Louise in the hollow echoing of their footsteps. Or maybe it was the prospect of calling Donna that depressed her. Her own faith in her powers of persuasion was considerably less than High's.

"Don't you ever air this place out?" she asked as she stepped inside the apartment. There was a strong, stale smell, partly cigarette smoke, partly something else—But High doesn't smoke, she thought; that's odd.

He had gone in ahead of her. Now he stopped, where the foyer widened into the living room. "Somebody's been in here." he announced accusingly. Papa Bear come to life. "Look at that." He pointed to the rumpled couch cover, the afternoon newspaper, the ash tray heaped with cigarette butts, the glass overturned on the floor. For an instant they both stood still, sniffing. Then in a rush they made for the kitchen door.

It had been wedged shut with a towel. On the third shove it flew open suddenly, sending High into a tottering half-sprawl. He crashed against the refrigerator, and hung there, staring. For once in his life he was incapable of action; it was Louise who turned off the gas jets and flung the window open.

Max was huddled in front of the stove, his head on the open oven door. He had wadded up his suit jacket for a pillow and taken off his shoes. He still looked uncomfortable, though. He also looked dead.

Of course he never had been the picture of health. But now the mushroom pallor of his long, lugubrious face seemed to have a bluish tinge. His half-open eyes were filmy. His drooping Balkan-spy moustache added the last despondent touch.

"But how did he get in here?" Louise asked. As if that were the one all-important, all-absorbing angle ... It was the only one she felt capable of dealing with at the moment. "Did he have a key?"

"I remember now. Sure. That time a couple of months ago when the plumbing broke down in his place and he stayed here. He still had the key." High's voice was abstracted. He had recovered from his momentary lapse and was back in business, bending over Max, prodding and hauling. "He's still alive. Weesie! He's not dead. Come on, help me. We'll get him into the bedroom, the air's better in there, I'll give him artificial respiration. You take his feet, Weesie. Okay? All set?"

Max made an inert, awkward burden. He was heavier than he looked. All bones and no meat. After they had deposited him on the bedroom floor, they remained kneeling for an instant, and their eyes met. Louise had one of her clairvoyant flashes; High's mind lay exposed to her, like a watch with the case open and all the little wheels busily spinning.

Busily and uselessly—he knew it as well as she did, and yet he could not stop the cogs from whirring. Each one activated the next, chain-fashion: artificial respiration to resuscitation to Max rescued not only from himself but from the police who had not thought to look for him here and probably never would

"No," said Louise loudly and firmly. She scrambled to her feet. "There's only one thing to do, High."

She went back into the living room and phoned for an ambulance.

4

By Tuesday morning the report from the hospital described Max's condition as good, recovering satisfactorily. Which was all very well as far as it went; the patient's state of mind was something else again, as High and Louise discovered the following morning, when they were permitted to visit him briefly.

The visit turned out to be even more distressing than Louise had expected. To begin with, there was the policeman. Large, impassive, immovable as a piece of essential equipment, he dominated the proceedings without participating in them. Max made doubly sure of this by tossing into the conversation references to Bright Boy and Meathead. These peevish, puerile little jabs—so typical of Max—seemed to have no effect whatever on the policeman. They made Louise and High squirm. So did the jabs that were aimed directly at them. For of course there were those too.

They stood side by side, looking down helplessly at his melancholy face propped against the pillows, his hands lying, abnormally clean and motionless, on the white cover. He stared back, daring them to befriend him.

The bouquet of tulips and iris was a mistake. "I'm allergic," said Max.

"Now don't worry about anything," High began bravely. "It's all going to be okay, Max, take my word for it. I've already got a lawyer lined up for you—"

"Why?" asked Max. "What's the use of a lawyer?"

"What do you mean, what's the use? How are we going to get you out of this without a lawyer?"

"The answer is you're not. Take my advice and save your money. The lawyer doesn't live that can get me out of this. It's an open and shut case, didn't you know? Just ask Bright Boy. He's got all the answers. Sure. All they needed was what they got Monday—me with my head in the oven. That wraps it up. Better than a confession."

"That's no way to talk. My God, Max, you're innocent! You didn't do it!"

"Who cares, innocent? I never had a prayer and I knew it. Why do you think I ducked out Monday morning?"

　　　　　　　　　　　　　　　

"I know, and I wish you hadn't. I wish you'd had the sense to stick around and tell them your side of it."

"Ha," said Max. "My side of it. We had a fight Friday night and I went out and got drunk. Ask Meathead what that adds up to."

"But you can't just lay down and give up. We've got to find out who really did it!"

Max closed his eyes. Beneath his drooping moustache his mouth quivered defenselessly. "It won't bring her back," he said, and for a moment even High was silent.

For a moment only, of course; despair—in himself or anybody else— was incomprehensible and intolerable. "All right, it won't bring her back. But if we don't get to the bottom of this, it makes it twice as bad. Two victims instead of one. She's beyond help, but you're not, and—"

"Please. Don't do me any more favors." Max's eyes were open again, and burning with hostility. "I might have known you'd come charging in there and turn me over to the cops."

"Listen, you ungrateful bastard, if it hadn't been for me you'd be dead! Weesie and I saved your life!"

"Thanks for nothing," said Max.

He then retreated into stony silence, and High stamped out sputtering with rage. A familiar finale, if not a fitting one; this was the way they often wound up. Louise, who was supposed to be the tranquilizing agent, lingered. Ruffled feathers she could deal with. But that was not what ailed Max. She looked down at his face—his baleful, obstinate, suffering face—and tried to believe that someday life would again seem possible to him, maybe even desirable.

"Donna's taking care of your cat," she said. "She wanted me to tell you." A pathetic offering, but the best she could do.

Nothing changed in his face. She touched his hand in a timid gesture of farewell and left him with the policeman, who was cleaning his fingernails with a pocket knife.

Out in the corridor High pounced on her the moment the door closed behind her. "Well. Did you get him straightened out? Of all the nerve, blaming me for charging in, that's what he said, charging in—As if it wasn't my own apartment, damn it, I'm the guy that pays the rent and lives there! Who does he think he is, trespassing on my private property and turning on the gas and then blaming me for saving his lousy life for him? Not only that, but I knock myself out getting him a lawyer that I'm going to have to pay out of my own pocket because don't kid yourself, the Peerless guys aren't going to come through with a nickel, and this is the thanks I get! Needs a punch in the nose, if you ask me." He jabbed at the elevator button instead. "I must say, you were a big help. Not a word out of you, you might at least have—"

"Shut up," she croaked.

"Now what's the matter?" He hustled her into the elevator with one hand and yanked out his handkerchief with the other. Then he waited, still gripping her arm and peering at her in mingled indignation, dismay and respect, the way he always did when she cried. "What the hell, I didn't mean it that way ... Weesie?" She shook her head violently; it was on account of Max, not him. At least he understood that much, though naturally he boiled it down to practical terms. "Come on now, Weesie, I'm not going to leave him in the lurch, no matter how sore I get at him. You know me better than that. By God, we'll get him out of this mess whether he likes it or not! He can't stop us, and neither can the police. We're going to get to the bottom of this whole business and come up with the guy that really did it. You'll see. I'm not giving up the ship. Not me. I've barely laid my shoulder to the plow."

Outside the office door Gladys paused, with the key in her hand and a chill creeping down her backbone. Not that she was superstitious, especially not this time of day, broad daylight, even if she believed in ghosts which she didn't. But she hadn't counted on being the first one here; that was what gave her the shivers, the thought of waiting all by herself with nobody to talk to. She couldn't help it, she happened to be gifted with a vivid imagination. Right now, for instance, she could *see* the murderer slithering through this very door, as he must have done Friday night ... The key clattered to the floor, and as she bent to retrieve it she heard, with a rush of relief, the elevator stop behind her.

"Oh, hello. Miss Popejoy, isn't it?" Beulah Hannaford came toward her, dressed—as she should be, and as Gladys was—in black, and smiling an appropriately restrained smile. "I wasn't sure whether anybody would be here or not. But I thought I'd stop by, just in case, to make sure you all knew about the funeral arrangements."

Gladys, who could have kissed her, settled for a handshake. Friendly but solemn, as befitted the forthcoming funeral. "So thoughtful of you. Yes, that's why I'm here. The office is closed officially, will be the rest of the week, but Mr. Dudgeon asked the staff to meet here and go to the services together." She laughed nervously. "I guess I'm the first one here. As usual. Oh dear, the key seems to be sticking. I don't know what's the matter with me today, I'm all thumbs."

"Can I help you? There." The door opened, and Mrs. Hannaford hesitated, not quite abandoning Gladys, not quite following her inside. "Well. As long as you do know. I don't want to intrude—"

"Nothing of the sort!" cried Gladys. "It's so nice to see you again. Do come in. The others should be along any minute. Mr. Robinson, anyway, he's almost as much a stickler for punctuality as I am. More than can be said for Mr. O'Brien. And Donna Hirsch of course just came out flat-footed and refused to have any part of it. Doesn't believe in funerals. Thinks they're barbarous. Can you imagine? That girl! You'd think she'd have the decency ..." With Mrs. Hannaford in tow, Gladys trotted down the hall to her cubicle, her backbone comfortably unchilled. "Little Patty's coming. And Mr. Dudgeon and Louise, of course. They were going to the hospital to see Max this morning. He's under arrest, you know, but that's the way Mr. Dudgeon is, give him credit, he won't turn his back on anybody that works for him, no matter how bad it looks."

"But surely Max wouldn't have tried to kill himself if he weren't guilty! That amounts to a confession, or practically. Especially when you add it to all the other—"

"I'm not so sure," said Gladys mysteriously. Having settled Mrs. Hannaford in the extra chair, she took up her usual perch behind her desk, bright-eyed, ready for a nice long visit. "Oh, I know, the police have their methods, and they've gone over every inch of this office with a fine-tooth comb without finding anything to change their minds about Max—it stands to reason, or they wouldn't be holding him, wouldn't have cleared out and allowed us back in here—but all the same, I'm not so sure. He's a peculiar boy, Max. Moody. But then you probably know him as well as I do. Maybe even better."

"No. I only met him three or four times." She closed her eyes for a moment; Gladys thought she looked tired, and as if she might have been crying. Well, naturally. "Do you mean it might have been just grief that drove him to suicide? I didn't realize he was that much in love with Fern."

"My point exactly. He's deep. Nobody knows what's going on with Max." Gladys' hands, rarely idle, fidgeted with her cameo brooch. Her head, topped with its black saucer hat, nodded smartly. "But he's not the only one. Oh no, I could mention one or two others around here that might know more than they're telling. It's a peculiar coincidence, the way Mr. O'Brien happened to be at that Publix party Friday night, right here on the same floor. Far be it from me to tell tales, and the police have no doubt made a thorough investigation, but I'm practically certain he keeps a bottle in his desk. Such an intelligent man, too. With his background and ability, you wouldn't think he'd be interested in working on an insignificant magazine like *The Compleat Angler*. Now with Mr. Robinson, of course, it's different. I can't help feeling sorry for him sometimes, the way Mr. Dudgeon bullies him, I've told him more than once, 'W. J.,' I tell him, 'the only way to get any place with Mr. Dudgeon is to stand up to him, otherwise he'll have no respect for you.' But he's too afraid of losing his job to do it. And there was a rumor—I don't know how much truth there was in it—but rumor hath it, as they say, that Fern would have welcomed an opportunity to try her hand at the Questions and Answers."

"Is that so?" said Mrs. Hannaford politely. But she was showing the signs of restiveness that Gladys so often detected among her acquaintances. She noted them now with a sinking heart, and at once decided to change her course.

"Well, there, we'll just have to wait and see. All I say is, until and unless they get a full confession out of Max, I'm not eliminating anybody. After all, anybody could have come back here Friday night. We all have keys, except Patty … I suppose Fern's relatives are here for the services?"

"What? Oh. No, her mother isn't well enough to make the trip. It's her heart, and you can imagine what a terrible shock this has been. So the stepfather felt he shouldn't leave her. No, there won't be any relatives. Unless you count George Villard," she added, and glanced at her wristwatch.

"I was wondering about him, whether he'd be there or not, I mean, in view of the divorce," Gladys chattered. No use: Mrs. Hannaford was on her feet and edging toward the door. "Tell me, how is your son? I do hope you've been able to spare him all this dreadful business. So upsetting for a boy his age. Though I suppose with all the newspaper publicity— Oh dear, did I say something wrong?" For to her surprise (still, it was gaining her a few extra minutes) Mrs. Hannaford's eyes filled with tears.

"No, no, it's not your fault. It's just that I'm worried about Michael too, on top of all the rest. The doctor says it's probably nothing serious, but I think I told you, he had rheumatic fever as a child, so the least little thing and I'm terrified …" She found a handkerchief in her purse and wiped her eyes. "He's been running this low-grade temperature, slight, but it hasn't cleared up, and I've taken him out of school for the time being. It couldn't have happened at a worse time, but I felt I simply had to have him here with me where I can keep an eye on him."

"I'm sure you're right. I'm sure I'd do the same. Poor boy, too bad he couldn't have been kept out of this."

"Actually, I think he's enjoying it," said Mrs. Hannaford, with a quick, unexpected smile. "It's not as if he were fond of Fern, he hardly knew her, so to him it's all very exciting, being this close to a murder investigation. The police even asked him a few questions. I can imagine how he's going to brag about that when he gets back to school." Another glance at her watch. "I must run along and meet George. We're going to the funeral together."

"Oh. I was going to say, if you wanted to join us—" Gladys began desperately. But then she caught the sounds she had been waiting for: the click of the outside door, voices. It was all right now. It was all right. She scuttled contentedly along beside Mrs. Hannaford. "We'll see you later, then. So nice talking to you, so nice of you to stop by."

Mr. Field was the lawyer's name: bald head, horn-rimmed glasses, slight paunch, briefcase, pipe and oilskin tobacco pouch. Donna had seen a million of him, and that was just about a million too many. She made a point of not shaking hands with him when she let him in. He sat on the sway-backed studio couch; she slouched in the canvas sling chair, eating a candy bar and scowling at him. He cast one coolly appraising glance around the room—poise, that was his middle name—and then gave her the same treatment. She was wearing thong sandals and a mustard-colored sweater with holes in the elbows. Blue jeans in between. Okay, so he didn't approve. But she had a disconcerting moment of wondering whether the look in his eye wasn't more a kind of confirmation than disapproval. As if this was very much what he had expected her to wear, the way she had expected his gray suit and conservative-stripe tie. Her scowl deepened.

"All right, Miss Hirsch," he began, opening his briefcase. "As I told you over the phone, I'm representing Max Sutter in this matter, and you're one of the few people we know of who saw him over the week end. Saturday night, to be specific. I just had a preliminary talk with him at the hospital, and apparently he remembers very little about that interview. So what I need from you is a full and accurate account of everything you can recall of the conversation you had with him. I mean everything. Don't hold back, even if there are parts that you think may possibly be damaging to Max's case. I need those too, if I'm going to defend him successfully. Give me the whole story, and let me take it from there. Okay?"

Silence, except for the crackling of Donna's candy wrapper as she wadded it up.

"This isn't an easy case, as I'm sure you realize." He had quite a voice, all right. More stops than a pipe organ. It sank now to mellow meditation, without losing any of its assurance or power. "I'll be frank with you, it's a tough case. A whole lot tougher than I like them to be."

"Okay, if it's so tough, why did you take it on?" she burst out fiercely.

"For the money," he said. Then, with an air of deliberation, he crossed his legs, took off the horn rims, and again looked her up and down. His upper eyelids were full and oddly peaked, so that his eyes seemed triangular in shape. Very shrewd eyes, the color of bitter chocolate. Their gaze was neither friendly nor unfriendly, simply observant. But when he spoke there was a crack of the whip in his voice. "There's something we have to get straight, Miss Hirsch, and right now. We can't afford to waste any more of each other's time. I didn't come down here to charm you or be charmed by you. Fortunately, because believe me it wouldn't work either way. But I've got more important things to do than spar with you. Like each other we don't have to. Cooperate, yes. Either you get down to business and tell me what you've got to tell, or I go out and beat the bushes for another witness. It's up to you whether you want to help Max, and incidentally me, or not. Make up your mind."

Thought he could bluff her, did he? That was all it was, a bluff, a clumsy try at bullying her. They always had to push you around. How else could they build up their revolting little egos? And wouldn't you know he'd make a crack about wanting to help Max, probably considered that a master stroke of subtle flattery. As if her version of Saturday night was going to turn the trick for Max! She couldn't see how it would make much difference one way or the other. And anyway, she wasn't taking orders from any stuffed shirt of a lawyer. No, thank you. Once he figured he had the upper hand he'd—

She watched, rigid with alarm, as he put his glasses back on, uncrossed his legs, and snapped his briefcase shut. It had to be a bluff. But what if it wasn't? What if she was underestimating her own importance as a witness and there wasn't anybody else to beat out of the bushes?

"Well? Do I go or stay?" he asked.

Her mouth stayed stubbornly shut. He stood up. Now he was putting on his topcoat. Adjusting his hat. (A snap brim. Naturally.) She held out until he had his hand on the door knob.

"Don't go." Her throat was too parched with panic for anything more than a whisper. She scraped the two words out again; she even managed to add "Please." It sounded—to her consternation—more arrogant than abject.

He turned, and she screwed up her eyes to shut out his face, which might so easily be wreathed in a fat-cat smile of gloating complacency. He was entitled, she supposed. Worse still, he might pull the patronizing fatherly bit. Pats. Phrases like that's a sensible girl, I knew you'd come round. In which case she probably wouldn't be able to keep from snarling at him all over again.

But he didn't do either. "Good," he said, and plunked himself back on the couch, ready for business.

It was a good thing that Max's cat chose that moment to come padding over to her. She scooped him up in her lap and bent her head over him, until the crisis was past. Because the revolting fact was that she was on the point of dissolving from gratitude.

"Take your time and concentrate," said Mr. Field. "Try to remember everything."

She could remember, all right. Her problem was telling it. Words, words. They seemed to pour out of other people. Not her. Might as well ask for a full, accurate account from Duke, who was curled up in her lap purring, and who had been there Saturday night too, watching and listening from his favorite spot on the window sill. She envied him: he was not expected to remember or report. He furthermore did not care in the least what happened to Max. Lucky Duke, he never heard of love.

She swallowed painfully and began. "Well, he was drunk. Stoned. He hardly ever drinks, but they had this fight, see, because she didn't like the way the week end trip was shaping up. Not fancy enough. So he went out and got looped Friday night, and stayed looped through Saturday. He called me Saturday night."

And the crazy part was that he hadn't sounded stoned over the phone; it wasn't till she saw him that she got the pitch. Falling down drunk, but still talking in that slow, meticulous way. Talking about Fern. As usual. That was about the only time he bothered with Donna—when he'd had another crisis with Fern and needed somebody to listen. So she listened, hoping each time (after all, she was human too) that this crisis was for real, but never letting herself believe it was. Because she had done that at first; she had learned her lesson. Even Saturday night she managed to cling to a reservation or two, in spite of the differences this time, the tempting signs that Friday's fight really was final. He had never gotten drunk before. And he had never been able to resist calling Fern the next day. Was it damaging to his case—in Mr. Field's revolting lingo—that Max had resisted? Would it suggest that he knew Fern could not be reached by telephone or any other means? That was for Mr. Field to figure out; his business. Donna's was to keep talking.

She went doggedly on: "He talked like he always did when they'd had a row. Only more so. But it was the same old jazz about he'd had it, this time he was through, she could find somebody else to string along, money, that was all she cared about. He wouldn't have talked like that if he had killed her. He couldn't have." Her voice rose passionately. "He couldn't have hidden a thing like that from me. Drunk or sober. Don't you see? I know Max, I would have known if he'd killed her!"

"Yes," said Mr. Field, and again she felt the rush of gratitude. He watched her thoughtfully, head cocked, eyes sharp.

"It was just the same, only more so," she repeated. "He even talked about finding another job so he wouldn't have to see her anymore. It bugged him to think of her and some other guy— 'my replacement,' he kept calling it—he knew she wouldn't waste any time, she'd probably been cheating on him all along. He always got off on the jealous bit. That's when he really blew his stack Friday night, I guess, when she got this telephone call—"

"Telephone call?" Mr. Field leaned forward. "Somebody called her Friday night? At the office? Who?"

Donna shrugged. "She didn't tell him. That's what burned him up. They were already fighting, see, so of course when she got this call he decided it was some other guy. He blew up and walked out on her."

"Let's see, this must have been well after regular office hours. The guard downstairs in the lobby checked Max out at eight twenty-seven, so the call must have been a few minutes before that. Switchboard would have been closed. What's the arrangement for late calls? They leave a line open?"

"To Dudgeon's office. She'd have to take it in there."

"I wonder. Did Max actually overhear any of the conversation? Fern's part of it, I mean?"

"Enough to convince him she was making a date with somebody else. Of course that wouldn't take much, the mood he was in. He could have overheard, from his office. It's next to Dudgeon's. There's no soundproofing. And it would be quiet. Nobody else around. Or he could have followed her into Dudgeon's office—" She paused. "It's important. Isn't it?"

"Could be. It's not going to be easy to trace that call. But if we can establish that she really did make a date with somebody else, somebody who showed up after Max left ... It must have been somebody she expected or at least knew. Otherwise she wouldn't have unlocked the door. Assuming it was locked."

"It might not have been," Donna admitted. Like Mr. Field, she leaned forward; disturbed and resentful, Duke gave her a warning dig with his claws. "It's supposed to be, after five thirty, but it isn't always. The way it usually works out, whoever leaves last snaps the lock."

There was a moment's silence, while they thought it over. "It's a point for us, either way," Mr. Field decided. "If the door was locked, okay, she was expecting somebody and let them in. If it wasn't locked, anybody could have turned the knob and walked in. We don't even have to prove she made a date."

"But they'd have to get past the guard downstairs. He's pretty strict about who he lets by. Especially that late."

"Sure he is, ordinarily. But don't forget the Publix party Friday night. I've seen the record for that night, the page where everybody's supposed to sign in or out, and I'd say things got pretty confused before the evening was over. Traffic to and from the twelfth floor was a lot heavier than usual, and a lot less orderly. Comedians all over the place, signing out as De Gaulle, Castro, so on. One bright boy—and what do you bet he's been shaking in his boots ever since—put down Jack the Ripper. With that kind of commotion going on, it wouldn't be much of a trick for somebody to get lost in the shuffle. Now then. Back to Max."

There wasn't much more to be squeezed out of Saturday night. She had poured the rest of the whiskey down the sink, and a can of tomato juice into Max. Had undressed him and shoved him first under the shower and then into bed. Out like a light the minute his head touched the pillow. So then she put out some food for Duke and opened the window and emptied the ash trays. That was all. Well, not quite all. "I kissed him good night," she added in a loud, challenging voice. "For your information." She had also left a note telling him to come over and eat dinner with her next day, if he wanted to. Not that she expected he would; and he didn't. Didn't either come or call. She hadn't seen him again until Monday morning in the office.

There she stopped. No more steam. Like an engine going dead.

"Monday morning," said Mr. Field gently. He waited.

"Well." She hooked her hair back of her ears. Her throat felt rusty. "He got in first. To the office. Monday morning. When I came in he was on the phone, talking to Dudgeon. Then he started to say something to me, only—only I'd already looked out the window, I don't know why, I just happened to look out the window ..." She bent almost double, as if in sudden pain, displacing Duke, who stalked off, mortally offended. "It was my idea. I was the one that told him he had to get out of there, quick, before—Stupid. Stupid. But all I could think of was the quarrel, and how they always arrest the boy friend. It was me. My idea. I thought I could cover up for him somehow, or they'd arrest somebody else, or—I don't know what I thought. I just didn't want him to be arrested!"

Mr. Field nodded. "And he went along with the idea."

"He was like a zombie. Like it didn't matter who told him to do what, he'd do it. Like a zombie. I said don't go home, get on a subway and keep moving, never mind where, just keep moving. And that's what he must have done. For a while. Till he sort of came to. Then he must have remembered he still had the key to Dudgeon's place, so he went over there and—" She swayed back and forth stiffly, now and then swiping at the tears that streaked down her face. "He could have died, and it would have been my fault! If they hadn't found him he'd be dead, and it would be my fault, I'd be to blame!"

"Maybe so," said Mr. Field imperturbably. He was busy packing up his briefcase. "But he didn't die. And if I'm not mistaken, he may have a good deal to thank you for before we're through with this business. So you can remove the hair shirt any time—unless, of course, you like wearing it. I'll give you a ring tomorrow. Okay?" His triangular, bitter-chocolate eyes met hers briefly, still neither friendly nor unfriendly. But as he let himself out the door he nodded cheerfully.

It was revolting, how much better that made her feel.

5

"How do you do, glad to meet you," said George Villard. He blew his nose; apparently the services—short, impersonal, and mercifully unpublicized—had affected him. A large young man, not yet flabby, with tan crew-cut hair, he seemed earnest as a missionary and eager to please as a puppy. It was impossible to imagine him married to Fern. "I thought it went off pretty smoothly, didn't you? Fern wasn't a religious girl, you know. She wouldn't have wanted it in a church."

She wouldn't have wanted it anywhere, thought Louise. George brought out the acid in her; she therefore felt an obligation to protect him, and was unnaturally kind to him. "Very smoothly," she assured him. "I understand you made the arrangements? They couldn't have been in better taste."

High, who had been eyeing George suspiciously, cast a glance, equally suspicious, at her. But he kept his mouth shut. For the moment. They emerged from the funeral parlor to the sidewalk and lingered under the awning, caught in the anti-climax and indecision common to such occasions. Besides the office contingent, George, and Beulah Hannaford, there were perhaps half a dozen others.

"It's Beulah that deserves the credit," said George. "She's been wonderful. After all, it was my responsibility. The least I could do. That's how I see it, anyway. Even though Fern and I weren't able to establish a permanent relationship."

"You mean you got a divorce," translated High. "Or rather, she did. Same thing with me and my wife. When she first started yammering for a divorce I was dead against it. But you want to know something? We get along better now than we ever did when we were married. No kidding. Whenever she's in town I take her out to dinner, and every once in a while I just pick up the phone and call her up."

Whatever he may have been hoping for in the way of full confessions or guilty starts, he didn't get it. George's expression remained pleasant and rather blank. "You're lucky to have made such a satisfactory adjustment. I'm afraid Fern and I hadn't reached that stage yet. Of course now we never will ... As a matter of fact, it's been at least six months since I saw her, and I think the last time I talked to her on the phone was around Christmas."

The look in High's eye grew even fishier. But before he could pursue the subject Beulah Hannaford said in that foggy voice of hers, "I don't want to hurry you, George, but I do feel I ought to be getting home to Michael. I don't like leaving him alone any more than I have to. I can take a cab if you—"

"No, no, I'll drive you home. No trouble at all. My car's just around the corner. Can I give you a lift, Mr. Dudgeon? Mrs. Clarke? Glad to, if you're going downtown."

High took the No right out of Louise's mouth and turned it into Yes. "Fine. Thanks. Sure we're going downtown."

They said their goodbyes to the rest of *The Compleat Angler* staff: Patty, still crying her uncomplicated little heart out; W. J. Robinson, stately as always, his booming voice temporarily hushed; Gladys Popejoy nattering along in her customary stream of consciousness style; Archie O'Brien, smelling of peppermint and holding himself rigidly upright.

Then, as they were about to set off, Ethel Jerome came up and spoke to Beulah. Louise had noticed her during the services; she was a tall, spindly-legged Negro girl. Beulah greeted her rather gushingly. "Why, hello, Ethel, I didn't expect to see you here. How are you?"

"Okay. I came with Miss Villard's friends. You know. The ones she sent me to after I left you."

"Oh, so you're still working for them. How nice."

"Yes. I'm still working for them." Ethel's voice was polite, yet somehow insinuating. Louise had a fleeting impression of hostility. "Terrible about Miss Villard. A terrible thing. Well. I just thought I'd say hello. How's Michael?"

"Not too well, I'm afraid. Nothing serious, but he's been running a slight temperature and I've taken him out of school for the time being."

"That's too bad," said Ethel. Again that puzzling undertone— resentment of Beulah's effusiveness, maybe, and mockery of it. Ethel disengaged her hand and stepped aside. "Well. Don't let me keep you."

"Nice to see you again, Ethel. So glad to hear you're doing so well. Good luck! Goodbye!" Still in a flutter, Beulah explained, on the way to the car, "Ethel Jerome. Such a nice girl, and an excellent maid. Wasn't it good of her to come today. Quite touching, really. She was devoted to Fern."

Uh huh, thought Louise. But not to you. Why try to cover it up with all this rattling?

By the time they reached Beulah's apartment, in the East Fifties, her composure was restored. "Won't you come up and have a cup of coffee?" she asked, turning toward the back seat to include High and Louise in the invitation. "Please do."

"Delighted," said High. He had been unusually quiet during the ride; no doubt plotting his strategy to expose George as the anonymous phone caller. Here was his chance. He popped out of the car like a cork out of a bottle.

And what did that double-crossing George do but decline! Much as he'd like to, he just couldn't take any more time, he'd had to skip all his afternoon classes as it was, but the boys were counting on him for softball and he didn't have the heart to let them down, it was a good hour and a half trip back to Lothrop Hall anyway, and what with traffic, et cetera, et cetera. High's face was a study in frustration; it was all Louise could do to keep from guffawing. The nuances of the situation were not lost on Beulah, either. There was a twinkle of amusement in her eye as she stepped out of the car. "So sorry. Michael will be disappointed too. Some other time, then. Do let's make it soon, George."

"Absolutely. I'll give you a buzz." George shook hands all around. "I wish we could have met under happier circumstances. Let's all get together again."

"We will," High assured him ominously. But George was too busy pulling away from the curb to get the message. With a wave and a smile, he was gone.

"Now for that cup of coffee," said Beulah cheerily. "Or maybe we'd better make it a drink."

The apartment house was geometrical and glassy, with banks of concrete terraces, plastic shrubbery, and mobiles in the lobby. Beulah's living room seemed all the pleasanter by contrast. It was spacious, uncluttered without seeming bare, a little too much gray, maybe, but vivid colors would not have suited Beulah's personality. The furniture, like her clothes, was in unobtrusive good taste. Michael lay on his back on the couch, his legs twisted into a complicated pretzel-like arrangement that served as support for the book he was reading.

"Michael darling, you'll ruin your eyes." Beulah crossed to him, flicking off the television set on her way, and laid the back of her hand solicitously against his forehead. "Are you all right, dear? I brought some friends up for a drink. They're from Fern's office. Did you remember to take your pill?"

He unwound himself and stood up, a knobby, undersized kid in slacks and a cashmere sweater. No shoes, argyle socks. Beulah probably spent her spare time knitting. Spotty complexion, prominent teeth, nose slightly swollen, as if from chronic sinus trouble. A straggle of limp blondish hair across his forehead.

He looked somewhat better when he smiled. And his manners were nice. He was even polite to his mother: patiently explaining that yes he had taken his pill, no his temperature was no higher, yes he was all right. His voice had the same engulfed sound as hers; otherwise they were nothing alike. Against her protests (he should be resting) he handed round the drinks—coke for himself, Scotch for the others.

"George Villard drove us home," Beulah told him. "But he didn't have time to come up. Had to get back to school."

"Duty calls," said Michael. "How they doing back at good old Loathsome Hall?"

"Now, dear. He was sorry not to see you. Said the other boys miss you and hope you'll be back soon."

"Stop, you've got me all choked up." He grinned at High and Louise. "My mother and her myths. She will cling to them. Like what a popular number I am among my assorted contemporaries. And Gorgeous George encourages her. What are you gonna do?"

"Gorgeous George?" asked High. "Is that what you call him?"

"You know how boys are," Beulah said. "It's against their principles to admit they like school or their teachers."

"Actually, old George isn't so bad," conceded Michael. "I've seen worse. I guess. Except he's got this dedication complex. Hey. You the ones that found Fern? Gruesome, wasn't it? The police grilled you too, huh?"

"Don't be ghoulish, dear. The whole thing's settled now, anyway."

"I'm not so sure," said High. "The police claim it's all settled, but they could be wrong. If you ask me, there's more than one loose end."

"Like what?" Michael gave an excited gulp and leaned forward, blinking rapidly. "Yeah, but the guy tried to kill himself. Like what?"

"Like why did he wait till Monday morning to cut and run, for one thing. Weesie, you'll bear me out on that, you're the one that figured it out. If he was guilty he'd've panicked right away and never showed up Monday at all. Like how come he hasn't confessed, never mind he tried to kill himself, he's fool enough to do that for any number of reasons. Like who was making those telephone calls, for another thing. Don't try to tell me it was Max Sutter. I've got my own ideas on that score. Okay, laugh," he added, with a bitter glance at Louise. "I don't care. It still makes sense to me."

"Excuse me, Mr. Dudgeon," said Beulah, who was smiling too. "I can't help it. It's just so fantastic to think of George—"

"George? You think it was George?" Michael's face shone with the light of unholy ecstasy. He came within an inch of falling off his chair. "Hey. How about that? Dedicated Teacher's Double Life Exposed. Like Dr.

Jekyll and Mr. Hyde. Confesses to Anonymous Phone Calls. Prime Suspect in Scissors Sex Murder—"

"Michael darling!"

"Yeah, but what if he's right, Mother? He could be. It wouldn't be the first time they arrested the wrong guy. Sometimes they even electrocute them and then twenty-seven years later there's a death-bed confession and come to find out they burned the wrong guy. No kidding, he could be right. Why not? It's a common psychological phenomenon. These hearty, well-adjusted types like Gorgeous George are the ones that go berserk. How do we know he didn't nip into town after the softball game, zip with the scissors, and back again to Loathsome Hall and his red-blooded American boys?"

"Maybe we don't know, but the police do," Louise pointed out. "They checked on George, along with everybody else."

"The police," said Michael scornfully. "Those geniuses. Besides, they'd already made up their so-called minds it was Max Sutter. You've got something, Mr. Dudgeon, sir. I'm with you." He shot across the room to High, who was looking slightly dazed, and thrust out his hand. "Look, now that I'm sprung from school I've got plenty of time to concentrate. *And* one or two lines of communication still open out there. I'm bound to come up with something and when I do you'll hear from me. We'll have a code. Like GeeGee for Operation Gorgeous George. Okay?"

"Well—" said High. He peered doubtfully at his self-appointed assistant, who was now scratching himself in various places, literally itching with eagerness.

"Now that's enough, darling. I mean it. I won't have you playing detective if it's going to get you this worked up. You know what the doctor said about taking it easy."

"Oh, Mother—" Michael turned on her, almost savagely. But she won: he flopped back into his chair and stayed there, nursing his coke (and no doubt his dreams of glory) behind a screen of lofty detachment.

"Funny kid," High offered tentatively, while he and Louise rode down in the elevator. They had not lingered after the first drink. "Of course I'm no judge. In the neighborhood where I grew up kids didn't go to private schools. Not many of us even made it through high school. What did you think of him?"

"Too much mother," Louise said promptly.

"Well. But she's a widow, he's all she's got. And then he's sickly."

"Spoiled kids usually are."

"I guess I never knew many spoiled ones, either. He got all steamed up about George, didn't he? Maybe because he's running a fever. Or maybe all kids get steamed up like that. I can't remember."

"You got him started."

"I know," he said uncomfortably. "He just might come up with something, though. After all, he does know George, and the set-up out at that school. Trouble is, how will I know whether he's really got something or just making it up for kicks?" After a moment of worried silence, he squared his shoulders. "Well. Face the music when I come to it. Where you going? Home? I'll drop you off."

Cruel and unusual punishment. A haunting phrase, thought Archie O'Brien. A phrase of peculiar poignancy; he was having his third drink with W. J. Robinson. How had this disaster come to pass? As simply and inevitably as all the other disasters that befell Archie. He had said Yes instead of No when W. J. suggested a drink after the funeral. Furthermore, he had let W. J. pay for that first drink, thereby committing himself to the second, just as he was now committed to a fourth on account of having absent-mindedly accepted the third. Cruel and unusual punishment. Not permitted by law. But there was no law against W. J. Robinson.

"What?" he boomed. "What's cruel and unusual punishment?"

Watch it, boy. No more thinking out loud. "Everything," Archie explained, with a sweeping wave of his cigarette. "Life. Death. Funerals. All a lot of mumbo-jumbo. There ought to be a law against funerals."

"I'm an Episcopalian myself," said W. J. "They have a very impressive—"

"Mumbo-jumbo," repeated Archie. Stay in the driver's seat, that was the ticket. Don't let the long-winded bastard take over again. "I don't care what the brand name is. All a lot of mumbo-jumbo. That business this afternoon. Nothing to do with Fern. What it does, it mars the image. Who do they think they are, trying to mar my image of Fern? Haven't I even got a right to remember her the way I want to?" The blurred glimpse he caught of his own face in the bar mirror impressed him. What pathos! How the man must be suffering!

Then his gaze switched to the unmoved, cold-eyed face beside him. And it had been a tactical error to end up with a question. W. J. was proceeding to answer it. "You have every right," he declaimed. "Your memories of Fern are your own, as mine are mine. And I think I can safely say—"

"Your memories! You didn't know her!"

"Possibly not." W. J. lowered the rockbound coast of his profile and peered into his glass. "Certainly my acquaintance with her differed from yours. In a number of ways. I would be the last to deny it. Nevertheless—"

"What do you mean by that?" Mistake again: another question. He hurried on. "You didn't know her at all. Not in any way. Didn't like her, either."

"Is there any reason why I should?" W. J. paused, then went on, ponderous and reasonable as always. "I'll be frank with you, Archie. Knowing her as intimately as you did—I don't think that's too strong a term, correct me if I'm wrong—you could not but be aware of the situation that existed between us. To put it bluntly, she was out after my job. What's more, she would in all likelihood have succeeded in getting it."

A tremor in that granite jaw? A faltering note in that inflexible voice? Archie must be imagining things. "Come now, I wouldn't go so far as to say that."

"I would. Oh yes. I know my limitations. I've never deluded myself about my capabilities, in this position or in any other. I've had a good many, you know. Almost as many as you. Not that I'm implying any similarity ... *The Compleat Angler* probably seems like pretty small potatoes to you. It's not to me. Or to High Dudgeon. He'd fire me—or any of his staff, for that matter—in a minute if he found somebody else that could do a better job. Right?"

"I suppose so." It was not an idea Archie liked to think about.

"You know it as well as I do. So did Miss Villard." W. J. smiled a shark-like smile. "You couldn't by any chance tell me where she kept the sample Questions and Answers column she was working on, could you? I have good reason to believe that's what she was doing."

"Couldn't prove it by me," said Archie carelessly. "Ask High. He probably knows."

"I don't think things had reached that stage yet. No. If he had seen it he wouldn't keep it a secret. He couldn't wait to wave it under my nose. Don't worry, if she had finished it I'd have heard about it before now."

"So she hadn't finished it." Archie thumped down his empty glass and signalled to the bartender. Number four coming up. Obligation fulfilled. "She never will now. So what's your problem?"

"No problem, no problem. Call it intellectual curiosity. Naturally I'd be interested in seeing how she handled my department."

"Sure. Naturally." Interested in cribbing from her, you mean, Archie thought, interested in passing off her stuff as your own. Son of a bitch, you'd steal the pennies off a dead man's eyes.

"It just occurred to me that she might have mentioned it, might possibly have shown it to you. Not that it matters, of course. I just thought if you did happen to know—"

"I don't happen to. And she didn't happen to." Archie closed his eyes; there was her disdainful face, the rich, unattainable curve of her breast.

Sorrow pierced him. The waste, the senseless waste, the fire turned to ashes, the brave music lost in the clinking of a million drinks, the maundering of a million petty-souled W. J. Robinsons ...

"Cruel and unusual punishment," Archie announced in ringing tones. Suddenly he surged to his feet. There was one wavering moment while he sought and found his balance. Then he stalked out.

Sometime later—however much time it took to walk himself damn near sober—he strode briskly into the familiar lobby, exchanged nods with the elevator starter and noted that the hands of the bronze wall clock stood at four twenty-one. So that was how much time it took. Very interesting. Except that he seemed to be a bit hazy about when he had started walking. However. Here he was, a man of decision and conscience, bent on cleaning up some odds and ends of work, even though *The Compleat Angler* was officially closed down for the rest of the week.

Conscience? Well, that might be stretching a point. But decision— definitely. Somewhere in the course of his long recuperative walk he had made up his mind that he was not going to expose himself to any more conversation today. This applied not only to Mrs. Archie O'Brien, who was never at a loss for words on the subject of Archie O'Brien's shortcomings, but to all the rest of the human race as well. Bar after bar he had passed, without so much as a twinge or a backward glance. Bars meant people; people meant talk. He did not care to listen to anybody else's troubles or relate his own. What he wanted, and what he was going to have, was solitude: the silence of his own four office walls, the bottle in the desk drawer, and, when the spirit moved him, the couch in High's office where on one or two previous and unpublicized occasions he had slept.

He could hardly wait to reach the twelfth floor and sanctuary. His hand shook as he unlocked the door to *The Compleat Angler* suite. Nerves. He had had a bad day. A bad week. A bad couple of decades, if you insisted on working it out to the last decimal point.

So maybe it was nerves again, the feeling he had when he stepped inside, the swift, strong impression that he was not alone in the office. It seemed to have no definite basis. Nothing seen or heard or even smelled. More like a disturbance in the air, as if, seconds before, someone had closed a door or ducked around a corner. Oh Lord, he thought wearily, W. J., he's probably ransacking the place for that so-and-so Questions and Answers sample.

"Hello?" he called. "Hey there?"

No answer. Only the echo of his own voice bouncing back from the row of cubicle doors. They all stayed closed. After a moment he moved on down the hall, rather self-consciously checking each cubicle as he passed. All empty. All in order.

That settled it. Nerves. What he needed was a drop of good old solitary bourbon to soothe his nerves. He returned to his own office and poured himself a generous drop. Rocking gently in his swivel chair, with his feet propped on the open desk drawer and the little fluted paper cup handy beside him, he felt lapped in tranquility. This had been an inspiration. Oh yes, he could still come up with one occasionally; even now, after months of fishing tackle and bait, the old O'Brien spark was not completely quenched. Give him a chance, and he'd snap out of this temporary slump and start rolling again. Onward and upward. Pretty small potatoes, W. J. had said—and that reminded him. He reached down and plucked from the bottom drawer the sample Questions and Answers column Fern had started but not finished. She had brought it along to show him that day last week, the last time they had a drink together.

Now he skimmed through it again. W. J. had a point, all right: lucky for him High hadn't seen it yet. Archie swivelled toward the window and gazed out beyond the parapet at the pattern of towers and spires against the translucent sky. He thought about Fern and that last drink together; and about W. J., poor old clod, he had never deluded himself about his capabilities. After a while he tore up the sheets of copy and dropped the scraps into the waste basket. So much for Fern's sample column. It would do W. J. no harm now. And no good, either.

Tranquility. Solitude. Silence ...

The sound was tiny and furtive, like the scurry of mice in a country house. Which this was not. He stopped with the bottle poised for his third refill. Listen. There it was again. Wasn't it? Was it? The back of his neck prickled. He waited, sensing—as he had when he first unlocked the outer door—the presence of another human being who, like himself, was listening and waiting and holding his breath. Nerves. He had checked all the cubicles. But not the mail room. He remembered it now. Not the mail room. Cautiously he set the bottle down and got to his feet. It surprised him, the way the damn floor lurched under him. He leaned against the desk, giving it time to get its bearings.

There was no doubt about the sound now. A rustle, a faintly scraping footstep right outside his door. He lunged to open it. "Who's there?" he yelled. But the instant before he emerged into the hall he heard the unmistakable click of the outer door closing. Again he lunged, and again he was just too late. The corridor was empty; the doors of the middle elevator were gliding shut; the red light of the arrow above it blinked out as Archie watched.

A lucky kid, whoever it was.

The luckiest kid in town; he had hit it right on the nose of five o'clock. At the other end of the corridor the Publix doors flew open and out rushed the first contingent of the liberated. The same thing was happening all through the building; for the next fifteen minutes the elevators would be jammed, and stopping at every floor. No chance in the world of singling out from all that horde one lucky kid who didn't belong there. He could of course be reported—

Yes, but first find out what there was to report. A sneak-thief, most likely, somebody who had managed to get hold of a key and had figured now was his chance, while the office was empty. But a peculiar sneak-thief, Archie decided after he had made the rounds—this time thoroughly. As far as he could see, nothing was missing. Twenty-odd dollars in the petty cash box. A good deal more than that in stamps. Three transistor radios, a couple of electric clocks, a drawerful of tempting gadgets in High's desk, more cash in Louise's, several cartons of cigarettes. All still there, and scattered throughout the office space, so that no matter where Lucky Kid might have been when Archie interrupted him he could have picked up something to make his visit worthwhile. Or so it would seem.

Archie wandered back to his cubicle and poured another drop. He squinted at the telephone.

Nobody's going to believe me, he thought. For a moment he wondered whether he believed himself.

6

"Oh, hello, Arch," Louise said into the phone. It had roused her from another of the spells of suspended animation that by now were familiar to her; she had been falling into them at intervals ever since Fern's death. They could not be called periods of meditation, or even reveries. The events of the past few days simply sat there in her mind, like a stew in a kettle with no flame beneath it to start it simmering. Coming home from the post-funeral drink at Beulah Hannaford's, she had dropped onto her living room couch and had stayed there, her feet on the hassock, her hands idle in her lap, her mind a mere receptacle.

"Is High there, by any chance?" Archie asked in the stately tone that meant he had had one or two more than the usual. "Or do you happen to know where I can reach him?"

"Sorry, but I don't. He had a dinner date with Max's lawyer, but I have no idea where they were going. Is something wrong?"

"That is the question," said Archie. "Two schools of thought. The situation calls for an independent opinion."

"What is this, anyway? You're talking like W. J."

"I *beg* your pardon." Looped, she thought. Lucky for him High's not around. But he was going on, briskly now, quite like himself. "Listen, Louise, do me a favor and come up here, will you? No kidding, this guy's giving me an inferiority complex."

"Up where? What guy? Where are you?"

"At the office. The detective. Good old doubting Thomas himself. From Missouri."

"I'm on my way," said Louise. "Be there in fifteen minutes."

She was, too. With a head full of wild surmises, including another body on the parapet. It did seem like an anti-climax, Archie's thin little tale of an intruder. Was it drunkenness that made him cling to it so stubbornly? He was certainly not the soberest man alive. He did not pretend to be.

"You say you came up here to work?" inquired the detective, with another thoughtful glance at the bottle and paper cup on Archie's desk.

"A euphemism," said Archie blandly. "I felt the need of solitude. And I didn't get it. Damn it, I *know* there was somebody here. I don't care if there isn't any sign of him, nothing missing or disturbed. Comes to that, I don't care if you believe me or not. Go ahead, brush me off, blame it on the bourbon. But you're making a big mistake. Louise can tell you. You know me, Louise, you know I'm not that drunk."

"Of course you're not," said Louise, more out of loyalty than conviction.

But that was before she spotted the sunglasses. They were on Fern's desk, a pair of dark green sunglasses with side pieces like blinders, and they changed the whole picture for Louise, converted her from neutral to fiery partisan. Archie's intruder was not imaginary: the sunglasses proved it. She was absolutely certain that they had not been there earlier in the afternoon, when everybody met in the office before going to the funeral.

"How can you be so sure?" asked doubting Thomas from Missouri. "After all, with half a dozen people milling around, anybody could have come in here and—"

"But nobody did!" cried Louise. "I mean, I was the last one. Arch, you remember, we were all at the door, ready to leave, and High couldn't find his reading glasses. Claimed he couldn't, they were in his pocket all the time, but anyway. I came back to see if he'd left them in his office, and of course that meant coming through Fern's, you can't get to his office any other way, and I had glasses on my mind so I would have noticed. I remember distinctly, I stopped here, right here by Fern's desk for a minute—it looked so terribly neat, with nothing on top but the telephone and the empty file box, not even a pencil. So terribly neat. Grim. Then High yelled that it was all right, he'd found his glasses, and I went on out. By that time everybody was outside in the corridor waiting for the elevator. Everybody but High, he was holding the outer door open for me. I was the last one out. And I would have noticed. I *know* there weren't any sunglasses!" It was the same phrase Arch had used, delivered with the same passion, and received with the same polite restraint.

"Somebody could have stopped in after the funeral," the detective pointed out. "Another member of the staff in need of solitude or with some other legitimate errand. I think you said you didn't come straight here after the funeral, Mr. O'Brien? So there would have been time. Suppose we check on it now."

"You can skip me and High," said Louise. "We stopped for a drink at Beulah Hannaford's and then went on home. And Max is out. Wouldn't you say?"

"I would," said the detective, poker-faced.

"So that leaves the rest of the staff. Donna sometimes wears sunglasses. She's the type. Wait a minute, while I find the complete staff list. Here it is, and their phone numbers."

They stood side by side, Louise and Archie, listening while the detective made the phone calls. No one had been in the office that afternoon. No one was minus a pair of sunglasses.

"There you are," said Archie with a summing-up flourish of the hand. "It was somebody that didn't have any business here. Otherwise why sneak around? Why not answer when I gave a shout? One of the staff would have answered, even if he was up to his neck in skullduggery. He'd be out of his mind not to, when all he had to do was make some excuse, any little old excuse." It was a good point; Louise wished he hadn't lurched so noticeably in making it.

"You never can tell what people will do when they're overwrought." The detective dealt them each a smile of tolerant good will. "We all get carried away now and then." He tucked the sunglasses in his pocket. Mentioned other possibilities: a cleaning woman, one of the maintenance men. Assured them that the matter would of course be thoroughly looked into. After that he departed.

"He didn't believe us," Louise said incredulously. "Didn't believe a word either of us said. You about the intruder. Me about the sunglasses."

"You protested too much. Yak yak yak. I kept trying to signal you to tone it down a little. That's where you made your mistake. Too positive."

"At least I didn't lurch!"

"What you need is a drink," said Archie. He took a firm grip on her arm and steered her down the hall to his office. He seemed suddenly sober and dependable, equal to the situation. "There we are. Cheers. I didn't expect him to believe me. Why should he? Why should anybody? Present company excepted, of course. But you've got to admit, it wasn't me that convinced you, it was the sunglasses. They didn't convince the detective because—"

"You told me before. Because I yakked too much."

"Not only that. Because he's not as gullible as you are, dear." Archie was watching her with the mixture of curiosity and amusement he so often turned on High. "It would never occur to you, for instance, that I might have left those sunglasses there myself."

"You! Archie O'Brien, if you—"

"As it happens, I didn't. But I could have, and if I had I naturally wouldn't admit it to the detective, especially not after you made such a production out of the damn things."

"You wouldn't admit it to me, either," said Louise in a hollow voice.

"Probably not. But I also wouldn't call it to your attention. I didn't leave them there, Louise. So help me. I was just giving you an example of the difference between you and the detective. Don't worry, it occurred to him that those sunglasses might be mine—or yours, as far as that goes. They're not, are they?"

"Mine? They certainly are not!"

"I didn't really think so," said Archie calmly. "So who's left? And what were they up to? It doesn't have to have any connection with Fern, you know. My first thought was a sneak-thief. Only nothing was missing. That's why I asked for the detective when I called, because it seemed so screwy …"

"It is screwy. A sneak-thief wouldn't have a key. He'd have to break the lock."

"Yes, but you know how High is about keys. Hands them out like they were free samples, and doesn't always remember to get them back when somebody quits or gets fired."

"That's true," Louise admitted. "And Gladys is always leaving hers in the ladies' room or on her desk, instead of taking it with her when she goes home at night. She forgot it again today. I noticed it on her desk. So somebody could have gotten hold of a key."

"A sneak-thief would have *taken* something, though, even if I interrupted him at the very beginning. Look, Louise. I checked the offices, so he must have been in the mail room when I came in. Why didn't he at least swipe the stamps? And he must have already been in Fern's office, because that's where the sunglasses were. Why would he have passed up the petty cash box? Answer is, he wouldn't have. So it wasn't a sneak-thief. Or a cleaning woman or maintenance guy—that's a lot of bull. They'd have answered me, the same as anybody on the staff would have."

"I wonder if Donna would have," Louise said, after a moment. "I've never been able to figure her out. Have you?"

"Never bent my mind to the problem. Another drop? Say when. Donna ..." Archie clasped his hands behind his head and rocked in his swivel chair. His expression was one of alert interest. The fading light was kind to his bloodshot eyes and hard drinker's flush. "It has crossed my mind that she's got a yen for Max. Dreary, isn't it? But I have now and then detected a gleam in Donna's eye. When she wasn't wearing her sunglasses. Wonder how she spent the afternoon. She didn't go to the funeral."

"Mr. Field had a date to see her, after he talked to Max. You know, the lawyer. He told High she hadn't sounded very cooperative over the phone but he was hoping to get something out of her when he saw her. If she's got such a yen for Max, she'd at least cooperate with his lawyer. Wouldn't she?"

"Sure, if it would help Max. But suppose she knows something that would do him more harm than good? Or suppose it's not just Max she's worried about, but herself too? If I'm right about the gleam in her eye, she had more of a motive than Max for wanting Fern out of the way."

"Oh come on, now. She was in Queens Friday night. Had dinner with her parents and stayed overnight. At least that's what—"

"I know. What she says and what they say. And the police see no reason to doubt it. Why should they, when they've got an ideal suspect like Max? They elected him, right at the start, and he hasn't done anything since to make them change their minds."

"He hasn't confessed, though," said Louise. "I can't help thinking he would if he was guilty. Just give up and confess and get it over with. He's given up, all right. What's the use of a lawyer, what's the use of anything, why did we have to turn off the gas ... But he hasn't confessed." She paused, aware of the deepening twilight and the silence. "If he didn't do it, Arch, then—then maybe it was the murderer you heard this afternoon."

"But why?" Archie switched on the desk lamp and peered at her crossly. "What would he come here for? Nobody's bothering him. The police are happy with Max. He's gotten away with murder. Why the hell not leave well enough alone?"

"He must have been looking for something. Something he forgot Friday night, like the sunglasses he forgot today, and the police overlooked it when they searched, but he's scared it will still turn up and he can't take the risk. It's something irrefutable," (a good word, and the way it rolled out, without a hitch; gratifying) "like a bloodstained handkerchief with his initials—"

"Please, Mrs. Clarke. A little more subtlety? The cops might notice blood. No. It's a package of letters, Fern was blackmailing him, see, and he couldn't find them Friday night because she'd filed them under M instead of B. No, wait. She was pushing dope in her spare time, she hid the stuff in her ball point pen, and—"

The phone in High's office rang, and they both jumped a foot.

"I'll get it," said Archie. But Louise was quicker on her feet, or maybe just nearer the door. It would be a wrong number, she told herself as she raced down the hall, or High might possibly try the office because he couldn't get her at home. No cause for alarm. Nothing necessarily sinister about a phone call, even if it was after hours and the office was supposed to be closed and a mysterious intruder—but not a murderer, that was just a flight of fancy—had been prowling around.

"Hello?" she said breathlessly.

"Is Mr. Dudgeon there?" The voice was foggy and unmistakably adolescent; she recognized it at once, and melted with relief.

"It's Michael, isn't it? This is Mrs. Clarke ... No, Mr. Dudgeon isn't here. Is there anything I can do? If you want to try him a little later at home I can give you the number."

"I've got it. Thanks, anyway," said Michael forlornly. "The thing is, I may not get a chance later. It's highly confidential." He hesitated, and added, in a sepulchral whisper, "Operation GeeGee."

"What? Oh. Oh yes, I read you. I'll probably be talking to Mr. Dudgeon later, if you want to get a message through to him. Can he reach you at home?"

"No! That's no good. Don't let him call me at home."

"All right. I understand." It would be tactless to specify the Master Mind's mother and the dim view she had taken of Operation GeeGee.

"I'll try him again tomorrow morning. Ten o'clock," said Michael.

"Right. I'll tell him to stand by."

Louise hung up and turned to Archie, who stood, swaying perceptibly, in the doorway. "So High's found himself a disciple," he said when he had listened to her sketchy account of the situation. "A real eager beaver, from the sound of him. I didn't know Beulah had a son ... Who is it she reminds you of? Her voice, I mean, that engulfed-cathedral voice. I've been trying to place it ever since this afternoon at the funeral. That's the first time I met her. To talk to, that is; I saw her once when she stopped by to pick up Fern. Is there some actress with a voice like that?

Never mind, it'll give me something to mull over when I can't sleep nights. I don't envy George Villard, with High and the kid on his tail. What was your impression of Fern's erstwhile spouse?"

"Not at all what I'd expect. He seemed so—I don't know. Earnest. Naive. I had the feeling I must be extra nice to him because otherwise I'd be extra not-nice. You know?"

Archie nodded. "And yet, if you want to get technical, he's the one who stood to profit if Fern died. I don't mean she left him any money. Doubt if she had any to leave. But she was into him for a nice chunk of alimony every month. He won't have to pay it anymore ... Ah, the hell with it. Let's have a drink."

"I'm hungry," said Louise firmly. "Any more to drink and I'll fall on my face. If you want my candid opinion, so will you."

"Okay, I'll buy you dinner." Again Archie seemed to have reached one of his plateaus of sobriety. His step was steady, his manner cheerful and responsible. As they went out the door he laughed, rather wryly. "So much for resolutions. I came up here with the avowed purpose of having no more conversation today, with anybody whomsoever, on any subject whatsoever. And look at me now. It's you, Louise. You'd charm a hermit out of his cave."

"Sure, sure."

"Why don't you and High get married and live happily ever after? He's in love with you, whether he knows it or not."

"It's a lovely idea. Only I happen to be married to somebody else."

"So you are. The seafaring man. I keep forgetting him."

Louise sometimes forgot him herself. Probably not as often as he forgot her, though. "Besides," she said, "it's not me High's in love with, it's *The Compleat Angler.*"

"Lucky High. I'm not saying you're right, mind you. But lucky High, anyway. All that enthusiasm. All that—faith. I used to have it too, you know. Only somehow or other I lost it in the shuffle." For a moment Archie's face looked profoundly sad. "Here's the elevator. Let's go."

The conference was scheduled for eleven o'clock the next morning in High's apartment, but Louise had been urgently requested to get there early. She did so, feeling a good deal less ragged than seemed logical. Dinner with Archie had stretched out to include more brandies than she cared to remember, and when at last she did get home, there was the phone ringing and High frantically wanting to know where she had *been* all evening. He had of course assumed that she would be waiting with bated breath to hear his report on Mr. Field, and was a little miffed to find that she had a more spectacular report of her own. Not for long, though: here was a fine load of fresh fuel for his Save Max campaign. A prowler in the office! Obviously the murderer returning to the scene of the crime. Who else? And Michael with who-knew-what to impart!

"Now try not to get carried away," Louise said when he had ushered her into his living room and settled her on the couch. He was wearing slacks and a terrible sport shirt with palm trees splashed all over it. Through the years she had managed to get segments of High's wardrobe under control—he no longer appeared at the office in perforated two-toned shoes or the striped-suit, checked-shirt, dotted-tie combinations that used to be his specialty—but when it came to casual clothes the lid was off. "Remember, Michael's just a kid. A bored kid, with a lively imagination. For all we know, he may be a compulsive liar. So whatever he says, take it with a grain of salt."

"Right. My feeling exactly. Here, have some coffee." His face shining with happy excitement, High wrestled the electric percolator free of its plug and poured Louise a cup and saucer full. He then upset the sugar bowl and sat down on the paper bag of Danish from the bakery. "Listen, I was a kid once myself. Dreams of glory. The cloak-and-dagger bit. I've been through it too. Don't worry about me getting carried away. Did you get any idea of what's on his mind? Me either. Not a clue. You look pretty this morning, Weesie. When you going to get a haircut? He just might come up with something, you know. I told you, didn't I, Field says Donna may not be a bad witness if he can get her to wash her face and comb her hair. She gave him the lead on this phone call Fern got Friday night. Max hadn't thought to mention it, trust him to skip anything that might do him some good. Where is the kid? He said eleven on the dot. Of course if his mother decided to stay home from work today ..."

At eleven on the dot Michael rang the doorbell. He came in noiselessly, wearing crepe-soled shoes, a rain coat with the collar turned up, and an inscrutable expression. But he was as full of nervous blinks and itches as he had been yesterday, and the submerged gulp of his voice surfaced occasionally into an uncontrollable squeak.

"The thing is, I got to thinking ... Hey, don't let me forget to call my mother at eleven thirty. If I don't, she'll call me at home and whammo that will be it. Friday night, that's when it happened. Right? Well, listen, who's got the scoop on Gorgeous George for Friday night? Me. That's who. Because I was with him, that's the night he drove me home from Loathsome Hall! How about that?" He stuffed half a Danish into his mouth and chomped; Louise averted her gaze.

"You didn't say anything about this yesterday," she said.

"I'm like that. A part-time idiot. But after you left I was trying to decide which of those jerks on the softball team might fill me in on George and

Friday night, and whammo, it hit me. I could forget the jerks. Who needed them? Poor old George didn't make the softball scene Friday night. He was stuck with me. And here's something else. I wasn't in any great sweat to come in. I could have stood another night out there. Friday night wasn't my idea. It was George's."

"And your mother's, I bet."

"Well, maybe. But she wouldn't have insisted. Because he was doing us a favor. He didn't have to drive me in at all. He could have picked his own time. He did. He picked Friday night."

"That's true," said High. He glanced at Louise, and added, "Of course it doesn't necessarily mean anything."

"Wait. Wait till I tell you." There was a pause while Michael took on another load of Danish. "So it's about seven thirty when George picks me up with my bags and stuff at the dorm and we bid farewell to lovely Loathsome Hall and its simple, kindly natives. And it's a quarter of ten when he dumps me at the old homestead. Now. It said in the papers she was killed 'some time Friday evening,' so that puts George here in Manhattan at the right time, doesn't it? Not more than ten minutes away from *The Compleat Angler* office, in fact."

They thought it over. Louise said, "But how about the guard in the lobby downstairs? Surely he'd notice a stranger—Oh, I forgot, the Publix party. I suppose it could still have been going on, even as late as ten."

"It was quite a party," High put in. "Field says the record for that night is a mess. You know, where they sign you in and out. Charlie was the guy on duty, and chances are he'd had a nip or two himself. So George wouldn't have had any problem there. You said seven thirty to quarter of ten, Michael? I didn't realize it was that long a haul."

"It isn't, usually. But we stopped for hamburgers and cokes, and for George to make this phone call—"

"Phone call! He made a phone call? When? What time did he make it?"

"Cripes, Mr. Dudgeon, I wasn't paying much attention. Is it important?" Michael was all blinks and innocence. "I'm not even exactly sure where we stopped ... Hey, that reminds me, okay if I use your phone to call my mother?"

Louise couldn't help noticing—even admiring—the artistry of Michael's conversation with his mother. Yes, he had taken his pill. No, his temperature hadn't gone up. He was just kind of lazing around, watching TV and reading. Okay, okay, he knew about the soup and stuff for his lunch. Yeah, and the milk. He sounded listless and plaintive and entirely convincing. A real pro at deceiving his mother. Well, weren't most kids?

She also couldn't help wondering how much he caught of what High was whispering during the course of his phone call: "Listen, Weesie, this could be it, the phone call Fern got just before Max left. Eight thirty, he claims, and Field says if we can track it down ..."

"That'll hold her for a while," Michael said with satisfaction, when he had hung up. "Oh brother, the things she can think up to worry about. Over-compensation, they call it. Like she's got to make it up to me because my father got bumped off."

"Bumped off?"

"Car accident. Whammo. Never knew what hit him. I don't even remember him. Now. Where were we? We stopped for hamburgers and cokes, and George made this phone call. Time, time, what time was it? Excuse me while I concentrate." He whacked his forehead, squinted, blinked, scratched, snuffled. Perhaps he also concentrated. "It was a diner, and the hamburgers were lousy. Gee, Mr. Dudgeon, the nearest I can make it is about eight thirty, but I could be off ten minutes or so, either way, I'm sorry I can't be more definite ..."

"It fits, Weesie," said High. "Max signed out at eight thirty, right after she got the call, that's why he walked out, the final straw. George and his phone calls! I had a hunch right from the start about those anonymous calls she was getting."

"Yeah," said Michael, "but this one Friday night wasn't anonymous. Whoever he was calling he told them who he was."

"How do you know? You mean you heard what he said?"

"Well, not all of it," said Michael modestly. "But the phone booth was at the end of the counter, right next to where I was sitting, so I couldn't help overhearing some of it. And I could see him in there, talking up a storm. You know. Like he was handing her a line."

"Her? So it was a girl. Did he call her by name?"

A tempting question, if Louise ever heard one; and Michael hesitated for an instant before he said, with genuine regret, "No, I didn't hear any name. He called her dear, so I figured it must be a dame. Unless old George is a queer. Hey, he could be, at that. Maybe that's how come Fern divorced him, because he—"

"Michael," said Louise, in much the same tone Beulah had used in her efforts to restrain him yesterday. But without the "darling."

"Okay, I was just woofing. He called her dear, and he said—yeah, he said 'Wait for me. I won't be too late.' That much I know he said. 'Wait for me.'" He shot a defiant glance at Louise. "You think he was talking to Fern, Mr. Dudgeon? He could have been. Honest, it wouldn't take him even ten minutes to get to the office from my mother's apartment. And he was in a sweat to get away, that's for sure. Didn't even come up with me in the elevator."

"You'd think he'd at least say hello to your mother," said High. "As good friends as they are."

"Sure. She thinks he's the greatest. Always has," Michael added, with a touch of bitterness. "But Friday night he just dumped me and beat it. Ask her if you don't believe me. She'll tell you." He scratched, once more in a transport of itchy bliss. "You going to the police, Mr. Dudgeon? Huh?"

"Not till I've talked to George. Eh, Weesie? Talk to George first."

"I should think so," said Louise drily. "Especially since he must have already given the police a satisfactory explanation of what he was doing Friday night."

"They had their eye on Max, though, right from the start," High reminded her. "I bet they didn't even ask George about the anonymous phone calls. And what about yesterday after the funeral? He claimed he had to get back to the school, but how do we know he didn't stick around town a while? Nobody's asked him about that."

"Yesterday?" Michael, who had been in the middle of putting on his rain coat, froze to attention. "What's with yesterday after the funeral?"

Louise gave High a warning look, and it worked. "Just something else I wonder about. We won't go into it now."

For once Michael yielded without an argument. A nice little tribute to High. "Okay, Mr. Dudgeon. I can research it for you, even if I don't know what you want it for. Yesterday after the funeral. I'll be in touch." He paused at the door, to add in a dreamy tone that did not match the craftiness of his expression, "Come to think about it, old George didn't seem like his usual happy carefree self Friday night. I wondered at the time what was eating on him. He didn't say two words, all the way in. Bye now. Be seeing you."

7

Louise was late getting back to High's apartment that evening. (He had wasted no time in phoning George Villard. Who, sounding a little puzzled but cooperative, had explained that he was coming in to Manhattan for the evening anyway, and would be glad to drop by for a drink.) So she was due there at six thirty. It was W. J. Robinson's fault that she didn't make it till seven.

Well, and her own. For being too good-natured, too weak-willed, too— gullible, to use Arch O'Brien's word. She had believed W. J. when he assured her, over the phone, that he wouldn't take more than half an hour of her time, not even that much, just a couple of details he wanted to get squared away. She should have known better: W. J. was perfectly capable of taking half an hour to say How do you do. By the time he stopped hemming and hawing and got to the point, Louise was exasperated almost to tears. She was also ashamed of herself for snapping at him, and, in spite of everything, sorry for him. He was a very worried man.

"I don't know how fully informed you are as to what transpired yesterday afternoon subsequent to the funeral services—"

"I know about the office prowler, if that's what you're getting at," said Louise impatiently. "I've already told you. Archie and I were both there when the detective called you and the others to ask about the sunglasses."

"Yes. Exactly. And it has since occurred to me, particularly in the light of certain confidential remarks I made to Archie prior to that, remarks which might be misinterpreted—"

"Look, W. J. Did you leave those sunglasses on Fern's desk and then lie about it to the detective? Is that what you're trying to tell me?"

"So he did accuse me!" For once W. J. dropped circumlocution in favor of straightforward venom. His cold blue eyes glittered. "Now it comes out. Now we know where we stand. Well, this time he's gone just a little too far. This is nothing less than defamation of character, and I intend to put a stop to it, even if it entails descending to his own mud-slinging level. I mean that, Louise. Archie's tongue wagged too, over those drinks we had together. Oh yes, he said a couple of very interesting things himself, if I cared to repeat them. At least I didn't mince words. I came right out and asked him about the Questions and Answers column Fern was working on. Well, why shouldn't I want to know where it is? You'd ask too, if you knew somebody was out to get your job. But to accuse me of sneaking back to the office and prowling around looking for it ..."

"Archie didn't accuse you," said Louise. "He didn't mention the column business or even that you had a drink together."

"Ha! Then perhaps you will be good enough to explain where you got the impression I was the guilty party." W. J. folded his arms and waited.

"I didn't mean it that way. I mean, I only asked you because—" But it would be too unkind to tell him the truth, which was that she had asked out of irritation and boredom. Too unkind and too much of a shock: he never seemed to have the slightest inkling of his own effect on other people. "I wasn't serious, really," she finished lamely.

"Please, Louise. Don't you start lying to me too. It's about what I'd expect of Archie, of course. He wouldn't even admit he knew what Fern was up to, when the fact is he probably was helping her write it. It's perfectly obvious he's been telling you a pack of lies about our conversation. As for this famous prowler of his, I'd be interested in knowing how many drinks he'd had when he heard whatever he heard."

"Several," said Louise. "And I'm sure you'll be pleased to know that the detective didn't believe Arch—or me, either—any more than you do. Relax, W. J. There's nothing to worry about."

"You can say that. Relax. Nothing to worry about. Of course there isn't—for you and Archie. You're both in solid with High. He thinks you hung the moon. And Archie went to Harvard, he can do no wrong. I don't happen to have those advantages. I can't afford to lose this job, Louise. I don't know where I'd find another one." It was a bleak, accurate statement of fact; for an instant W. J.'s dignified air changed from counterfeit to genuine.

"But you're not going to lose it!" cried Louise. "At least not because you're suspected of prowling around the office. Arch didn't accuse you, honestly he didn't. Not to me, not to the detective, not to High. Your name didn't even come up. You don't have to *worry*, W. J.!"

"Possibly not about that." The look he turned on her was cold and searching as a winter wind. "But it still leaves the little matter of Fern's column. I wonder if I could ask a favor of you, Louise." He was smiling now, the half-obsequious, half-sly smile that always put her off. "Just for my own information, I'd like to see that column before it reaches High's attention. We all know the key position you're in, and particularly now that he's without a secretary everything will pass through your hands for routing. So I was wondering if you would mind—"

"Doing your snooping for you? Yes, I would mind. Very much. You're in such a twitch about this column you say Fern was writing. Well. You can damn well look for it yourself—if you haven't already."

"And you still insist nobody accused me." He stood up. His face was white with rage. "Go ahead. Run to High with this little tidbit too. He'll believe you. Sure. The same way he believed everything Fern told him. The same way he believes a drunken bum like Archie O'Brien. Did anybody think to ask him what *he* was doing in the office yesterday afternoon? Him and his memories of Fern. He had them, all right. He wasn't lying then. More memories than he cares to live with, if you ask me. They might very well constitute cruel and unusual punishment."

"What are you talking about? Are you suggesting that Arch—"

"I'm not suggesting anything. I'm simply quoting what he himself said. He seemed to have cruel and unusual punishment on his mind. His brilliant Harvard mind. Interesting, isn't it?" At the door W. J. turned and loosed his parting shot. "Another interesting point that you may or may not have forgotten. It just so happens that he was in the building Friday night, too. Never a dull moment when Archie's around, is there?"

"Shut up," whispered Louise. Unnecessarily: the door had already closed behind him, she was alone with her shaking hands and the lump of angry tears in her throat. She swallowed them doggedly. There was no time to cry. No adequate reason, either. Really! To fly into a rage herself simply because W. J. blew his top and spouted a lot of spiteful nonsense about Arch ...

But he had been in the building, right there on the same floor at the Publix party, on Friday night. He could have left the sunglasses, which had seemed to Louise such convincing proof of his intruder story. To Louise, yes. To the detective, no. "Because he's not as gullible as you are, dear." Arch's light, pleasant voice echoed in her ears; she saw again his smile, the odd flicker of curiosity and amusement, as he watched her. Could he have been testing her gullibility at that moment? Revelling in the virtuoso skill of his own glib tongue?

She pressed her palms against her temples, as if to keep her head in one piece. Nonsense. Arch couldn't possibly be that devious.

But until a little while ago she would have said that W. J. couldn't possibly be that violent or vindictive. It just showed how little she knew about anybody. Because at one point the gleam in his eye had seemed to her positively murderous ...

She snatched up her coat and fled.

"You're late," said High. "Where the hell were you? We're having a drink. Want one?"

"Quarrelling with W. J. Scotch, please. Hello, Mr. Villard."

She saw at once that High had already jumped in with both feet. His hair (thinning now, and no particular color) was standing on end, his glasses were crooked, and his forehead was puckered into a nervous frown. George Villard also showed signs of wear and tear. The expression in his round eyes was one of helpless surprise. A light film of sweat glistened along the edge of his tan crew-cut; his hand too, when he shook Louise's, felt moist. He smiled at her anxiously, as if he were hoping for help but not counting on it.

"Mr. Dudgeon was just telling me that Fern had been getting anonymous phone calls? Yes. I guess you knew about them, too. Well, I didn't." His voice took on a blustering note. "This is the first I've heard of them, and the idea that I might be responsible for them is absolutely preposterous, the most ridiculous thing I ever heard in my life. Nobody who knows me could possibly make such a suggestion, or take it seriously if somebody else made it. I can't take it seriously myself. You must be joking. Why, anonymous phone calls—they're on the same level with poison pen letters. People who do things like that are sick, they're disturbed, they need help! I ask you. Do I look like the type?" He thumped his broad chest, as if it were the conclusive proof of his wholesome, undisturbed psyche.

"Okay." High straightened his glasses, maybe to get a better look. "I just asked was all. I didn't say—But somebody was making those calls. Threatening her, trying to scare her. The question is, who?"

"I don't know," said George. But his eyes shifted. "Maybe some sneak-thief, checking to see if anybody was home. I've heard they do that. Fern and Beulah were robbed, you know, not so long ago."

"But this bird knew where Fern worked. It couldn't have been just somebody looking for an empty apartment to rob."

"Then I have no idea who it could have been. I told you before, Fern and I didn't keep in touch. I sent her her alimony check every month, and that was it. You know more about her personal life than I do, who her friends were. And her enemies." He sat down, hulking and somehow forlorn in his madras plaid jacket and gray slacks. "I keep forgetting the enemies. What about this fellow they've arrested? Max? Why couldn't he have been making the calls?"

"Because he couldn't, that's why. He certainly didn't make the one she got that day in my office. I remember distinctly, he was there when the phone rang, we were having an argument, and Fern told us to pipe down so she could hear. That's one thing they can't hang on Max. They're not going to hang the murder on him, either, if I have anything to say about it."

"Oh," said George, like a balloon collapsing. He took out his handkerchief and patted his hairline. "But just because he didn't make the calls. I mean, that doesn't prove he didn't kill her. The police didn't seem to have much doubt about his guilt. At least that was the impression I got when they questioned me."

"The police," said High impatiently. "Listen. After what I told them about those phone calls, and then they didn't even ask you about them, didn't even mention them to you. That's the police for you!" Again George's eyes shifted. He had evidently convinced High that this was the first he had heard of the phone calls. But Louise wondered.

"Well, of course I was pretty upset at the time. I don't remember everything that was said. I know they asked about the divorce, and what our relationship had been since then. That sort of thing. And about Friday night, the way they must have asked everybody." He smiled tentatively. "Lucky for me I had an alibi, I guess, and Michael to back it up. That was the night I drove him in from school to his mother's apartment."

High's face turned red with embarrassment. Was he going to make one of his lightning switches and wind up, no longer George's assailant, but his passionate defender? This might just do it, this guileless, misguided expression of George's trust in Michael.

"Yes, he told us," said Louise, to fill in the silence. "We met Michael yesterday, you know, after the funeral. Too bad he's not well enough to stay on at school."

"It seemed the best thing to do, to bring him in to Beulah's," said George. He inspected his hands. "Well. To get back to the police. That was mainly what they asked me. About Friday night. It was while they were talking to me that word came in Max had been found, so—"

"So naturally that settled it." Louise could see, from the set of High's jaw, that the crisis was past. No switch. "Why question you or anybody else any further? Case dismissed."

"I'd already told them all I had to tell."

"Yeah. Including the phone call you made on the way in?"

"What? Oh. That's right. When we stopped at the diner." George's manner was pleased and approving: High might have been a bright pupil, coming up with a detail Teacher had overlooked. "No, I don't think I mentioned it. No reason to. It wasn't of any significance."

"Just a personal call, I suppose?"

"A personal call, yes. Look here, what is all this, anyway?" Belatedly, George's eyes sharpened. "How did you know about it? Did Michael— But why would he even remember a thing like that, let alone mention it to anybody? Who cares if I made a phone call on the way in?"

"Max might, for one. According to him, somebody called Fern at the office just before he left. That's why he left, in fact, because it sounded to him like she was making a date with some other guy."

"Listen. Did that little bas— Did Michael tell you I called Fern Friday night?"

"He didn't say who. He didn't hear you call her by name. Just 'dear,' so he figured it was a girl."

"I see. Just 'dear.' No name. And what else did he hear me say? Don't tell me, let me guess. 'Stay right where you are, dear, I'll drop in later and kill you'? Something to that effect? Well, for your information—" He rose up, majestic in his wrath. "—I did not call Fern Friday night or any other night in the last four months, and furthermore, it's a physical impossibility for Michael to have heard one word of the phone call I made from that diner because he was sitting at the other end of the counter, as far away from the phone booth as he could get, even if I hadn't kept the door shut, which I did, and furthermore, the juke box was blaring so I could hardly hear myself! Put that in your pipe and smoke it!"

"Now wait a minute." It was interesting to see High, that noted creator of scenes, playing the role of mollifier. Made a nice change, thought Louise. "The kid didn't say all that, what you said, about killing her. All he said was you called somebody about eight thirty, which was about the time somebody did call Fern—"

Somebody had to extricate him; Louise said, "You don't like Michael much, do you, Mr. Villard?"

The question seemed to jolt him. "I like all my boys," he said stiffly. "Whatever Michael told you, I'm sure he was motivated less by malice than by mischief. Yes. He has a lively imagination, and it's been overstimulated by all this violence, and ... I didn't mean to imply that he's a bad boy. Certainly not. There's no such thing. He has his problems, who hasn't, a few areas where he needs to make a more satisfactory adjustment, a certain amount of hostility toward me because—" He stopped short and swallowed resolutely. "It's normal for adolescents to manifest hostility toward any established authority and the individuals representing it, teachers, parents, so on. What else did he say?"

"Well," said Louise thoughtfully. She had liked George much better in his fit of honest anger. "Well, that you were unusually quiet Friday night on the way into town, and seemed in a great hurry to get away, didn't even go up in the elevator with him. We did wonder a bit about that, under the circumstances. Michael being ill, I mean, and Beulah worried about him."

"Oh, for—In the first place, I was double parked. I helped him unload his stuff and get it in to the elevator. He wasn't all that sick, that he couldn't go up by himself. Beulah understood the situation. And I was in a hurry. I had an appointment with—with the friend I called from the diner. The police know about it. They have her name and address. She can confirm the call and appointment both."

A girl friend. Naturally. An attractive young man like George—well, reasonably attractive—would of course have a girl friend to confirm call and appointment. And to marry, especially now that he was through paying alimony to Fern. "That was about all," Louise said, "except for yesterday afternoon. You were in a hurry then, too. Let's see, you must have gotten back to the school by—what time? Three thirty or so?"

"Yesterday afternoon? As a matter of fact, no, I didn't go straight back. There was, uh, something I wanted to do here in town. So it was about seven when I got back to school." Once more George swabbed his hairline. Then he asked, "Why?"

"Apparently somebody paid an unofficial visit to *The Compleat Angler* office yesterday afternoon. It may not mean a thing. Just sort of mysterious. I suppose you had another appointment with your friend?"

"I—As a matter of fact, no. What I did, I went to the library. I'm doing some post-graduate work in psychology, and whenever I have a little extra time—" He gestured toward the briefcase he had left on the hall table. "I know I said I had to get back. To tell you the truth, I wasn't in the mood for socializing. What was stolen from *The Compleat Angler* office?"

"That's the mysterious part. Nothing. Do you ever wear sunglasses?"

"Sure. Often. Here—" He reached in his breast pocket. "No, I guess I didn't bring them today. I usually do. Or maybe I left them in the car. What about it?"

"Somebody left a pair on Fern's desk yesterday."

"I get it," said George. "And what did Michael darling overhear this time? Did I kill somebody else? Or was I just revisiting the scene of the crime?"

Here we go again, thought Louise. Good. "He doesn't even know—"

"Well, let me tell you, he's going to hear plenty from me! I'm going over there right now and give him an earful he won't soon forget. Him and Beulah both. What I ought to do is take him by the scruff of his scrawny little neck and shake the bejesus out of him." On his way to the door he stopped in mid-stride. "I suppose he's been peddling this beautiful bill of goods to the police too?"

High, who had been joggling anxiously on the edge, spoke up. "Just us. Listen, Villard, don't be too hard on the kid. I'm as much to blame as he is. More. I'm the one that started him off in the first place."

"Bull," said George. "I know Michael." He grabbed coat and briefcase. The door slammed behind him.

"Knows Michael, and has no use for him." High's expression was chastened and unusually thoughtful. "And it's mutual. Why do you suppose they hate each other? That's what makes it tough. Damn it, now I don't know who to believe! The kid could have been making it all up out of spite, and yet he sounded so plausible. But then so did George. Weesie? Didn't he sound like he was telling the truth?"

"He did when he was mad," said Louise. "Excuse me, when he was manifesting hostility toward Michael. Maybe that's what Michael can't stand, the gobbledegook he talks." Absent-mindedly she straightened the hall rug, rucked up by the storm of George's departure. Her eye fell on the table. "Hey! He's gone off with your briefcase instead of his! Look, High, this is his, his initials."

"Come on, maybe we can catch him." As always, High was cheered by the prospect of action; by the time he had jammed on his hat, hustled Louise into her coat, and out of the apartment, he had recovered most of his normal bounce. But when they emerged from lobby to street, there was no sign of a middle-aged green Chevy, or of a large young man in a madras jacket, carrying a briefcase that didn't belong to him. "We'll grab a cab at the corner," said High. "My case is full of office stuff. If we miss him at Beulah's God knows when I'll get it back. Did you buy that business about the library? No way of proving it, I guess ... Hell, Weesie, he could be lying. They both could be."

"Everybody could be," said Louise. Herself included: during the cab ride to Beulah's, she gave High (because he remembered and asked about it) a quick run-through on her conversation with W. J. She didn't lie exactly, but she edited right down to the bone. Things were already confused enough, without introducing a Questions and Answers column that Fern might or might not have been writing and that W. J. might or might not have ransacked the office for—assuming, that is, that Arch was not lying and somebody really had ransacked ...

She closed her eyes and leaned her head against the cab seat cushion. "Poor Weesie, you're tired." High patted her cheek tenderly. "Hey, here we are. And that's his car, isn't it? I just hope he hasn't killed the kid yet. Well. Beulah wouldn't let him. She's probably raising holy hell with everybody." He grinned wanly. "Especially me."

The doorman, perhaps remembering them from yesterday, nodded cordially as they whizzed past him. The self-service elevator was waiting to bear them silently and swiftly upward. Even before they reached the door to Beulah's apartment, which stood ajar, they could hear the voice of George Villard, raised in righteous anger. "I'm warning you, I'm not going to stand for this kind of persecution. Letter or no letter. I don't care about the damn letter—" Then Beulah and Michael both speaking at once, the two foggy voices—protesting? placating? threatening?— merged into an unintelligible gargle. Then, as High pressed the bell, the melodious, sprightly chime; a sharply hissed "Sh!" from one of the three inside; an instant's hush; muffled footsteps.

Michael pulled the door all the way open and peered out at them. His face—ordinarily rather impassive—seemed at this moment like a kaleidoscope, so varied and rapid were the expressions that crossed it. But of them all, the one that stuck in Louise's mind was a kind of demure excitement, the look of a scared but happy bride. It, too, vanished; Michael produced a snuffling "Hi" by way of greeting. He did not invite them in.

Neither did Beulah, who appeared with George in tow while High was explaining their errand. (Her expression was simply harried; his irate.) There was an awkward exchange of "sorry's" and "thanks a lot's", along with the switch in briefcases. "A good thing Weesie noticed it," High said, as they edged away from the door. "I don't know about yours, but mine's work I brought home from the office. I don't even know what's there myself. Haven't had time to go through it. But it's no good to anybody but me. Well. Thanks again. So long."

George had already retreated into the living room. Glancing back, Louise saw Beulah and Michael still standing in the doorway, their faces oddly alike for the moment, frozen in identical—and to her unfathomable—expressions.

Down the hall and around the corner, they found that the elevator had gone about its business; High pressed the button and turned to her, all agog. "Damn it, Weesie, why did I have to ring the doorbell? We could have—"

Footsteps thudded behind them; it was Michael, flapping his arms like some large, agitated bird. "Oh man, is he in a sweat! Old George is really flipping this time! Wait'll you hear!"

"Listen, Michael, what did he mean about the letter? What letter?"

"He tell you about that? No? I bet he didn't! He's going to have a tough time talking his way out of that one. Wait'll you hear."

"That's what we're doing, waiting," said High curtly. "Quit stalling and tell us."

"Who's stalling? I haven't got the whole bit yet myself. He was just going good when you—" Michael's voice sank to a portentous whisper. "It's something about Fern, see. Man, is he in a sweat to get hold of it! Look, I've got to get back before they send out the bloodhounds. I'll call you in the morning. Okay? Just hold everything till then." He darted off. The elevator glided to a stop. They rode down in deep, busy silence.

<h2 style="text-align:center">8</h2>

On Friday morning W. J. Robinson awoke, as usual, to the sound of his wife's voice; an alarm clock was a superfluous piece of equipment in the Robinson household. "Yes, dearie," he mumbled, and heaved himself up groggily before he realized that the voice was, for once, not aimed at him.

She was having one of her little chats with her sister on the telephone. "... that's just what I said, might be just the spot for Arthur, I've always thought it was a shame he never did anything with those art courses he took, more talent in his little finger than ... Even if it doesn't pay quite what he has in mind to start with ... Exactly what I said, worth it if he finds himself ... Art Director, that's the title. The fellow that killed her, yes, that's right, under arrest, so they'll have to replace him, and as I told Woodrow, I said, all you need to do is put in a good word for Arthur, that's all it would take, one word in the right quarter ..."

W. J. (who would never be anything but Woodrow at home) put his distinguished white-haired head in his hands and groaned. He had been sleeping badly of late; last night worst of all. Now, after an hour's fitful doze, he was once more at the mercy of his worries, which gathered like a swarm of gnats whining spitefully in his ears. A good word in the right quarter for his nephew Arthur, once more between jobs—Yes, but who would put in a good word for W. J. himself? No one; after yesterday, not even good-hearted, easy-going Louise Clarke would find anything to say in his defense. He remembered wistfully the favors she had done him in the past. There would be none in the future. Even if she had not turned into an outright enemy, she was lost to him as an ally.

And he still did not understand quite how it had happened. Why should he suddenly lose control at hearing what, after all, he had expected to hear? For he had known that Archie O'Brien would tap him as the office intruder; that was his purpose in going to see Louise, to convince her it was a lie, to explain, calmly and reasonably—

He groaned again, and stumbled into the bathroom.

"Morning, dearie," he said when he emerged. She had finished talking to her sister and was locked in combat with the vacuum cleaner, jamming its clanking joints together to show it who was the boss.

"Look out for the ironing board," she said. "I hope you don't want an egg because there aren't any. I knew I should have done the marketing yesterday myself. You never pay any attention to the list. Might as well not give it to you. I thought you'd be sleeping late this morning, with the office closed. You can help me with the living room drapes."

She was mounting a major attack, then, not just the usual daily skirmish. Living room drapes meant the big push. W. J., edging past the ironing board and into the kitchen, where battle preparations were clearly in evidence, considered his own position and decided on orderly retreat. "Afraid I can't, dearie, not this morning. High asked me to look in at the office and go through the mail for him." He sloshed the contents of the glass coffee maker—only slightly muddy—and turned on the gas. "I couldn't very well say no. Somebody's got to do it. Not just anybody either. Somebody with a sense of—"

She switched on the vacuum cleaner. "The way you let that man push you around," she yelled above its roar. The subject was a favorite of hers. She covered it at some length, and from it made a smooth transition to Arthur and the one good word that was needed to put him on *The Compleat Angler* pay roll and solve everybody's problems. W. J. leaned against the sink and sipped his coffee. Through the years he had developed a protective device, a sort of internal hearing aid which could be turned off at appropriate moments like this one. It left him free for his own worries, of which Arthur was the least. Now that he had plucked it out of thin air, the office errand seemed to him quite an inspiration. As long as he was already branded as sneak and intruder, why not make an honest man of Archie O'Brien for once in his life? He had nothing to lose. He might even find what he was looking for.

Slight though the possibility was, it buoyed him up. He stepped out into the street a few minutes later with a brisk air—not merely a refugee from the living room drapes, but a man with a mission. It was all he had ever asked of life, really, a niche to call his own, a cubicle, a desk, with luck a title—yes, that was nice, his name on the mast head, and after it Associate Editor, Questions and Answers, it gave him an identity. So little to ask. And yet so much to lose.

Maybe if he called Louise and apologized? With one of his rare flashes of perception, W. J. decided not to risk it, at least not yet.

While he waited in the office building for the elevator, he explained to Charlie, who was on duty this morning, about going through the mail. In his own mind the line between fact and fiction was by now comfortably blurred. Besides, this open approach was proof that he had nothing to hide. "I understand there's some talk of a mysterious prowler up there the other day?" he added.

"Yeah, the detective was asking me." Charlie shrugged. "A building this size, and I'm supposed to keep track of who comes and goes? Can't prove anything by me. I did notice what's-his-name, O'Brien, come in. Looked to me like he'd had a few over the quota. But beyond that I don't know from nothing. The lock wasn't broke, and there wasn't anything stolen, so what's their beef, anyway?"

"Right," said W. J. "You're absolutely right."

The postman had left the bundle of mail outside the office door; he picked it up on his way in. Inside, all was unnaturally quiet and orderly. He went down the hall, past the cubicles and through the anteroom that had been Fern's, to High's office. There he removed his hat and topcoat, and there he began his search. He worked his way methodically through High's desk, through Fern's, and was about to tackle Archie's as the next best bet when the phone rang. It startled him; maybe because of the emptiness of the place, maybe because of his own mildly questionable activities. His first reaction was not to answer it. But supposing High or Louise had tried to reach him at home and had been told he was here? He did, after all, have the mail as an excuse. He went back into High's office and picked up the phone. "W. J. Robinson speaking," he intoned.

"Is this Miss Villard's boss?" It was a woman's voice, rather timid.

"Mr. Dudgeon isn't in today. Can I help you?"

"I don't know exactly what to—I thought maybe her boss. Somebody on the magazine."

"I am on the staff. Associate Editor. In charge of Questions and Answers."

"Oh." The woman laughed, a pleasant, spontaneous sound. "Then maybe you're the right one. I've got a question, all right. Maybe you can give me the answer."

"I'll be glad to try," said W. J., a little stiffly. "May I ask who's calling?"

"Oh. Ethel Jerome. I used to work for Miss Villard, a while back, and I thought being's I was in the neighborhood, right around the corner, if you weren't too busy, I mean, Miss Villard's boss—"

"As it happens, I have some free time; in fact, the office isn't officially open. So if you'd care to come up I can give you fifteen or twenty minutes."

"Fine, that would be fine. I can be there in two shakes. I'd appreciate it, Mr.—"

"Robinson," said W. J. "Just take the elevator to the twelfth floor. I'll be on the watch for you."

Five minutes later he was opening the door to Ethel Jerome. He remembered seeing her at the funeral: a tall, lean Negro girl, with her hair skinned up all around and a black velvet pancake hat pinned on top. She followed him shyly down the hall to High's office. He had decided that was the best place, in case of any more phone calls. And then it was bigger, more impressive. Not of course that he had any idea of passing it off as his own.

"Now then," he said, tipping back in High's chair and clasping his hands behind his head. He smiled across High's desk at Ethel Jerome. "Now then, what can I do for you?"

"Well, the thing is," she began. She pulled nervously at the cuffs of her blue suit; the sleeves were not quite long enough. "The thing is, Miss Villard loaned me some money a while back when I needed it, and now I—"

"Yes?" His smile began to congeal.

"Oh, I'm all right now. Don't you worry, Mr. Robinson." Again she laughed in that spontaneous way. "I didn't come up here to put the bite on you. The thing is, I still owe some, and I don't know who to pay it back to, now that she's gone. I ought to pay it to somebody. Don't you think?"

W. J. thought it over. "Yes, I see what you mean. A debt outstanding. I should imagine to the decedent's estate, though I'm not sufficiently well versed in the legal ... Hmmmm. May I ask, uh, how large an amount is involved?"

"Oh, it's not so much. I was paying her back in installments, like, and

I'd got it down to twenty-five dollars." She fumbled in her handbag and produced an envelope. "The thing is, I get my pay on Saturday, so I put it aside and I was going to call her Monday, only here it was in the paper about her. Well. I didn't like to ask Mrs. Adams, that's where I work now, Miss Villard got me the job. But I thought I ought to find out from somebody because it's not my twenty-five dollars." She eyed him sternly. "I'm not keeping what don't belong to me. That's all."

"Exactly. A commendable attitude, and one in which I heartily concur." It was the truth; whatever W. J.'s failings, they did not include dishonesty in financial dealings. "As I see it, the question we are faced with is, to whom is the money now payable, in view of Miss Villard's—"

And as so often happened, just when he was coming to grips with a subject, he was interrupted. In the middle of one of his better phrases. Ethel Jerome turned toward the door, listening, as he was listening, to the quick, light footsteps coming down the hall.

"Hi! So it's you, W. J. I wondered—" Louise Clarke, in her customary hurry, skidded to a stop in the doorway. She looked (also customary) somewhat windblown: pink coat hanging open, briefcase in hand, curly hair dishevelled, face delicately flushed, big eyes wider still in surprise. Not a pretty woman, really, but she often gave the effect.

"Good morning, Louise." W. J. remembered the mail, and gestured toward it. "Yes. It occurred to me that it might be helpful if I—"

"Hello," Louise was saying to Ethel Jerome. "I can't think of your name, of course, or where I—Oh yes, at the funeral. I'm Louise Clarke."

So W. J. was not even permitted to perform the introductions. He did, however, manage to get in a few words of preliminary explanation before Ethel Jerome took over. Louise flung off her coat and perched on the edge of the desk, facing Ethel, and from then on W. J. might just as well have not been there for all the notice he received. The conversation was completely out of his hands—and a very peculiar turn it took, in his opinion. The problem was primarily legal in nature, but neither Louise nor Ethel seemed to grasp this fact, or, if they grasped it, to feel any concern about it. The angle that caught their attention—women!—was utterly irrelevant.

"I should have thought you'd ask Beulah Hannaford," said Louise. "After all, you worked for her too, didn't you? Seems to me she's the logical one to ask."

"Well, Mrs. Clarke, to tell you the truth." Ethel twitched at her cuffs and looked off into space. "Well, I guess I just never thought of her."

"You could still ask her, of course. I expect she knows the name of Fern's lawyer, assuming she had one." W. J. was glad to hear at least one reference, however brief and casual, to the crux of the matter. "So

Beulah Hannaford's the one to—"

"I'd just as soon not, if it's all the same to you." After a pause, Ethel added bitterly, "She'd say it was fifty dollars I owed instead of twenty-five."

"She'd what? Why in the world would she say a thing like that?"

"Because according to her I'm a thief. That's what she called me. A thief. Oh, not to my face. Not her. Behind my back. I wouldn't have minded so much if she'd come right out with it. But oh no, all this sweet talk about how sorry she is, dear Ethel, you do understand don't you, I wouldn't feel right if I didn't take What's-her-name, this other maid, back now that she's available again ... And the other day at the funeral, sweet as pie, she's so glad I'm doing so well. She thinks I don't know what she was up to, behind my back. Huh!"

"Wait a minute, you've lost me." And W. J. as well, when it came to that. The difference being that he didn't care, whereas Louise seemed to find this domestic squabble, whatever it was, of absorbing interest. "If it was all behind your back, this thief business, then how do you know she said it? I mean, who—"

"Miss Villard. And that's another thing. How do you think it made me feel, asking Miss Villard to help me get another job when here come to find out she'd been told I was a thief? Why, I was never so embarrassed in my life! I could have sunk right through the floor!"

"She couldn't have believed it, though. Because she did help you get the job you have now, didn't she? Yes, and lent you money besides."

"That was afterwards, after we got together and compared notes. But when I first called her, you should have heard the way she laced into me. I had a nerve, asking her to recommend me when I'd been discharged for stealing, I could consider myself lucky I wasn't in jail. All like that. Well, it was the first I'd heard of it, me being a thief, and of course she realized I must be telling the truth once she thought it over. Because I'd have to be some kind of a nut to call her at all, let alone expect a reference. Anyway. We finally got it straightened out. No thanks to Mrs. Hannaford. If it had been left up to her, Miss Villard would have gone to her grave believing it was me that took all that jewelry and stuff from their apartment."

"So that was it, the apartment robbery," said Louise. "Were you there the day it happened?"

"Sure. Sure I was there, in the morning. But if you think—"

"I don't," said Louise hastily. "Believe me, I don't think so."

"Okay. It just gets me so mad, every time I think about it." Ethel took a deep breath. "The way it was, I went there three mornings a week. Mondays, Wednesdays, and Fridays. That way it was cleaned up for the week end, and after, and once in between. And gave me time for other jobs, afternoons. So this Wednesday Mrs. Hannaford hadn't gone to work yet when I got there, she was waiting to let me in. Because they'd had the lock changed, see."

"You mean whoever robbed them had a key?" asked Louise.

"Well. The lock wasn't jimmied. Mrs. Hannaford said they could have come in through the fire escape window. Said it was open when she came home Monday night and discovered there'd been a thief. Said I must have forgotten to lock it when I left Monday. But they'd had the lock on the door changed, anyway, just to be on the safe side. She just kind of brushed the whole thing off—oh well, these things happen, could have been worse, they had insurance. All like that. Not one word about thinking it was me. She hadn't gotten around to having an extra new key made for me, so she said she'd either wait for me again on Friday or leave me a key with the doorman. Well. I never went back, Friday or any other day. Because that night she called me with this story about the other maid turning up, the one that used to work for her, she's so sorry, she'll mail me a week's pay, so on. It never even dawned on me that there was any connection—Not till a month or so later, when I was kind of up against it and I called Miss Villard."

"She was the one you called. Not Mrs. Hannaford."

"That's right. Because I—Tell you the truth, I liked her better. She was tougher to work for, in a way. More particular. But she didn't gush the way Mrs. Hannaford did. You knew where you stood with her."

"Yes, you did," said Louise thoughtfully. In all fairness (not that anyone asked his opinion) W. J. had to agree: Fern Villard had been nothing if not open about her designs on his job. Too arrogant for dissembling, he thought; that had rankled too. "How about Mrs. Hannaford's son?" Louise was asking. "Did you like Michael?"

"I don't really know him. Never saw him but once or twice." Ethel looked off into space again. "Seemed to me like she spoiled him. It happens that way sometimes where it's an only child. I didn't dislike Mrs. Hannaford, you understand—not till after I found out she was trying to put if off on me, about the robbery. But that's something I'm not going to forget, somebody calling me a thief. If she'd even said it to my face—"

"But she didn't," said Louise. "Just to Fern. Did she mention it to the police, I wonder?"

"Miss Villard said not. Said if it had been her, she would have, but by the time she got home the police had been and gone, and Mrs. Hannaford said let it go, they couldn't be absolutely sure it was me, think how awful to tell the police if it wasn't, so on. Best just to fire me and get the lock changed. So that was how it was. And that's why I'd just as soon not have anything more to do with Mrs. Hannaford. Only I don't know what to do about the money."

"I can ask George Villard," said Louise. "He must know whether Fern left a will. I understand she didn't have any money to speak of, just a small checking account. She didn't even own much furniture. Sold it all when she and George broke up. But she did have a few pieces of jewelry, and of course a lot of clothes. That's where Fern's money went. She loved clothes."

"Knew how to wear them, too." Ethel sighed and stood up. "Is it okay if I leave this with you? I'd appreciate it. Whoever it belongs to, I want them to get it." Her laugh rang out. "Even if it's Mrs. Hannaford."

She remembered W. J. and shook hands with him too in farewell. At the door she turned, as if on an impulse, for one last message to Louise. "Mrs. Clarke, I know good and well I never left that fire escape window open. I checked it, like I always did, the last thing before I left, and it was shut and locked. I told Mrs. Hannaford so. Maybe that's why she— I guess maybe she didn't like me contradicting her like that about the window. I mean—"

"I know what you mean," said Louise, and W. J. had an odd second of feeling that there actually was a current of understanding between them, something unspoken and—as far as he was concerned— unshared. Women! Always making a mountain out of a molehill, always investing the most trifling events with some deep, mysterious significance. His own mind was once more engaged with the ticklish issue of his presence here in the office: whether or not a fuller explanation was in order, whether or not he shouldn't, after all, tender some sort of apology to Louise for yesterday's indiscretions. In the end, he decided to take the initiative on the theory that offense constituted the best defense.

"May I ask what brings you to the office this morning?" he asked, when Ethel Jerome had departed. He smiled, to indicate that she might, if she so desired, take the question as a gesture of jocularity.

"What?" Her expression was abstracted, her voice tinged with impatience. "Oh. High asked me to go through the mail." She stared blankly at the bundle on High's desk, with its twine binding still intact.

"The phone rang before I had a chance to get at it," said W. J., in case he was being criticized. "Apparently we both had the same idea about the mail. Two minds with but a single thought, ha ha. Seriously, though, I'm glad of this opportunity to correct any possible misapprehensions arising from our little visit yesterday. I'm afraid I may have spoken a little too hastily, said a number of things that were better left unsaid.

I hope you won't hold it against me ..."

"Of course not. Forget it," said Louise absently. And then, abruptly: "How did she strike you? Did you believe her?"

"Who?" With an effort W. J. shifted gears. "Ethel Jerome? Why yes, I'd be inclined to believe her. No reason not to. What could she hope to gain by telling a long rigmarole like that if it wasn't true?"

"Exactly," said Louise. Her eyes looked very big and bright. Without another word she snatched up her coat and plunged off down the hall, leaving W. J. openmouthed with astonishment. The next moment she was back. "High's briefcase," she explained. "I took it home with me last night because the handle's loose, and there's a very good repair shop in my neighborhood, I meant to leave it there this morning, and of course forgot, walked right past with it under my arm ..." She grabbed the briefcase, and was gone again. This time for good.

Well, she always had seemed to W. J. a rather unstable type. Or, if that was too strong a word, disorganized. No telling what had sent her flying off like that: it might very well have no connection whatever with Ethel Jerome. Hummingbird mentality, thought W. J. The phrase pleased him.

So did the situation. With Louise out of the way, he could continue his search at leisure.

9

"Is Mr. Field expecting you?" asked the efficiency expert behind the desk. She switched off her electric typewriter and removed her glasses, which were leashed around her neck by a black cord; after a couple of bounces they dangled helplessly against the imposing slope of her bosom. Everything under firm control—glasses, bosom, blue-white hair, voice, expression.

"No," said Donna.

"No appointment? I'm afraid Mr. Field has a very busy—"

"Is he here?"

"No, he isn't," said the expert with satisfaction. "May I have your name?"

"I'll wait," said Donna, and sat down on the black leather couch across from the desk. There were three doors, all closed, leading no doubt to the private offices of Mr. Field and his partners, and all no doubt firmly controlled by the expert.

"It may be some time before Mr. Field returns. As a matter of fact, I don't really expect him until after lunch."

"That's all right." Donna slid farther down on her spine and began rooting for a cigarette in her good old saddlebag-sized purse. She also took the letter out and held it in her hand, for comfort.

"If you'll tell me what it's in reference to, I may be able to help you."

Donna decided to let that one lie where it fell. She brushed the hair out of her eyes to get a better view of the expert controlling her temper. It took a minute or two, and considerable mouth tightening and deep breathing. Then the glasses were switched from bosom to nose, the re-activated typewriter began clicking up a storm, and the show was over except for an occasional baleful glance in the direction of the couch.

It was a comfortable couch, a better place to wait than home. Besides, this way she was sure of catching him. It wouldn't take him long to read the letter; his precious busy schedule wasn't going to suffer. Good, he would say. Very good, this clinches the case for us, this is all we need to clear Max, he has a great deal to thank you for, Miss Hirsch.

They might not even transfer him from the hospital to the jail. Might release him immediately. He could sue them for false arrest, why not, and wind up with a bundle, enough to live on happily ever after ...

Donna sank luxuriously into reverie. Now and then she roused enough to re-read the letter, which she already knew by heart. She smoked several cigarettes. Ate a candy bar. Nibbled her fingernails. The expert receded to the outer fringe of her consciousness, no more worthy of notice than the distant hum of traffic. She very nearly forgot Mr. Field himself; when the door opened and he sailed in she blinked at him as if he were an intruder.

"Miss Hirsch!" he said, breaking in on the expert, who of course had started a great bustle and flap about the events of the morning. "Come on in, Miss Hirsch. What's on your mind?"

Donna scrambled to her feet, stole one glance at the expert (controlling her temper again), and followed him into the inner sanctum. "I got this letter," she said. She thrust it at him. "It's from Max. A suicide note."

"Suicide! Good God! Don't tell me he's—"

"No, no, it's from Monday. He wrote it last Monday, before he went up to Dudgeon's, only I didn't get it till this morning because he got the address mixed up, 332 instead of 323. See?" She jabbed her finger at the envelope, on which somebody had thank God made the notation: Try 323.

"He didn't mention any letter," said Mr. Field. "But then that's our boy, that's Max. No blabbermouth he." He peered at the envelope, front and back. With what seemed to Donna maddening deliberation he took off his topcoat and hung it on the rack before he settled down at his desk. And still he delayed, to dart at her a look of sharp alarm. "This isn't a confession, is it?"

"Of course it isn't! Do you think I'd be here if it were? Anyway, he's innocent!"

"I think so, yes." Mr. Field sighed. "It's just that he—"

"Read it," she said between clenched teeth. In her mind she read it with him: the barely legible message Max had scrawled—on the subway? in a post office?—no matter, she was the one he had thought of, in the last extremity he had turned to her. "No use ... Nobody can help me. You did your best. At least this way is quicker. I know I haven't got a chance anyway, so what's the difference ... Whoever killed her, damn him to hell. It wasn't me, it wasn't me. Take care of Duke. Thank you for ..." And then it just trailed off downhill to the initials M. S.

"It's important. Isn't it?" Donna demanded. "People don't lie when they're going to kill themselves. Why should they? They've got nothing to lose. This proves he didn't do it. They'll have to let him go now. Won't they?"

"I wouldn't go so far as to say that," said Mr. Field. His calm air, and his plump, useless-looking hands folding the letter—her letter—and returning it to its envelope, reducing it to Exhibit XYZ, threw her into a sudden fury.

"Give it to me then! It's mine. Give it back, if you're not going to use it, if you haven't got the brains to see—You're supposed to be defending him, and you don't even believe he's innocent! You said yourself, it's just the money, yes, and you expected it to be a confession, that's how much you—Let go of me!" For she had been wrong about his hands; snatching at the letter, she felt her wrist caught in a no-nonsense grip. And the look in Mr. Field's bitter-chocolate eyes matched it.

"What's the matter with you?" It was his whip-cracking voice. "Stop acting like a maniac and listen to me. You want me to lie to you? I'm not going to. This letter won't clear Max. It will help. Add it to what else we've got, and it will help considerably. It substantiates your story about the way he acted when you saw him Saturday night—the behavior of a distraught man, distraught but innocent—and incidentally, when you tell that story in court I hope to God you're not planning to throw a fit of hysterics, because if you do, so help me, I'll—"

She put her head down on his desk and sobbed.

"Go ahead," said Mr. Field. "Get it out of your system. Lay off the telephone, will you? I'd like to be able to get at it, in case it rings."

It was jabbing into her breastbone anyway, so she laid off it. Certainly not because he asked her to. She could hear him rustling through some papers. Then he got up and went outside to confer with the expert. By the time he came back Donna had pulled herself together enough to sit up and blow her nose.

"Now then," he said with one of his cheerful, reassuring little nods. "We've got something else good. Even better than this letter. A couple of women who were at the Publix party, and the Lord bless and keep them, they saw Fern in the ladies' room after eight thirty."

She stared at him blankly. His triangular eyes were snapping with excitement. "Max signed out at eight twenty-seven," he said impatiently. "Now do you get it? They saw Fern after he left. She was alive, and they remember the time because her watch had stopped and she asked them. It was eight thirty-five. How's that for a break?"

Her head bobbed up and down. She could not get out a word.

"They'll make good witnesses, both of them. Salt of the earth types, not lushes. One of them doesn't drink at all. They'd left the party and were going out for dinner. They didn't know Fern by name, of course, but there's no doubt at all it was her. They described her—both of them, separately—down to the last detail. Clothes, hair-do, jewelry, the works. Even Max brightened up a little when I told him about them. Not much. But a little."

"You saw him again, then. Is he—"

"Still in the hospital. Till tomorrow at least. He asked about you."

She swallowed. Even if it was a lie—No, Max might well have asked about Duke, and that would lead to her. Anyway, Mr. Field didn't lie to her. He really didn't. Revolting as he was in some ways; and he needn't expect her to apologize. She stood up and said, in a loud, quarrelsome voice, "They're not the only ones. I don't care what you think. I'll make a good witness too."

"You'd better," he said, and opened the door for her.

Having made a beeline for the public phone booth on the corner, Louise realized that she couldn't call Beulah Hannaford, after all: she had no idea which insurance company Beulah worked for. High might know. But High was not available this morning. He had been summoned to an extraordinary session of the Peerless Board of Trustees to explain the presence on his staff of a murderee and murderer, and she only hoped he was keeping his voice down.

So that left Michael. For some reason, she felt reluctant about talking to Michael. But she would have to, at some point; he must be bursting to elaborate on the letter business they had overheard last night. He had probably been trying to get High all morning. She dialed the number, and was so astonished to hear Beulah answer (and with the speed of lightning, in the middle of the first ring) that for a moment she was struck dumb.

"Yes?" Beulah sounded strained. "Who is it?"

"Louise Clarke. I didn't expect—"

"Is it about Michael? Have you heard from him?"

"No, I haven't. Is something wrong, Beulah? I thought you'd be at the office. That's why I was calling, to get your number. There's something I'd like to ask you about."

There was a peculiar little gulp at the other end of the line. A hiccup, perhaps. Then Beulah said, in her normally foggy voice, "I decided to stay home today. I'm not feeling quite up to par. Nothing serious. Just fatigue, I guess. What was it you wanted to ask me?"

"It's kind of complicated. Of course if you're not feeling well enough to see me—" She let it dangle. So did Beulah, but for only the space of a breath.

"Oh, I didn't mean that. If you'd like to come over, please do. How soon can you make it? Ten minutes? Good. Be nice to see you."

It must be more than just fatigue; when Beulah opened the door to her, Louise got the impression that she was on the verge of collapse. She was puffy-eyed and pale, and her hair, usually so impeccably neat, looked as if she had been running her hands through it. If not tearing it. She wore a long, limp, pale-blue housecoat, with one ripped pocket and the belt inside out. These signs of erosion gave her an unexpected appeal; ordinarily her appearance was too tidy and composed to be very interesting.

"I'm afraid I'm not very presentable," she said, and Louise, following her into the living room, decided that her first impression had been false. Beulah's manner was completely normal. She no longer seemed tottery or trembly. She just hadn't done her hair or gotten dressed yet, that was all. "Would you like some coffee? I'm not really ill. Nothing that a day at home won't cure. Delayed reaction, I guess. It's been a bad week for all of us."

Louise agreed. "Where's Michael?" she added.

Whatever it was that flared in Beulah's eyes—fear? anger?—it was instantly quenched. "He's not here just now. He'll be back later. Are you sure you won't have some coffee?"

"No, thank you." It was a point of honor with Louise: she drew the line at drinking Beulah's coffee while she launched this attack—if that was the right phrase for what she was about to do. She thought it was. "What I wanted to see you about—I just had a talk with Ethel Jerome."

"Ethel Jerome?" Beulah repeated. "How on earth did that happen?"

"She called the office to ask what she should do about the money she still owes Fern."

Beulah sank back in her chair and closed her eyes. "Oh," she said.

"You know about it, I expect. It was a month or so ago, shortly after your apartment was robbed, when Fern helped her find another job."

"I knew about the job. Not the loan. What did Ethel ..." Her eyelids fluttered open wearily. "I can guess what she told you. All right. I admit it now, I was wrong to suspect her. But honestly, she was the logical one. She was here the day of the robbery, you know. Naturally I thought of her. Wouldn't you?"

"Sure. But if I really suspected her I would have said so. To everybody, not just to Fern. I certainly would have told the police. You did call them, didn't you?"

"Of course I called them." A dark, ugly flush rose in Beulah's face. "Why wouldn't I?"

She was still leaning back in that listless attitude. False. Even across the room Louise could sense the tension in her. Her own back ached in sympathy. "Because—" she began, and stopped on the brink of the chasm that separated thinking from saying. It was unexpectedly wide and deep. She might just possibly be misinterpreting what Ethel Jerome had said. Or rather, what she had left unsaid; that was the significant part. Even without it, though, the peculiarities of Beulah's behavior remained. There had to be some reason for her variations on the theme of the robbery. Ethel had supplied a very good reason; it was up to Louise to leap the chasm. She took a deep breath. "Because—"

The phone at Beulah's elbow buzzed, and was immediately scooped up. "Yes? ... No, nothing. Have you?" Beulah's face sagged; once more there was the tremor of imminent collapse. "I see ... No, apparently not. I can't understand ... Yes, please do. And thank you, George, thank you." She hung up, gave Louise one wild, blind look, covered her face with her hands, and burst into tears.

"Beulah! What is it? What's the matter?" Louise bounded out of her chair and stood by in helpless dismay. There was no response to her questions or to her timid pats. Beulah continued to cower in her chair, her shoulders hunched and heaving. It seemed to Louise an alarmingly long time before the sobs tapered off into gulps (like the one she had heard when she called from the phone booth; Beulah must have been crying then).

And finally it came out, in a burst of foggy misery: "He's gone. I don't know—I don't know where he is!"

"Michael?" said Louise, unnecessarily. Of course Michael. "You mean he's disappeared? But you should have told me, Beulah!"

"I didn't want to bother you. I keep thinking it's just—But I've tried everyone I can think of. You'd know if he was with Mr. Dudgeon, wouldn't you?" Beulah's drowned eyes fastened on her imploringly. "You wouldn't keep it from me if you knew anything?"

"Of course I wouldn't. High's at a board meeting, so Michael can't be with him. What about George?"

"Nothing. He's here in town, but he called Lothrop Hall for me to see if Michael might be out there—"

"George didn't go back to school last night? How come?"

"He's taking a long week end off. He and his girl are planning to get married next week, you know. But he hasn't heard from Michael, and neither has anybody out there." The painful sobs threatened to start up again. "I don't know where he is. I don't know what to do."

"Now, now," said Louise. "How long has he been gone? All night?"

"He slept here, at least for a while. It must have been about nine when George left, and about an hour later when Michael went to bed. I stayed up, reading, till eleven thirty. Before I went to bed I looked in on him to make sure he was all right, and he was asleep, or I thought he was asleep. If only I hadn't taken that sleeping pill—But I've been having one of my bouts with insomnia, and I just felt I couldn't face the office today if I didn't get some rest. That's why I didn't hear him leave. It didn't put me under right away, I remember hearing the clock strike twelve, and then twelve thirty, and the next thing I knew the alarm was ringing, seven thirty, and then when I looked in his room and saw he was gone—"

"You've checked his clothes, I suppose. Did he pack a bag?"

"No. He wore his rain coat. Slacks and a plaid shirt. Just his regular clothes. There's nothing else missing."

"How about money?"

"I don't know exactly how much he had. Maybe five or ten dollars."

"Not enough to take him very far." But Beulah's eyes had shifted a little when she answered that one. Even so, no luggage probably meant no trip. "Look, Beulah, kids sometimes do nutty things. Maybe he just suddenly felt like seeing the sun rise from a Staten Island ferry boat or walking across Brooklyn Bridge or something."

"But not even to leave me a note, when he knows how I worry ... It's not like him. Michael's not like that. If anything's happened to him I'll never forgive myself. Never. It's all very well for George, he doesn't understand how sensitive Michael is, much more sensitive than the ordinary type of boy. That's why I've always been so careful not to be too severe with him. I should have known how he'd react last night when George—" She caught her breath. "Well. You already know George was annoyed with him."

"That's putting it mildly," said Louise. "He sounded off to us before he came over here last night. High feels it's his fault, he's the one that got Michael started. But George wouldn't listen. Can't blame him, I suppose.

What was that business we overheard about a letter?"

"Oh, I'm not blaming him exactly. But Michael didn't mean any harm. After all, he's still only a child, it was just a fantasy to him, a sort of— Letter?" Beulah shoved her hair back from her temples and sighed. "That was just more of the same. Last month I think it was, George was late with his alimony check, and he wrote Fern—she told me about it, that's how I know—asking for a little extra time. It hasn't been easy for him, on his salary, and Fern wasn't the type to make allowances. Michael was working that into the fantasy, you see, building the letter up into a quarrel between George and Fern. Ridiculous, of course. George shouldn't have taken it so seriously."

"I see," said Louise. But she was remembering that *The Compleat Angler* office really had been searched, and on an afternoon when George could have been the searcher. He wasn't wasting any time marrying his new girl, either, now that he was relieved of the burden of his alimony payments to Fern. Not that the two facts were necessarily connected; still, there they were. Fern really had been murdered, and if you accepted the premise of Max's innocence ... "Maybe George actually did have a quarrel with Fern. If he did, it would explain why he's so upset about all this. You don't think it's possible?"

"Of course not. Ridiculous. Even if he quarrelled with her, George wouldn't ever—If that's what you're suggesting."

Louise decided not to pursue it. "So last night you sided with George when he scolded Michael?"

"It must have seemed that way to Michael. Because I didn't stop George, you see, even though I knew he was being too harsh. To tell you the truth, I couldn't have stopped him. He scolded me too, you know. Oh yes, I came in for my share of the blame. He said it was my fault for not cracking down on Michael, I shouldn't be so lenient, so permissive ... He had a right to be angry, I suppose. But you can't expect a child to realize, it's not as if he were the rugged extrovert sort that can shrug off criticism. Michael broods over things."

It didn't quite fit with Michael as Louise saw him, certainly not as he had seemed last night, when he followed them to the elevator to report gleefully on old George's state of mind. But she knew better than to argue. "How does George feel about it now? I mean, does he blame himself?"

Beulah shook her head hopelessly. "He thinks I'm making too much of this. Oh, he didn't say so, but I know how George's mind works. I can tell he thinks it's just a trick of Michael's, his way of getting even, of punishing us. Especially me, because he can count on me to overreact ..."

Yes. Louise had heard some of George's psychological double-talk too. Only for once he might be right. She could see Michael as he might be at this moment, snuggled down in a movie theater somewhere, munching popcorn and contentedly picturing to himself how much his mother must be suffering.

It was as if Beulah could read her mind. "You don't understand!" she burst out in a wail that was both accusing and entreating. "People like you and George, you don't understand Michael, you don't know what it's like for me. Something terrible's happening to him, I know it, something terrible's going to happen, and I can't …" This time she did not cover her face; Louise had no choice but to watch her struggle with the terror that threatened to engulf her again. The wild, blind stare was back in her eyes; the muscles in her neck knotted and strained against the sobs. In the end she won. She sank back, exhausted, and whispered, "I'm sorry. I didn't mean to give way like this. Forgive me. I'll be all right now."

"But there must be something we can do." It no longer mattered to Louise whether Beulah was "overreacting" or not. Misery was misery, never mind how unsound its basis. She could not bear to think now of what she had come to say to this distraught woman. Thank God Michael's mother had been spared that. "Beulah. Do you want me to call the police for you and report him missing?"

"George says it's too soon. If there's no word by this afternoon, four o'clock or so …" Beulah closed her eyes at the prospect. It was only noon. "You've been very kind. Thank you."

A dismissal: Beulah obviously preferred to do her waiting alone. Louise had no wish to stay, and yet it seemed cruel, an act of abandonment. "I hate to leave you like this," she said. "Look. I'll be at— No, it's better if I go to High's instead of home. Isn't it? Because no telling when the board meeting will end, and Michael might call there. That's probably it, he's probably been trying to call High all morning. I have a key, so that's what I'll do, go over to High's and wait there. I'll call you the minute I hear anything, of course. You can get me there. I mean, even if you just want to talk to somebody—"

"Thank you. You've been very kind," Beulah repeated. She got to her feet unsteadily and followed Louise out to the foyer. "You've been a big help. Really."

"Try not to worry—Oh, High's briefcase!" cried Louise, and dashed back to the living room after it. "The second place this morning I've almost left it."

"The wayward briefcase." Beulah managed a wan smile. "That's the same one George took by mistake last night, isn't it? Full of Mr. Dudgeon's office papers?"

"Not anymore. It's empty now. He noticed last night, the handle's loose, and I'm supposed to get it repaired. There's a shop near my apartment, only this morning I forgot to stop in and leave it. There's no rush about it. Tomorrow will do. He uses a shopping bag half the time, anyway."

She lunged off down the hall, pausing at the corner for a last glance back at Beulah. She stood in the doorway, still managing her smile, still hanging on to the shreds of social amenities. Her hand lifted in a hostess' gesture of farewell. For some reason that brought Louise nearer to tears than anything else she had done. That damned kid, she thought; wait till I get my hands on him.

Unless, of course, Beulah was right, and something terrible was happening to Michael.

10

"That damned kid!" It was George, exploding at the other end of the telephone; Louise's ear crackled, even when she held the receiver a foot away. "No, of course I'm not worried about him. Beulah's the one I'm worried about. I just talked to her again. Poor woman, she's practically out of her mind."

"I know," said Louise. "That's why I'm staying here. Because he might call High." She glanced at the clock on High's bookcase. After three, and not a squeak out of Michael—or High either, when it came to that. Surely the Board couldn't still be in session?

"You'll see, he'll come strolling in just when she reaches the breaking point, and she'll be so relieved to see him that she'll fall on his neck and promise never to cross him again. The same old story. And don't think he doesn't know it."

"You mean he's disappeared like this before?"

"Whenever she tries to discipline him. Which I admit isn't very often. Nowhere near often enough."

"She didn't tell me that." But then of course Louise hadn't asked her. There were other things she hadn't asked Beulah, too. Could she ask George instead? Maybe; given the right opening. "She's convinced something terrible's happened to Michael."

"Something terrible will," said George darkly, "if he doesn't mend his ways. One of these days he's going to go too far and wind up in real trouble. I mean it. Beulah can't go on protecting him forever."

There would never be a better opening. Louise snatched at it. "Real trouble. I have a feeling he came pretty close to it, not too long ago, only Beulah managed to cover up for him. That is, if Ethel Jerome meant what I think she meant."

"Ethel Jerome?" He sounded puzzled. Also wary.

"You know. She used to work for Beulah and Fern."

"Oh. Oh yes. She was at the funeral, wasn't she?"

"Yes. I had a little chat with her this morning. She was telling me about the time Beulah and Fern were robbed. She was working for them then, and—Listen, George. Could Michael have been the thief?"

Silence at the other end. Such a long silence that Louise began to wonder if they had been cut off. Then George said, "We'd better have a little talk. I mean, not over the phone. You going to be there for a while?"

"Sure. In case Michael calls. Come on over." Poor dedicated George, she thought, this business was leaving him precious little time for romance. No wonder he was annoyed with Michael. And yet, while she waited for the doorbell to ring, she couldn't quite suppress a qualm or two. Michael might be a thief—George's reaction left little doubt on that score—but that didn't necessarily make him a full-time liar. Some of the things he had said about George could still be true. High believed them. Well, naturally: High, being whole-heartedly convinced of Max's innocence, had to find somebody else to hang the murder on. As for what Louise herself believed ... She wished High was here. That was all, the one thing she knew for sure.

George wasted no time, either in showing up, or, once there, in getting to the point. "Now then," he began, "what's all this about Ethel Jerome?" Louise talked, and he listened, his expression solemn and intent.

"It all adds up," she finished. "There has to be some reason for the peculiar way Beulah behaved, the different stories she handed out to different people. I bet she never called the police at all. Because she knew perfectly well it was Michael, and she was determined to protect him. The trouble was Ethel might know too, or guess. So Ethel must be dismissed. But not antagonized—that explains the week's pay and the story about the other maid. Which wouldn't do for Fern, of course. She probably suspected Ethel, anyway; it was easy enough for Beulah to go along—throwing in the open fire escape window just to keep things nice and iffy. It was just a fluke that Ethel and Fern ever got together and compared notes. Otherwise it would have worked. Who tipped you off? Fern?"

The question caught him off balance, as she had counted on it to do. He blinked and shifted in his chair. "What makes you think I—" Then, with a deep sigh, he surrendered. "Oh hell, you've already got it figured out anyway. Sure it was Michael. Nobody tipped me off. I found it out on my own, early last week, when I caught him trying to unload some of the stuff on another kid out at Lothrop Hall. Don't ask me why he'd kept any of it for six weeks, but he had. Anyway, I recognized one of the charm bracelets. I ought to, I gave it to Fern myself. Well, that tore it. After all, you've got to draw the line somewhere, even with these problem kids, they've got to take a little responsibility if they're going to achieve any measure of maturity. I'd gone out on a limb for Michael, he'd never have gotten into Lothrop or any other school if it hadn't been for me. Okay, I did it partly for Beulah's sake, but partly for Michael's, too, because I thought he deserved another chance. I should have had my head examined. What that kid deserves is a stretch in the reformatory."

"How do you mean, you went out on a limb? He's been in scrapes before?"

George uttered a good old mirthless laugh. "He's been kicked out of three schools for stealing. Those are just the ones I know about. God knows how many other boyish pranks Beulah's managed to sweep under the rug. I pulled strings and juggled the records to get him into Lothrop, and the little bastard knew it. That's what he was counting on, you see, he thought I'd be scared to expel him for fear of what might come out about the record juggling. Well, he found out different."

"That's why he's got it in for you, then," said Louise. "Because you did expel him."

"I didn't exactly expel him." George avoided her eyes. "I mean, not technically. What I did was tell Beulah to get him out of there. In no uncertain terms. I'd had it with Michael and I didn't care how she worked it, just so he was gone by the end of the week. She dreamed up the fake illness, and I finally agreed to go along with it. For one thing, I felt sorry for her, she's had a rough time of it ..."

And for another, you didn't want to lose your job. Louise didn't say it aloud, either.

"I was wrong," George said flatly, and Louise had another of her moments of liking him. Naturally, he couldn't leave it at that. "In the first place, it's not doing Michael any favor to keep on insulating him from the results of his own actions. It's only postponing the inevitable, because some day it won't be possible to insulate him any longer, and it's going to come as a shock to him, a real traumatic experience. In the second place, I might have known he'd find some way of getting even, and he has. All this business of trying to connect me up with what happened to Fern—"

The door opened, and in bounced High. "Weesie! I wondered where you were. Been trying to call you." He caught sight of George, and switched his radiant smile to dim. "What's up? What are you doing here? Listen, Weesie, I just talked to Max's lawyer, and he's got hold of something good, proof that Fern was alive when Max left her. Didn't I always say that boy was innocent? Let's have a drink, let's celebrate. I need one, anyway. Have I had a day! I don't mind telling you, it was touch and go there for a while with those Peerless guys. I managed to calm them down, don't ask me how. Then I got trapped into lunch with the old man himself, naturally I couldn't refuse after the way he'd stood up for me, that's why I'm so late ..." Without missing a syllable, he had flung off coat and hat and was already thumping and clattering at the bar. "Why doesn't somebody tell me what's going on? How come you're here, anyway? I thought you'd—"

"If you'll shut up a minute," said Louise, "I'll tell you. I'm waiting in case Michael calls. He's—"

"He hasn't turned up yet, huh? Well, I told him it might be four or after."

"You've seen Michael? You know where he is?"

"What do you mean, where he is?" Suddenly aware of the two pairs of eyes staring at him, High stared back. "I didn't see him, no. He called me this morning about eight thirty. Caught me just as I was going out the door, so I didn't have more than a couple of minutes to spare. He didn't want to talk on the phone, anyway. Claimed he had to see me, and when I explained about the board meeting, he said okay then, later this afternoon. What is all this? What's the matter with you two?"

"Didn't I say there was no cause for alarm?" George looked both triumphant and bitter. "Beulah's been worried sick all day because she didn't know where he was. That's what's the matter. It's a sure-fire stunt of Michael's when he's sore about something. He goes off without letting her know where, so she'll agonize over him."

"The hell you say." High looked uncertainly from George to Louise, no doubt trying to gauge whether or not she shared this view of Michael. Well, of course she did. So would High when he heard about Michael's career as a criminal—or at least as a juvenile delinquent. "You mean he wasn't at home when he called me this morning?"

"He was already gone when Beulah got up at seven thirty," said Louise. "No way of knowing what time he sneaked out. I'll call her and tell her—"

"Wait!" cried High. "He didn't want his mother to know he'd called me. I promised not to tell her."

"Well, I didn't promise. She's gone through enough on his account. Sitting there all day long imagining the worst. I'm going to put her out of her misery."

"And speaking of promises," George put in, "what about the one he made Beulah and me last night? He gave us his word, no more playing detective. So the first thing he does is call you with another load of lies."

"What lies?" A stubborn flush rose in High's face. "He didn't say anything except he wants to see me. That doesn't necessarily mean—"

"No? What else could it mean?"

"I don't know exactly. I just think he's entitled to the benefit of the doubt, is all." It was a sentiment in keeping with George's ideology—he liked all his boys, there was no such thing as a bad boy—and it gave him pause. Behind his earnest, furrowed brow theory struggled visibly with natural human impulse.

"It's about the letter business, I expect," said Louise brightly, with her hand on the telephone. There, that ought to tip the scales in favor of George's honest—if ignoble—feelings. She expected an explosion. Rather looked forward to it, in fact.

"Letter business?" George said, on cue.

"The letter you wrote Fern about the alimony. You know, asking for extra time."

"So that's what it was!" cried High. "Who told you, Weesie? How'd you find out?"

"Beulah." She added, for George's benefit, "We overheard something about a letter last night, when we followed you over to Beulah's. So this morning I asked her, and she said Michael was—how did she put it?— working that into the fantasy. It was ridiculous, she said, you shouldn't have taken it so seriously."

George just stood there, looking at her in a dazed way, not exploding at all. "But that wasn't—" Then, as his eyes flickered toward High, he broke off and straightened his shoulders grimly. "Okay. He's entitled to the benefit of the doubt. We'll see when he gets here. We'll wait and see. Go ahead, call Beulah."

The phone rang just as she reached to pick it up. But there was no response to her "Hello." She repeated it several times before the line clicked and went dead. Michael? she wondered. Though it didn't make sense that he wouldn't recognize her voice and speak to her—unless he had gone off on a new tangent that excluded her from his conferences with High. She shrugged and dialed Beulah's number.

"Yes?" Beulah answered instantly, her voice frayed with anxiety. And when she had heard Louise's news: "He's coming there, you say? Then if Mr. Dudgeon doesn't mind, could I—"

"Sure. Come on over," said Louise. "A good idea." Whatever Michael had to say, he could say it to everybody. And about time, too.

"Listen, Louise." It was George, at her elbow, speaking fast, and in an undertone. High was in the kitchen, crashing around with the ice cubes. "When Beulah gets here—she is coming, I take it?—well, listen, no need for her to know that you figured it out about Michael and the apartment robbery. Is there?"

"You mean no need for her to know you told me," Louise amended.

"Well, but you already knew. I wouldn't have told you otherwise." He cleared his throat. "So I wasn't really breaking my promise to her. If it was just Michael, I'd say broadcast it, the hell with him, but Beulah … Someday, of course, she's going to have to face the facts. I just don't want to be the one that clobbers her with them. That's why I agreed to keep my mouth shut if she'd take Michael out of school."

Not to mention the other consideration, that he might very well lose his job if the truth about Michael's record came out. Still, he had taken the risk in the first place out of the goodness of his heart. "Okay," said Louise. "I won't tell anybody. Not even High."

"Good girl." He added, in an expansive burst, "That's the letter we were really talking about last night, the one I wrote Beulah, promising not to—"

He didn't finish on account of High, who bustled in just then. The glance he cast at them was bright with curiosity; he had an instinct for secrets. Perhaps he had even caught the word letter, for he said, with a transparently casual air, "Incidentally, George, this letter you wrote Fern. What became of it?"

"She destroyed it," said George promptly. The look he gave Louise left no doubt as to which letter he was referring to. "Naturally she wouldn't want—" He paused, and finished lamely, "I mean, I suppose she did. Fern wasn't the type to keep stuff around, old letters or anything else."

They sat down with their drinks. A silence fell. Even High seemed to have nothing to say. It was an unexpected opportunity for a little quiet meditation, and Louise did her best to make the most of it. But her brain was like a ball of hopelessly snarled twine; whenever she found a loose end to pull, she only tightened the knots. Out of the jumble of the day's events, what did she know for sure? That Michael was a thief, and that his mother, naturally enough, was bent on hiding this fact. That George was willing to play it her way because he was good-hearted and didn't want to lose his job and had furthermore been brain-washed with a strong solution of not-bad-just-sick solution. But from there on it was a tangle of contradictory stories, one person's word against another's. Like the letter business. Two letters, if you chose to believe George; he had not denied the letter to Fern, he had simply dismissed it as the one of no significance. Whereas it was the only one Beulah and Michael had mentioned. Again, naturally enough: to admit the letter to Beulah would be to admit that Michael was a thief. And still another knot. George said both letters had been destroyed; Michael claimed otherwise.

Louise stole a speculative look at George's solid figure, his large, solemn face. That letter to Fern, she thought; if Michael did happen to be telling the truth about it, then here was the answer to practically everything. Bitter quarrels between George and Fern. Threatening phone calls. A letter (undestroyed by Fern) not only revealing the bitterness, not only asking for extra time on the alimony payments, but actually—why not?—spelling out the threats. So that after Fern's death George, whether or not he was guilty of murder, would be very much interested in retrieving that letter. Fern must have tucked it away somewhere in the office; otherwise the police, even with their attention focussed on Max, would not have missed it. George couldn't take any chances on their still finding it, so he had managed to get hold of an office key and had made his own secret search.

A nice, neat answer, Louise decided; all you had to do was believe Michael instead of George. It wasn't easy. Beulah herself had referred to Michael's "fantasy," had sided against him in last night's row. All right, that may have been to keep George from blowing his top and telling the truth about Michael. But she had also sprung to George's defense right at the start, before Michael was involved in any way. Ridiculous, she had said. Nonsense to suspect George of anonymous phone calls or any connection with Fern's death. And yet, if Max was innocent ...

"Why doesn't the kid show up?" High rattled his drink impatiently. "It's after four. Do you suppose he's caught on we're all going to be here? That might scare him off."

"You mean he has us under surveillance?" asked Louise. She laughed. But it wasn't so fantastic, really, to imagine Michael skulking behind the shrubbery, spying on them—and not just as part of the cloak-and-dagger game, either. He was bright enough to know he had pushed George pretty near the breaking point, if not beyond, and that by now his own name might be mud. To everybody except his mother, of course.

"You know, I've been thinking," said George. He stared at Louise, again with that dazed expression. "About Michael, I mean. I wonder if—"

Beulah rang the doorbell at that moment, so he never finished. She was still haggard, but she had pulled herself together since this morning. Her hair lay in its customary smooth waves; her clothes were once more tidy and her manner composed. It cracked a bit, though, when she caught sight of George.

"George? I didn't expect to see you here," she said. There was dismay in her voice, and a flare of fear in her eyes. Louise knew what she was afraid of: Had George broken his promise and exposed Michael as a thief?

He carried it off quite well. "I told you I had a hunch Michael would head this way sooner or later. So I kept calling and finally got Louise," he explained, truthfully enough. "I came over because—well, frankly, Beulah, I'm up to here with this detective bit of his, and I don't altogether trust him to keep the promise he made us last night. If he has anything more to say about me, I want to be here when he says it."

"I see." She flushed slightly. But then she held out her hand, and he took it. "I don't blame you for being angry with him, George. But he's only a child, don't forget, he doesn't realize what he's doing ..."

George sighed. "He's fourteen. Old enough to start realizing."

"It's my fault as much as his," said High. "I got him started on this. Though I must say he ought to be ashamed of himself, giving you such a scare."

"He sounded all right when you talked to him this morning?"

"Sure. Fine. I thought he was at home, of course. Don't worry, he'll be along any minute now. How about a drink? You look as if you could use one."

She accepted a small one, and went through the motions of listening politely while High and George urged upon her the importance of taking a firm hand with Michael when he appeared. Crack down on him. Lay it on the line. Let him know who's boss. Quite possibly she recognized the soundness of the advice they were giving her. But that didn't make her capable of following it, thought Louise; nothing could change the pattern now. Perhaps the terrible thing that was going to happen to Michael had already happened.

He called at four thirty. High answered, and after saying "yes" a couple of times, he turned toward Beulah. "Michael. He wants to talk to you."

She was across the room in a flash; with a little whimper of relief she snatched the phone and clasped it to her cheek as if it were her boy himself. "Michael darling, are you all right? I've been so worried, dearest... How could you ... Why didn't you let me know ..."

It was an abject performance. The fact that they had all three expected something of the sort made it no less embarrassing. George groaned. Louise whispered, "You shouldn't have told him she was here." High looked shamefaced and helpless. After that they avoided each other's eyes.

She hung up. "He'll be here in fifteen minutes," she told them joyfully. Then the radiance began to drain out of her worn face. "That is, if—if—there's nobody here but me. He seems to feel that you've turned against him, he's so sensitive about these things, and ..."

"You mean we're supposed to get out, just to suit him?" High erupted. "Then why the hell did he call me in the first place? All that business about something he had to tell me. What's happened to that?"

"Three guesses," said George bitterly. "I know what he had to tell you, all right, and now he's had time for a few second thoughts, it's dawned on him that I might just possibly have meant it last night when I told him—"

"George!" cried Beulah. "Please. You promised!"

"So did he."

"But don't you see, that's what he's trying to do, keep his promise, if you'll only give him a chance. He doesn't want to talk to Mr. Dudgeon anymore. He sees now that he was in the wrong, I know he does, he just doesn't want to have to face everybody all at once. It's not too much to ask, is it?" With the sure instinct of desperation, she turned to High. "I realize it's an imposition, Mr. Dudgeon, and I'm sorry. I should have told him to meet me at home. If I knew where to reach him—But I didn't even think to ask where he was calling from. I was just so glad to hear his voice and know he was all right. Please. Half an hour, that's all I ask. Just give me half an hour with him first, and then I don't care how much you scold him. That's what I intend to do myself, of course. Scold him, because you're quite right, it's time I took a firmer hand with him ..."

"We can go to my place," said Louise. She had already invited High for dinner, anyway. And George's poor girl friend must be getting a little tired of sitting around waiting while he coped with juvenile delinquency.

"A firm hand," he was saying, more in sorrow than in anger. "And so you let him set the terms. If we don't clear out he doesn't come back, I suppose. He's put you through hell today, he's done his best to get me arrested for murder, and you still let him set the terms." He picked up his coat. "Okay. I had my chance, and I let it go. Next time I'll know better."

"What's he talking about?" High asked in an undertone. Louise and he had already reached the foyer; he paused with his hand on the door, craning to see past her shoulder into the living room. "Weesie? What's he mean he had his chance?"

"When Michael was out there at his school, you dope. He could have drilled some sense into him then. Ready, George? Oh lord, that so-and-so briefcase, I almost forgot it again. It's been haunting me all day." She tucked it under her arm while High unlatched the door.

"I can't thank you enough," Beulah began, but he cut her short. There was still that tinge of embarrassed pity in the air, with a feeling of defeat added now, and an eagerness to get away. All this hassle, thought Louise, and where had it gotten them? Not even the letter business was sorted out. And what's more it might never be. She had no faith whatever in Beulah's firm hand. But it was obvious that Michael now saw for himself the risk involved in his whispering campaign against George and had decided to drop it while he was still ahead of the game. They would get no more out of him, true or false.

"Half an hour," Beulah promised anxiously as they filed out into the corridor. "I'll call you. Or better yet, Michael will. You'll see, he'll apologize ..."

The afternoon had turned dismal; they stepped out into a twilight of threatening skies and chilly wind. Louise lagged behind, pulling her scarf up over her head, while George and High moved down the broad, shrub-bordered steps of the terrace. She paused a moment, listening to their voices—they were starting the inevitable, gloomy rehash—and looking out past them and beyond the avenue, where a strip of dull, pewter-colored river was visible. Then she too started down the steps.

When the wallop caught her, she had an instant's impression that the steps had somehow tricked her, the way they do in dreams, by shifting beneath her feet. But it came from behind, she thought. And there was nothing dream-like about the yank at the briefcase under her arm or the thud of running feet.

Then she crashed against the cement and stopped thinking.

11

She was out for only a couple of minutes. Or so they informed her afterwards; it seemed like the next day to her when she opened her eyes to find a largish, roundish object hovering not more than a foot above her. It turned out to be a face. George's face. She didn't care for him at such close quarters. Didn't care much for him at all, in fact.

"Go away," she said thickly. But he either didn't hear or pretended not to. When she started hoisting herself up, there he was, with his arm under her shoulders, shoving and hauling at just the wrong angle, more hindrance than help, and making solicitous noises that also annoyed her.

"Are you sure you're all right?" he kept asking; a question so patently idiotic that there was nothing to do but ignore it. The one fact she was sure of was that she was not all right; the reasons escaped her. Then, as she achieved a sitting position, the ache in her head shot from dull to piercing, and her obscurely disgruntled feeling sharpened to outrage.

"Somebody hit me," she said accusingly. From behind, though—she remembered now—so it couldn't have been George. He and High had been in front of her, and that was another thing: Where was High, why wasn't he here when she needed him?

Before she could ask the question out loud, there was a commotion in the bushes at the corner of the building, a sort of surging crash, and the next instant a figure streaked past, up the terrace steps, through the glass door, into the lobby—and close on his heels High, also crashing and panting and pounding. And yelling: "Stop him! Get him!" while she sat there on the steps and George squatted beside her, both of them open-mouthed and becalmed. By the time he got himself up off his haunches a third man had run past, this one in the uniform of the grounds patrol.

Then she was alone, and not quite sure whether she had actually seen that lightning-swift procession or only imagined it. No: there were the trampled, flattened bushes to prove it, and from inside came a confusion of voices and slamming doors. She tottered to her feet, stumbling against an empty coke bottle in the process, and with the aid of the wrought-iron balustrade made it to the glass door. She was wobbly in the legs, and her head still hurt, but otherwise—thank you very much, George—all right.

The front part of the lobby was deserted. She shuffled around the jog and past the mail boxes before she reached the scene of action. Several of the other ground-floor tenants had popped out of their doors and were asking each other what all the racket was about. George was alternately beating on the door of High's apartment and ringing the bell, hollering for Beulah to let him in. At the far end of the hall, near the door that led to the storage room for bicycles and baby carriages, High and the patrolman seemed to be converging on their quarry. Their backs were to her, their heads thrust slightly forward, their hands outstretched as if ready to pounce. They looked stiff and wary, like hounds pointing. She moved up, trying to see past them, just as Beulah flung open the door to High's apartment.

Somebody gasped, "He's got a knife!"

The hounds shifted cautiously, and now Louise could see him. He was backed up against the storage room door; it was evidently locked, and he was trapped there, a pathetically undersized figure in a rain coat, clutching the briefcase in front of him like a shield. His face was white with panic, and light flickered, wicked as a snake's tongue, along the blade he held at chest height. Nothing else moved; they all stood as if frozen, in a brief, curious hush.

Then Beulah's voice—not fogbound, for once—rang out in a wild shriek. "No, Michael, no! It's empty, there's nothing in it!"

At the same moment High lunged; the knife whipped in a gleaming arc before it clattered to the floor; the patrolman's arms flailed and then closed in what appeared to be an impassioned embrace; George sprang forth, a belated thunderbolt; everybody yelled or grunted or whispered or sobbed.

Louise was one of the yellers. "High!" He heard her and turned. He looked rumpled and all askew, like one of his own inexpertly wrapped packages, and he was smiling in a shocked way. There was blood on his shirt front; she saw it and fainted.

This time when she came to she was in High's apartment, stretched out on his bed. He was sitting beside her, with his shirt off. The doctor was there, too, or anyway some fellow clanking around with a little black bag.

"Did he kill you?" she asked.

"He meant to. I can't get over it. He meant to kill me." High sounded awestruck. "It's just luck he got me in the shoulder instead of the heart. And clobbering you with that coke bottle. He could have killed you too. Weesie honey, when I saw you laid out there—you looked dead, honey, I thought you were dead."

"We're not, though." She sat up and kissed him.

"Now let's have a look at that head of yours," said the doctor genially. He prodded. "Mmm. Quite a bump you've got there."

"Thanks. Listen, High ... Ouch. Where is he? What was he—"

"In the living room. They're all out there. The cops and all. I don't know what he's telling them. The point is, what did he want the briefcase for? What did the little bastard think was in it?"

"Whatever it is, Beulah must know. Because she yelled at him that the briefcase was empty. I told her this morning, you see. Ouch! Stop it, will you?"

"Now just a minute," the doctor began, not quite so genially.

She managed to slip free of him and on to her feet, leaving him stranded on the other side of the bed. High was right; Michael hadn't been after the briefcase itself, of course, but something that was in it. Something he thought was in it.

"It was just stuff from the office, some folders I grabbed off my desk and Fern's and brought home. I don't even know what's there myself. The police okayed it," High said. They hung on to each other, caught up in mutual remembrance: the mysterious office prowler—if Arch O'Brien could be believed—who hadn't stolen anything; the letter business; the one George was supposed to have written Fern—if Michael could be believed, and how could he be now? "I dumped it all into a shopping bag last night, when I noticed the briefcase needed fixing. Remember? And left it in here, beside the bed, in case I couldn't get to sleep right away. Here." High dived down between bed and night table and came up with the familiar Horn & Hardart shopping bag. There were perhaps half a dozen file folders, plus the usual assortment of clippings, which High seemed to accumulate the way a magnet picks up tacks. They spread everything out on the bed between them.

The doctor tried again with his now-just-a-minute line, and at that moment George stuck his head in the door. "How you doing? You okay, Louise? Hey. What's going on?"

Louise looked up briefly. "What's going on out there? What's Michael telling the police?"

"Not much of anything, so far. Beulah's doing most of the talking. Claims he's sick, delirious, didn't know what he was doing. I don't know how much of that they're buying. They want to talk to you when the doctor finishes with you."

The doctor made some remark, not at all genial, to which nobody paid any attention.

"'Letters to be Signed,'" High read off, from one of the neatly labelled folders. "Oh lord, these should have gone out Monday. Where's my pen? 'Pending.' Nothing there, just junk I keep putting off. The trout fly article, that's for Arch, he's going to work it over. 'Photographs.' Nothing there, either. What's that, Weesie? What you got?"

"This is it," she said. The folder was labeled "Material to be Copied." There was a good deal of such material lately, on account of the new Xerox duplicating machine, which fascinated the entire *Compleat Angler* staff. Fern had kept this folder on her desk, and it was easy to see how the police—who had been preoccupied with Max from the beginning—could have let the important letter get past them without recognizing its significance. It was buried in a miscellaneous collection of official and unofficial business, including letters from subscribers, W. J. Robinson's latest bill (disputed) from Macy's, a recipe for rhubarb pie, and a memorandum from High's accountant about his income tax. All duly processed, with Xerox copies clipped to originals.

"This is it," Louise repeated. She straightened up. High and George crowded in on either side of her, peering at the papers in her hand.

"It's the letter I wrote to Beulah!" George burst out. "I told you, Louise. The one about Michael. What's it doing in here?"

"Wait. Lemme see." High, who had not been told, grabbed the letter and sank down on the bed to absorb it.

"Fern got hold of it somehow or other." Louise was stammering a little with excitement. "She may have had an inkling about Michael and the robbery, even if Ethel Jerome didn't come right out and tell her. The same way I had. Ethel didn't really tell me. And she was going to the police, because that's the way Fern was, she wouldn't fool around."

"And Michael knew it," George went on with it while she paused for breath. "She must have gotten wise to him before I did, a couple of weeks ago. Only she didn't have any proof. Just suspicions. She wasn't the type to keep them to herself, not Fern, so he tried to scare her off with those phone calls—it's a common behavior pattern with disturbed adolescents, I should have spotted it right away—only of course she didn't scare. She still didn't have any proof, though, not till she got hold of my letter to Beulah. He had to get it back, because if the police ever saw it he'd be in the soup but good. He didn't find it, that day he sneaked into the office—"

"Of course not. How could he, when High had already brought it home in his briefcase? When he found out about the briefcase last night, he figured that's where the letter must be, it couldn't be anywhere else. He's been waiting ever since for a chance at the briefcase, and all the time it was empty, only he didn't—"

"Listen." High lifted to them a face dazed with discovery. "This kid, why, he's nothing but a pill, this kid. Robbing his own mother's apartment. It's not the first time he's stolen stuff, either. He's been doing it for years, and getting away with it. It's all right here in black and white, the whole damn story."

"I know it," George reminded him. "I wrote the letter."

"That's right. Yeah." The first shock passed. High was once more himself, ready for action. "Well, he's not going to get away with it this time. His mother's covered up for him long enough. Stealing from her and Fern is one thing. But it's something else again when he clobbers Weesie and pulls a knife on me. Come on. I'm showing this to the police." He sprang up, clutching the letter.

Before they followed him into the living room, Louise's eyes met George's, in a glance of extraordinarily clear communication. His face was dough-white; she had a feeling hers might be, too.

"Oh no," he mumbled. "He couldn't have. Could he?"

But they were both thinking that he could have. Michael himself had pointed out, when he was tossing around his insinuations against George, that his mother's apartment and *The Compleat Angler* office were only ten minutes apart. The letter—provided he had known Friday night that it was in Fern's hands—certainly gave him as good a motive as any he had dreamed up for George. His actions that afternoon proved how reckless he could be, how violent. And how panicky: Louise remembered all too vividly the look on his face when he had stood, backed up against the storage room door, trapped there, with the knife in his hand.

Now he sat on the couch in High's living room, in an attitude of sullen defiance—head lowered, hands pressed between his bony knees, shoulders hunched as if to ward off a blow. (Though if the police had roughed him up any, Louise thought, they would have had Beulah to reckon with.) At the same time there was an air of elation about him, an exulting glitter in his eyes, as if he were secretly having the time of his life. He was getting plenty of attention, all right: in addition to the patrolman, there were two regular cops, one towering on either side of him. They did not look friendly. But he was no doubt counting on his mother to get him out of this difficulty, as she had always done before.

"So you don't remember anything," one of the policemen was saying, in a disgusted voice. "Mind's a blank, huh? No recollection of mugging anybody. You just all of a sudden came to and here were these two guys ganging up on you and you couldn't imagine why. Oh yes, and you all of a sudden had this knife in your hand that you'd just happened to find on the subway. Tell us, buster. You get these blackouts often?"

"I can't remember. Sir," said Michael. He ducked his head to hide the grin he could not quite suppress.

"I told you he's been ill all week." Beulah gave almost no sign of the wild anxiety that must be raging in her. Only her hands, which she held clasped in her lap, grappled with each other in an occasional, uncontrollable spasm. "Under the doctor's care. You can't hold a boy in his condition responsible. He's been wandering the streets all day, with nothing to eat ... That's my responsibility, my fault for not keeping him at home. And no one's been hurt seriously, nothing's been damaged or stolen—"

"Now wait a minute." Unable to contain himself any longer, High advanced, waving the letter. "Here. Take a look at this. This is what he was after when he clobbered Weesie. He thought it was in the briefcase, he didn't know I dumped everything out last night because the strap was loose. Blackout nothing. He's been itching to get his hands on this letter ever since he found out Fern had it. He knew damn well he was in for it if you fellows ever saw it. And if somebody hadn't killed her, don't think you wouldn't have seen it, long before this—"

"Wait a minute. Who's Fern? Somebody killed her?"

"Sure. Fern Villard. Only good secretary I ever had."

"Villard!" Both cops stiffened, as at the touch of a live wire. They exchanged a look. Then one of them made for the telephone. The other one said, "You're connecting this kid with the Villard murder?"

"What?" said High. Suddenly he sat down. After a moment he said, in a stricken voice, "I guess I am, all right. I guess that's what I'm doing."

12

"Me?" The sound Michael made started out as a laugh but wound up as a gasp. His eyes darted from one face to the next to the next; abruptly, he stopped enjoying the attention he was getting and bumped up against the grim reality of why he was getting it.

But he could still count on his mother to shield him, of course. High's words had drawn from her a choked wail and had sent her rushing to Michael's side, to clutch him in her arms. "You can't be serious!" she cried. "This is ridiculous. It's fantastic. It's—George! George, you know Michael, you know this is impossible!"

Poor George stammered and turned red. "I don't know what to say, Beulah. I don't understand how Fern—You told me you destroyed the letter."

"I threw it away, but she must have found it in the waste basket. What difference does it make, anyway? Michael didn't know she had it. Nobody knew. The letter's got nothing to do with anything."

"But then why did he snatch the briefcase? And another thing, Beulah, you—"

"He didn't know what he was doing!" She was no longer appealing to George, she was scorning him. He belonged with the enemy now: this roomful of heartless adults bent on persecuting a poor ailing child who had been running a fever all week. Her glance raked them each in turn, and they each in turn—even the policemen—shifted in their chairs, or shuffled their feet, or looked at the floor.

But it had been a fake fever, Louise remembered. According to George. A trumped-up excuse for getting Michael out of school without exposing him as a thief—and, incidentally, without endangering George's job.

After the one withering glance, Beulah focussed her attention on Michael. Her face melted into tenderness. "Don't worry, darling," she said, with a dreamy kind of serenity. "No one's going to hurt you. There's nothing to worry about."

"Who's worried?" said Michael, pulling away from her and craning his neck in embarrassment. (Like a normal boy, thought Louise, instead of a monster.) "They can't pin anything on me."

"I wouldn't be so sure, buster," said the policeman.

Their old friend the detective got there a few minutes later, and set everybody straight on just how much could be pinned on Michael. There was no question about the coke bottle attack on Louise, the snatching of the briefcase, or the knife wound inflicted on High. Michael did not deny them. He had blacked out? He was ill? The doctor was called forth from the background where he had been sulking to investigate the state of Michael's temperature. Normal, he reported, though naturally he could not vouch for what it might have been half an hour ago.

"It fluctuates," said Michael airily.

So, apparently, did Michael's mood; again Louise got the impression of daredevil elation. His attitude toward the detective shifted from insolence to sullenness to bored condescension: Was it sheer perversity that made him insist on striking all the wrong notes? Did he have too little imagination, or too much conceit, to realize the predicament he was in? Or did he realize it all too well and behave as he did out of desperation? Whatever the reason, the result was the same. It was painful to watch, even for one, like Louise, who had little sympathy for him; for his mother it must be agonizing. Yet Beulah's composure did not crack. Her hands had stopped their spasmodic grappling. She listened with her eyes lowered and her head slightly tilted, as if in detached, polite interest. Numb with shock, Louise decided.

She was wrong, of course. When the true reason for Beulah's serenity came out—as it did in a few minutes—she could not understand why she had not seen it coming from the start. It was that obvious. And that inevitable; Beulah must have decided that this would be her course of action some time ago, certainly before the detective got there. If "decided" was the right word for something that no doubt seemed to Beulah as natural and instinctive as breathing. Nothing to worry about, she had told Michael, no one's going to hurt you. It should have been crystal-clear right then to all of them that Michael's mother was determined to shield him from the consequences of his own actions, no matter what they might be, and no matter what it cost her.

By now the detective had dropped the side issues and was getting down to business—business being, for him, the investigation of murder. And the connection being the letter, George's letter to Beulah, which had somehow fallen into Fern's hands and which she undoubtedly would have turned over to the police if someone had not killed her first. Fortunately for Michael. Who insisted, more and more shrilly, that he did not know Fern had the letter, had not snatched the briefcase under the mistaken impression that it contained the letter, had not ransacked *The Compleat Angler* office in search of it. Sunglasses? Yes, he sometimes wore them. No, he had not lost a pair recently, at least he didn't think so ...

He snuffled and was silent. At that moment he looked like what he was: a scared young punk in trouble, with—give him credit—enough brains to know how bad the trouble was.

The detective stood up and said, with ominous gentleness, "All right, Michael. Let's go. I'll have to take you in for further questioning."

That was when Beulah came out with her confession.

She delivered it very glibly, as if it were a memorized recitation. Her voice did not rise above its usual foggy, well-bred level. Her face remained calm; her posture—she stayed where she was, on the couch— lady-like and poised, back straight, ankles crossed, one hand lightly closed over Michael's.

Listening to her, Louise felt a rush of exasperated sorrow. He's not worth it, she wanted to cry out, can't you see he's beyond saving now, can't you see the damage you've already done him with your misguided love?

But that of course was the point: Beulah was blind to everything but her own fanatic, futile determination to keep her son from suffering, even if it meant dying for him.

Michael himself had apparently not expected her to go this far. Of all her audience, he seemed the most dumbfounded. His jaw dropped open. He blinked. He looked almost idiotic.

Well, High wasn't looking any too bright. Louise probably wasn't either, though she was in no position to know. George sat with his head lowered and his hand over his eyes. The detective listened poker-faced. He was the first one to break the silence after Beulah stopped talking.

"Mrs. Hannaford, you realize what you're saying? You're telling us you killed Fern Villard to keep her from—"

"I knew she had the letter, you see," said Beulah evenly, but with just a touch of impatience. "It came that Friday morning before either of us left for work. I didn't think she saw it, didn't discover till I came home that night that she had stolen it out of my purse and taken it to the office with her. She'd been watching for it. For a couple of weeks—ever since Ethel Jerome got hold of her and gave her the idea—she'd been after me to find out if Michael was away from school the day our apartment was robbed. She threatened to check with George herself if I didn't do it. Fern was that way. Vindictive. Naturally I kept putting her off—"

"Naturally?" said the detective. "So you must have known yourself that Michael was the thief, and you were protecting him. Okay. Naturally."

"Lots of children take things if they're tempted too far. It's a stage they go through. It doesn't mean they're criminals. As things turned out, nobody needed to check with George, anyway. He found it out on his own and called me early in the week—Monday, it was. All upset. But he finally agreed to let the matter drop if I took Michael out of school. Everything would have been all right—I could have handled Fern, as long as she didn't know for sure—only then he wrote the letter, and she got hold of it, and that gave her what she wanted. Proof. As soon as I found it was missing from my purse, I realized what she was up to. She made no bones about having stolen it, or about what she was going to do with it, either. That was after I'd called her at the office and gone up there. I tried to persuade her, but she wouldn't listen. Wouldn't give it back to me. Wouldn't even tell me where it was. After—Afterwards, I started looking for it, but then I thought I heard someone coming, and I panicked and left without it. Of course I turned the apartment upside down hunting for it, on the off-chance she'd hidden it somewhere at home. I had the whole week end. They didn't find her till Monday morning." She paused, and added, "I'm sorry about Max Sutter. It didn't occur to me they'd suspect him."

Not sorry enough, though, to speak up until now, thought Louise. Naturally not; to speak up would have been to expose Michael as at least a thief. With that at stake, what was a little thing like Max Sutter's life?

"Let's see," the detective was saying. "That was the night Michael and Mr. Villard drove in from school. They reached your apartment about nine forty-five. Shortly after you got there, I suppose? How much of all this did you tell Michael?"

"Nothing."

"Please, Mrs. Hannaford. You'll be telling me next that it was you, not Michael, who knocked Mrs. Clarke out to get the briefcase and then pulled a knife on Mr. Dudgeon. I can understand your desire to protect him, but—"

"All right. I told him about the letter. I knew it must still be in the office, and I kept thinking the police would find it and start asking questions. It seemed to me it would be better if Michael was prepared, instead of having them spring it on him without any warning ... He had no idea there was any connection between the letter and the murder. I just said—which was perfectly true—that I was worried for fear it might turn up."

"Michael? That right?"

He nodded dumbly. He even found his voice, hoisted it up from some deep interior cavern: "I already knew Fern was gunning for me, anyway. That's why I—"

"Michael, darling."

But the detective was on it like a terrier. "Go ahead. Why you tried to scare her off with those anonymous phone calls? Is that what you started to say?" Another dazed nod from Michael. "Only she didn't scare, so then you had to do something else to stop her. Even if you didn't already know on Friday that she had the letter, and that's something we'll get back to later on, even without that you couldn't let her keep on gunning for you."

"He didn't know! It was me. I killed her. Why can't you leave him alone?"

The detective sighed. "How about the prowler in *The Compleat Angler* office? I suppose that was you, too? ... Be careful, Mrs. Hannaford. We have the sunglasses, you know. That's one thing we can check on. There are other things, too, now that we know what to look for."

It might be true, thought Louise. Whether it was or not, Beulah believed it; her face turned gray. "But it was only a game to him! He didn't realize—A sort of cloak-and-dagger fantasy. He enjoyed it, the same way he enjoyed playing detective, dreaming up evidence against George. That was all make-believe, too. Just a game." Not to mention a neat way of getting even with George, in case anybody believed him. "I got the key to the office. That was my doing. I lifted it from Gladys Popejoy when I stopped there before the funeral. It was too good a chance to resist. I ran into her in the hall, you see, and she was having a little trouble with her key, it stuck in the lock ..." Beulah's voice trailed away.

"I see. And later that afternoon Michael used it to get in and search the office."

"He talked me into letting him. He was the logical one, he said, because if anyone happened to notice him, they'd take him for a messenger. When he came home and told me he'd almost been caught— but that just made the game more exciting for him. He didn't realize. It was no use, anyway. The letter wasn't there. We found out last night it had been in Mr. Dudgeon's briefcase all the time. At one point it was actually in our apartment, if we'd only known!" She gave a short laugh. "Funny, isn't it? We had it right there, if we'd only known in time."

"That brings us to today," said the detective. "Michael's disappearance. Supposing you clear that up, Michael. You must have had some reason for turning up missing."

Again Michael delved into the inner depths and dredged up his voice. "It made me sore, the way they jumped on me last night. Mother and George. Both of them, yammering at me just because I—"

"But don't you see, darling, I had to! I couldn't let you go on annoying George! If you pushed him too far, he could get you into trouble with the police."

"Not if he wanted to keep his stinking little job," said Michael spitefully.

George made a spluttering sound, but the detective intervened. "You mean you skipped out just to get back at them for scolding you? What did you do all day, anyway?"

"Fooled around. Went to the movies."

"And called Mr. Dudgeon. Why were you so anxious to see him? To give him another load of your make-believe evidence against Mr. Villard? I don't think so, not after the way he cracked down on you last night. No, it was the briefcase you were after, wasn't it? Because you thought the letter was still in it. That's what you've been waiting for all day, a chance at the briefcase. No use denying it now. Your mother's already told us—"

"I told you I killed her!" Beulah burst out wildly. "What more do you want? You can't hold Michael, now that I've confessed. I did it, I tell you. You've got to believe me!"

"Mrs. Hannaford," the detective began. He tried again. "Mrs. Hannaford ..."

At that moment the doorbell chimed, several times, a succession of lilting peals. High bounded to his feet, then paused, teetering, until the detective nodded. From where she sat Louise had a clear view of the narrow hallway, the door at the end, and, when High opened it, of who was there. Archie O'Brien, in his beat-up all-weather coat and his hat with the brim turned up in front. He looked jovial and surprisingly clear-eyed, considering the time of day. Or perhaps he had reached one of his recurrent plateaus of sobriety.

"Good. You're home," he said. "Hope I'm not intruding. So there I was at my in-laws, right around the corner, when it came to me. For whatever it's worth. So I thought why not pop in and try it out on High ... Anything wrong? You look a little out of touch."

"I'm fine," croaked High. "Something came to you, you said?"

"I knew it would, of course." Except for Louise (whom he had not yet noticed) the occupants of the living room were out of Archie's range of vision, but in the hush his light, pleasant voice reached them with bell-like clarity. "If I waited long enough. The direct attack's no good in these cases. Patience, that's the ticket. Just a matter of biding one's time, waiting for the shy little creature to venture forth from the jungle of the subconscious, as it inevitably, eventually will." He steadied himself against the wall and lit a cigarette. "The O'Brien method of total recall. Unconditionally guaranteed."

"Look, Arch, would you mind giving it to me straight? I'm sorry, but I—"

"Not at all. Not at all. The Hannaford woman's voice. It's been plaguing me for days now. I knew I'd heard it before. But where? When? That's what just came to me. She was in the building, in the elevator, the night Fern was killed. I'd been to the Publix party, remember, and in the welter of departure—there was a moderate-sized mob milling around in the corridor—I assumed she'd been there too. We had a cozy little chat on the way down. About time tables. I happened to be obsessed with the subject at the moment, and she was kind enough to help me with the fine print. It was a fitting touch, somehow, that engulfed-cathedral voice bonging out the hours of departure. As I say, for what it's worth. Hell, maybe she really *was* at the Publix party, you couldn't prove it by me. The elevator I'm sure about. So it does put her on the scene, so to speak … High? High, what goes on?"

What went on was that High, gasping like a beached fish, was propelling him into the living room, where the hush still held. But for a moment only: a low, sad sound like a gust of wind swept through the group Archie faced. Then the detective stepped forth and began rapping out questions.

Louise did not hear them, or the answers. Her attention was fixed on Michael. He was drawn back as far as he could get in the corner of the couch, his legs twisted around each other, his arms tight against his body—a knobby, stringy lump of desolation. He stared at his mother as if he had never seen her before; his face, stripped of everything but shock, was defenseless and for once completely unself-conscious. His lips moved in the soundless question: "Mother?"

He hadn't believed her until now, either. Watching him, Louise knew that this was it, the terrible thing that was going to happen to Michael.

But Beulah, who had predicted it, seemed unaware of it, or—more likely—incapable of recognizing it. Her own face, as she stood up and held out her hand to Archie, was radiant.

"Thank you, Mr. O'Brien," she said, in that memorably foggy voice of hers. "Thank you very much."

THE END

The Man with the Cane
by Jean Potts

ONE

It wasn't often that Val got in or out of the house without being waylaid by one of "the girls," as he called them. They listened for him—never confusing his step with that of the other two male tenants, sterner types than Val—and popped out with their little pleasantries, their little favors to ask. Would it be too much trouble for Mr. Bryant to pick up an evening paper on his way back, or a package of soda mints, or one egg? Only, mind you, if he happened to be going past the grocery store anyway … They repaid him with crocheted neckties and dishes of fruit-jello salad or chocolate pudding for his supper—because they knew how it was, a man doing for himself didn't bother with the little touches that made all the difference.

Today it was old Miss LaTour. Her bony, red-nosed face, with its scalloped edging of pale-blue hair, appeared the moment he reached the second landing on his way down. "Afternoon, Mr. Bryant," she called in her cracked chirp of a voice. "Now I won't keep you a minute, I know you're in a hurry, because it's The Day, isn't it? I can just imagine how excited you must be, going to see your little girl again, after all this time. How long did you say it's been?"

"Three years. More than three years. She's been out in California with her mother." (And with Monroe too, of course, but Val guessed he didn't need to go into that.)

"Think of that! Oh, and you're taking her a homecoming present! May I see?" Miss LaTour's hand, misshapen with arthritis, reached out eagerly.

"It's a panda," said Val, unnecessarily. Quite a bit of panda; even though he had decided, after a quick mental calculation, on the six fifty size instead of the nine ninety-five. He held it up so that Miss LaTour could see the panda's steadfast button eyes and his bright-red, felt tongue. "Do you think she'll like it?"

"Let me see, you said she's six, a little past six?" Miss LaTour assumed her professional retired-schoolteacher air. Then, her voice ringing with authority, she said, "She'll love it. Just the thing for her age group. You couldn't have made a better choice."

That was what the saleslady had said, too. So it must be okay. But there was still the other question, the one he had not been able to ask the saleslady, or Miss LaTour, either, though it seemed to tremble all around him. *Look, will she remember me?*

More than three years. A long time to Val, and how much longer to

Annabelle! Half of her lifetime—and even in the long-ago half when she used to see Val, it had been only once a week. (That was the way he and Doris had fixed it in the divorce, that he could visit her once a week.) So how could she be expected to remember, no matter how fond she had been of him once?

She always used to come pelting down the walk to meet him. Her plump legs, terminating in minute white oxfords, twinkled; her brief pigtails bounced on either side of her rosy, beaming face; she stretched her arms out wide. He remembered her best that way.

Or no. The best way was when he swooped her up in his arms, and she threw back her head, making crowing, laughing sounds, and reaching for his moustache. Her cheek, when he kissed her, was like a—well, all right, like a rose petal ...

"How's Val's girl? How's Val's little girl?"

For of course she didn't call him Daddy. They had been all washed up, he and Doris, before Annabelle was born; and by the time she started to talk Monroe was in complete charge. So naturally she called Monroe Daddy. Val was just somebody who came to see her Saturday afternoons. Like today.

Val's coming to see you, they must have told her today. Val? she had probably asked. Who's Val?

Why, Val is—

"Now don't you worry, Mr. Bryant," chirped Miss LaTour, exuding, along with her encouragement, a smell of liniment and menthol drops. "You're going to have a perfectly lovely afternoon. I can feel it in my bones. Don't you worry for a minute."

He was ashamed of how grateful he felt to her. "Can I mail your letter for you ?" he asked, catching sight of the envelope in her hand.

"Would you mind very much? I don't want to put you to any trouble ..."

Letter in hand, panda tucked under his arm, he ran on down the stairs. It still surprised him, at times, to realize that he had lived on the same street, in the same small, rather down-at-heel house in the Village, for all of three years. An old settler, you might say. He had even stuck to the same job for more than a year now. Not that it was such a hot job; assistant to the art manager on a middle-sized magazine. Miracle Man Monroe (who was something impressive in television, trust Monroe to get in on the ground floor) would no doubt sneer at it. So would Doris, with her career in advertising. Even in the old days, her salary had been almost double Val's; by now she must be making a very pretty penny indeed. Still, it suited Val. Not too much responsibility. Not too much money, either. But he hadn't ever missed on the payments for Annabelle, and that was the important thing. Because if he ever did miss, Doris and Monroe would be just too damn delighted for words ...

There was something to be said for staying put, after all, he thought as he emerged into the pale November sunshine. It seemed to him that the street itself (he *must* be strung up!) was cheering him on, comforting him with its shabby familiarity, and he felt grateful, in the same shame-faced way he had felt grateful to poor old Miss LaTour. Nuisances though she and the other "girls" were at times, they gave him an illusion, for what it was worth, of belonging somewhere.

He and the panda took a bus uptown to the streamlined new apartment house where Doris and Monroe—who always had the right connections when it came to finding apartments, or buying new cars, or practically anything else you could name—had established themselves for the winter. The park was wonderful for Annabelle, Doris had reported when she told Val about it over the phone. And there was a good school, a really good school, nearby. Eventually, of course, they planned to move out of the city, Westchester or Connecticut, but not until they found exactly the house they wanted. For the present, Doris had said in her celery-crisp voice, this place would do very nicely. They had been lucky enough (naturally!) to get a large apartment, which they needed, because Doris' mother was with them now.

At the thought of his ex-mother-in-law, Val relaxed a little. She was an unlikely sort of mother for Doris to have: rattle-brained, improvident as a grasshopper. But he remembered Maudie with affection; in a way, he supposed, they were kindred spirits. Or so Doris had seemed at last to regard them—as though they formed a league especially designed to exasperate her with their incompetence. As a matter of fact, he and Maudie *had* occasionally shared guilty little financial secrets.

He hoped, as he rang the doorbell, that it wouldn't be Doris who answered. And it wouldn't be, he felt pretty sure, if she could help it. The rare occasions when they had met since the divorce had been a strain on both of them. It was sad but true: all that remained of what they had once called love was a barely controlled irritability.

No. Today of all days, he hoped it wouldn't be Doris. He didn't need any witnesses, in case Annabelle didn't remember him, but the one witness he especially didn't need was Doris.

He crossed his fingers and waited for the door to open.

TWO

The street where Barbara lived was only a couple of blocks away from Doris' and Monroe's apartment. In physical distance, that is; in atmosphere it was a world away. There was nothing new or shiny or spacious about Barbara's side street, or about its houses, which were cramped and grimy, and which duplicated each other with depressing monotony. Several of them had Furnished Room signs; they all had the forlorn look of places where rent is paid by the week and the tenants are no more permanent than the pieces of dirty paper flapping along the pavement.

But Barbara liked being near Doris and Monroe. And Maudie and Annabelle. They were not even her in-laws anymore (she and Doris' brother had been divorced six months ago) but they were all the family she had. They were aware of this pathetic fact; it made them all the more conscientious about helping Barbara "get herself organized." That was Doris' phrase. Not that the divorce had been a bitter affair. Not at all. Still, said Doris, it was always a wrench; especially to a shy girl like Barbara.

She did not find the street or her room depressing. Certainly not on a day like this. Because today was one of her pink days.

She had all colors. Mondays, for instance, were apt to be a harsh, nagging yellow: a new week staring her in the face, pulsing with the pressure of the things they said she ought to do—get a job, find a decent place to live, take a course, develop outside interests. The restful, muted greens and blues came later in the week. There was no predicting the purple days (oh, dreadful) when the world and everything in it seemed swollen and livid. They might come any time, even on one of the Saturdays she spent with Annabelle.

But today, this Saturday, was pink. The inside of a shell, apple blossoms, a kitten's tongue, a baby's curled-up fingers. The color of hope and promise.

She sat by the one window in her room, eating her sandwich ("But why don't you go *out* for lunch?" Doris was always asking) and there was a ruddy glow on the pavement down below, a delicate blush on the houses across the street. When she put the crumbs out on the window sill, two rosy-footed pigeons fluttered down, iridescent pink shimmering along their necks.

Oh, it was a day for wishes to come true, a day for miracles to happen. Even to someone like Barbara? Yes, even Barbara, the-girl-everyone-felt-sorry-for, might break out of her prison of loneliness and fear on a day like this.

In a burst of unwonted confidence (usually she was too timid for any sociable gesture) she picked up the telephone, which sat on the rickety table beside the sway-backed bed, and dialed Doris' number. Doris' "hello" was prompt, and edged with irritation. "I'm waiting for Mother," she said. "She promised to be back by two, because it's Val's day with Annabelle, you know—"

"Oh, that's right. It had slipped my mind."

"And I have this appointment. But you know how Mother is, never got anywhere on time in her life. You don't happen to know where she went, do you? Not that it matters, really. Val will be here any minute, and I can turn Annabelle over to him and run."

"If you want me to come over and stay with her till Val comes ..."

But it was too much to hope for, even on a pink day. "Thanks, Barbara, but he'll probably be here even sooner than you can make it." And now, a little later than usual, came the familiar, hearty question. "What are you up to today?"

They always asked that. And it always threw Barbara into a flurry of guilty mental scrabbling for something acceptable to be "up to." (Just sitting here enjoying her pink day would never pass with Doris.) She found herself lying again; her own glibness on these occasions never failed to astonish her. "I'm going to look at an apartment. I just happened to hear about it, from the waitress, while I was eating lunch today, and it sounds good, at least worth looking into."

"Well, good for you, Barbara! That's marvelous. Where is it? In the neighborhood?"

"No. It's downtown." (The approval in Doris' voice spurred her on to giddier efforts.) "That's one thing against it, because I do like being up here, close to you. But I've decided you're right, I can't go on living in a furnished room forever."

"I've felt that way all along, only I didn't like to say too much. I've been through this divorce business, too, you know. I understand how you feel, all at loose ends. But honestly, Barbara, a nice place to live would make all the difference. And wherever you are, we'll always keep in touch. Annabelle's devoted to you. We all are. That's why we're so anxious to see you get yourself organized."

She was safe. Another crisis past. She closed her eyes, not listening anymore: after all, she had heard Doris' pep talks many times before. When this one was over, she said, "I thought I might drop in later, if you're going to be around."

"Of course. We'd love to see you. Monroe and I are going out for dinner, but not till seven or so. Come for a drink, and you can tell us all about the apartment— There, that must be Val at the door now, I've got to dash. See you later, Barbara, and good luck."

"Give Val my regards," said Barbara. But Doris had already hung up.

She lay back on the bed and reached for the pillow, the plump, lozenge-shaped pillow she was so fond of. A pink haze suffused the ceiling above her, tenderly blurring the cracks and stains. It was as if she were floating, gently rocking toward the land of her heart's desire ...

A land undreamt of in Doris' philosophy. For a moment the tables were turned; it was Barbara who felt sorry for poor, wholesome Doris, whose vision never lifted higher than a nice place to live, a "stimulating" job, and the good old reliable outside interests that she was always recommending. She meant so well. And if she insisted on regarding Barbara as a forlorn, disorganized creature, clinging to her ex-in-laws because she had no one else—well, where was the harm in that? Even when they had been real, legal sisters-in-law, Barbara had been an outsider. The divorce only made her more so in Doris' eyes. But more defenseless, too. More of a responsibility.

Val, she thought, gazing up at the pink hazy ceiling, Val had been an outsider too. Not on so hopeless a level as Barbara. Still, there had been a wordless bond between them; she remembered him with warmth and gratitude, because he had been kind to her, and at a time when he must have been acutely unhappy himself.

The telephone shattered her rosy, floating feeling. She did not dare let it go unanswered, even though she was practically sure...

He so often called on Saturdays. She knew it was her own fault; she lacked the personal force to convince him that his calls were hopeless. They were. Quite hopeless; and she had told him so. But not with the right words, not in the right way—because he still did not believe it. He would not let go of her. He still called.

She knew by heart what he would say. She had listened, so many times, to his desperate outpourings—he loved her as no one else would ever love her, he knew her as no one else would ever know her, he could not live without her—and invariably, as she listened, a kind of paralysis clamped down on her, a monstrous embarrassment that reduced her to whispering, over and over, "No ... No ..."

But not today. Not this time. Her hand, reaching for the phone, was steady as steel, and inside she was steady too, cold and hard as a sword.

THREE

"Any messages?" asked J. Monroe Ward, pausing at the chromium and glass stall where the switchboard girl sat. She was doing her fingernails. Somewhere down the hall a lone typewriter clicked haltingly; otherwise the hush of Saturday afternoon was unbroken.

She blew on her fingernails and shuffled gingerly through her collection of slips. "Just this one. A personal call. He didn't leave his name. A friend of yours, he said, and he might try later."

A friend of yours. Monroe flinched at the phrase. But only inwardly; outwardly he managed to preserve the inscrutable expression that was habitual with him. Anybody might use that phrase, he told himself firmly. You heard it all the time.

You certainly did. It was only lately that he had realized how all the time you heard it.

"Thank you," he said in the deep, measured voice that went with the inscrutable expression. "Don't bother to put through any but personal calls this afternoon, please. I've got a tricky contract to go over, and I don't want to be disturbed."

"Righto, Mr. Ward." She flashed her professional smile at him, and he went on down the corridor to his office. His feet made no sound on the carpeted floor. The door gave a little gasp, hardly more than a sigh, as it shut behind him. He was alone in the atmosphere of majestic restraint that distinguished his office. It was done in gray and yellow, and it smelled slightly of furniture polish. When he had hung up his topcoat and homburg, Monroe sat down at his vast desk, which was shaped something like a blunt-edged fin and was unsullied by anything except his marble desk set, the two telephones and a small photograph of Doris. She was looking at him and smiling. He closed his eyes.

There really was a tricky contract. He laid it out in front of him and stared at it for a minute or two. Then he unlocked the second drawer.

The letters were still there. He had tremulous moments when he almost believed they wouldn't be, when he was half-persuaded that they were part of an ugly dream. But they were there, all right. Eight of them. They came twice a week, on Mondays and Fridays. Perhaps at this very moment next Monday's was being slipped into a mail box somewhere near Grand Central. Or it might already be in the post office, gliding along a conveyor, looking as respectable as any of the other thousands and thousands of letters that were being sorted. Wherever it was now, he knew where he would find it Monday morning—on his desk, unopened, because it would be marked Personal, and Miss Simmons would no more think of opening a letter marked Personal than she would think of following him into the men's room. He would find it, and—instead of dropping it unread into the waste basket as he would do if he had any sense—he would open it.

He no longer struggled against the ignominious fact: he had no sense about the letters.

He read them through methodically, beginning with the first one. He could not help himself. They fascinated him. They had a quality of rollicking innocence, as if the writer had no inkling of their real significance. You might have thought he was spreading the gladdest tidings in the world. They were a tantalizing mixture of the explicit and the vague. No names were named (except Doris'), and yet there were descriptions that Monroe found definitely recognizable. Oh, there was no lack of concrete details; the writer, whoever he was, knew Doris, knew her thoroughly. And that was another angle—the chummy tone he took with Monroe, as if they were in the same boat ...

They might be, at that. It made a crazy kind of sense. Because spite was what made people write anonymous letters, and who was more likely to give way to spite than a discarded lover, someone who wanted to get even with Doris because she had cast him off? The theory was terribly double-edged: to accept it meant accepting, along with it, the fact that Doris was indeed untrue to him—if not with the nameless character or characters indicated in the letters, then with the nameless writer himself.

"No," said Monroe aloud. "No." He had an abject impulse to put his head down on his desk and weep.

But what more plausible theory was there? The last letter seemed to set the seal on it. "You know, Monroe, we really ought to get together. We have so much in common. How about if I call you one of these days and we meet some place for a drink?" It was signed, like the others, A Friend of Yours. And it was typed on the same ordinary white bond paper, folded in thirds to fit into the ordinary stamped envelope, the kind you buy at the post office.

If only the fellow would call! If only Monroe could see him face to face; wring out of him the truth; rid himself, once and for all, of these agonizing doubts!

They raged through him. He remembered how often, when he called Doris at her office, the report came back: "Sorry. Mrs. Ward is not at her desk." And all the times when she "got stuck" and had to work evenings. The headaches. The excuses (surely they had been flimsy?) for not spending that weekend in Maine with him. Right down to this afternoon, when she had told him she was going shopping, so as to leave the coast clear for Val and Annabelle. He was almost sure he had overheard her mentioning "an appointment" to her mother, earlier this morning.

He should have taken her up on that one. Just as he should show her the letters, drag the whole thing out in the open, give her a chance to explain. Ah, but supposing she admitted her infidelity, or—even worse—tried to lie, so clumsily that he would know she was lying?

He picked up the photograph, searching her face. She did not look faithless or wanton. Her eyes met his frankly, her head had the assured tilt that was characteristic of her, and her lips were parted in the spontaneous smile that had charmed him from the beginning.

But anyone could wear a mask. In a sense, everyone did. Who should know this better than Monroe? The front he presented to the business world—the dead-pan, the impressively deliberate voice, the smooth gestures—was one he had spent years in building up. It was a mask, and behind it cowered the real Monroe, riddled with uncertainties, shamefully indecisive. An emotional incompetent, no matter how much money he might make or how brilliant his achievements as an executive.

That front, after all, was what Doris had seen first. And maybe that was all she wanted from him. Money. Security for herself and Annabelle ...

The lone, lame typewriter down the hall had started up again. For a moment it seemed to Monroe to be a part of him, like something broken inside him, still clicking forlornly.

It must have been quite different, when she married Val. No money or the promise of security there. No possible motive but love. Well, Doris had told him so. "We were just a couple of love-struck kids," she had said. "We didn't have any business getting married. Why, we hardly knew each other—and by the time we discovered we didn't really like each other much it was too late, Annabelle was on the way. It was hopeless from the start, an unqualified mistake of a marriage."

And Doris was too smart to make the same mistake twice. Love-struck, thought Monroe wistfully. You didn't have to be a kid to be love-struck; he had found that out. But it helped. Look at the way Doris and Val had shrugged off the collapse of their marriage, while the thinnest shadow of such a possibility was enough to turn Monroe to jelly.

That was the true significance of the letters. Somebody, for some reason, was conspiring to destroy his marriage. He must face it. He could face it. What he could not face was the terrifying chance that "A Friend of Yours" might be telling the truth about Doris. It paralyzed him. He knew that there were ways of finding out; one black Friday he had spent an hour mulling over the list of detective agencies in the classified phone book. "Matrimonial Matters Discreetly and Expertly Handled." Oh yes, he could find out. But, if it turned out to be true, he could not bear to know it.

He must go on like this, then, harrowed by doubts for the rest of his life? He discovered that he was praying, the way he used to do in moments of crisis, when he was a kid. Oh God, please make it not be true, please ...

The phone at his elbow whirred politely. Once. Twice. He felt the sweat break out in his hands as he reached to pick it up.

FOUR

Val uncrossed his fingers and took a deep breath. No luck. It was Doris who opened the door. All ready to go out, very trim in her fur jacket and stylish hat, and looking—yes—a little irritated. Had he done something wrong already? No; her first words set him straight. "I'm in a rush. Mother was supposed to be back by two, but you know our Maudie." She gave him the bright, quick smile that had once enchanted him, and held out her hand. It felt compact and cool in his. Their eyes didn't quite meet. Hers, he was sure, had not missed the beat-up state of his topcoat. "Well, Val. It's nice to see you again—even if it's just for a minute. Do come in, Annabelle's waiting for you in her play room. You'll hardly know her, she's grown so."

And there was the question, trembling in the air again, as he followed her into the big, expensively uncluttered living room. *Look, will she remember me?* But it was even more impossible to ask it of Doris than of Miss LaTour or the panda saleslady. Even if she weren't preoccupied—as she was—with something else.

"Oh, and Val," she was saying, "Annabelle's due at a birthday party at five o'clock. I don't know whether you planned anything special for this afternoon ..."

No, he hadn't. He felt at once that he should have. But again Doris set him straight.

"That's fine, then. I mean the party won't interfere. Would you be a lamb and deposit her there at five? It's right in this building. The name is Grierson. Apartment 14D. Can you remember that?"

"I doubt it. You'd better print it in block letters and pin it to my coat." She flushed. "I didn't mean—"

"Okay, skip it. Grierson, Apartment 14D, five o'clock. I'll get her there."

"Fine. I wouldn't ask you, except I'm not sure I'll be back by five, and you know how Mother is. She may turn up, and then again she may not. If you and Annabelle want to go out, there's the park. Don't forget, she's allergic to chocolate ..." She opened the play room door, and stepped aside as he followed her in. "Annabelle, here's Val to see you." Just a faint stress on the word Val, like a reminder.

All he could see at first was Annabelle's legs, carrying her, without haste, across the play room floor toward him. Slightly gangly legs, not thin, but no longer babyishly round. Six-and-a-half-year-old legs, brown from the California sun, with scars and scratches on the knees.

The panda ... It wasn't the sort of thing, a panda, that you could slip out of sight. It seemed to be growing bigger in his arms; more monstrous, more enormously a mistake ...

"Thank you very much," said Annabelle politely.

It wasn't as big a panda, it turned out, as the one Daddy had given her a year ago. "Oh, but much cuter," Doris insisted. "Much, much cuter. Isn't it, Annabelle?" Daddy's (the nine ninety-five size; trust Monroe) was sitting up on the top shelf, with the other toys that Annabelle probably never played with anymore.

"Hasn't she grown!" cried Doris. "You were nothing but a little bit of a thing, dear, no bigger than that, last time Val saw you."

(Why don't you just kindly depart, Val inquired silently. Why don't you just kindly get the hell out of here.)

But after she had gone, he couldn't think of much of anything to say to Annabelle, except had she liked it out in California? Her head bobbed up and down. She hoisted herself up on the window seat and made a prim little gesture of pulling down her skirt. Her hair (he could see all of her now; not just her legs) was different. No more pigtails. Bangs in front, and the rest of it fell, half-curly, almost to her shoulders. But it was the same cinnamon-brown color, like her eyes. She had the same round, rosy cheeks, and that shy half-smile that she used to give strangers and was giving him now.

Yes, she liked school. And yes, she knew how to read. (Doggedly he went on asking the dead-end questions; they were all he could produce in the way of conversation.) And yes, she had learned to swim in California.

"Once, out in Los Angeles, I swam miles and miles. There was this island, and I swam all the way out to it. In the middle of the night. Mommy and Daddy nearly went out of their *mind*. They were on the beach, watching me. But they were scared to come after me, on account of the sharks." She paused, testing her audience.

"Is that a fact," said Val.

"So they sent the life guard after me." Annabelle swung her legs; her eyes darkened with the excitement of the creative artist. "And you know what? He drowned! Well, not drowned dead. They gave him artificial respiration."

"The suspense is terrible," said Val. "Tell me, did the sharks get you?"

She clapped her hands over her mouth, but it was no use, the giggles burst out. "You're funny," she said. "Want to hear a riddle? Why is it bad to write on an empty stomach?"

"I give up. Why is it bad to write on an empty stomach?"

"It isn't so bad, but paper is better." She inspected him anxiously. "D'you get it?" He laughed to prove that he did, and here came another one. "What did one wall say to the other? 'I'll meet you at the corner.' D'you get it? What's black and white and red all over?"

"I know that one. It's a news—"

"No it isn't. No, it isn't!" She sat on her hands and bounced in triumph. "It's an embarrassed zebra!"

"I get it," Val said hastily.

"I know lots of riddles. Cane told me lots of them. And we played Old Maid, and I beat him every time but once. And then we had cocktails, and he played like he was drunk, and it was more fun! Do you know him?"

"I don't think I do. Was he out in California too?"

"Oh no. Here in New York. That's not his real name. That's just what I call him. He's got eyebrows, they're like little moustaches, and he's got whiskers in his ears, and he has a cane." Val noticed that her eyes were beginning to darken again. "I take hold of his cane, and he swings me way up. Way up to the ceiling. Way up to the sky. I'm going to a birthday party."

"I know. I'm going to take you to it. Meantime, you know what we can do? We can go to the park and go ice skating. That is, if you'd like to—"

"Can we? Honest and true?" She skipped across the room and stood close to him, rigid with excitement. He felt pretty exuberant himself. "Oh boy! I've never *been* ice skating!"

He was doing okay. Whether she remembered him or not, he was still doing okay. But he mustn't let himself get carried away. He must think—as Doris always did—of practical things like mittens and leggings and keeping track of the time, so she wouldn't miss the birthday party ...

"Now take it easy," he cautioned Annabelle (and himself) while they struggled with zippers and buttons. "Leave us pause for a short period of interlude while we concentrate." Annabelle giggled. "We'll go straight to the birthday party from the park, because there may not be anybody here to let us in. So we mustn't forget anything. Concentrate, Annabelladonna. Are we forgetting anything?"

"Birthday present! We have to take the birthday present!" She raced across to the book case for the small, festively wrapped package. "You know what it is? It's a charm bracelet. It's got all kinds of precious stones!"

"Just a little bauble you picked up at Tiffany's, I suppose."

"You're funny," she said again. "Oh, and we have to take the panda."

"The panda?"

"He wants to go ice skating too. We have to take him." She cocked her head, in its little plaid hood, at Val, taking his measure.

It didn't matter that this might be only a bit of coquetry, the eternal feminine instinct to flatter and please. Val felt his heart dissolving.

"We're having fun, aren't we?" Annabelle told him, as she put her hand trustfully in his.

FIVE

Half of Maudie seemed to have turned into a solicitous nurse, bent on administering to the other half, who was too shaken to look out for herself. Nurse Maudie kept up a cheery line of chatter: Well, isn't this nice, here's our bus already, a nice empty one, we'll get a seat by the window, now if we can just find our fare ...

Obediently the stricken Maudie fumbled in her purse for the right coins, dropped them in the box, and stumbled down the aisle to the seat by the window.

Oh my, look at the time, we *are* late, aren't we? Doris is going to give us what-for, and no mistake. But never mind. We'll think up an excuse. A traffic jam. We'll say we grabbed a cab, just to be on the safe side, and wouldn't you know, we got into this awful traffic jam. Doris will have left for her appointment by the time we get home, anyway. If anybody's there it will just be Val and Annabelle, and we've always liked Val, like we say, he's our favorite ex-son-in-law.

But the thought of a kind word, a friendly face, was too much. Tears welled up in Maudie's eyes; it took all her will power to keep from dissolving right here in public.

She hadn't cried, back in the hotel lobby. She clung to that one shred of her tattered self-respect: at least she hadn't cried in front of him. Not even when he said naturally it was money he wanted—what else?— from an old bag like her ...

Now, now, gabbled Nurse Maudie, we mustn't let ourselves get upset.

We mustn't think about it.

She *couldn't* think about it, she found. All she could do was stare in horror at what had happened to her, was happening, was going to happen. What a fool! Oh, what a fool she had been, to swallow his flattery! Hook, line and sinker. So much so that she couldn't believe her ears at first; this afternoon she had sat there dumbfounded, while he explained in words of one syllable. Exactly what kind of a scoundrel he was; and exactly what kind of a fool she was. She believed it now, all right. It made her crawl inside. Inside. Secretly. That was the one thing that made it bearable. If it ceased to be a secret, if Doris ever found out …

That was where he had her, of course. She would die, if necessary, to keep him away from Doris. Surely he knew that? Surely he hadn't taken her pitiful little bluff seriously? "And supposing I haven't got any money?" she had quavered. Of course he knew. It startled her, some of the things he knew—not just about her, but about Monroe and Doris and Annabelle. Almost as if he had already been up there.… Oh, if he had dared, if he had dared! She might as well face it: he was capable of anything, and she was twice a fool if she tried any more bluffing. (She must call him tonight; make it quite, quite clear that she had no such intention.)

Though he must know already, because he had laughed, and that was when the outlandish truth dawned on her. Blackmail. She was being blackmailed.

Oh, not for any fantastic amount. He had found out—with Maudie's whole-hearted co-operation; no mystery here—just how much the traffic would bear. In other words, just how much her insurance checks amounted to. (That was where Doris got her head for figures and money, from her father. He had left Maudie all this insurance that came in regular as clockwork. A good provider, even from the world beyond; and Maudie was duly grateful, even though she sometimes thought, wistfully, of what fun she would have had with one great big gorgeous lump sum.)

The insurance checks made her feel independent and, for a couple of days each month, wealthy. It always amazed Maudie, how quickly the money melted away. A special treat or two for Annabelle, a shopping spree for herself, the payments due on last month's shopping spree, some little gift for Doris or Monroe or Barbara—she never knew quite what happened. Well, from now on she would know. All too well. He wasn't going to get rich off Maudie, but then she might not be his only source of income. Why, yes. Why shouldn't he have a whole string of foolish old women breaking their necks to pay him hush money? She swallowed hard.

It was one thing for Doris to think of her as flighty. She did; she always had. And what was that other word? Gullible. "Mother, how can you be so gullible? Really, I should think you'd have learned by now!" She said it impatiently, but affectionately, too. Because flighty and gullible were forgivable traits. There was nothing disgraceful about being a well-meaning nitwit. But not for one minute would Doris put up with a mother who was an old tramp.

She'd turn me out, bag and baggage, thought Maudie bleakly. She'd never let me speak to Annabelle again as long as I live. And I don't blame her. I may be a nitwit, but I raised her that way, her and Clyde both.

The thought of her son, like that of Val, brought the tears to her eyes. But she could not appeal to Clyde for help, either. In the first place, he was too far away. Cleveland. That was where he had gone, after he and Barbara were divorced. Even if he were here, she could not have told him, any more than she could tell Doris. She might make up some story and ask him for a temporary loan. But she couldn't go on, manufacturing a new financial crisis every single month, and knowing all the time that she was never going to be able to pay back these "temporary loans."

Never? Didn't blackmailers ever go away, or get tired of the whole thing, or drop dead?

Through a haze of misery, she heard her other self, Nurse Maudie, yakking away: Well, can you beat that! Look at what we've done, ridden two stops too far. Aren't we the ones. Never mind, we can walk back, it's pretty along here, the park and all …

As she got off the bus, a forlorn gust of hope struck her. Maybe *she* could go away, just disappear for a while, get a job somewhere, change her name, dye her hair a different color. But the buoyancy that had always before kept her afloat was gone, along with her self-respect and her independence and her couple of wealthy days a month. Only the grim realities remained. Hide from him? Disappear? There was no surer way to send him galloping to Doris. A job? Years ago, the summer before she got married, she had "helped out" in the bake shop in her home town. She hadn't been very good at making change.

She bent her head against the chilly November wind. For the first time in her life Maudie felt like an old woman, with no hope left, no zest, not even any tears.

The apartment was empty. She walked through it aimlessly. After a while she remembered to take off her coat and hat. Then she sat down in the living room and waited. For nothing.

"Why, Mother, what are you doing, sitting here in the dark?" cried

Doris, when she came in—later, probably quite a while later, because Maudie saw that sure enough it was dark, or very nearly. She flinched a little, when Doris turned on the light. She could not think of anything at all to say.

But Doris didn't seem to notice. She was over at the window now, pulling the drapes shut against the early dusk. She turned, and Maudie saw that her eyes were shining, it was one of those infrequent moments when Doris looked—not merely smart; she always looked that—but pretty. Pretty because she was happy.

"Tired, dearie?" She patted Maudie's cheek. "Have a nice lunch?"

"Oh, yes. Lovely," said Maudie, because that was what she usually said. Funny. No lunch, and still she didn't feel the least bit hungry. Remembered guilt stirred in her. "I'm sorry. I mean about being late. I grabbed a cab, just to be on the safe side, and wouldn't you know, we got into this awful traffic—"

"Late? Oh, yes. I'd forgotten." Even in her benumbed state. Maudie felt a thrust of surprise. It wasn't like Doris to forget, when you were late. It wasn't like her, either, to toss her jacket and hat on the couch, or to stand still in the middle of the room, suddenly smiling at nothing.

"Mother," she began impulsively. But then the doorbell rang: it was Barbara, and right afterwards Monroe came in (looking anything but happy, himself), and everybody had a drink. Maudie, remembering her empty stomach, hesitated over hers. But not for very long. She might as well be drunk as the way she was. Much better, in fact. She was proud, rather startled, to hear herself chattering away in her usual gay fashion. Just as if the terrible afternoon had never happened. A great little actress. Give the old tramp credit, thought Maudie: a great little actress.

SIX

So there he was, as he might have foreseen, stuck with the damn panda after their ice-skating session. Because it seemed that the panda didn't want to go to the party; he wanted Val to take him home.

"But there may not be anybody there to let me in," protested Val. (On the other hand, there might be everybody, including Monroe, there to let him in. Old Home Week.)

"Oh yes, Doris is back," reported Mrs. Grierson, who had opened the door of Apartment 14D at their ring. A big help, Mrs. Grierson. "She stopped in on her way up a few minutes ago, to say that you were bringing Annabelle."

That took care of that. Oh well, thought Val as he got into the elevator, it wouldn't take more than a minute; he could just hand the panda to whoever opened the door and take himself off …

Except that it was Maudie who opened the door and, with a shriek of joy, fell on his neck. Maudie with a slight flicker on—that was no doubt what made her seem so frantically gay—and with her mind made up. No two ways about it: he had to come in and have a drink with his poor old ex-mother-in-law. The sight of her filled him, as it always had, with a warm kind of amusement. Her hair was as defiantly golden as ever; her plump little body appeared to have been melted and poured into her kelly-green wool dress. (For Maudie operated on the sanguine and completely groundless theory that she was going to lose fifteen pounds in the next two weeks, so why buy something that in no time at all would be too big? Just ordinary common sense.) There was something different about her eyes, though. They were as round and brown as ever, but the expression Val remembered—the young girl's look of hope and wonder—seemed to have faded.

Meanwhile, he was being drawn irresistibly down the hall to the living room. And everybody was there, all right. In a word, Monroe. He unfolded his narrow length from the couch (he had always reminded Val of a praying mantis) and advanced, hand outstretched. Civilized as all hell. "Val, old man, it's a pleasure to see you again. How've you been?"

"Fine, thanks. I stopped in to leave Annabelle's—"

"We're just having a drink," said Doris, without getting up from the couch. "Won't you join us?"

"Thanks, but I've got this dinner—"

It was against the law, apparently, for him to finish a sentence. "Don't anybody listen to him," cried Maudie. "Of course he's going to have a drink with us! A martini—isn't that right, Val dearie? With lemon peel."

"Martini with lemon peel," repeated Monroe, already smoothly busy at the bar. Val might still have stuck to his guns, except that Monroe added, with a dip of his head toward the window, "You remember Barbara, don't you?"

"Barbara?" And sure enough, there she was, in the big chair in the corner; she had always avoided the limelight. As he turned toward her, Val caught her unfinished gesture, as if she had been about to stretch her hand out to him and then changed her mind, for fear of seeming too forward. She was smiling tremulously.

"Why, of course I remember Barbara!" Who could forget that sad madonna-face, as pale and smooth as a flower, or its quality of mystery and depth? It might be true—as Doris had once said, in a waspish moment—that there were no depths to be plumbed in Barbara, that soulful effect was a simple accident of bone structure and low metabolism. Moonlight, too, could no doubt be explained in technical terms; and moonlight still was haunting.

So was Barbara—without seeming to be in the least aware of it. She was so unsure of herself socially that even the smallest, most informal party threw her into a near-panic. How she must suffer, being married to somebody like Doris' brother! For Clyde was as noisy and gregarious as a crow; he loved crowds, baseball, night clubs, conventions, loud, fast music ...

"Here we are," said Monroe, and it was too late to escape now, Val was trapped, for at least the length of the martini he held in his hand. It would be an impeccable martini. Naturally. Look who had mixed it. He put the panda down and, without taking off his coat, perched on the window seat.

Automatically he lifted his glass toward Doris, as he had done so often and often in the past. Was it possible, that bitter-sweet year they had spent together, that snarl of time so queerly shot with shreds of happiness? It must seem even more unreal to her than to him; he had no second marriage to crowd out the memory of the first. But Doris had Monroe. J. Monroe Ward, the wonder husband who never lost jobs or spent his money without being able to account for every last cent. They sat side by side on their chartreuse couch, looking sleek and poised, like the successful young married couples in the advertisements. The lamplight fell warmly on Doris' glossy reddish-brown hair (did Monroe ever wash it for her, the way Val used to?) and on Monroe's dead-pan face, his chalk-stripe suit and immaculate shirt.

Maudie was rattling on at her usual pace: "Did you and Annabelle enjoy yourselves? I know what they say about doting grandmothers, but I do think she's just the cutest thing. And smart! Well, she always was way in advance of children her age—"

"Now, Mother," said Doris. But she was smiling. "I hope she behaved herself, Val. She gets awfully fresh sometimes."

"She was fine. We went ice skating."

Everybody made pleased, admiring sounds. Ice skating! An inspiration! (And it had been; the afternoon had been a great success. So why should Val feel annoyed when they said so?)

"I bet she talked your ear off," Maudie went on. "The things that child comes out with! She must have had a field day, telling you all about California, and the trip back, and school."

"Yes, she gave a pretty full report," said Val. They all smiled at him expectantly and encouragingly—for it wouldn't do to let the conversation die; this was neither the time nor place for companionable silence. "She told me about somebody she calls Cane, too," he added, simply for the sake of keeping the show on the road.

Right away he got the strangest feeling of tension, as if they were all holding their breath. Or perhaps just one of them. Only which one? And why? For the life of him, he couldn't nail it down.

"Who?" said Doris. "Cane? Who in the world is Cane?" She laughed nervously.

"A great guy, according to Annabelle." He seemed to have put his foot in it; nothing to do now but flounder on. "He tells her riddles, plays Old Maid with her ..."

Again he had that feeling of a breath being held, of somebody in the room (who? why?) thinking fast. And again it was Doris who broke the silence.

"Do you know who this character is, Monroe?"

"I have no idea," said Monroe evenly. "Have you?"

"Would I be asking you, if I had? I can't imagine. Because we haven't left her with anybody but Mother and Barbara since we've been back. Unless—" She took an absent-minded sip of her drink and set it down on the coffee table. "Well, of course that must be it! She's simply made him up. She does things like that, you know. Remember that little playmate she dreamed up for herself in California? She's simply done it again!"

Everybody relaxed; you could practically taste the relief. "Like I said, the things she comes out with," Maudie pointed out. "The imagination." And Monroe explained, for the benefit of any dopes who might be present: "It's very common, especially with impressionable children like Annabelle. It's a phase they go through. They confuse fantasy with reality."

"Don't we all?" said Val. So Cane was a fabrication of Annabelle's imagination. Like the swimming episode. He was willing to take their word for it. He finished his drink and stood up. From this vantage point he saw, with a thrust of keen pleasure, that Monroe's hair was getting thin on top.

"Thanks for the drink. I've got to be going."

He was rather surprised to see Barbara rise too. "So must I," she said. "I mean— We can ride down in the elevator together." There was a little gust of laughter, and she blushed.

"Barbara has a thing about self-service elevators," said Doris. "She's depending on you for moral support."

So it wasn't his magnetic personality. All the same, Val found the idea of Barbara's depending on him somehow pleasing. She wasn't too shy of him for that.

For a moment he and Doris were alone in the hallway. Maudie had bustled into the bedroom after Barbara to help her with her coat. And Monroe made a point of busying himself again at the bar.

"I'm afraid I disrupted your cocktail hour," said Val. "Sorry. It won't happen again."

"Don't be silly." She paused. "Val—" There was a puzzling note in her voice. She kept her head lowered, as if she were searching for the right words. She did not find them in time. Here came Maudie and Barbara.

"Goodbye, Val." Her quick, bright smile flashed between them like a shield. "It was nice seeing you."

In another minute the door closed behind him and Barbara. "You see?" he said, when he had pushed the right buttons and the elevator began its serene descent. "There's nothing to be afraid of."

"It might not stop," she whispered. It did. But her smile—and then it was a wan one—did not appear until she had stepped out into the lobby. "I'm afraid of lots of other things too," she said. "Subways, airplanes, even escalators ..."

"And people. Some people, that is. I hope you're not afraid of me."

"No, not of you." As they went out the door, she added softly, "You're afraid of some people, too."

"You think so?" He turned it over in his mind, wondering whether his resentment of Monroe might stem from an obscure kind of fear. He didn't really believe it. To distrust a guy—and for no sensible reason he did mistrust Monroe—was one thing; to be afraid of him was something quite different. But if she meant Doris ... Yes, he supposed he was afraid of Doris, the way you are afraid of someone who has hurt you once. "Not of you, though," he said, smiling. "So that makes us even. Are we going the same direction? I don't know where you and Clyde live anymore."

"Oh, we're not—I mean, Clyde and I are divorced." She spoke matter-of-factly, but her great dark eyes looked off into space—a space, Val felt sure, where the ghosts of lost hopes wandered, mutely grieving. She couldn't have been very happy with Clyde, she might not even have loved him. All the same, the ghosts would be there. "It doesn't surprise you, does it?" she asked.

"No. But I'm sorry it didn't work out, even though you and Clyde didn't seem exactly suited to each other."

"We weren't, were we? Not suited at all. I don't understand why Clyde ever married me."

"I do. You're beautiful, Barbara." He was embarrassed to hear his voice break slightly, with the weight of sincerity. Above her shabby polo coat her face, as flawless as a flower, was lifted toward him with a look of breathless wonder. "Other people must have told you so. I can't be the first. What I don't understand is why you married Clyde. I don't mean that he's not a good guy—"

"Yes. That's why. A good guy," said Barbara dreamily. "Such a good, normal, average guy, and I thought—somehow I thought I could turn into that kind of person, too, if I married him. A house in the suburbs, I thought, just like everybody else's house, and shopping at the supermarket with all the other wives, and having other couples in for bridge and television, just like everybody else ... Silly of me, wasn't it ? To think just marrying Clyde was going to turn me into the kind of wife he ought to have."

"Probably. But Clyde didn't turn out to be the kind of husband you ought to have, either." Not that Val was at all sure of what kind of husband Barbara ought to have. Someone as off-beat as herself? That might be as disastrous, in a way, as a bouncing extrovert like Clyde, who had simply flung her into the uproarious current of his own life and expected her to learn to swim in it.

"But Clyde never intended to change," she said. "That's what makes the difference. It wouldn't ever occur to Clyde to try to be anything but himself."

What an odd mixture of directness and shyness she was! They had paused at the street corner, and there they stood in the chilly twilight, talking as intimately as if they had spent hours together in cozy seclusion.

"Let me see you home," said Val. "Which way do we go?"

"But your dinner date," she murmured.

"I haven't really got one. I just invented one, to get us all off the hook."

"Oh. I see." She seemed impressed by this bit of social skullduggery. "I live just a couple of blocks away. It's nice, being nearby like this. I can stay with Annabelle, nights when they all want to go out. It's nice, being near somebody you know."

Certainly there was nothing else to recommend it, thought Val. It was a dreary street. She must be living in a furnished room—just for the sake of being near her ex-in-laws. But hadn't she any friends? He looked down at her face, that pure oval that seemed almost luminous in the dusk, at her heavy-lidded eyes and long hair, which she wore pulled straight back from her brow and done in a knot low on her neck. Yes. Beautiful. It didn't seem possible that she should have no friends at all.

"They've been back for a month," she said. "Did you know that?"

"Yes. Doris— We thought it would be better for me to wait to see Annabelle until they were settled."

"Poor Val," she said. "Once a week isn't very often to see her. Your own little girl."

"I'm not complaining. It's better than nothing." He must have spoken rather curtly; anyway, he felt her stiffen beside him, as at an actual rebuff.

"I'm sorry," she murmured. "I shouldn't have said anything."

"Nothing to be sorry about." He tucked her hand under his arm; she did not resist, and he felt pleased and flattered, as if he had taken another step toward gaining the confidence of some timorous little woodsy creature. Did he dare ask her to have dinner with him? Better wait, he decided. Maybe when they got to her house she would give him an opening, ask him up for a drink or something.

She didn't, though. When they reached one particular set of steps with the regulation garbage cans on either side and the dingy-curtained door at the top, she stopped and said, "This is where I live. Thank you for walking me home."

The stilted words took him right back to the first-date agonies of his high school days. "Look," he said hurriedly, "I'd like to take you to dinner. Sometime soon. Like—well, like now."

"Now?" she echoed in alarm. "Tonight? Oh, I couldn't. Not tonight."

He sighed. Patience, he told himself, patience and fortitude. There were six other days in the week; if he had to, he supposed he could work his way through every last one of them. "How about tomorrow, then?"

"Tomorrow?" Again the echo of alarm. "Why, I—"

"Tomorrow. That's Sunday. Or maybe you're tied up with other friends on weekends—"

"Oh no," she said, with touching candor, "I haven't any other friends. I think—" She drew a breath and took the plunge. "I think tomorrow would be very nice."

"Fine, then. I'll stop by for you about six thirty. Okay?"

She nodded. There was a faint flush in her cheeks. "Thank you, Val," she said. Still she paused, on the first step, so that her face was on a level with his. He kissed her gently; her lips were smooth and fresh as petals, and as he watched her run up the steps the magic of dusk worked a little miracle of transformation, so that the grimy house and even the harsh street sounds seemed momentarily brushed with beauty.

SEVEN

It wasn't at all according to plan, and Doris always resented it when her plans went awry. But most of all she felt baffled. What had set everything off on the wrong track like this? It was all very well to blame Val for bringing up the subject of Annabelle's gentleman caller, but who in their right mind would expect it to cause more than a few harmless ripples?

Instead, it had touched off a full-dress quarrel, and a fight with Monroe today was the last thing, the very last thing, Doris had planned on. Not with what she had to tell him …

And she had been so happy when she first came home. (It was like a voice inside her, mourning and grieving.) Yes, so happy; right or wrong, she had felt scarcely able to contain her secret bliss. It was all gone now. Evaporated. Dissolved in the acid of this ridiculous, unscheduled, frightening row with Monroe. Who was being—as always, on the rare occasions when they quarreled—ferociously polite. Monroe never hollered. He just goaded *her* into hollering.

Well, she wasn't going to give him the satisfaction. "I thought we all decided that it was just Annabelle's imagination," she said. "Somebody she made up."

"That's one theory. Yours, if I'm not mistaken. And a very interesting theory, too. Very convenient from your point of view. Let me congratulate you on your ingenuity."

"*What* are you talking about?" She couldn't help it; her voice soared. She jumped up and glared at him. He was standing up too, leaning against the book case with his hands in his pockets. No expression. His face might as well have been an egg. Only his upper lip twitched, just a little. "Answer me, Monroe. What is all this?"

"You haven't any idea, have you? Not the slightest."

"I certainly haven't! And I'm getting good and tired of all these dark hints, whatever they are. Either come out with it or—"

"Or what? Do go on."

"Or drop it. Change the subject."

"An excellent idea. Let's talk about your shopping trip this afternoon. What did you buy?"

"I—I—" How she hated herself for stammering! But how impossible it was to do anything else, caught off guard as she was! "Nothing. I didn't buy anything."

"You astound me," said Monroe.

She wet her lips. "Here we go again. What do you mean by that?"

"Just what I said. You astound me. A whole afternoon of shopping, and not a thing to show for it. Not so much as a handkerchief. I should think you'd find it exasperating, to waste time like that. I'm sure I would. But not you. I noticed when I came in tonight how happy you looked. Gay as a lark. I naturally assumed you had come home loaded with bargains."

She was really rattled now, beyond all shrewdness or even caution. "Well, I didn't," she snapped. "And I'm not gay as a lark any more. In case you're interested, I'm—"

It was Mother who saved her. Poor Mother, a captive and restive audience of one, whose presence Doris had forgotten. She piped up now, just in the nick of time: "My, look at what time it's gotten to be! Almost time for me to go get Annabelle. If you'll excuse me ..." Laughing merrily, she scuttled across the no-man's-land that separated Monroe and Doris, and down the hall to her own room. She shut her door against the possibility of continuing battle.

Only a moment, but long enough for Doris to pull herself together. (She had actually been on the verge of blurting it out. The narrowness of her escape left her shaky. Shaky, but once more in her right senses.)

"I've had enough of this," she said. "In case it's slipped your mind, we're due at the Russells' tonight for dinner. I'm going to get dressed and go. Do you intend to join me?"

"By all means," said Monroe. "I wouldn't miss it for the world."

In icy silence they marched into their bedroom and dressed for the dinner party. When she was ready, Doris went down the hall and tapped on Mother's door. Apparently Mother was in the middle of one of her long-winded telephone conversations; Doris could hear her saying, "Of course I'll be there. Anything you say. Anything ..." There was quite a little pause before she called, "Come in, dear," and when Doris opened the door she was sitting in her chintz-covered chair with a magazine in her lap. Dear old Mud, with her innocent little intrigues. And trust her to make a great business of pretending there had been no quarrel. "My, how smart you look," she chirped. "Nothing like black, I always say."

Doris twitched at her velvet skirt and started pulling on one of her long gloves. "We're about to leave. I've left the number beside the phone, in case catastrophe strikes. The Russells, down on Tenth Street."

"I know. Don't worry about a thing. I thought I'd give Annabelle another five minutes of birthday party before I bring her up."

"Poor Mud. I do impose on you—"

Mother pooh-poohed, the way she always did. "That's right. Just call me Maudie the Martyr. Run along now, and have fun."

"Fun," echoed Doris. She felt as hollow as her voice sounded. "I wish I had the nerve to call them up and say I couldn't come. Mother, you heard that nonsense out there in the living room. Do you know what Monroe was talking about?"

"Well," Mother hedged. "Not really."

"What do you mean, not really? You either know or you don't."

There, she was upsetting Mother. And to what purpose? God knew she couldn't stand sympathy from Mother or anybody else, any more than she could stand girly-girly confidences. All wrong. Nothing according to plan. She tugged at her glove irritably.

"What I meant was—" floundered Mother. "Of course I didn't hear it all. But it sounded to me like he didn't believe you'd been shopping this afternoon."

She waited. Well. What did she expect? Let her wait.

"And you did tell me, that is, I got the impression that you had some kind of an appointment this afternoon—"

Doris flashed out at her: "Don't *you* start in on me! I've had enough, without that! An appointment, shopping—what's the difference what I did this afternoon? Do I have to be put through the third degree just because I—"

She realized, with horror, that she was on the brink of tears. She shrank from Mother's outstretched hand and made a desperate rush for the door. Paused there, with her back to Mother, till the crisis was past.

"Don't mind me, Mud," she croaked. "It's not your fault. Skip it. See you later."

And inside her the voice went on mourning: I was so happy, before. It's all spoiled now. He had to spoil it all. I was so happy ...

EIGHT

All the way downtown on the bus, Val's mind was busy with the financial and aesthetic aspects of where to take Barbara to dinner. He couldn't manage a real splurge; still, if he waited till after pay day to pick up his laundry and cleaning ...

He got past the second floor, for once, without encountering Miss LaTour. But as he passed Mrs. Pomeroy's apartment, on the third floor, he noticed that she had forgotten and left her keys in the door again. She must have just returned from her week's visit with her sister upstate. Val hesitated. In a way, Mrs. Pomeroy was his favorite of "the girls," but she was also the gabbiest. If he stopped to tell her about her keys, he'd be lucky to get away from her in less than half an hour. On the other hand, if he didn't tell her she'd be sure to get into a state when she couldn't find her keys. (For, often as she absent-mindedly left them in the lock, it always came as a complete surprise to her to discover that she had done it again.)

He tapped on the door. "Left your keys in the lock, Mrs. Pomeroy."

A muffled voice bade him come in. He pushed open the door, and stopped dead in surprise. Because it wasn't Mrs. Pomeroy—unless Mrs. Pomeroy had switched from her genteel, flowered prints to dungarees, and unless she had suddenly developed a young and shapely posterior. That was what the dungarees enclosed, without an inch to spare. The owner of this posterior was bent over an open suitcase in the middle of the floor.

"I beg your pardon," said Val. "I thought Mrs. Pomeroy—"

"Oh, hello," said the girl, straightening up. "What did I do, leave my keys in the lock? Thanks a lot. You must be Mr. Bryant. I've heard all about you from Aunt Fan—Mrs. Pomeroy. I'm her niece."

And every bit as gabby, Val soon found out. Within two minutes she had informed him that Mrs. Pomeroy was in an upstate hospital with a broken hip, wasn't it a shame, she simply stepped off a curb and wham; that her niece had jumped at the chance to take over her apartment because she'd been living at the YW (gruesome) and it might be months before poor Aunt Fan got out of the hospital; and that the niece's name was Helen but everybody called her Hen, which was revolting but what were you going to do?

There was a brief pause. But only while she got her breath. "Come on in. Please do. I'll rassle us up a drink to celebrate. Poor Aunt Fan, but isn't it enchanting to have a place of my own? Here, let me get some of this stuff out of the way so you can sit down." She shifted an armload of books and a goose neck lamp from the chair to the couch and—without giving Val a chance to say ay, yes or no—got busy with ice and liquor in the minute kitchenette, where Mrs. Pomeroy had never "rassled up" anything stronger than a cup of tea. Already the little apartment seemed to have changed, from an atmosphere of fussy, old-lady refinement to one of headlong vitality. The brocade drapes (a left-over from that opulent, distant era before Mr. Pomeroy passed away) were pulled back to let in the air; the frail little bird's-eye maple desk was cluttered with costume jewelry and cosmetics; a hat with an impertinent feather was perched on top of the glass bell of the clock.

Besides the tempting posterior, Mrs. Pomeroy's niece had a face that—while not exactly pretty—was still very engaging and lively. She was short but sturdy looking, and her sandy hair, cut short at the sides and back, fell down over her brow like a pony's forelock. As a matter of fact, she reminded Val of the Shetland pony he had owned when he was a kid.

She shut up long enough for him to say, as he lifted his glass, "Here's to your new home. Happy days in it."

She flashed a warm, pleased smile at him. "And to Aunt Fan," she added. "I suppose you know you're the original fair-haired boy in her social circle. They all think you're just the nicest young man. Miss LaTour, the one downstairs, went on and on about you. I stopped in to tell her about Aunt Fan, and I thought I never was going to get away from her."

"That's me," said Val. "Old ladies love me. Also dogs and children."

"Oh, that reminds me. Did she remember you? Your little girl? Miss LaTour was worried sick for fear she wouldn't."

"So was I." It seemed a long time ago that he had set off with the panda under his arm and the question that he didn't dare ask trembling inside him. Its urgency had dissolved, somewhere along the line; after those first bad moments with Annabelle he hadn't thought of it at all. And then all the other happenings of the afternoon: Maudie, Doris and Monroe, Barbara ... There was a contrast for you. Barbara and Mrs. Pomeroy's niece, who was about as glamorous as a pane of window glass. When the subject of dinner came up, as it inevitably did, she simply stepped behind the screen that separated the living room from the bedroom alcove, exchanged her dungarees for a skirt, slapped on some lipstick, and announced that she was all set. No panicky hesitation, no flushed cheeks or radiant eyes—and of course no thrill of excitement, either.

But Hen was a nice kid, a nice, happy kid, still fresh enough from the country to find New York full of marvels. It was going to be cheerful, having her around to liven things up in the old house.

"It's a quiet place. A quiet street," said Val while they were walking home from the neighborhood restaurant where they had lingered, after dinner, to drink a beer or two and listen to the classic jazz records that were a specialty of the house. "Nothing much ever happens. Oh, now and then a drunk," he added, for they were passing the church now, and a dishevelled figure was sprawled on the steps. Not an uncommon sight, especially late on a Saturday night like this; quite often drunks strayed over here from the Square and passed out in the peace and comparative darkness of this block. "Don't let it bother you. He'll come to and move on eventually."

Hen kept looking back. "He doesn't look like a bum," she said doubtfully. "I mean, what if he isn't drunk? What if he's had a heart attack or something, and we just walked past without bothering to help him?" She had been walking more and more slowly; now she came to a full stop. "He doesn't look drunk," she said. "He looks—funny."

"Oh now, Hen." But it was true: the man didn't seem to be a derelict. His clothes, as nearly as Val could make out in the dim light, were decent enough, and they were all there, even to a hat crumpled beside him. Of course respectable people sometimes got drunk and passed out, too … There was something about the man's attitude, something not relaxed but downright contorted, as if—far from collapsing—he had been transfixed in the middle of a struggle. He was on his back, with one knee drawn up; his body seemed almost arched on the steps.

They started back. Against Val's better judgment, but Hen wasn't going to rest until they did. As they drew near the church steps, he felt her take hold of his arm. It was very still. There was a tree in the little church yard with a few withered leaves left that ticked against each other in the chilly wind. On the second step, below the man's feet, they half-stumbled over something: a cane. Then they were close enough to see his face.

Hen didn't scream. Her breath drew in, as if she were going to, but the sound that came out was a sort of ragged whisper.

"Oh my God," said Val.

Because the man was dead. Violently dead. His face was convulsed; his eyes glared up at them from under beetling brows; his mouth was drawn back, as if in agonized protest against whatever it was that had happened to him.

"What'll we do?" whispered Hen. "Oh my, what'll we do?"

Val stayed there on the steps while she ran home to call the police. It didn't seem right to leave the man alone, now that they had found him. Not that there was anything they or anybody else could do for him. It just didn't seem right.

Torn between reluctance and curiosity, Val stared down at the man on the steps. Not an old man; about thirty-five, he guessed, and strongly built. His clothes were neither very cheap nor very expensive. Trench coat, tweedy suit, shoes recently shined, tie a little on the flashy side … That was where the damage was. The man's neck; rather, his throat. Could he have fallen somehow, struck his throat against the edge of the step? But in that case he would be lying face down—wouldn't he?— instead of in this fiercely, desperately exposed attitude. One hand was flung out and clenched, as if to deliver a blow. And the face itself had a rigid urgency, as if, even in death, the man were trying to convey a message. It was fantastic, but in the few moments before Hen got back, and the police came, Val had an eerie feeling that the message was for him personally and that by failing to grasp it he was breaking faith with the stranger on the steps.

An unreasonable notion; but so strong that Val found himself bending closer, straining to understand, and succeeding only in memorizing the man's features. Glassy eyes; bushy brows; close-cut hair, very dark, very thick; a strong jaw, shadowed by what would have been a heavy beard, if left to itself.

And something else eerie happened. Val heard Annabelle's clear, piping voice: "He's got eyebrows, they're like little moustaches, and he's got whiskers in his ears, and he has a cane. I take hold of his cane, and he swings me way up ..."

Then Hen came racing back, and a couple of minutes later a radio car zoomed to a stop at the curb, and two policemen strode up the church steps and took over. One of them, after snapping a series of questions at Val and Hen, went off to summon swarms of his colleagues. At least swarms of them—cops, detectives, technical men, a doctor who announced solemnly and superfluously, "This man is dead"—turned up shortly afterwards. But in the interval of waiting, the other cop, a more expansive type than the question-snapper, volunteered a few comments. "Looks like somebody belted him across the throat with something," he observed. "Maybe with the cane. You people touch anything?"

They had been asked this before. No, they had touched nothing.

"However it was, he sure got his," said the cop philosophically. "You people know who he is?"

They had been asked that one too, and before the night was over they were to be asked it again and again.

"No," said Val firmly, perhaps more firmly than was necessary. "We never saw him before. Haven't any idea who he is."

NINE

"I thought they never were going to stop asking questions," said Hen. "Much more of it and I'd have confessed we killed the poor guy, just to get them to shut up."

It was the next afternoon, as bleak a Sunday afternoon as Val remembered, and he and Hen were sharing a pot of coffee in his apartment and rehashing the night's events. Weary as they were of the subject, they could not let it alone. Neither of them had had much sleep; it had been almost dawn when the last detective asked the last question and told them to go home. Miss LaTour (agog, like all the rest of the neighborhood) had been lying in wait for them, and they had wound up drinking tea in her apartment. Tea that had a faint flavor of liniment, like everything connected with Miss LaTour. She had turned out to be a veritable mine of rumors, in possession of more information—or possibly misinformation—than Hen and Val.

Yes, indeed (Miss LaTour had it on good authority) the victim had been struck across the throat with his own cane. Shattered the poor fellow's larynx, said Miss LaTour. The cane was because he was slightly lame, a mild case of polio, no doubt. No question of its being anything but murder. His wallet was gone. Not a scrap of identification on him. Though of course that didn't mean a thing; why, look at what had happened to Miss LaTour herself just the other day when she called at the post office for a piece of registered mail, she had never been so mortified in her life, not one bit of proof with her that she really was Miss LaTour ... The missing wallet pointed to a simple case of mugging. Juvenile delinquents all over the place these days. But Miss LaTour was plainly not going to be contented with any such humdrum explanation as that. Visions of espionage on an international scale danced in her head. She had it on good authority that the man was a secret agent, obviously a foreigner, that was why the police were being so chary with the information they gave out. It wouldn't surprise Miss LaTour if they recognized the man from the beginning but were keeping his identity secret for reasons of state. Then there was the fascinating question of time. It was midnight when Hen and Val made their shocking discovery, but at least an hour before that somebody who lived across the street had noticed the body on the church steps and had thought nothing of it, assumed it was what Miss LaTour called a sot. And who knew how long he might have been lying there before that? Only the medical examiner could estimate the time of death, and it was Miss LaTour's understanding that even he wouldn't be able to pinpoint it.

Slumping in their chairs, listlessly sipping their coffee, Val and Hen went through it all over again, point by point. It was like being on a treadmill.

"What gets me is that we have to wait to read about it in tomorrow's paper, like everybody else," said Hen. A jaw-cracking yawn overtook her. "Just as if we weren't the ones that found him. Doesn't seem fair."

"They've probably got it all cleared up by now. Who he was, and who killed him, and why."

Val was assuring himself, he found, more than anybody else. Because there was still the nagging memory of those moments on the church steps when Annabelle's voice had seemed to pipe in his ears and he had felt the crazy conviction that the man was trying to get some message across to him. He hadn't mentioned Annabelle's story to anyone. How could be repeat anything so flimsy—the prattling of a six-year-old with too much imagination—to the police, who were nothing if not factual minded? They would have made him feel like a fool. It was simply one of those queer twists of coincidence, and he was as bad as Annabelle, trying to make something out of nothing.

But he could not quite put it out of his mind. How would it sound to Hen? Would she laugh at him too? She was a sensible soul; last night, when plenty of girls would have gone hysterical on him, Hen had kept her head. But she had an imagination too. After all, she was the one who had insisted on investigating the man on the church steps.

"Make me stop talking about it, will you?" she was saying now. "As a matter of fact, you'd be doing me a favor if you put me out. That way I couldn't talk about it. I'd just sit down there in my own place and think about it."

"Stick around," said Val. He glanced at his watch. Four thirty. Two hours till his dinner date with Barbara. Even that prospect failed to strike a spark for him. "We might as well be miserable together."

"Any time I make like a good citizen again," said Hen. "Where does it get you? It gets you haunted."

They stared dully into space.

"Hen," Val heard himself saying. "Hen, something funny happened yesterday that I haven't mentioned before because I'm sure it doesn't mean a thing, just one of those crazy—" The peal of the doorbell stopped him. "Oh hell," he said as he hoisted himself out of his chair to push the buzzer, "they've probably thought of some more questions they want to ask us."

"Maybe it's a reporter," Hen offered. "Maybe we can pump him, for a change."

It wasn't. It was the last person in the world Val expected to see. Barbara. She stopped in the doorway, overcome with shyness, and yet glowing with some inner excitement.

"Forgive me," she stammered. "I know how inconsiderate it is, interrupting you like this, and I wouldn't have, except that I—Please forgive me."

"Nonsense. I'm delighted, Barbara." He was also flustered—by the presence of Hen (for some obscure reason) and by the state of his living room, which had seldom looked more shabby or cluttered to him. Not, however, to Barbara. She was gazing around, starry-eyed.

"Oh, how nice it is," she murmured. "That's why I dropped in. I mean—" She drew a long breath, and her exciting news came out in a rush. "I just took an apartment of my own! It's right in this neighborhood, and I wondered if you'd mind looking at it and telling me what you think. I've already paid the deposit, but maybe there's something wrong with it that I didn't notice—"

"Of course I'll look at it. Why, Barbara, this is wonderful!" His heart had leaped at her phrase, "right in this neighborhood "

Hen said it was wonderful, too, and Barbara responded to her enthusiasm with a timid smile. It's all right, thought Val with relief (again for some obscure reason); they like each other. It's going to do Barbara a world of good, knowing someone like Hen.

In the flush of her happiness, she was talking much more than usual. "Doris is going to be so pleased," she said. "She's been telling me and telling me that I ought to move. And of course she was right, only I don't know, the idea scared me. But she made me feel so ashamed that yesterday I—well, I lied to her. I told her I thought I'd found a place, and it wasn't true at all. So when I saw this ad in the paper today I thought, it won't be a lie if I take this one. Or anyway, not so much of a lie." She laughed tremulously. "I don't suppose it makes any sense to anybody but me."

"It does to me," said Val. "Sometimes Doris affects me that way too. How about a cup of coffee before we make our tour of inspection?"

The bleakness of the day was illuminated for him. He felt as if he were entertaining some fairy creature from another world who had appeared without warning and might vanish at any instant. But in the meantime she was here, sipping coffee from one of his few unchipped cups, smiling her luminous smile. She was bareheaded, as she had been yesterday, and she was wearing the same plain, sand-colored dress. She made Hen look more than ever like a Shetland pony.

No, Hen said, she'd have to put off seeing Barbara's new apartment till some other time. (What a good kid she was!) "I just moved myself," she said, getting to her feet and hitching up her dungarees. "I've got a million or two domestic chores to do downstairs. So give me a rain check on today. I'll see you again, I hope, and good luck." Her grin, as she said the good luck part, was aimed primarily at Val.

Then the door closed behind her, and he was alone with enchantment.

The apartment Barbara had found was indeed right in the neighborhood, only three blocks away. This fact alone was enough to make it ideal, in Val's eyes. The bedroom was small, but the living room had big casement windows and a built-in book shelf. There was a hole-in-the-wall kitchenette and a bathroom, painted a shrieking shade of cerise.

"I can paint it for you," offered Val. "No trouble at all. This is great, Barbara, just great. Doris herself couldn't have done better." The mention of Doris brought to mind practical details like electric outlets, the hot water supply, and closet space. Dutifully he checked; as far as he could see (though like as not he was overlooking something vital), all was in order.

"I won't have to buy furniture." All Barbara had needed, apparently, was his stamp of approval. She bubbled with plans. "I put some things in storage when Clyde and I broke up. Oh, I can hardly wait to move in!"

They lingered, rhapsodizing, until what little light the dismal day had provided was gone. They decided to have dinner at a nearby Italian restaurant, a pleasant place of mellow lights and leisurely atmosphere.

"I've been here before," Barbara said when the waiter had settled them at one of the choice corner tables and brought their cocktails. "Clyde and I used to come here sometimes. We lived in this part of town for a while, you know. Until we—lost the baby."

Her face changed; it grew blank, almost ugly, with remembered grief. Val had forgotten about Barbara's baby. Now he recalled dimly that something had gone terribly wrong and the baby had been born dead.

"He'd be almost Annabelle's age—a little younger—if we hadn't lost him." Her long hands lay, upturned and empty, in front of her on the table. "It might have made all the difference, if he had lived. Or if I could have had another baby."

At a loss for words, Val reached across and touched her fingers in mute sympathy. She shouldn't brood about it like this. But—being Barbara— she would of course brood about it, probably till the day she died. She wasn't geared to take either sorrow or happiness lightly.

"You're very fond of Annabelle, aren't you?" he said at last.

At once she brightened. "Oh yes. I couldn't have stood it without her. It's strange, isn't it? You'd think it might make it worse, being so close to somebody else's baby. But it didn't, with me. She's all that kept me from—" She stopped short of putting it into words.

"To Annabelle, then," said Val, lifting his glass. "I'm fond of her myself. Even if she does let her imagination run away with her."

For a moment Barbara looked puzzled. "Oh. You mean the tale you mentioned yesterday. The man she made up."

"That was what Doris said, that she must have made him up. And I expect she was right. Doris usually is."

There was a touch of mischief in her laugh. Val leaned back, relaxed and comfortable. Time, and the pleasure of being with Barbara, had restored his perspective: the man on the church steps was something shocking that he and Hen had happened to stumble on. That was all.

He told Barbara about it, later, while they were having their coffee. He did not mention those few eerie moments before the police came.

After all, why take a chance on upsetting Barbara over nothing? Somehow the telling of the rest fixed it even more firmly in its proper place, in the realm of stray, grotesque experiences that you were bound to collect if you lived in New York long enough. A conversation piece, for people to shudder over, as Barbara was shuddering now.

"How awful! It couldn't have been an accident? I mean—No, I suppose not. And nobody knows who he was?"

"They've probably found out by now. Once that's cleared up, they can figure out who would want to kill him, and why. Unless, of course, it was just a plain mugging ... There, let's talk about something else. It's nothing to do with us."

So little to do with them that—what with Barbara's plans for moving and her no longer hesitant acceptance of him as a friend, surely more than a friend—he did not think of it again all evening.

TEN

And then the next evening, Monday evening, he found the note in his mail box.

By that time, of course, he knew from the papers that the man on the church steps had indeed been identified. His name was John Custer; he had lived for the last six weeks at a decent, middle-priced hotel in the twenties; he wrote magazine articles; he had no relatives, and apparently no close friends, in New York. His sister, who lived in Philadelphia, sobbed, "Who would want to kill John? He's never been in any kind of trouble. Not an enemy in the world ..."

Val never bothered to look in his mail box in the mornings because he left for work before the arrival of the postman. So he didn't find the note until Monday evening. Whoever left it (for it had been delivered by hand) had probably stuck it halfway through the slot, but it had slipped all the way inside. There it was, shuffled in between a couple of advertisements. It was written on a page torn from an address book, in a hasty, masculine-looking scrawl: "Saturday P.M. Val Bryant— There's something I want to tell you for your own good. I'll try again tomorrow morning." That was all. No signature or address or telephone number to follow up.

Val read it over several times before his mind began to click. "Saturday P.M." could mean any time from six or thereabouts, when he got back from his afternoon with Annabelle and ran into Hen until—well, any time from then on. It had been Sunday morning before he came back to his own apartment. "I'll try again tomorrow morning." He had been in all day Sunday. It must have been at least five before he and Barbara left. No one had rung his doorbell morning or afternoon. Of course the guy, whoever he was, might have changed his mind, anything might have come up to prevent him ...

Like an encounter on the church steps, only a few doors away from here, with someone determined to prevent him from coming back? An unpleasant shortness of breath gripped Val. Now wait, he told himself, don't lose your head. All right, you found the body of a murdered man, and now you find a note in your mail box. There doesn't *have* to be a connection between the two facts. And all right, you had a funny feeling while you were waiting for the police. Sure. Who wouldn't?

He read the note once more. Unsigned as it was, it still didn't have exactly the ring of an anonymous letter. The fellow might not have signed it for the simple reason that his name would mean nothing to Val. Or it might be the work of some waggish friend. Offhand, he couldn't think of any friend quite that waggish. But the writer addressed him as Val Bryant, not V. T. Bryant, which was the way his name appeared on the mail box. So it was someone who, friend or not, knew of him as Val. The blunt announcement—"something I want to tell you for your own good"—seemed less and less friendly, the oftener he read it.

None of this was helping his shortness of breath. He closed his eyes, and at once the man's face flashed into his memory, straining up at him from the church steps with that queer effect of urgency. It was all there: the desperate eyes, the bristling eyebrows "like little moustaches," the cane. And here in his hand the message that still conveyed nothing ...

He could not stand being alone with it for another minute. He went downstairs and tapped on Hen's door.

"Hi," she said. She had just gotten in with a load of groceries; hadn't yet taken off her coat or hat. It was the one with the perky feather. "What's the matter with you? Hangover?"

"No. I found this note," he said in a hollow voice, and held it out to her. When she had read it he told her the whole fantastic business, beginning with Annabelle's report on the man she called "Cane" and ending with the few unsubstantial conclusions he had been able to draw from the note itself.

"Do you think I'm maybe nuts?" he finished hopefully. "Go ahead, make fun of me."

But Hen wasn't laughing at him. For once she wasn't talking, either. At some point she had given her hat an abstracted shove; it looked comic above her solemn face.

"Stop doing that," he said at last. "Stop biting your fingernails."

"I'm not. I haven't for years." She clasped her hands guiltily in her lap. "You could tell the police, I suppose. Show them the note, tell them all this stuff you've just told me."

Val swallowed. Several times.

"But the thing is—" Hen was picking her way along the precarious route. "If John Custer really was Annabelle's man, then that means that it was—that it might be one of those four people. Doris, or her mother, or her husband, or Barbara."

They stared at each other, and at the dismaying implications. "Listen," said Val, "it's impossible. Doris is one of the most irritating—and irritable—women in the world, but she's not a murderess. Neither is Maudie, for God's sake. She's a perfectly harmless, perfectly sweet nitwit. You've met Barbara. Do you think *she's* capable of killing anybody?"

Hen shook her head. "Not even in self-defense. That leaves what's his name. Monroe."

"Monroe a killer?" Val paused, sorely tempted. "It grieves me to state it, but I honestly don't think so. I can see somebody killing him, all right. But this way, no. He's too damn *controlled*. And too damn smart to get himself into a fix where he'd have to kill somebody."

"All the same," Hen persisted, "if it was Annabelle's man—"

"That's the point. If. You've got to admit the whole thing is pretty thin, Hen. But supposing I did go to the police, and supposing they did investigate, instead of checking me off as a crackpot, and then supposing it turned out to be all Annabelle's imagination, as it undoubtedly would turn out to be—" He stopped for breath. Hen was still with him. "Well, I wouldn't have accomplished a thing except to stir up a hell of a lot of trouble for people that I don't want to stir up trouble for. I don't want to get Annabelle dragged into a mess like this. Or anybody connected with her. That even goes for Miracle Man Monroe."

"You don't have to holler," said Hen. "I agree with you. I don't think you should go to the police yet, either."

"What do you mean, yet?"

"I mean not unless you're sure there really is some connection between one of those four people and John Custer. When you get right down to it, Val, you're in a better position to find that out than the police because you know all four of them. You'll be seeing Maudie and Barbara anyway, so all you have to do with them is make a few discreet inquiries. With Doris and Monroe you'll have to dream up some excuse for having a talk with them, about something else, and—"

"You mean I'm supposed to question Monroe? Grill him?" Val gave a hoot of laughter.

"Well, you've got to do something!" snapped Hen. "If you're not going to the police, what do you have in mind? Just ignore the whole thing? The note, and all the rest of it? It may be thin, but it sent you tearing down here with your hair in a braid!" She took off her hat and sent it kiting across the room to the studio couch. "If there's anything I can't stand it's somebody that can't make up their mind."

"If there's anything *I* can't stand it's a bossy woman," said Val. She was making him feel just the way he used to feel with Doris. Inadequate. "You don't seem to realize—"

"I realize perfectly well. You want to protect Annabelle and the rest of them, and that's all very well, but somebody *killed* that man. It isn't very nice to think it might be somebody you know, but then murder isn't ever very nice. When it comes to that, it isn't very nice to think of a murderer left at large, hanging around Annabelle the rest of their life, all because you're too scared of your ex-wife's husband to do anything!"

Val's first impulse was to stalk out of the room without answering her. But then he saw that—bossy as she was (like Doris) and ornery as she was (like the Shetland pony of his boyhood)—there were tears flashing in her eyes. It jolted the anger right out of him. And she really did have a point ...

"I never said I wasn't going to do anything. What if I snoop around and louse everything up, somehow or other? What good is that going to do?" He realized, with a sinking heart, that he was committing himself. Or very nearly.

"You're not going to louse it up." Hen blinked; the tears had never been there. She leaned forward, all eager excitement. "The way you'll do it, they'll never suspect what's going on. Don't you see, Val, you're the perfect one, just because you'll keep it natural and unofficial. You're not horning in on the police—"

"You're damn right I'm not," Val assured her.

"You're just making a—a preliminary survey to find out whether it's a police matter at all. Which dollars to doughnuts it isn't. Start with Maudie. She sounds like the easiest. You can get her to gossiping, can't you?"

"Feed her a couple of drinks and you can't keep her from it," said Val. He felt his heart lift a little. Maybe he hadn't committed himself to anything so drastic, after all. Even he had no doubts about his ability to pump Maudie.

"So feed her the couple of drinks and let her gossip. Family stuff. How Doris and Monroe get along. What they did Saturday night after you left. What's the score with Barbara. All like that."

"Maudie won't be any problem," Val admitted. "It's the others that I—"

"Time enough to worry about them after you've worked on Maudie. Chances are she'll give you all the angles you need."

"Well. All right." Val heaved a sigh. "You've talked me into it, I guess. Does it make you happy?"

"Don't be bitter, dear." Hen grinned at him smugly. "You'd have come around to the same conclusion, all by yourself. I just lit a little fire under you. Cheer up. It could be a plain case of mugging, after all. You probably won't dig up a thing to connect any of them with John Custer."

"But if I do?"

Hen wasn't grinning any more. "If you do, then you'll have to go to the police," she said. "Even if it turns out to be—I mean, whoever it turns out to be."

ELEVEN

"Maudie, you're looking great." It was the first thing Val said when they met in the lobby, and now that they were settled in the cocktail lounge at a table near—but not too near—the little orchestra, he repeated it. Already his conscience was bothering him (unaccustomed as he was to the role of secret investigator) and it was a comfort to start off, at least, with the pleasant, unvarnished truth. "I mean it. Saturday it seemed to me you were looking a little tired. I'll admit it, I thought to myself, can it be that time's catching up with the old girl at last? But now I see I needn't have worried for a minute. You're the same ravishing kid."

"Oh, well, Saturday. *That* day," said Maudie, drawing off her gloves and looking around her with the open delight that made it such fun to invite her for cocktails or any other little treat. "If I looked anything like the way I felt, I'd have been to bury. I think I'll have—yes, a frozen Daiquiri, just by way of celebration."

"Okay. Fine. Incidentally, what are we celebrating? The passing of Saturday? Poor old Saturday. What did you have against it?"

"If I told you, you'd never believe me," said Maudie, fussing happily with her furs. She was wearing a black suit tonight, very restrained for her. But trust Maudie to let herself go on her blouse, which was pale pink and ruffly, and on her hat, which was a giddy froth of pink roses. Below it her face was radiant, wide-eyed, like that of a child who knows a secret.

"What is this? You're holding out on an old pal like me? Maudie, I'm surprised at you." (What surprised him even more was that he didn't choke on his own false comradeship. And it might all be wasted effort:

like as not Maudie's secret would turn out to be nothing more significant than a well-deserved scolding from Doris.)

"Now, now. It didn't amount to a thing, really," said Maudie airily. But her eyes shifted, just a little. "One of those days, you know. To cap it all off—as if there hadn't been enough, without that—Doris and Monroe got into this *violent* altercation—"

"What? Why, I didn't suppose Monroe ever lost his temper like us vulgar types. He's so poised it's poisonous."

"That's what you think," crowed Maudie. "Oh, it's not like when you and Doris were married. Gracious, the fights you two used to have! But don't think Monroe doesn't get mad, just because he doesn't yell. And personally, I think he'd be better off if he did yell. It's not healthy, keeping things bottled up. You never know where you stand, with a person like that."

"No, you don't. What was eating on him Saturday?"

"I shouldn't be telling you this, but ..." Maudie proceeded to tell, with relish, and what she told so absorbed Val's attention that he forgot all about his guilty conscience. It was a provocative tale, all right. Assuming that Maudie for once had gotten things straight, it opened the lid on a little treasure trove of possibilities. What kind of deception might Doris be working behind Monroe's back? The obvious answer was a clandestine affair with some other man. It didn't seem very likely to Val, but it must be what Monroe believed. Nothing else would have thrown him into such a turmoil. He can't be so sure of himself, after all, thought Val with surprise; not if he's jealous.

"I just don't understand it." The spring of Maudie's confidences bubbled on obligingly. "Why should he all at once be so suspicious of every little thing? Gracious, what's the difference if Doris did fib about going shopping? I'm almost sure she mentioned an appointment to me, but like she told me afterwards, she's got a right to spend the afternoon the way she wants to without being put through the third degree."

"She didn't tell you where she really went, then?"

"Well, no. No, she didn't. And I never was one to pry. Not with Doris, anyway. You know how she is. Flies off the handle at the drop of a hat. Besides, you don't think for one minute that I'd suspect Doris of doing anything out of the way ..." She paused, all outraged loyalty.

"Sounds like Monroe does, though," said Val. "He must have some reason for his suspicions, whatever they are. And I suppose he could be right. I don't mean Doris is a tramp. I know she isn't. But she's bright and attractive, and she works at a job where she must meet plenty of what they call desirable men. Who knows, maybe even more desirable than Miracle Man Monroe—"

"Now Val, you're being naughty." So was Maudie; she couldn't suppress a delighted chuckle. "All right, maybe he isn't everybody's idea of a barrel of fun. All the same, Monroe's been a wonderful son-in-law, good as gold to me always, and good as gold to Annabelle too. Doris could have gone farther and done a lot worse."

"I know it. I was just pointing out that it could happen. That's all." He was remembering how quickly, with what relief, Doris had come up with her explanation of Annabelle's visitor. Supposing she was involved in an affair with "Cane," John Custer (if they were indeed one and the same), and supposing Monroe had found it out

Val took a nervous sip of his drink. No doubt about it: it would give Monroe a good old-fashioned motive. His mind made another wild leap. It might conceivably give Doris a motive too. If you were going to start supposing, there was also the possibility of a lover's quarrel. Doris might have found herself in deeper than she wanted to be, might have wanted to call the whole affair off and run into resistance from "Cane." She had never taken kindly to resistance in any form; Maude's phrase, "flies off the handle at the drop of a hat," was nothing if not accurate.

"What did they do Saturday night?" Val caught the waiter's eye and signalled for a repeat order on the drinks. It wouldn't do to stop priming now. "Just stay home and fight?"

"They went to this dinner party at— What's those people's name? Old friends of Doris', you know them, I'm sure. They live down in the Village. Russell, that's their name. Down on Tenth Street. Oh now, dearie," she protested, as the waiter whisked away her empty glass and replaced it with a full one, "another drink? Do you think I ought to?"

"Bird can't fly on one wing," said Val. The Russells. On Tenth Street. Not too far from the church steps where somebody had struck John Custer down. Not too far at all. "I'm a real rat, Maudie. I must be, or I wouldn't get such a kick out of hearing about these little family spats up at the J. Monroe Wards. I suppose it's all blown over by now."

Maudie looked blank. "Why— Come to tell the truth, Val, I don't know whether it has or not. I was out most all day Sunday, and let me see, last night they were neither one home for dinner, and tonight of course I'm here, so I haven't seen much of them. It slipped my mind, what with all the rest I've had to worry about—I mean, think about."

"You don't look as if you had a worry in the world," said Val. In his preoccupation with Monroe and Doris, he had forgotten what Maudie had started off with—the hint that she was harboring some kind of a secret. She had already given him his money's worth; were there more startling revelations to come? It was highly unlikely. Secret Operator Bryant could now relax. He did so, smiling fondly at his subject.

"Oh, I haven't," said Maudie. "Not anymore."

"Attagirl. Get right down to it, most things aren't worth worrying about."

"This was." Maudie's eyes grew solemn. "Oh Val, if you had any idea of what goes on in the world. The wickedness! The people that take advantage of you because you're friendly, and then use it to rob you—"

She caught her breath, and Secret Operator Bryant suddenly stopped relaxing. "Maudie, don't tell me somebody's been trying to rob you!"

"I'm not telling you a thing. Period." Again the airy tone, again the slight shifting of her eyes. "But it's taught me a lesson I'm never going to forget. I'm a very lucky girl. It scares me to think of how lucky. I've never been one to wish anybody else harm, but if a man ever deserved it he did, and when I saw it in the paper Monday morning I could have gotten right down on my knees and thanked God—"

"The paper Monday morning! You mean the fellow that was—"

"Did you see it too?" Maudie seemed abruptly aware that she was doing what she had resolved not to do. She was telling. Too late, her hand went up to her mouth. "But you couldn't have! I mean you couldn't have known! Because it didn't even mention my name!"

Val took a firm grip on the edge of the table. Maudie's face—that oh-so-innocent, oh-so-ingenuous face—reeled before his eyes. "Maudie," he said quietly, "are you talking about what I think you're talking about? I mean, what *I'm* talking about?"

She was rattled. Her voice quavered reproachfully. "I didn't mean to talk at all. I wouldn't have, only you—you tricked me. Just because we've always been friends, you think you can worm anything you want to out of me, and I don't think it's fair. They didn't even mention my name, so how could you have known it had anything to do with me?"

"I didn't. I still don't know, but I intend to find out. The fellow I'm talking about was murdered."

"Oh," said Maudie. Val could not interpret the expression in her eyes. Was it relief? Dismay? The panic of someone caught in a trap, desperate for a way out? "You said—murdered?"

Val nodded. "Murdered on the steps of the church a few doors from where I live. I was the one that found him."

"You're not mixed up in a murder, Val!" cried Maudie in alarm.

"Of course not. That is, I don't think so." A fine kettle of fish: Maudie asking him if *he* was mixed up in a murder. How had things managed to get so out of hand? "The question is, what are you mixed up in? This business of seeing something in the paper that didn't even mention your name— Did it have anything to do with John Custer?"

"John Custer?" Maudie paused, seeming to consider. "That isn't the name he used with me. But then he used so many different ones, you know. At least half a dozen aliases, it said, and not one of them his real name. And he seemed like such a nice young man! I just can't get over it."

At last, thought Val, they were getting somewhere. "Where did you meet him?" he asked.

"Why, in the— Val! You've got no business making me talk like this! I wasn't ever going to breathe it to a living soul. On account of Doris. I mean it, Val, I'd do anything, I'd die before I'd let Doris find out. And of course he had it figured that way. Oh, he worked all the angles. One of the slickest con men in the country, it said in the paper." Her voice took on a note of something like pride.

"Did you lend him a *lot* of money, Maudie? Now, now. I'm not going to tell Doris. You know me better than that. I just mean, if you're not in too much of a fix maybe I can help you out."

"You're a lamb." Obviously touched—almost to the point of tears—she reached across the table and squeezed his hand. "And I'll admit it, I may have to take you up on that, just to tide me over till the first of the month. It wasn't a loan, with him. It was— It was blackmail."

Val couldn't help laughing at the way she brought out the word—like a solemn child. Besides, the idea itself was absurd. "You're making this up, Maudie. He couldn't really blackmail you."

"Oh yes, he could. If Doris had ever seen those letters—" The radiance drained out of her face; for a moment she looked the way she had last Saturday. Old and scared. "I'm such a fool, Val. I should have known that a young fellow doesn't take up with a—with an older woman like me just for fun. Only it *was* fun, having somebody make a fuss over me like that, and I— But it wasn't like it sounded in those letters. Honestly it wasn't. Honestly." The tears brimmed up in her eyes. "Oh Val, you'd never believe what I've been through. The things he said to me—"

"My God, Maudie. You should have gone to the police. I mean, you could have told me. I could have—"

She gave a tense little shake of her head. "What could you have done? He'd have made a bee line for Doris with the letters. I'd sooner give him every penny for the rest of my life, I'd sooner die, than have Doris know. She wouldn't think I was just a fool. She'd think I was a tramp, an old bag. She'd never speak to me again as long as I lived. And I wouldn't blame her."

There wasn't any answer to that. It was the truth. They stared at each other bleakly.

"That poor woman that was in the paper," said Maudie. "She went to the police, and bless her for doing it, but I wouldn't be in her shoes for anything on earth. I don't see how she can *face* her family   but then maybe her family isn't like Doris. God help her if they are."

"You weren't the only one, then? This was a regular racket with him?"

"Oh yes. He had quite a string of us. No fool like an old fool, you know." She tried out a tremulous smile, found she could manage it, and was suddenly beaming again. "That's where I was so lucky. Because he found out they were on his trail, and when they nabbed him he had already destroyed some of the evidence. There wasn't a word about my letters, so he must have burned them. That's what he was doing when they caught him, burning stuff in the fireplace. Didn't want to get stuck with any more than he had to, I suppose. Well! Talk about hair-breadth escapes!"

"Yes," said Val thoughtfully. "You're sure it was your pal, not somebody else?"

"Of course it was him! There wasn't any picture, but I could tell from the description. And then it was the same hotel, and he'd slipped up and used the same name with one of the others that he did with me. Oh, it was him, all right, and I can thank my lucky stars I got off so easy. Gives me the chills every time I think of it."

"It ought to. If I ever again hear of you taking up with a handsome young stranger—I suppose he was handsome?"

"Well, not what you'd say handsome," said Maudie judiciously. "But nice looking. Real manly, you know. And lovely manners. I just never would have dreamed …" She heaved a wistful sigh.

"He didn't by any chance carry a cane?"

There was a moment of blank silence. "A what? Why do you—Oh, I remember. That story of Annabelle's. Isn't she the limit, the things she comes out with? And that reminds me—" She glanced at her wrist watch. "Gracious, dearie, look at the time! I've got to get home to Annabelle. It's my night to baby-sit. Barbara's with her now, but I know she wants to get away this evening. She's up to her ears getting ready to move. Isn't it nice about her new apartment? She's going to be a neighbor of yours, she tells me." Her brows arched roguishly, and Val felt as if he might be blushing. "Oh, you needn't think you can keep any secrets from Maudie! I could tell, the look in your eye when you saw her Saturday."

"What look in my eye? And anyway, you don't see as good-looking a girl as Barbara every day. And anyway, she's probably got a list of beaus from here to the corner—" He paused hopefully, and Maudie came through with flying colors.

"Nothing of the sort. You haven't got one scrap of competition, my boy.

Strange as it seems. But then Barbara always was different. The last girl on earth you'd think Clyde would pick to marry. Oh, don't get me wrong, I *like* Barbara. Think the world of her. I just don't understand her, that's all. Why a girl with her looks doesn't get out and have herself a whirl while she's young enough to enjoy it—"

"My point exactly," said Val. He might as well come clean with Maudie. She had it all figured out anyway. "As long as the whirl is with me."

"Well, I'm all for it," said Maudie heartily. "You may be just the one to shake her out of it. Comes to that, she may be just the one for you, too. I've always felt that the trouble with you and Doris was that she was too independent. Didn't need you to take care of her."

"And a good thing too, I guess," said Val ruefully. "Broken reed, that's my middle name."

"I'm not so sure. You've never had anybody that needed to be taken care of. You might surprise yourself."

He might, at that. Certainly part of Barbara's charm lay in her effect of helplessness, of needing a strong arm and an understanding heart. And maybe you drew forth from those who loved you what you needed— even if it hadn't been there to begin with. It was a new idea to Val. And an exciting one. He looked at Maudie with considerable respect.

She was busy with her gloves, her purse, her furs. "I wish I didn't have to run like this, but I really must. It's been lovely, Val. Just lovely."

"Let's do it again some time."

"Yes, let's," said Maudie gaily. She gave him an odd, straight look before she added, "Some time when you want to pump me again."

TWELVE

Val walked more than half of the way downtown. A long walk, but it was a crisp evening with a bright fingernail clipping of a new moon hung low in the sky, and after the overheated atmosphere of the cocktail lounge, the cold, clean air felt good to him. A substitute, no doubt, for the compulsive washing that was supposed to be a sign of guilt. Yes. That parting shot of Maudie's—"Some time when you want to pump me again"—had made him feel guilty. Ashamed of himself. And deflated: he had fancied himself as quite the clever fellow, unobtrusively extracting information from his unwitting subject. Well, Maudie's remark made it clear just how unobtrusive, and just how unwitting, everybody had been. If it was as obvious as all that to a scatterbrain like Maudie, how could he hope to work his smart little game with Doris and Monroe?

And yet he must try. Hen was right: he couldn't just ignore murder, any more than he could turn the police loose on Doris' family circle with no more justification than his own and Annabelle's flimsy imaginings. All right. So he must try. Call this interview with Maudie a practice run, a try-out which—if nothing else—had taught him what not to do. Change his tactics and try again.

Clumsy as he may have been with Maudie, he had still managed to accomplish his mission. His spirits lifted a little as he checked over his take. Friction between that model couple, the J. Monroe Wards— Monroe making like a suspicious husband, Doris possibly telling fibs. Certainly there was food for thought there. Maudie and her hair-raising little brush with blackmail. (No wonder she had looked her age, Saturday afternoon!) And then, as a bonus, there was the information— strictly personal to Val, thoroughly gratifying—that he didn't have a lot of competition cluttering up the field with Barbara. That alone was worth the price of admission.

He was feeling better and better. Nothing like a good brisk walk to cheer you up. He decided that he would stop in for a quick dinner along the way, and then—why not?—take a chance on finding Barbara at her new apartment. Maudie had said she was up to her ears in moving; she might very well be working at the new place this evening. Maybe he could help her lift things or pound things or something. In any case, it would be a neighborly sort of gesture, and— Oh hell, who was he kidding? He just plain wanted to see her.

There was an answering buzz when he rang her doorbell, and once he had started up the stairs, Barbara's voice, tinged with apprehension, floated down to him: "Who is it?" She had come out onto the second floor landing; he could see her face in the dim light, peering down at him. "Oh, it's Val! I couldn't imagine—How nice!" No more apprehension. In its place so much pleased surprise that Val made the second flight of stairs in record time. She had on a smock with torn pockets, and there was a smudge of dust on her cheek. She looked lovely.

"Hi," he said, and took both her grimy hands in his. "I was hoping I'd find you here."

"Everything's a shambles, but do come in. We're in the middle of cleaning the closets."

We? His eyes switched to the doorway behind her, and there stood Doris, with a mop in her hand and a curious, dryly amused expression on her face. "Hello, Val. You're just in time to lend a hand. Take off your coat and roll up your sleeves. The more the merrier, I always say."

The light touch. Light to the point of being brittle. Val found himself falling in with it; Doris had always had a knack for setting the pace. And it was probably as comfortable a pace as any for this particular set of circumstances. Doris had her good points, all right. Coming down here and helping Barbara with the dog work, for instance. How many women as busy as Doris would do that for an ex-sister-in-law?

"Doris has been wonderful," Barbara was saying. "She's so good at managing things. I don't know what I'd have done without her."

"Nonsense," said Doris. But it was perfectly clear that she was indeed in charge. Barbara's furniture had arrived from the storage company; it was Doris who pointed out that the sofa really wouldn't do there ("You won't be able to get at the radiator, to turn it on and off. And it will ruin the upholstery.") She set Val to unrolling the rug ("Look, it goes this way. *This* is lengthwise.") She showed Barbara how to unpack the dishes without getting excelsior all over the place. And, having polished off the closets and the bathroom and hung up Barbara's clothes for her, she announced that they had done enough, it was time to call it a day.

"Not bad at all," she said, sinking down in one of the easy chairs with a cigarette. "You're all set, except for stuff like pictures and curtains. Fibre-glass, I should think. One of those off-white shades ... Maybe another lamp."

"I'm going to stay here tonight," Barbara told Val, with shining eyes. "I'm really moved! It doesn't seem possible." Tired as she must be, she could not sit still. She wandered around her miniature castle in a joyful daze, straightening the cups that hung on their little hooks in the kitchenette, once more testing the faucets, patting the sofa as if it were the arm of a long-lost friend. It was touching to watch her. Even Doris' face softened into a half-smile.

It was that half-smile of Doris', the apparent mellowness of her mood, that turned Val's thoughts toward his secret operator duties. He was going to have to tackle Doris some time. Why not tonight? He couldn't ever hope to catch her in a better humor; and he couldn't ever hope for more propitious circumstances, either. It would seem natural, tonight, to suggest seeing her to a cab or the bus. Just as it would seem natural, once they were down stairs, to suggest a drink or a cup of coffee. And then? Well, he would simply have to let luck and instinct be his guide— which was, after all, what he would have to do, no matter how much planning he might attempt ahead of time. Might as well get it over with.

The only hitch came from Barbara, of all people, whose face seemed to fall (though maybe it was only wishful thinking on Val's part) when he offered to leave with Doris. She had to go out herself, she said, to get some things for breakfast at the delicatessen, so maybe she'd come along ...

"Let me get them for you," said Val hastily. "No trouble at all. I'll be glad to. Save you a trip."

"Take the nice man up on it," said Doris. The glint of dry amusement was back in her eye. "I won't keep him long."

So that hurdle was past, and then, when they got down on the street, Doris took the words right out of his mouth by saying, "How about stopping in for a beer? We ought to be able to stand each other that long. Two civilized people like us."

"Why, sure. Great. I was going to suggest it myself." He could hardly believe his luck.

"I'm parched," said Doris. "Trust Barbara not to think of anything hospitable like offering the hired help a drink. Poor girl, she always was the world's worst hostess. Remember that awful cook-out she and Clyde gave? Well, all their parties were pretty awful, but this was the worst. About half enough hamburger to go 'round, and not even half enough buns."

Yes, Val remembered. Everybody but Barbara had wound up by getting drunk—Clyde out of mortification, the guests out of sympathy and hunger. But Doris didn't need to make such a thing of it. "You never did like Barbara," he said. "Did you?"

"Not really. I don't dislike her, either. She's just not my dish of tea. I never could understand why Clyde married her."

"Could be because she's beautiful."

"Well, but he didn't have to *marry* her! I mean— There. I'm being bitchy." (Val wasn't going to argue with her on that point. Or on any point. He hoped. But it wasn't going to be easy; it never was, with Doris.) She was going on, as unsparingly candid about herself as about others. "I suppose it's as simple as that. The female primeval. I suppose I'm just plain jealous of Barbara."

"You shouldn't be. You've got so much that Barbara hasn't got. Your job, your home, Annabelle ..."

"But she's got more of the old basic appeal. I know I shouldn't begrudge it to her. But I do. She's not only sexy, she's a sexy clinging vine. And that's what's wrong with me. I don't know how to cling. Everybody thinks I'm so damned self-sufficient."

"Well, you are," said Val. But that wasn't tactful; he added hurriedly, "Nothing wrong with being self-sufficient. Who says anything's wrong with you?"

"You used to, if memory serves. In the old days. Before you got so gallant."

"Time has mellowed me," he said. Thank God for the light touch; they had been a little too close to fundamentals for comfort. "After all, it's turned out for the best. Here you are, married to Monroe and living happily ever after ..."

He let the pause stretch out and out, and so did Doris. At last she said, "Yes," in a small, absent voice. The waiter had already brought their beers; after taking a sip, she leaned her head back against the imitation leather of the booth and closed her eyes wearily. For Val, the chance gesture struck an elusive, reminiscent chord: when, in the past, had she done just this, with just this same look—all the more poignant because it was so unusual in Doris—of vulnerability? When had he said before what he was saying now?

"You're tired. You shouldn't have worked so hard."

At once her eyes flew open. "Nonsense," she said crisply (as she had said that other time.) Then the instant of almost-remembering slipped out of Val's grasp, leaving only the uncertainty of the present. For Doris' voice was edged, ever so slightly, with irritation. Of course. He should have known better than to say anything that smacked of sympathy. "I didn't work at all. Even if I had, it would be worth it, to see Barbara settled in a decent place at last. I've been trying to get her out of that dump uptown ever since we came back from California."

"She liked being near you and Annabelle."

"Oh, well! For heaven's sake, she can still see Annabelle whenever she wants to! It's time she quit brooding and started living a life of her own. Speaking of Annabelle—" She shot a puzzling, oblique glance at him. He was instantly on the alert. What was she up to? "Speaking of Annabelle," she repeated, casual as all get out, "isn't it weird, the things she makes up? I mean that character she told you about Saturday afternoon."

His heart gave a little jump. This was what she was up to. This was why she had suggested having a beer. She wanted to pump him about Annabelle's Cane character. Which made it a very small world indeed; and now if only he could keep his wits about him, if only he could manage not to fumble

"Oh, that." He laughed, carefully. "I don't know why I even mentioned the guy. I have a hunch I shouldn't have, somehow. At least, that was the feeling I got at the time, that I was talking out of turn. Hell, I didn't mean to step on anybody's toes—"

"Of course you weren't stepping on anybody's toes " Doris broke in. "How could you have been talking out of turn? Nobody else had ever heard of him. He's just somebody she made up. I said so, right away."

"Yes. I remember you did."

"Well, so did everyone else." Her voice threatened to go shrill. She took out a cigarette, and by the time Val lit it for her she had things back under control. "I've always been interested in Annabelle's imaginary people. She dreamed up a dilly of a little girl, when we were out in

California. What else did she say about this one? Cane, I think you said she calls him?"

"Yes. Cane. Her name for him. Not his real one, she said. He has a cane, and she takes hold of it, and he swings her way up to the ceiling. Let me see what else. He plays a good rousing hand of Old Maid, he's a real tiger when it comes to riddles, and when they had cocktails he played like he was drunk. Great sport."

"A cane." Doris was too absorbed to remember her role of casual inquirer. She chewed her lip and frowned. "Does that mean he's lame?"

"We didn't go into that. Maybe he just carries a cane for show."

"But didn't she describe him? She must have told you what he looks like."

"Bushy eyebrows," said Val. "And—how did she put it?—whiskers in his ears. Do you recognize the description?"

She didn't seem to. Unless she was shamming, with her puzzled expression, Annabelle's Cane was nobody she knew. Not even an acquaintance, let alone a hypothetical secret love interest. But she must have some reason for being so all-fired curious. He ought to be able to tell whether she was shamming. He knew Doris; damn it, he had once been married to her, so he ought to be able to tell.

"Why are you looking at me like that?" she said sharply. Her whole face seemed to sharpen as he watched. Her face that he knew so well— stylishly pale, haughty-nosed, with the pointed chin and the bright-brown eyes that had always before seemed so frank but were now unfathomable. "She just made him up. Of course I don't recognize him. For the very good reason that he doesn't exist."

Val made a sudden decision. "He doesn't now," he said, still watching her. "I'm not so sure he never did."

There was the tiniest pause, almost imperceptible, before she shot the question at him. "What do you mean by that?"

"I had kind of an unnerving experience Saturday night. Late, about midnight. I found the body of a man on the church steps a few doors from where I live."

"You— What?"

He took a drink of his beer and nodded. "The police say he was murdered. Somebody had clipped him across the throat with his cane." He let that sink in, and then went on. "Like I say, it was unnerving, especially with Annabelle's description so fresh in my mind. I got a good look at him, and he fit—bushy eyebrows, whiskers in his ears, cane and all."

"But that's fantastic," whispered Doris. All at once she stiffened; like a bow string drawn taut, she leaned toward him, both hands clutching the edge of the table. "Val! You didn't tell this to the police!"

"No. I didn't tell the police." (Her hands loosened and slipped down into her lap, limp with relief.) "It's such a far-fetched story. They'd have decided I belonged in Bellevue. And they might be right, at that ..."

Doris wet her lips. "Who was he?" she asked at last. "The man you found, I mean?"

"They didn't know, at first. His wallet was gone. No identification. But they traced him, the way they do, through his clothes, or laundry marks, or—"

"I know how they trace people," Doris broke in impatiently. "Who was he?"

"Turned out to be a guy named John Custer. A free-lance writer from Philadelphia. They still haven't figured out who killed him, or why. I guess you didn't happen to notice it, in the paper." He took the clipping from his wallet and slid it across the table to her.

"No. No, I didn't. John Custer." It was as if she were trying the name out on someone else. All the time she was reading the clipping, she kept smoothing her hair back from her temples in the familiar, nervous gesture. Then, catching Val's eye on her, she became once more her crisp self. "No great mystery about why he was killed, if his wallet was missing. It sounds like just another mugging. Practically an everyday occurrence, especially on those dark little Village streets. I'm not the scarey type, but I couldn't help thinking, the other night when I left the Russells', how easy it would be for someone to follow me and—"

But surely Monroe had been with her? What in the hell could she have been doing, leaving the Russells' by herself? Val only hoped he was keeping his expression suitably blank.

She must have sensed what he was thinking, though. She was talking so fast. Almost chattering. "You remember the Russells, of course. They're just as mad as they ever were. In a nice way, I mean. I've been devoted to Sally for years. The amazing thing is that Monroe likes them too. I remember what grave doubts I had, when I introduced them. But as it turned out they hit it off beautifully, right from the start."

"How nice," said Val. Frustration settled on him, like a clamp. He had been so close to something—he didn't know what, but something significant—and yet he had fumbled it, he had let her slip away into the safety of this aimless gabbling. He lashed out, any which way. "Good old Monroe. Maybe he isn't so stuffy, after all."

It was all he needed to say. They were off in a cloud of dust.

"He's not in the least stuffy," snapped Doris. "That's the trouble with you, you jump to these completely illogical conclusions, and nothing on God's earth can jar you loose from them. Stuffy! According to you anybody's stuffy that happens to hold down a better than average job. Just because Monroe makes more in a month than—than lots of people do in a year—"

"I know what a big shot he is. You don't have to tell me again," said Val coldly. "He's a great big successful executive, so of course he can do no wrong. Oh no. You and Monroe never get into anything vulgar like a fight—"

"So Mother told you about that. She would, you and she always did see eye to eye on such things. And you'd listen, too, wouldn't you? As if it was any of your business, or anybody else's, how I happened to spend Saturday afternoon!"

"None of my business at all. I couldn't possibly care less. Let good old Monroe figure out his own problems, in his own un-stuffy way." That thrust had hit home, all right. He watched, with satisfaction, while Doris jabbed her arms into her coat sleeves and gathered up her purse.

"I might have known," she said. "There's no use trying to have a friendly, sensible conversation with a person like you. Go on back to Barbara. She's just your type. Wouldn't contradict you if you said black was white. And don't forget the groceries for breakfast."

Trust her to have the last word. The perfect, cutting retort would no doubt come to Val in the middle of the night, when it was too late.

She flounced out, and he stalked after her, grimly determined to do his duty and see her into a cab. He flagged one at the corner, and in stony silence helped her into it.

"Thanks for the beer," she said bitterly, as the cab door slammed shut.

Just like old times, he thought … And in the middle of the thought, for no reasonable reason, his mind clicked, and he had it in his grasp—the tantalizing half-memory that had eluded him earlier, when they were sitting in the booth. He recognized that weary gesture of Doris' now, and her look of vulnerability that still had the power to touch his heart, and something careful and preoccupied about the way she carried herself, even at the end when she lost her temper.

Why, she's pregnant, he thought. She's just starting a baby.

It gave him such a jolt that he stopped right in the middle of the street. A passer-by jostled him and a car honked, good and loud, before he collected his wits and moved on.

THIRTEEN

But the jolt was only momentary. It didn't have a chance—nothing did—against the acute irritation Doris always managed to stir up in him. He was smarting inwardly when he climbed Barbara's stairs again with his load of groceries. (And it didn't help any to realize that he would most likely have forgotten them, without Doris' sharp-tongued reminder.)

This time Barbara wasn't waiting for him in the hallway. She responded, in a muffled voice, to his tap on the door, and when he walked in he found her curled up forlornly in the corner of the sofa.

"What's the matter?" he asked at once. Then he blurted it out: "Barbara! Why, Barbara, you've been crying!"

"I thought you weren't coming back," she whispered—against his shoulder, for by this time he had dumped the groceries on the table and rushed to take her in his arms. "You went away with her, and you were gone so long ..."

She was so like a frightened child that he could have wept himself. (He could also have jumped up and down and whooped his elation: she's jealous, bless her heart, jealous of me and Doris!) "Now wasn't that a silly thing to think." Her hair was ruffled; he smoothed it down tenderly. "I told you I was coming back. Didn't I? Of course. So of course here I am."

"But you were gone so long," she repeated shakily.

"Not really. Just long enough to get into a cozy little scrap with Doris. We can manage that in less time than any two people you ever saw. Practice makes perfect, you know." The inner smarting was gone, magically cured. He felt fine again. Confident and masterful.

And Barbara was on the verge of smiling, even though one last tear still trembled on her lashes. Her mouth was a little swollen from her fit of crying; this accented, even more than usual, the haunting fragility of her features. "But why would you and Doris get into a scrap?"

"I haven't the slightest idea. A case of mutual allergy, I guess. The crazy part of it is that fundamentally I like Doris, in a lot of ways I admire her ..."

"Oh yes. So do I. Only she scares me, a little. She's so good at everything, she makes me feel like such a hopeless dud. I am, you know, compared to her. A complete all-round failure."

"I like you the way you are," Val told her huskily. Yes. She was his idea of what a woman ought to be, with none of the bright, hard surface that made Doris at once attractive and forbidding, none of the ruthless drive or strength. Here she was in his arms, all quietness and depth and mystery, with her half-veiled eyes and her swollen mouth waiting, ready to respond ...

What was it that stopped him? He knew that she was his for the taking, and yet ... Perhaps it was something he saw, or thought he saw, in her face: a secret, involuntary flicker as if she were determined not to flinch at what she was waiting for. Or perhaps it was the echo of Doris' voice: "Well, but he didn't have to *marry* her! I mean—" What she meant had been crystal-clear: Barbara was a pushover, not only Val's for the taking, but anybody's. Crystal-clear then, and crystal-clear now, and perhaps he was holding back out of spite, a compulsion to prove—no matter what it cost him—that Doris was wrong.

He kissed Barbara chastely, on the left cheekbone. Then he stood up and said he didn't know about her, but personally he felt like a cup of coffee. (That wasn't all he felt like, but let it go.)

"Yes," she said faintly, and he set up a ludicrous bustle with the groceries and the coffee pot. She stayed where she was, on the sofa. He could not bring himself to look at her. She might very well be laughing at him. Or maybe she was angry, or contemptuous. Or—he felt a wrench of self-reproach—maybe he had only succeeded in making her feel more than ever like a failure.

The coffee turned out several horsepower stronger than necessary; he had let it perk overtime, dreading the moment when he must pour it and face Barbara. She was sitting as he had left her, with her feet tucked under her. Only her head was lowered now; she seemed to be staring at her hands. He set her cup down on the table beside her, and here it was at last: her gaze, luminous and steady, stopped him in his tracks.

"Why did you act—the way you did?" she asked. "What did she tell you about me?"

Women, he thought, in helpless surprise; just try to predict what tack they were going to take. "Who? Doris, you mean?" he hedged. "Why should she tell me anything about you?"

But there was no talking away the sorrow, the ancient knowledge, in her eyes. "She doesn't want you herself, and yet she won't quite let go of you," she said desolately. A great sigh shook her. "I shouldn't have said that. It's not true. Or else it's too true. Either way, I shouldn't have said it. Only tell me straight out, Val. Are you still in love with her?"

"Good Lord, no! Now you *are* being ridiculous! Why, we can't spend five minutes together without getting into a fight!"

"Sometimes people do that because they're in love."

"Not me. And not Doris, either. Look at the way she and Monroe get along. Never a cross word." He paused, wondering how much Barbara knew about Doris' private life. Not much, he suspected. But at least the subject might divert her from her own dark broodings. "Well, hardly ever. Maudie tells me they had kind of a dust-up Saturday."

"Yes. Maudie talks quite a bit. She told me too." Her smile, wan at first, brightened into a real flash of mischief. "Wouldn't Doris be wild, if she knew!"

"She does know. That's one of the things that set her off tonight. I don't remember just how it came up. I made some crack about Monroe, I guess, and she immediately leaped to the conclusion—correct, of course—that Maudie had been unloading all the family dirt for my benefit."

Barbara's eyes widened with interest. "What did she say?"

"She said it wasn't any of my business, or anybody else's, how she happened to spend Saturday afternoon. Which I couldn't agree with her more. Do you actually believe, Barbara, that Doris might be carrying on with somebody behind Monroe's back? Now don't get me wrong," he added hastily. Hypersensitive, as he was just now, to the mysterious workings of the female mind, he saw what might be made of this. "I'll tell you why I'm asking in a minute. It's not because it's anything to me personally. Do you think she might be?"

For a long minute Barbara hesitated. "She did tell me, you know, that she had an appointment Saturday afternoon. And— But after all, that doesn't necessarily mean anything. It doesn't seem a bit like her. She's so out in the open with everything she does. Poor Monroe."

"What's poor about him?"

"It's awful to be jealous," murmured Barbara. "The awfullest, the most destructive feeling there is."

"I suppose so. Okay, poor Monroe. But look, Barbara. He isn't the congenital jealous type. He can't be. You know, and so do I, that Doris wouldn't put up with that kind of nonsense for a minute. I don't like the guy, but he's no screwball. He wouldn't be jealous for no reason at all. No. He's got some damn good reason for believing what he does."

"Seems so," said Barbara. "I've never known him to be like this before, and with Maudie around, I guess I'd have heard about it. It's so silly, isn't it? All Doris had to do was tell him where she really was Saturday afternoon—"

"If she's innocent, you mean." Val thought about it. "She might be innocent, though, and still not tell him. Out of pure cussedness. I know how contrary she can be. Brother, do I know. Well. It beats me. And I wouldn't be worrying my pretty little head about it if I didn't have this half-baked hunch that it might be mixed up with the fellow I found on the church steps Saturday night. You remember, I told you about it. The fellow that was murdered."

She stiffened beside him. Her mouth opened in a wordless gasp. "He looked like the man Annabelle described to me. The one she calls Cane. It—it gave me quite a turn."

"You didn't tell me this Sunday, when you—"

"It seemed so crazy. Still does. I figured it was just my imagination working overtime. But then Monday I found this note in my mail box, and I got the wind up all over again."

"A note in your mail box?" she repeated faintly. And her eyes grew enormous, enormously dark, while he told her what the note said, when it had been left, what alarming possibilities it had stirred up in his mind.

"You see why I want to know whether Doris is really mixed up with some other man," he finished. "If she is, it still wouldn't explain the note, because why would anybody come tattling to me? But it would explain the funny feeling I had up there Saturday afternoon, when I mentioned Annabelle's Cane. As if I'd set off some kind of a bomb. Or maybe I imagined that, too—" Barbara's expression told him that he had not imagined it. "No. You felt it, the way I did."

"But the police," she faltered. "They're investigating the murder. They'd find out, if there was any connection. There *can't* be, Val! Doris and Monroe and Maudie—why, they're my family!"

"Poor Barbara." He touched her cheek contritely. "I've scared you. I should have kept my nightmares to myself."

"No. I'm glad you told me." Her face took on a sudden radiance. "I'm glad about—everything, the way everything happened tonight."

"I'm not so sure I am," said Val truthfully. "Barbara, I—"

"No. This way it's going to be right. I don't want it to be one of those easy-come, easy-go things. Two people that don't even know each other. I'm not any good at that sort of ..."

"I know you're not. Darling. I know."

"I think maybe you do. Oh, please do. Please try to understand. I know I'm different, I'm not always very—sensible about things, but don't be cross with me when I'm not. It's only because I—I'll try, if you'll only help me. It's going to be right this way. Let's keep it this way—"

They weren't going to keep it this way if he didn't get out of here quick, thought Val. He stood up and pulled her to her feet beside him. "Okay," he said unsteadily. "However you want it, that's the way it's going to be. When can I see you again? When can I call you?"

"Soon. Any time. Here, I'll write my number down for you. Because it's unlisted."

"Unlisted? Who you hiding from?"

"Oh, I'm not," she said very quickly. She blushed. "It's just that when you're a woman living alone, like me, sometimes—people call you up, and you'd rather they wouldn't, so it's simpler to have an unlisted phone."

"Look, if somebody's been bothering you—"

"Oh, he won't anymore. Now that I've moved and left no address. Now that my phone isn't listed. It was my own fault, anyway. Other girls seem to know how to brush people off in a nice way. Why can't I?"

"Because you're not other girls," said Val.

Other girls didn't have her disturbing, haunting quality, he thought as he started down the stairs (after a discreet good night kiss at the door). Other girls didn't leave him feeling at once sad and rapturous, as if he were bound in some kind of a spell. They didn't have faces like hers—he looked back, when he was halfway down the stairs, and there it was above him, like a rare flower blooming in the shadows of the hallway.

No. Barbara wasn't other girls at all.

FOURTEEN

It took a little research. But not too much: Doris was clever at such things. She was also lucky. Yes, John Custer had had a literary agent; the editor who had bought one of his recent articles obligingly supplied the agent's name. It was a woman. Good. A woman was more likely to be talkative.

Doris waited a moment, marshalling her thoughts, before she dialled the agent's number. (She had fabricated an errand for her secretary. This was one day when she preferred to make her own calls, with no one to overhear.) She made the most of her very pleasant telephone manner— just enough authority, just enough personal charm.

"Hello," she began, when she had the agent on the wire, "this is a friend of John Custer's. Well, maybe I should say an acquaintance. I haven't really seen much of him lately. But I was so shocked when I read about his death in the paper—"

"Wasn't it awful?" The agent's voice rushed back to her, warm and eager and chatty. The kind of voice she had hoped to hear. "And just when he was breaking into the big money, too. He started out writing for the pulps, you know, worked his way up."

"Yes, I know," said Doris. "It makes it even worse, somehow. I couldn't believe it at first. I still can't. John, of all people, to be murdered ...

Because he always struck me as the quiet type. I can't imagine John getting drunk and winding up in a brawl."

"Of course not. No one who knew him could. As I said to the police when they asked me about him, that's what makes these juvenile delinquents so absolutely terrifying. You never know what they're going to do, or why. No rhyme nor reason to them."

"It is terrifying," Doris agreed. "I gather the police are convinced it was just another mugging?"

"There's no other explanation. His wallet was missing, and then they haven't turned up a single lead in his personal life. Why, he didn't have any close friends, let alone enemies, here in New York. That's why he liked to come here, because he could hole up and work without interruptions. Oh, it makes me wild to think of it! He was killed with his own cane, you know. Most likely, that is. According to what the police told me, a strong man could have done it, just with the edge of his hand. But with a cane anybody could have done it. Even a child, if he happened to hit just right."

"And of course it could have been a gang," said Doris. "Probably was, in fact. Poor John. He was so interested in his work. So serious about it."

"Serious, and absolutely dependable. You could always count on John to do a thorough, accurate job, and to get it in on time, too. I never knew him to miss a deadline. He certainly didn't have any enemies among his editors. They loved him."

"Yes. Those articles he did about prison life, several years ago—didn't he actually go to jail for a couple of weeks, just to get the feel of it?"

"He did indeed. Same thing with his mental hospital article. That's what made his stuff seem so real."

"I was just wondering—" Doris put forth her suggestion tentatively. "He wasn't working on anything right now that might have been dangerous, was he? I mean, like an article on gangsters, or exposing some underworld racket, where he might have gotten mixed up with crooks? I'm sure the same thought must have occurred to the police ..."

"You're so right," John Custer's agent assured her. "When they found out what kind of a writer he was, they thought they had something for sure. But it couldn't have been that. Because he wasn't doing anything particularly spectacular. Nothing in the personal experience line, that is. It was a piece on poison pen letters, he had it almost finished ... Beg your pardon? Did you say something?"

"No," said Doris. She closed her eyes and took a deep breath. "We seem to have a noisy line. Poison pen letters, you said?"

"I haven't seen the article—the police finally turned all his papers and other effects over to his sister in Philadelphia—but John and I discussed it several times. He was digging into all the psychological angles. Who writes such letters, and why, and the different ways different people react to them. John was a great lad for psychology, you know. Ate it up. I used to kid him about it. You've missed your calling, I'd tell him, you ought to be a psychiatrist instead of a writer. And he'd laugh. But not very hard. He was really quite hipped on the subject."

"Yes, I remember he was," said Doris. "Well. So much for my inspiration. It doesn't seem very likely that an article on poison pen letters would have any connection with his being killed. And I was pretty sure the police would have covered it already. I'm sorry to have taken up your time with it."

"Quite all right. It's been nice talking to you, anyway. What did you say your name was?"

"Mrs. Anderson," said Doris.

She could hardly wait to hang up. She felt as if a powerful motor had started racing inside her; all her nerves hummed with the urgent need for speed, for action. But she made herself sit still for a minute or two and think. To gallop off without direction, just for the sake of galloping, would be worse than useless.

The coast was clear, both at home (Annabelle was at school; Mother, she remembered, had a lunch date with one of her cronies) and at Monroe's office (he had left early this morning for a business trip to Washington.)

Home first, she decided; there would be less risk of running into Mother, who might conceivably get back from her lunch early, for once, and find Doris there. Even if that happened, she could make some excuse, say she was looking for some office papers she had left at home. Mother wouldn't be a problem.

The cab seemed to her to crawl its way uptown. Actually, it was only a matter of fifteen minutes or so before she let herself into the empty apartment, tossed off her coat, and began her search. She worked her way methodically through all the bedrooms, even Mother's, through the play room, the living room, the kitchen, the closets in the foyer. She did not find what she was looking for. But there was still Monroe's office. And the physical action in itself was a relief to her, a means of keeping her thoughts at bay.

It was two o'clock when she walked into Monroe's office and explained to his secretary—smoothly, with wifely assurance—that she had stopped in to pick up a folder of hers that he had borrowed and then forgotten to bring home, such a nuisance, but she really needed it ...

"Certainly, Mrs. Ward," said Miss Simmons, turning on her perfect-secretary smile. "Can't I help you find it?"

Doris had to be quite firm. She wouldn't think of taking up Miss Simmons' time. (Thank God the woman had a separate office of her own.) She was sure she would have no trouble finding it, thank you very much, et cetera.

Her second search took nowhere near as long as the first one. Almost immediately she found a focus for it. The second drawer of Monroe's desk. It was locked, and the other drawers were not. Poor Monroe, thought Doris, he no doubt carries the key with him and thinks he's being very, very shrewd, what a simple soul he is. Because of course all she had to do was pull the top drawer all the way out and reach in.

And there they were, a tidy packet of letters, conveniently arranged in chronological order. She read them through, and as she did so the most peculiar feeling spread through her. More than detachment. Complete numbness. Like the feeling her imagination had conjured up when, as a child, she had heard the expression "creeping paralysis."

She did not move until Miss Simmons, helpful to the end, stuck her head in the door. "Did you find your folder? Anything I can do to—" She broke off, blinking, her professional smile melting like butter over a flame. "Is something wrong, Mrs. Ward? You look so pale. Are you all right?"

"Fine, thank you. No trouble at all. Yes, I found my folder." She put the packet into her bag, closed the drawer, stood up. She even smiled. "Thanks a lot, Miss Simmons. You've been very helpful."

Her mind began to work again when she was back in her own office, at her own desk. She faced several facts, among them her own inability to stay here and go through the motions of her ordinary life. It was simply impossible. She had to do something, even though the only something she could think of to do might be hare-brained, a waste of time and energy.

She made two long-distance telephone calls. Then she dialled the apartment number. Mother ought to be back by now, she must be, she had to be … She was.

"Hi, Mother." Doris spoke even more briskly than usual; business-like airs always had an overwhelming effect on Mother. "Look, something's come up at the office and I've got to rush off to Boston. You can hold the fort, can't you? Monroe's due back tonight anyway."

"Of course, dearie. Now don't worry about a thing. Boston? Where will you—"

"Same place I always stay. Monroe knows. I've got my overnight case here at the office. Luckily. Because I haven't a minute to spare. Take care, Mud dear."

"But when will you—"

"I'll call you the minute I get back. Really, Mud, I must run. Give Annabelle a kiss for me ..."

She swallowed a sudden sob as she hung up. No time now for tears. And a good thing too; tears would not help. What she was doing might not help, either. There was the possibility, if you wanted to go on from there, that nothing at all would help.

But she was going to try.

FIFTEEN

Nothing like a nice quiet evening at home, thought Hen as she turned the corner and headed for the familiar shabby apartment house. Nothing except another nice quiet evening at home. She ought to know; she had had quite a few of them lately. Not so many, really—this was Thursday, no word from Val since Monday—but it seemed like quite a few.

He had no doubt been busy with his unofficial investigating. Which, she reminded herself, was more her idea than his. Well, then, he might at least report. Hen herself had little to report, except for the long, chatty phone conversation she had had last night with Aunt Fan in the upstate hospital. Poor Aunt Fan, so cheered with the news that Hen and Val had already struck up an acquaintance, so transparent about setting her little match-making wheels to whirring. Even murder, fascinating in its way, had been only a side dish to Aunt Fan.

One thing about it, Hen was *not* going to break down tonight and try to call him, as she had done last night. (No answer. Busy investigating.)

Oh, wasn't she? Then how did she explain the extra chop she had bought just now, when she stopped for groceries on her way home from work? Or the excuses she had made to that fellow in the accounting department when he asked her to go bowling with him tonight?

Bowling, she thought bitterly. You bet. She was the red-hot favorite when they had good clean fun on their minds. But just let their thoughts stray to moonlight sails or dancing, and Hen promptly became the original forgotten woman.

Why? She too had the necessary curves to fit inside a glamorous party dress, and the starry eyes, and the tremulous soft lips. Not to mention the romantic heart yearning and aching. But somehow on Hen it didn't show. What they saw when they looked at her was—damn, damn, damn—a good kid.

Well, there it was, her own particular cross to bear, she supposed she ought to be getting used to it by now.... She opened the outside door and began the routine fumbling for keys in her purse.

"Hello," said the man who was standing in the foyer with his hand on the knob of the inside door, apparently waiting for someone to push the buzzer and let him in. A largish, breezy type man. Hen felt him watching her while she rummaged, around the sack of extra chop and other groceries, for the keys that must be somewhere in her purse. (For the door was a perverse thing: often unlatched when it made no difference, always firmly locked at moments like this.)

"Got your hands full and your pants to hold up, haven't you?" the man observed cheerfully. He was chewing gum. "Here, let me hold that for you."

"I guess you'll have to," said Hen. "They shouldn't make purses this deep. Thanks a lot," she added, when at last she succeeded in cornering her keys.

"Don't mention it." Still holding on to the door knob, the man reached over and pushed one of the bells. Hen was busy opening her own mail box, but not too busy to notice whose bell he pushed. It was Val's. "Nobody home, I guess."

"He doesn't usually get home till six thirty or so," Hen volunteered, a little to her own surprise. But after all, why not? The man, whoever he was, had offered her a helping hand. No harm in returning these little favors.

He cocked his head at her. His eyes were extraordinarily blue, with thick, fair lashes; what she could see of his hair under his hat was fair too, though probably not so thick. He looked to be just on the verge of the thinning-hair, thickening-waistline stage. But attractive, in spite of his chewing gum and his tie, on which blue and green rockets exploded.

"Oh," he said. "So you're a friend of Val's."

"Sort of," she admitted. "In a small house like this, you know, you get acquainted with the other tenants."

"How is old Val, anyway? I haven't seen him in a coon's age. Don't very often get to New York anymore. Just thought I'd take a chance and ring his bell, beings I was in the neighborhood. Just thought I'd buy him a drink if he was around."

That was when Hen began to get—not exactly suspicious, but curious, alert as she had not been before. He was making such a point of being offhand. She couldn't help wondering what was behind this determined casualness. And she discovered that he was watching her with a wary interest that matched her own.

"He's fine. That is, he was last time I saw him. It's a shame you've missed him. Of course you can try again later. Or you could leave him a note." (If she could get him to do that, and if his handwriting should turn out to be the handwriting of last Saturday night's note-writer … Well, it ought to prove something, Hen didn't have time right now to figure out what.)

"Yeah. I guess I could." But he made no move to do so. He took out a package of cigarettes and offered her one ; she took it, with the idea of spinning out the encounter—which might, of course, be of no significance whatever, he could very well be a guy on the make and nothing more—until she was sure, one way or the other.

The man's next remark settled the matter, as far as Hen was concerned. "From all I hear, you been having some excitement in this neighborhood, haven't you?"

All she could do was stand there like a dope, with her mouth hanging open. Wondering whether she was imagining things, whether he might be talking about something else entirely.

"Wasn't it right in this block? The fellow that was murdered on the church steps? Why, sure. That's how I happened to notice it, in the paper. The address. I thought to myself, damned if that isn't right close to where Val lives, or did live, the last I heard. Course, I could be wrong, being away from New York for so long."

"No. It was in this block, all right." Hen was thinking, why not jump right in? What have I got to lose? "We were the ones that found him. It didn't give our names in the paper. But we were the ones. Val and I—"

"*What?*" The man's eyes popped at her. "You mean Val was in on it?"

"I didn't say he was in on it. I just said we found him. That's all. Of course Val wasn't in on it. Neither one of us knew him from Adam. Nobody else did either, at first."

"Yeah. I remember that's what it said." He made a grab at his original, casual manner, trying to hide the fact that he was still shaken. "Well, how do you like that! I can't get over it, Val finding him. You and Val finding him. Poor devil. Why would anybody want to do him in?"

"Was he a friend of yours?" asked Hen. "Somebody you knew?"

His face turned very red. And he sputtered. "Who, me? Hell, like I said, only reason I noticed it was the address." He shook his finger at her, clumsily waggish. "You know what I think? I think you're trying to make like a detective. That's what you're up to. Can't fool me."

"You brought the subject up. Not me. Maybe you're the one that's trying to make like a detective." He could be, at that. He knew John Custer, Hen would bet on it. Friend or foe? The writer of that cryptic message Val had found in his mail box? The murderer, come back for some obscure reason …

"Some detective I'd make!" He guffawed, as at a huge joke. "But look here, I'm holding you up. Keeping you from your dinner. Or probably you've got a date." He eyed her speculatively, on the verge, she could tell, of asking her to have a drink with him. But not quite daring. She had scared him off with that direct question: "Was he a friend of yours?" If only she had waited!

But the damage was done. He gave a regretful sigh and held out his hand. "Well. Well, no hard feelings, I hope. If you see Val tell him I was looking for him. Maybe I'll give him a ring later on."

"I don't know your name," she reminded him.

"Oh. Yeah. Just tell him—uh, tell him Charley. He'll know."

If he *is* the murderer, she thought, he'll never get away with it. As transparent a liar as she had ever seen.

She stalled on fixing her dinner, hoping that Val would turn up so she could tell him about Charley. The more she mulled it over, the more certain she became that he had had something more on his mind than simply looking up an old pal. But it was almost nine before she heard Val's step on the stairs. At once she bounced out, full of her news.

"Did he get hold of you? He said his name was Charley, but I don't believe it for a minute, and he said he might give you a ring, so hurry up, Val, let's go up to your place in case he does call ..."

"Now wait a minute. Charley who? What is all this?"

But he let himself be shooed upstairs, and listened while she poured it all out. The only Charley he knew was small and dark, a fellow from his office. He couldn't think of anyone from college, or the army, or anywhere else, who fit the description Hen gave him.

"If you'd only found out more about the guy, whoever he is," he complained.

"Oh sure. Naturally it's all my fault." Hen was stung into remembering her own grievance. "At least I've told you all I know. More than can be said for you. Where have you *been* since Monday night?"

He flushed slightly, so right away she knew the answer. Barbara. That lucky Barbara. Men didn't tell *her* she was a good kid, or ask her to go bowling. "I would have stopped in tonight anyway," Val was explaining. "I've been meaning to bring you up to date, but Tuesday night it was too late, and last night Barbara and I— Here, have a cigarette. Sit back and listen. Please don't be mad at me."

Sweet talk, thought Hen. But it worked. She didn't know what it was about Val ... Nothing wrong with his looks, if you cared for the wiry, boyish type. Hen never had, until now. It was partly circumstances; apparently murder made you want to huddle close to whoever was handy. But before that, from the very first minute, she had felt drawn to Val, and even now, absorbed as she was in his report on Maudie and

Doris, she was aware of the underlying current, stronger than ever.

He was such a gentle soul. So naively unwilling to believe that someone he knew might be mixed up in murder. It shocked him when Hen went through Monday's paper, checking on Maudie's story about the blackmailer who had been nabbed by the police. Shocked him even more when Hen, having spotted the story, said, "Of course, if she nipped downtown Saturday night and killed John Cane Custer for reasons of her own, she might just be using this story as a decoy. You admit she's shrewd, in kind of a rattle-brained way. Maybe it was Cane, not the guy they nabbed, that was blackmailing her."

And he was more than shocked, he was indignant, downright insulted, when she said, "What about Barbara? Maybe she was mixed up with John Cane Custer somehow or other."

"Are you suggesting that Barbara— You're out of your mind!"

"Well, but she could be." Misery had always had a stubbornizing effect on Hen, and she was suddenly conscious of a sharp, nameless misery. "We're thinking suspicious thoughts about everybody else. Why skip her? Maybe she was mad for Cane, or he was mad for her, and—"

"And so naturally, as a token of affection, she killed him?" Val laughed stiffly. "How fantastic can you get?"

Pretty fantastic, Hen supposed. She sighed. "So go on. Anything else?"

"Well, yes. I got to thinking about how Doris talked, as if she'd been by herself when she left the Russells Saturday night. So tonight after work I went down to Tenth Street, the block where the Russells live. I honestly don't know whether I had anything definite in mind or not, but anyway, who should I run into but Sally Russell with a load of bamboo—"

"A load of bamboo?"

"Sally always has these projects. Leather punching, or hammering stuff out of brass, or something. So she asked me to come in for a drink. And I pumped her for all I was worth."

He looked so ashamed of himself that Hen had to laugh. "And?"

"Well, Doris and Monroe didn't leave together. According to Sally, he sat and gloomed all through dinner, and Doris chattered. She always does when she's nervous. There were two other couples there; otherwise Sally would have insisted on getting the fight out into the open. She's opposed to repression in any form. Matter of fact, I'm surprised she let a little thing like other guests stop her. She must be slipping. Anyway, after dinner, she missed Monroe and found him out in the hall, pacing up and down like a caged tiger—that's the way Sally talks—a seething mass of unwholesome repressions. She couldn't get him to open up. All at once he said, 'You'll have to excuse me, Sally. I've got to get out of here. Tell Doris, will you?' And off he went."

"Just like that," said Hen. "Did she say what time?"

"About ten. No telling, of course, whether he went straight home or not. Doris left shortly after he did."

"Then they could both have been roaming around. Couldn't Sally get anything out of Doris either?"

"Not a hell of a lot. When she told Doris Monroe had left and asked her point blank what went on, Doris stuck out her chin and said, 'Why, not a thing, dear. Not a thing. I just happen to be married to a maniac who's convinced himself that I'm wallowing in illicit love.' She might have gone on, only just then somebody asked where Monroe was, and Doris jumped up and said he'd been seized with one of his blinding headaches and had had to go home, and they must excuse her too. Exit Doris. Curtain. Poor Sally. She's never been so frustrated in her life."

"She must have some theory. Knowing them both as well as she does. She ought to be able to tell if Doris is carrying on with somebody else."

"I ought to be able to tell too," said Val unhappily. "I never realized before how little I know about the people I know. I don't think Doris is the philandering type. But then it might not be philandering. It might be—to quote Sally—the real thing. The one point Sally and I both feel sure about is that Monroe is no maniac. He wouldn't be on this jealous-husband kick for no reason at all."

"It could be so many reasons," said Hen despondently. "He could have seen her with somebody else, or overheard a telephone conversation, or found some letters. And when you came out with your story about Annabelle and Cane, he must have thought Cane was the guy, and that Doris had had the gall to see him right in Monroe's own home. That's why he worked himself up into such a state over where Doris was Saturday afternoon. I must say, she hasn't helped any, the way she's been acting."

"No. But for a smart woman Doris can do some of the damnedest things. Especially when she gets sore. And Monroe's suspicions would make her plenty sore. If she's innocent, that is. If she's guilty ..."

"If she's guilty, you'd think she'd have a slick little ready-made explanation for everything. Wouldn't you?"

"She did have an explanation for Cane," said Val. "She said right away that Annabelle must have made him up. And they all broke their necks agreeing with her."

"Well, sure. Because none of them wanted their own particular skeleton dragged out of the closet in public. Monroe certainly wasn't going to air his suspicions in front of you, of all people. And poor old Maudie must have been scared out of her wits on account of her blackmailing pal ... Hey, Val!" Hen had been slumping on the middle of her spine; now the power of her idea brought her bolt upright. "Who was *with* Annabelle when Cane turned up? One of them must have been there too. Who?"

"Yeah," said Val. But then his face fell. "It's probably too late now, though. I suppose whoever was there—if there *is* any funny business going on—has already bribed her or scared her into clamming up. Oh Lord, what a shambles it all is! I haven't cleared up one single thing with my 'unofficial investigating.' I've just got myself tied up in bigger and better knots. I wish I'd never started it."

"You had to," Hen told him relentlessly. "And there's still one to go. Monroe."

He closed his eyes and swallowed.

"We'll figure out some angle," Hen began with hollow assurance.

Then the phone rang, and she nearly jumped out of her skin. "There he is now. Charley. It's got to be Charley. Hurry up, Val. Hurry *up!*"

He already had the phone in his hand. "Hello," he was saying, and then—Hen could have howled, it was such a let-down— "Oh, hello, Maudie. Yes. Sure. What? Speak up, Maudie, I can hardly hear you ... No, of course she isn't." There was quite a long pause before Val, frowning as he listened, worrying his moustache, said, "Why, I guess I can. Sure, if you want me to. Now, Maudie, take it easy, there's probably some perfectly simple—I'll be right with you."

Still frowning, he hung up and turned to Hen. "Maudie's in a flap. They don't know where Doris is. I *think* that's what she said—she was practically whispering, because she didn't want Monroe to hear her calling me. He's in a flap too. She wants me to come up there, only I'm supposed to make some excuse, like I just happened to drop in—"

"You forgot something when you were there Saturday," Hen improvised automatically. "Left your glasses, or something."

"Great. I don't wear glasses. By the time I get there, of course, Doris will have turned up from wherever she is, just to make me feel more of a fool than ever—"

"You've got to go," said Hen. "If only to find out what it's all about."

"I know it. Only why in the name of common sense would I just happen to drop in there, of all places?"

"You've got something of Maudie's," offered Hen tentatively. "*Her* glasses, maybe. Somehow you picked them up by mistake while you were having a drink with her the other night. And tonight you happened to be in the neighborhood, so you thought you'd return them."

"How did I happen to be in the neighborhood?" Suddenly Val snapped his fingers and grinned. "I took you out to dinner, that's how! Why not, Hen? With you along, we can really make it seem casual. And you can divert Monroe while Maudie gives me the low-down. You're a smart little apple, maybe you can figure out a way to pump him. Wouldn't surprise me a bit if you got more out of him in two minutes than I could if I tried the rest of my life!"

"You shameless dog. Trying to sweet-talk me into doing your dirty work for you." But Hen was grinning too: she knew she was going with him. Even if she hadn't been too curious to stay away, there was something about Val.

He was watching her eagerly, his eyes kindling into open elation as he saw that he had won her over. "You'll do it!" he cried. "Won't you, Hen? You'll come with me. Won't you? That's my girl! That's my—"

"Only because you're a feckless creature that can't be trusted out alone," she told him. "Only because I'm such a good kid."

There, she had beaten him to it. If that was any satisfaction to her. It wasn't much. But maybe (so brainless was hope, so tough) maybe just because she had said it first, for once, her luck would change, and it would turn out that he had been about to say something quite different …

"You are, you know." Val's voice was warm with sincerity. "One of the best. I don't know what I'd do without you."

She gritted her teeth, thus managing not to wince as he reached over and touseled her hair.

SIXTEEN

"Of course she hasn't really disappeared," whispered Maudie. Once her welcoming exclamations were out of the way—what a nice surprise, having Val and Hen drop in like this, she loved impromptu visits, didn't Monroe? and she had been simply *lost* without her glasses—she had whisked Val off to the kitchen to help her make a cup of coffee. "We just don't know where she is, that's all."

"But Doris wouldn't just go off without a word to anybody," said Val. Patience, he reminded himself. Maudie had her own quaint way of presenting facts.

"Naturally not. She called me yesterday afternoon, in a great rush, because she had to make another trip to Boston. She goes there quite often, you know, this new drug account she's working on. I *know* I got it straight. Boston. Because when I asked where she'd be staying, she said the same place she always stays, Monroe would know. He was away himself. Didn't get back from Washington till late last night."

"Now, look, Maudie, she only left yesterday afternoon, and it's quite a haul to Boston. No wonder she isn't back yet. What's all the fuss about?"

"That's what I'm telling you. Monroe says she isn't *there*. He's the one that's making the fuss. I didn't think a thing about it until he called me this afternoon. Was I sure she'd said Boston? Whereabouts in Boston? Got me so rattled I wasn't even sure of my own name. Finally I put it to him straight, 'Now look here, Monroe,' I told him, 'you may not think I'm very bright, but I'm her own mother and I've got a right to know what's going on if anybody has.'" She paused, breathless with indignation, and peered dubiously at the scoopful of coffee she discovered in her hand. "Oh dear, now I've lost count. It set him back on his heels. For once. He actually came out with what was on his mind, or part of it, anyway. 'What's going on is that she isn't in Boston,' he said, and mad as I get at the man, I couldn't help feeling sorry for him, the way he said it. 'She's not registered at the hotel, and her office doesn't know anything about a trip to Boston or anywhere else.'"

"I'll be damned," said Val. So it wasn't just one of Maudie's false alarms, after all. He began to feel profoundly uneasy. "Does Monroe always check up on her when she goes away?"

Maudie shook her head. "That's the one other thing I got out of him. Miss Simmons—that's his secretary, Miss Simmons—told him Doris came into his office yesterday afternoon to pick up some papers that belonged to her. Only there weren't any such papers. She took something else. I don't know what, but it must be important, whatever it is, to set Monroe off like this. I thought to my soul I'd go out of my mind, Val, he's been pacing the floor ever since he got home. Didn't eat a bite of dinner. Pace, pace, pace. And then he'd start in again on me. Just exactly what did Doris say to me on the phone, did she sound any different than usual … Well, after I got Annabelle to bed I decided I couldn't stand it another minute, I just had to call somebody, and you were a dear good boy to come, Val."

"I don't know what good I'm going to do," said Val bleakly. "I suppose we could call the police, the Missing Persons Bureau."

"Monroe says not yet, not unless we haven't heard from her by tomorrow morning. If she didn't intend to come back, he says, she'd have taken Annabelle with her. She'd never go away and leave Annabelle."

"Even though she might go away and leave Monroe." That must be what was in Monroe's mind: Doris off on a stolen-fruit trip (with Cane? But Cane was dead), perhaps making plans to leave Monroe for good. But if I was right the other night, thought Val dazedly, if she really is pregnant … That must be in Monroe's mind too. along with all the other agonizing items. He had plenty to pace the floor about. He had seemed, when Val and Hen came in, not so much jittery as rigid. Hen was no doubt having a madly gay time, trapped in the living room with the

Great Stone Face.

"That's a real nice girl you brought with you. Cute as a button," Maudie was saying. She had apparently had one of her lightning changes of mood—shadow to sunshine, her worries disposed of by the simple means of telling them to Val. "I haven't met her before, have I?"

"I haven't known her very long myself."

"Aren't you the one! Fast worker, aren't you?" She beamed at him. "If I'd known you had a date I'd never have— Oh my, Val, I do hope I haven't got you in a fix! Because I called Barbara too, she's coming up too! And here you are with another girl!"

"What of it? They've already met each other. Even if they hadn't—" But it might be just a little bit awkward. Not on account of Hen. Well, of course not on account of Barbara either. "Anyway, Maudie, this is no time to be fussing around about the romances you think I'm juggling. We've got to concentrate on Doris. *Did* she sound any different than usual yesterday?"

"She was in a hurry." At once Maudie had grown solemn, like a child anxious to be good. "But then she usually is. I can't believe it, Val. I can't believe that Doris would— What was that? I thought I heard Annabelle."

She bustled out of the kitchen, with Val at her heels. And she had thought right: Annabelle, in rumpled, fuzzy pajamas, was standing in the doorway at the other end of the living room. She was clutching Val's panda; her eyes, bright and round with curiosity, were fastened on Hen.

Maudie made sputtering noises. "Now, Annabelle, you get right back in bed. What are you doing out here?"

"I want a drink of water," said Annabelle automatically. Her owlish gaze shifted. "Hello, Val."

"Hi." He went over and picked her up. Long-legged as she was, she still felt warm and soft as a kitten in his arms. "That's Hen over there, and you can ask her one riddle before I put you back in bed."

Annabelle needed no urging. "What goes up the chimney down but can't go down the chimney up? Give up? An umbrella! D'you get it?" She laid her head against Val's shoulder and suddenly yawned. "Is it Saturday? You're not supposed to come till Saturday."

"You're not supposed to be sashaying around at this hour of the night, either," he said when he got her into the play room and deposited on the bed.

"What's sashaying? Who's Hen?"

"What you were doing. She's a girl. Here's your glass of water. Mud in your eye."

This brought down the house. "Sh," said Val. "Your Gran's going to be mad at me if you don't quiet down. Give us a goodnight kiss and then shut your eyes and go back to sleep."

"Stay and talk to me. Please, Val," coaxed Annabelle, snuggling under the covers. "Please. Just five minutes."

"Just five minutes, then. No more. What shall we talk about?"

"You choose."

"All right." He touched her rosy cheek and offered up a silent prayer for forgiveness. "Let's talk about Cane. Remember you told me about him the other day? How he came to see you and told you riddles and played Old Maid with you? You didn't tell me who else was here when he—"

The chime of the doorbell reached them faintly. Maudie's footsteps as she hurried to answer. A murmur of voices.

Annabelle was all ears. "That's Aunt Barbara," she decided.

"I hear Aunt Barbara talking."

"So do I." Barbara was no doubt trotting out her little excuse, whatever it might be: she just happened to be passing by, just happened to be in the neighborhood.... He wondered if Monroe was too frozen in his misery to recognize Maudie's fine Italian hand in this rash of unexpected callers. Wondered what expression had crossed Barbara's face when she caught sight of Hen. He turned back to his unfinished business. "The five minutes is almost up, and you haven't told me yet who else was here when Cane came to see you."

Annabelle was putting up a valiant fight, but she was no match for her opponent, sleep. "Cane?" she repeated drowsily. She pulled herself together. "Who's Cane? You're making up stories, and that's bad, you shouldn't make up stories ..."

Well, it was just exactly what he deserved. What he had expected, too. He looked down at the innocent child-face, the heavy eyelids drooping, stubbornly lifting one last time before they shut for good. Her hand loosened and fell back, the fingers still slightly curled from holding his. She gave him a dreaming-angel smile before he snapped off the light and went back to the living room.

The atmosphere there was fairly normal, considering everything. Barbara was helping Maudie pass around the coffee, so they all had something to do with their hands, plus a subject of conversation that might not be scintillating but was absolutely safe. Cream? Sugar? Two lumps, please. Thank you very much.

"Hi, there, Barbara. Fancy meeting you here," said Val, and let it go at that. She looked a bit abstracted, he thought—as well they all might—but Hen's presence didn't seem to have had any soul-shaking effects on her.

Hen herself had what struck him at first as a wicked gleam in her eye. But when he looked again, she was the picture of pussycat demureness, sipping her coffee and listening to Maudie's variations on her favorite theme—Annabelle.

"She's got a real crush on Val. Can't pry her loose from that panda he brought her." She went rattling on, so that no one but Val heard Monroe when he spoke. They were over by the window, Monroe standing, staring blank-faced into his coffee cup, Val perched on the window seat.

"I brought her a panda once, too," Monroe murmured, as if to himself. But then he looked straight at Val. The Great Stone Face. With eyes, though, that were alive and suffering. "Maudie told you about Doris?" he said.

"Look, Monroe, it's probably nothing. Maudie's always getting things mixed up. Doris simply isn't the type to ..." His voice trailed away to nothing. There was too much that he wasn't supposed to know. And then there were Monroe's eyes. The guy looked human, for once. He looked like the poor kid with his nose pressed against the window, watching the rich kids' party. Val felt a queer inner lurch. It was easy enough for him, now, to flaunt his trust in Doris. He wasn't married to her anymore, he wasn't in love with her, as he once had been. If she were still his wife, would he be so sure of her? Barbara's words came back to him: "It's awful to be jealous. The awfullest, the most destructive feeling there is."

Monroe sighed. "She's not the type to leave Annabelle, no. But if I haven't heard by morning, I'll have to—"

The doorbell chimed, two sprightly notes that struck everybody, even Maudie, dumb. She was a close second, but Monroe got there first. He flung the door open. This is all we need, thought Val as he caught sight of the husky, florid-faced man who stood there with his hand outstretched, beaming at the room in general.

"Clyde!" shrieked Maudie, and scrambled past Monroe to embrace her son.

"Clyde," whispered Barbara, and sat motionless, her face white as a gardenia, while her former husband boomed out hearty greetings.

"Clyde to everybody else," Hen was saying, under her breath, to Val. She had gotten out of her chair and was standing beside him at the window seat. "Not to me. Charley to me."

SEVENTEEN

There was a good deal of hullabaloo. There usually was, Val remembered, whenever Clyde hove into view. He just naturally produced noise, the way a fish makes bubbles. He picked Maudie right up off her feet and kissed her audibly. He slapped Monroe on the back. Val got an added bonus: Clyde addressed him as you old horse thief.

But even he didn't seem to know quite how to cope with Barbara. He took her hand (how limp and defenseless it looked in his big paw) and finally stammered out that she was looking great, it was great to see her again.

And there was still Hen, waiting and ready. "How do you do, Clyde," she said politely. "You don't mind if I call you Clyde, do you? I believe we met earlier this evening."

He took it in his stride. "Bet your life we did. What happened, folks, when I hit town there I was, right near Val's old stamping grounds, so I thought why not ring his bell, shoot the breeze with him and get your new address—"

"But I wrote you!" cried Maudie. "I know I gave you our new address!"

"I been on the road. My mail hasn't caught up with me for a month or more. So anyway, Val wasn't home, but I ran into this young lady in the hall. Came within an ace of asking her out to dinner. Only you know me, the shy type. It wouldn't have done me any good, I guess, looks like Val already had her dated up. I know better than to try to beat that guy's time. So there it is. Small world, like I always say." He settled down on the couch beside Maudie and gave everybody his disarming smile.

Funny, though, thought Val, funny he should try to get in touch with me first. He and Clyde had always hit it off well enough, but they weren't that kind of buddies. Usually Clyde didn't bother to look him up at all when he came to town. Funny that he should make such a point of it this time, or that he should have been so curious about a murder that had been given no great play in the newspapers. And why should he palm off a phoney name on Hen? Charley. Unless it was habit, pure and simple. Standard traveling salesman procedure: never tell a dame your real name if you can help it. It still seemed funny to Val.

By this time Monroe had supplied Clyde with a highball ("Go ahead, twist my arm," he had quipped when the subject came up) and Monroe himself was having a straight shot. Poor bastard, he needed it.

"So how's everything?" Clyde asked genially. "How's the wonder grandchild? And—hey, I knew something was missing. Where's Doris?"

"That's just what we—" began Maudie, but Monroe caught her eye and she gulped. She fluffed her hair. Grew very airy indeed. "Why, she's out of town. Business. This new drug account she's working on. Isn't it a shame, when you get here so seldom! If you'd only let us know, Clyde. But you always were a great one for dropping in out of the blue."

"Secrets, huh?" said Clyde. "What's Doris done? Eloped with the iceman?"

Monroe's shot glass clicked against the coffee table. The rest was silence. They sat like a circle of wooden Indians, motionless and blank-faced. Except, oddly enough, for Clyde, who looked—neither pleased with his little joke nor bewildered at its effect, as Val might have expected—but appalled at what had come out of his own mouth. His ears turned scarlet.

There was the sound of a key turning in the lock. All the wooden-Indian heads swivelled.

Doris came in briskly, the way she always moved, and smart, as always, in her russet coat and little velvet hat. But she was very pale. Shadows under her eyes.

"Well!" she said, as she put down her bag. "Look who's here! Clyde! It's Old Home Week for sure." She held out her arms to Clyde, who recovered enough to bounce up and kiss her. "Hi, Monroe. Hi, everybody."

Monroe had leaped to his feet the instant he saw her. Now he stood still, his guard down, audience or no audience; his obvious first reaction of relief giving way—like that of the worried parent who greets his lost child with a slap—to vexation.

"Where in the *hell* have you been?"

"Why, I called Mother and told her—"

"I know what you told her. A great little pack of lies. You weren't in Boston. You weren't anywhere on business. Where were you?"

Doris set her jaw. Once the bridle was off her temper (and it came off pretty damn easy), she didn't care if she had an audience, either. "I might have known you'd check up on me. Typical of you. Typical of your low, suspicious, sneaking mind." She jerked off her gloves as if they were contaminated.

"I wouldn't talk about low sneaking minds if I were you. Not after the way you sneaked into my office and broke into my desk."

"Broke into your desk! Ha!"

"Now, Doris," quavered Maudie. "Now, Monroe." Neither of them flicked an eyelash in her direction.

"And you." Doris' voice dropped to a furious purr. "You believed those letters. Didn't you? That's how much you trust me. So much that you're ready to believe anything anybody says about me. I must say, it's nice to know how I rate with you."

That one hit Monroe where he lived, all right. Something dangerous flashed in his face. But when he spoke it was with cold, measured politeness. "Let's get back to the point. Do you mind? The point being that you lied about going to Boston. God knows what else you've been lying about. Or why. What I want to know right now is where you went."

"All right, then. Put it this way. I've been on a wild goose chase. I've been—" Her eyes were fixed on Monroe's in an agony of watching; she looked, Val thought, ready to snap from strain. "I've been to Philadelphia."

"Philadelphia!" The word burst out of Clyde like a cork popping from a bottle. Even Doris and Monroe turned toward him. "Why, that's where— I mean, I just came from there!"

Some of the nervous tension in the room dissolved into a ripple of foolish laughter. Small world, like Clyde always said. Clyde said a lot of things, Val was thinking, some of which he wished he hadn't. Like the crack about Doris eloping with the iceman. He had nearly done it again, just now, had switched just in time. Val was sure of it. Philadelphia. John Custer had been from Philadelphia ...

"I know, Clyde," said Doris. "That's one reason I went, because I wanted to see you. When I called your head office in Cleveland they told me you were due there, and the Philadelphia hotel said you were registered. Only by the time I got there you were gone."

"Sure. I checked out yesterday afternoon and headed this way. Made several calls on the way, in Jersey, so I didn't hit New York till late this afternoon. Well, how do you like that! We must have just missed each other. If you'd only left a message at the hotel, so I'd have known you were on the way—"

"I guess I wasn't thinking very straight," said Doris. "I had quite a bit on my mind."

"I'm sure you did." Monroe smiled icily. "So you dashed off to Philadelphia on this innocent little trip to see your brother, naturally leaving word that you were going to Boston on business ... You certainly weren't thinking very straight, or you'd have realized that I wasn't going to be quite so gullible about this particular business trip. Not after I found out you'd taken the letters."

"Letters?" It was Maudie, finally dredging up the courage to repeat the fearsome word. More fearsome to her, with the bruises of blackmail so raw in her mind, than to anyone else in the room. "What— What letters?"

"Monroe has a pen pal," snapped Doris. "Why don't you tell them, dear, about the fascinating letters you've been getting? And while you're at it, tell them how quick you were to believe every bit of dirt you heard about me. What? You're not proud of it? I can't understand why not."

She was doing what she used to do with Val. Pushing too far, and knowing it, and not being able to stop. Val remembered so well the defiant tilt to her head, and the sparkle in her eye. But now he could be objective about it: the defiance was only a shield against her own suffering; the sparkle came from unshed tears—of despair as much as fury.

Monroe didn't have Val's advantage. "I'll stop believing the letters when you stop lying and hedging. Or is that something else you can't understand? You and your Saturday afternoon shopping! And your trips to Boston that turn out to be Philadelphia instead, because all of a sudden you want to see your brother! Do you seriously expect me to believe that?"

"Well, hell, I believe it." Clyde bumbled onto the battlefield, complete with one of his all-purpose jokes. "Why not? Dames are always chasing me. That's why I carry a baseball bat, to beat 'em off with. No kidding, what's all the fuss about? So Doris decides to take a little trip to see me, and there's some kind of a mix-up, a little misunderstanding about where she's going—"

"Why yes, just a little misunderstanding," Maudie echoed loyally. "I'm always getting things mixed up. Poor old Mud, she means well but she ain't right bright."

"Stop it, you two," said Doris. She closed her eyes wearily. "There wasn't any misunderstanding. I lied. I don't know exactly why. Those awful letters, and I thought if I could just see Clyde. Because—"

"Do go on," said Monroe softly. "We're all ears."

"Because Clyde knew John Custer, that's why!" She flung the name out, and having flung it, caught her breath in terror. Again silence struck, like a blight. Again all the faces went blank. Too blank to be true.

"And who might John Custer be?" asked Monroe, in the same soft voice. "A friend of yours too, no doubt?"

Doris put her hands up over her eyes and stumbled to the nearest chair.

"John Custer!" piped Maudie. "Why, that's the man you told me about, Val, the one that was killed, and you and Hen found him ..."

"All right, so I knew him!" said Clyde loudly. He shifted from one foot to the other. "You don't all have to look at me like that, just because I knew a guy that was murdered. That's no crime."

"Answer me," Monroe was saying to Doris, bending over her as if to draw it out of her with his two hands. "You knew him too. Didn't you?"

"So what if she did?" asked Clyde. "What of it? Lots of people knew

John Custer."

"But not the way you knew him." Again Monroe addressed Doris, though she had not spoken, had not even uncovered her eyes. Suddenly he reached down and pulled her hands away from her face, forcing her head up. "Isn't that so? He was the one. Wasn't he?"

"Now look here. You better not try any rough stuff if you know what's good for you," warned big brother Clyde. He took a couple of steps toward Monroe. But his eyes, Val noticed, were fixed on Doris, trying to push across some unspoken message to her. Whether she got it or not was something else. Val caught only a glimpse of her white, distracted face. Her guilty face? He couldn't have said. Not if his life depended on it.

"I don't know what you—" she whispered. "You mean the one that wrote the letters?"

Monroe gave an ugly laugh. "That's for you to tell me. You knew him. I didn't."

"Not at all? You never even saw him? Never even spoke to him?" In Doris' tone there was a beseeching quality, and a touch of her old assurance, curiously mixed together. Monroe seemed to find her steady gaze disconcerting. He took a wary backward step.

"I don't know what you're getting at. Of course I didn't know him or see him or speak to him. I never even knew the fellow's name."

"Please, Monroe. Please. Don't be cagey any more. I can't stand it! Because I—" She swallowed hard. "That last letter. He said he was going to call you up some time. You've got to tell me if he ever did. I've got to know."

Never mind why she had to know, for the moment; the sheer impact of her sincerity shoved the question aside. Even Monroe felt the force of that impact. The Great Stone Face didn't actually crumble. But erosion appeared to be setting in. There was quite a long pause before he said carefully, "As a matter of fact, yes, he did call me. Last Saturday afternoon, at the office. We made a date to have a drink." He added, even more carefully, "On Sunday. The date was for Sunday."

"Sunday," said Doris, on a long breath of relief. "Then you didn't—"

"I never saw him. He didn't show up."

For a very good reason, thought Val. The same very good reason that had kept him from calling Val on Sunday, as he had promised to do in the mail box note. Once more he saw in his mind's eye John Custer's dead face, staring up at him from the church steps.

Of course, Monroe might be lying. So might Doris. On a variety of points.

"Look here, Monroe," he said. "Did he give you his name over the phone? I gather these letters you've been getting were anonymous. So how did you know the guy that called you was the guy that wrote the letters?"

"I assumed he was." If Monroe was putting on an act, it was a good one. He went on thoughtfully, intent, to all appearances, on telling all he knew. "I asked him several times, but he wouldn't give me his name. He said, 'There's something I want to talk to you about, Ward.' I remember he called me Ward. He didn't sound tough. Just sort of flip, in a nervous way. I got the impression he was very nervous. I said, 'What do you want to talk to me about? If it's about those letters—' And he said, 'Let's just say it's a family matter.' So then we made a date to meet at the Commodore Sunday. I said, 'How will I know you?' and he said, 'Don't worry, Ward. I know you.' And then he hung up. That was the end of it. He didn't show up on Sunday."

"Because he was dead," murmured Val. "That is, if it was John Custer."

It sounded reasonable enough, at first glance. But there was only Monroe's word for the details of the date he had made with his unknown caller. Supposing it had really been for Saturday night somewhere down in the Village. Supposing that was why Monroe had gloomed all through the Russells' dinner, why he had suddenly left by himself.... Something else occurred to Val. Did anonymous letter writers ever decide to stop being anonymous? Val wouldn't have thought so. But this one had—provided you were going to assume, along with Monroe, that letter writer and telephone caller were one and the same. It seemed like a natural assumption. And while you were on the subject of assumptions, there was Doris jumping to the conclusion, for reasons of her own, that John Custer had been the poison pen author.

Monroe's thoughts must have been following the same trail. "If it was John Custer," he repeated. He whirled again on Doris. "We're right back where we started. You knew him awfully damn well, didn't you? So well that as soon as you saw the letters, you knew he had written them. Or is that just another one of your lies? Another handy little smoke screen?"

"No, no. I mean, I didn't know him that well, I didn't even recognize his name when Val told me. I mean, I'm not lying—"

"I can tell you how well she knew him." It was Clyde to the rescue again, Clyde the staunch defender of womanhood. "She just barely met him once or twice, years ago, when I first got acquainted with him. You want to make something out of that?"

But Monroe was not to be deterred. "When Val told you what?"

"About—" She faltered; quickly recovered. "About how he and Hen found this man murdered. He showed me the clipping from the newspaper, I hadn't noticed it—why should I?—because it wasn't even the same name. He was writing for the pulps when I met him, using another name. John C. Lee. Something like that. And the way it described him didn't mean anything to me, either."

"She means the cane," Clyde contributed. "He wasn't lame when I first knew him. But then he got polio, and it left him with kind of a hitch in his left leg."

It was clear from the way Doris hurried on that she would just as soon not stress the cane angle. "Afterwards, though, it dawned on me that John Custer was this free-lance writer friend of Clyde's. You used to mention him every once in a while, Clyde, and I remembered some of the articles he had written. Personal experience stuff—'I Was a Jailbird for Two Weeks,' or a mental patient, or some such. It made me wonder if he could have been murdered on account of some article he was working on. So I checked with his agent, and she said he was doing a piece on poison pen letters. That's when I—"

"Hey," said Clyde, "I never thought of that. That was pretty bright of you, you know it?"

Yes, pretty bright. And she had done some pretty fancy footwork in telling her story, skipping lightly over one particularly large gap. A good try, but she wasn't going to get away with it; Monroe's next words showed that.

"You mean you did all this eager-beaver investigating simply because a man you had 'just barely met' years ago got himself murdered? How public-spirited of you!"

"Well, I—" Doris wet her lips. "Naturally I was interested. Of course the police had had the same idea, and of course there was nothing to it. Nobody's going to murder a man for writing an article about poison pen letters. I realized that."

"And still you charged up to my office and found the letters and then charged off to Philadelphia ... What do you take me for, Doris? Do you expect me to believe this cock-and-bull concoction?"

She flushed. "Believe what you want to. I couldn't care less. It's the truth."

"The truth. There's just one thing I want to get straight. You still insist that John Custer wrote those letters? You're convinced of it?"

"I think so. Yes. I think he wrote them."

"Then he can't possibly be somebody you just barely met, once or twice, years ago. Whoever wrote those letters knew practically everything there is to know about you. So you've been seeing him right along, ever since we came back to New York. All the evenings when you had to work late. All the Saturday afternoon shopping trips. You even let him come up here. Didn't you? Of course you did, because Annabelle knew him too.

The fellow she told Val about. Cane. He was John Custer. I thought you were awfully damn quick with the business about Annabelle's imagination."

"No. No." Doris had been listening like a woman in a daze. Now she shook her head helplessly. "I wasn't lying. I thought she made him up. Until later, when Val told me about the murder."

"Yes. You really got the wind up then, didn't you? Because Val recognized the guy from Annabelle's description. You knew you couldn't make the imagination story stick any longer. If you didn't do something quick, I was going to get wise to your little game. Well, there's one way to settle part of this, and that's to find out from Annabelle—"

Doris shot out of her chair. "You're not going to drag Annabelle into it! I won't have it, Monroe. I will not have it."

"You're afraid she'll tell me the truth—"

"I'm *telling* you the truth!" She looked around wildly. Ready to bust everything wide open, thought Val; the bridle was off for sure. "I haven't been seeing John Custer behind your back! I haven't, I haven't! If you want to know who was with Annabelle when he came up here, I'll tell you. And if you want to know where I was Saturday afternoon, I'll tell you that too. I was at the doctor's, finding out I'm going to have a baby!"

"You what?" said Monroe.

"I kept wanting to tell you, only I wasn't sure how you were going to take it. And you've been in such a vile mood, you never gave me a chance …"

Now she tells him, thought Val. He had a crazy impulse to laugh. It was so exactly like Doris to pick the very wrongest moment possible, especially when she meant to pick the right one. He remembered all the other disclosures she had made tonight, all the gaps she had tried to skip over, all the things that needed sorting out. He didn't feel like laughing anymore.

She had that rare vulnerable look of hers. She was waiting, her eyes fixed on Monroe. "Are you—glad?" she asked.

"Ecstatic," said Monroe. "Too utterly ecstatic."

That was when Barbara began to scream at him.

EIGHTEEN

"No, No!" screamed Barbara. "I can't stand any more! Stop it, stop! I can't stand it!" She beat her fists against her knees; her eyes were squeezed tight shut, and even after her breath gave out her mouth went on forming those violent "No, no's!" The echo of them twanged in the air like plucked fiddle strings.

Val rushed to her side. So did Clyde, though why he should imagine himself as a soothing influence … Anyway, there he was on the other side, and between them Barbara, trembling and rigid, her fingers like icicles under Val's, sweat breaking out on her forehead, along the lovely hair line. Clyde kept making idiotic crooning noises, but it was Val she turned to when, with a shudder, she got a grip on herself and opened her eyes. Their pupils were dilated. Two mirrors, reflecting nothing but blackness.

"I shouldn't have— What did I say?" she whispered. "I'm sorry, I'm afraid I …"

"She can't stand scenes," Clyde explained. (He ought to have a pointer. And a set of slides. He ought to go into the illustrated lecture business.) "Never could. High-strung, you know. It's all right, Baby. You just kind of blew up. You didn't say anything."

Baby!

"Don't worry, Barbara." It was Doris' voice, clear as a bell, ringing above the confused murmuring sounds the rest of them were making. "You didn't say anything. I think maybe you could have. But you didn't. Of course it's not too late, even now. Or would you rather I said it?" Her bright, hard stare impaled Barbara.

"But why do you want me to say it?" Barbara's hands lifted, in a gesture of piteous bewilderment. "I'm only trying to—"

"Only trying to keep your own nose clean, aren't you? Never mind what it does to me. What do you care if Monroe thinks I'm a tramp, if my whole life blows up in my face? Let it blow up. Let the sky fall, just so long as none of it falls on you!"

"What are you talking about?" said Monroe sharply.

"Ask her. She knows better than I do. Just ask her about John Custer and who was with Annabelle the day he came up here. See what she says. It ought to be interesting. It ought to be very interesting."

"You mean it was Barbara," said Monroe. He turned and looked at Barbara, and so did everyone else. A firing squad of stares—Doris' still bright with malice, the others' startled and curious—all aimed at Barbara, who sat with her defenseless head uplifted. Val felt her quail; he tightened his grip on her hand.

"Yes. It was me." The words came out in a timid rush. "Is that what you want me to say?"

It was too much for Val. But he got no further than the first word of protest. Barbara herself stopped him, with a tremulous shake of her head. "No, Val. It's true. I was here. I was with Annabelle that day."

Monroe snapped it up with bitter triumph. "Annabelle didn't just make him up, then. This proves it."

"It doesn't prove anything!" cried Val, with more heat than logic. "When I asked Annabelle about it tonight she said *I* was making up stories, she never heard of Cane!"

"Naturally," said Doris. She was still watching Barbara. "That's what Barbara primed her to say. It's what Annabelle told me at first. I asked her, too, after I came to my senses and realized that Cane wasn't one of her imaginary characters. By that time Barbara had gone to work on her. Only I know Annabelle. It took some doing, but I pried it out of her. It's something else I'm not going to forget, Barbara, that you tried to use my little girl as a cover-up."

Barbara flushed. She looked straight ahead of her. "I never tried to do that, Doris."

"But you admit you saw Cane. Don't you? You admit that, afterwards, you tried to bribe Annabelle or scare her—I don't know which—into keeping still about him." Without waiting for an answer, Doris pushed on. "Why? It's gone too far, I'm not taking the rap for you any longer. What are you hiding? Why haven't you spoken up before now?"

"Because I—" Again Barbara made that piteous, bewildered gesture. Her eyes were luminous. "I don't understand why you're making me do this. Don't you know it was for your sake?"

"For *my* sake?"

"I didn't want to make things any worse for you," faltered Barbara. "I kept thinking you'd explain it all away, and that if I just kept still nobody was going to find out I knew about it. I *didn't* want to know about it. I tried to make him stop telling me, that day. I tried not to listen." She put her hand up to her mouth in dawning horror. "You didn't know he told me! That's why, that must be why ... And now I've done it all wrong!"

"What did he tell you?" asked Monroe quietly.

Silence. Barbara shrank back in her chair, her scared eyes fastened on Doris.

"You might as well go on," said Doris, even more quietly than Monroe. "No point in stopping now."

Still Barbara hesitated, as if searching Doris' face for guidance, or perhaps for some sign of forgiveness. She got neither. As she began to talk, her fingers twisted tighter around Val's. She spoke in a monotone.

"He seemed all right, at first. I thought he was a friend of—of Doris' and Monroe's. He said he was. Gave me his name. Not John Custer. Something else, I can't remember. Said he must have gotten his wires crossed, because he thought Doris was supposed to be home that day. He was so nice. So nice with Annabelle. He asked about Maudie ... I mean, he seemed to know all about the family, the way a friend would.

But then, when Annabelle went out to play with the little Grierson girl, he got—he got all worked up ...." The monotone faded to nothing.

"Go on," said Monroe. "Worked up about what?"

"Because Doris wasn't there. She'd promised, he said, but he might have known, she was always breaking promises lately, but he'd show her whether she could brush him off. I didn't know what to do. He talked so wild, and I couldn't make him stop. Part of the time he was cursing her, and then all at once he'd switch and say he couldn't live without her ..." Suddenly she wrenched her hand out of Val's and covered her face. "That's all I know! Don't ask me anymore. I didn't want him to tell me, I didn't want to know about him and Doris! I didn't want to tell, only you made me!" She swayed back and forth, sobbing.

Doris stood very still, waiting for Monroe's question. "Is this true?"

"How should I know what he told her? I wasn't here." She flipped out the answer automatically. Then, as if aware—too late—that this was no time for brittleness, she drew a long, ragged breath. "No. Of course it's not true. I told you the truth. I haven't seen John Custer—Cane, John C. Lee, whatever you want to call him—since I met him years ago. I don't know why he came up here. Do you think I'd have pulled all this out of Barbara if I'd known she was going to—"

But that exit was blocked, too. She obviously hadn't known what Barbara was going to reveal. Out of fear, or an impulse of loyalty, Barbara had kept her secret too well. She had given no sign, even to Doris, of the confidences John Custer had poured into her unwilling ears. From Doris' point of view she had, in her own words, "done it all wrong."

"You don't believe me," said Doris dully. She looked all around the room, checking each face in turn. Not hoping. Just checking. Then she got to Barbara, and fury flickered in her eyes. "Are you happy now? Pleased with yourself and your pack of crazy lies? Why are you crying? You've won. They believe you, not me. Well, you know what you can do, now that you've won?"

"Doris ..." Barbara raised her head, imploringly.

"You can get out. I won't have you on the place. Get out and stay out. Don't you ever dare come near me again, or I'll fix that pretty mouth of yours for you. I'll fix it so it will stay shut forever." Hands clenched, she advanced on Barbara, who had stumbled to her feet and stood frozen, like a terrified rabbit.

"Didn't you hear me? Get out. I mean now. This minute."

Val never forgot what followed—Doris' slow, stalking steps as she edged her prey toward the hall; Barbara groping her way backward, her hands lifted in front of her as if to ward off the words that were flung at her like stones. He never forgot it, and yet while it was happening he did not believe it; a glaze of unreality held him fast. The others, too. No one moved. Only Doris and Barbara, in their strange, slow-motion flight and pursuit.

"I'll fix you. You'll wish you'd never been born. I'll—"

Halfway down the hall Barbara turned at last, in a flurry of panic, and made a dash for the door. The sudden movement shook them all out of their glaze. In a flash they were on their feet, jostling each other in the narrow hall, gasping out their incredulous alarm.

"Chrissake, somebody stop her." That was Clyde, who had reached the door first after Doris and seemed wedged there, doing nothing himself and bottle-necking everybody else.

"Now, Doris," quavered Maudie. "Now, dearie ..."

"She's going to kill her," whispered Hen in Val's ear.

"Move, will you," said Val, shoving against Clyde's meaty shoulder.

They burst out into the corridor. In time to see Doris make a lunge (her hand reaching out like a claw) and Barbara break away. Val caught a glimpse of her face, wild with fright. She headed first for the elevator. Veered sharply. (She had a thing about self-service elevators. "It might not stop," she had said. And, "I'm afraid of lots of other things too ...") She made for the heavy door marked "Stairs" at the other end of the corridor, and yanked it open, with Doris streaking after her, just out of Val's reach. He caught the door as Doris whisked through, halfway shutting it in his face.

There was a clatter on the iron stairway, a muffled scream, a thud. In the dim light Val saw Doris standing at the head of the stairs, arched there, with one hand gripping the rail and the other thrust out in midair. Barbara lay in a huddle on the landing.

Before Val could get to her, before he (or anyone else; they were all milling around behind him) could say a word, Doris whirled and faced them.

"She fell," she said defiantly. "I didn't push her. She fell."

NINETEEN

She was alive. She stirred in his arms, her eyelids fluttered open and closed again in a spasm of pain. But she was alive. Val's heart gave one more lurch and then steadied.

"Val," she said faintly. She smiled.

"What happened? Where are you hurt? Don't be afraid, darling. Tell me what happened. Did she—"

Above them Doris' voice cut through the air like a knife. "I know what you're all thinking. It isn't true. I didn't push her. She fell."

"She didn't push me. I fell," murmured Barbara. She sat up tentatively. "See? I'm all right. Just my ankle." It was bruised and already swollen. The heel had been torn off her pump; her stockings were in shreds. "I caught my heel and fell." She lowered her eyes before his searching gaze.

Clyde came pounding down, all set to take over. "I've got her," said Val. She seemed lighter in his arms than Annabelle. Clyde tagged along, carrying her slipper and clumsily trying to keep her ankle from jarring on the trip up the stairs.

"I fell," she told him. "I caught my heel and fell." She repeated it when they got to the top of the stairs. Maudie and Hen fussed around, exclaiming and sympathizing. Doris said nothing at all. Neither did Monroe.

Then they were back in the corridor, and Barbara was whispering, "Don't take me inside. I mean, Doris—"

"Oh, bring her in," said Doris. "What's the difference? *I* don't care what you do with her!" She slammed into the apartment ahead of everyone else. Her heels clicked down the hall, past the living room. The door of her bedroom banged shut.

"I know about first aid," volunteered Hen, and when Barbara was deposited on the couch she peeled off the remains of the ruined stocking and inspected the damage. "I can tape it up for you until you get to a doctor. Of course you ought to have it checked. But I don't think anything's broken."

"There's a doctor in the building," said Monroe. "If I can just think of his name." He sounded very remote. That was how he looked, too, standing in the middle of the room, trying to focus his mind on the doctor's name.

"No, no. Please don't. I'll be all right if I can just get home, I can call my own doctor tomorrow. Please."

It was what they all wanted—to get out of here. Maudie's offer to come home with Barbara sounded rather feverish. "You'll need help tonight, and in the morning. No reason why I can't come down and look after you. I could sleep on the couch. Really, dear, I'll be glad to. More than glad."

Everybody agreed that it was a good idea, and Maudie bustled off eagerly to get her things together.

Fine. Great. But it struck Val that some of tonight's developments couldn't be settled just by getting out of here. You could skip (as they were all busily doing) the question of whether or not Barbara's fall had been pure accident. In view of the stand Barbara was taking, you couldn't very well do anything else. And she hadn't been seriously hurt. All right, then, skip that part of it. But you couldn't just walk away from the rest—the apparently undeniable links between Doris and Monroe and John Custer. Because John Custer had been seriously hurt, he had been murdered. And murder was a matter for the police.

He left Hen and Clyde to their first aid chores and moved over to Monroe, who was still standing there looking remote. "What are we going to do about all this?" he asked.

"All this what? What do you mean?"

"You know damn well what I mean. If Doris is right and John Custer did write those letters to you, don't you think the police might like to know about it? It's just possible it might throw some light on why he was murdered."

Monroe eyed him stonily. "Are you accusing me of murdering him, by any chance? Because if you are—"

"I'm not accusing anybody of anything. I'm saying that whatever the connection is between you and Doris and John Custer, the police have a right to know about it. And that goes for you, too," he added to Clyde, who must have overheard, because here he was, breathing down Val's neck. "You've known the guy for years. I should think you'd want to do anything you could to help solve his murder."

"Well, sure. Sure I do. But what the hell, Val, I wasn't even in town when he was killed. I got nothing to go to the police with."

"Maybe not. But Doris and Monroe have. As I understand it, Monroe, you think Doris was involved up to her neck."

"What I think is my own business. The whole thing's my business. You seem to forget. Doris is my wife, not yours. I'm married to her, and if anybody goes to the police, we're the ones to do it."

"I couldn't agree with you more." It was a distinct pleasure to find that he could, for once, outstare Monroe. "Just bear in mind that we all heard what went on tonight. I can't speak for the others, but there's a limit to how much I'm going to keep still about. Or how long."

It couldn't be the expression on Monroe's face; except for an almost imperceptible quiver, it remained its usual deadpan self. And it couldn't be anything Monroe said; he didn't utter a word. But something produced in Val a sudden thrust of sympathy. He wished he hadn't assumed quite such an irate-citizen pose. Not that it wasn't justified. And not that Monroe hadn't asked for it. But if he were in Monroe's shoes would he be so militantly conscious of his civic duties? Would he be in any great rush to spread the news that his wife was mixed up with a man who had been murdered? "Doris is my wife, not yours." There it was, in a nutshell.

"If you'll just leave it to me," Monroe said at last. "If you'll just give me a chance to—"

Annabelle was peering out the play room door again, frowning in disapproval, like a schoolteacher dealing with a fractious class. "Everybody keeps talking," she scolded. "Why do they all keep talking, Val?"

"Because Aunt Barbara sprained her ankle. We're going to take her home. You hop back in bed and we promise not to disturb you again."

"You carried me before," she said.

"Okay." He went over and picked her up. "Just call me Val the patient pack horse." He turned, as Doris' door opened. She achieved some kind of a smile for Annabelle.

"Hello, darling. Did you know I was back? And Uncle Clyde's here. I bet you didn't know that, either."

That brought Clyde over, of course. Hugs. Kisses. Assorted whoops. In the shuffle Annabelle wound up on Clyde's shoulder, and Val found himself being drawn to one side by Doris.

"Look, Val," she whispered. "Will you do me a favor and get Annabelle out of here for tonight? Please? No telling when she'll settle down now, and I just can't— I've got to get things straightened out with Monroe."

He saw what she meant. Saw, too, that she was perilously near the breaking point. "Sure, if you want me to. I can take her down to my place. Maudie's going to Barbara's, you know. Sure. Might be a good idea, all around."

"Yes. I don't suppose anybody—trusts me with her after what happened tonight, anyway." Before he could answer that one, she had her voice back under control. "Skip it. Only ... Thanks, Val."

Annabelle was enchanted. To get dressed in the middle of the night! To pack her toothbrush and pajamas in her little case! To stay overnight at Val's! In her excitement she would have forgotten to kiss Doris goodbye.

"No goodnight for me?" asked Doris, and held her arms out hungrily.

She was lighting a cigarette when Val looked back on his way out the door. Monroe was standing a few steps behind her. Her face was set; she looked hardly at all like the girl Val had fallen in love with long ago.

TWENTY

"Oh, my aching back," said Clyde, settling down in Val's arm chair so thoroughly that it creaked. "What a night!"

"Feels like morning to me," said Val pointedly. Not that he had any false hopes about Clyde's getting the point. What he would have liked—

now that they had seen Barbara safely home and left her in Maudie's charge, now that Annabelle was stashed away in Val's bedroom, asleep at last—what both he and Hen would have liked was a chance to sort out the happenings of the evening between themselves. But they weren't going to get it. They might as well face the fact: Clyde was there to stay. Val sighed. "Actually, it's one thirty. Anybody want a drink?"

"Go ahead, twist my arm," said Clyde. One thing about him, he was dependable. You always knew what to expect in the way of conversation.

"Me too," said Hen. "Why not? We've earned it."

"You can say that again. Oh, brother. That Monroe's a real tiger when he gets started, isn't he?"

"Doris isn't any tame little housecat, either," said Val. There was a rather cautious silence: all three of them wondering just how candid they could afford to be.

Hen was the first to make up her mind. Apparently she reasoned that as long as they were stuck with Clyde, they might as well get what they could out of him. Because she said, with a flirtatious air, "And you. You're a fine one. Telling me your name was Charley. Aren't you ashamed of yourself, misleading a simple country girl like me!"

"Oh, that." Clyde had the grace to look embarrassed. But pleased, too; no doubt he saw himself as quite the lady's man. "Well, you know how it is. A guy can't be too careful. How did I know you were a simple country girl? You look pretty sharp to me."

The two of them laughed like anything. A great wit, Clyde.

"No kidding," he said when he had sobered up, "if I'd had any idea you were—you know, Val's girl friend—"

"Who, me? Why, Val's got his eye on Barbara. Didn't you notice?"

"On Barbara?" echoed Clyde. To his annoyance, Val felt himself flushing. They didn't have to look at him like that—Hen with mockery, Clyde with a kind of bumpkin curiosity. "Well, blow me down. I guess you're right, at that."

"Oh, sure. Hen's got everything all figured out. She thinks." Val glared at her.

"Not everything," she said. "But I can get a point when I'm beaten over the head with it. You're not very subtle, Val. Nowhere near as subtle as Clyde." She gave them, along with this outrageous remark, a shameless flicker of her eyelashes. "Now there's a real man of mystery. Charley, he tells me his name is, when all the time it's Clyde. And oh no, he never heard of John Custer, when all the time they're buddies from way back."

This time Clyde really did look embarrassed. "Not exactly buddies. Matter of fact, it's always been kind of a puzzle to me, the way John kept in touch, all this time. How we got acquainted, we worked for the same outfit. Electric appliances. Only John couldn't sell for sour apples. He got canned inside of three months, and after that he went in for this writing racket seriously. Wild West stuff. Cowboys. He turned it out by the yard, and it was damn good, too. Not that I'm any judge of literature, you understand."

"You just know what you like," said Val.

"Yeah. Later on he got off the cowboy pitch and into articles. But what I mean is, you wouldn't think two guys like John and myself would have anything much in common. And yet every so often here would come a letter from old John, or he'd turn up in person. Never had a hell of a lot to say, but he'd always look me up if he was anywhere near my neck of the woods. Same thing with me. That's how I found out what had happened to him," he added with another shamefaced glance at Hen. "When I hit Philadelphia I tried to call him, thought he might be back from New York, and his sister told me. It threw me. It really threw me. Last guy in the world anybody would want to murder." He brooded, staring into his drink.

"What kind of a guy was he?" asked Val.

"Quiet. You know, the studious type. Always reading these books on psychology. Never got married. Far as I know, never got het up about any particular dame."

"How about—Doris?"

Clyde was instantly on guard. No longer expansive. Wary as a fox scenting danger. "That's a lot of bull. Pardon my French."

Both Hen and Val tried, but all they got for their pains was a variation on this unproductive theme. At the same time, Clyde showed no signs of taking himself off and leaving them free to air their private views, if any. He interrupted one of Val's groping questions to say, "Hey, how about a refill? A person could die of thirst around here."

There was nothing to do but mix him another drink. Hen gave up. "Not for me, thanks," she said. "I'm going down and get some sleep before I fall on my face. Night, Val. Night, Clyde. Maybe I'll run into you again someday when your name's Charley."

"No maybe about it, if I have my way. Whatever my name is." Clyde lumbered to his feet. He didn't just shake hands with Hen; his other hand gripped her arm and administered a lingering squeeze. And she didn't draw away. The lady's man in action, thought Val. He remembered her description of the mysterious "Charley." Kind of attractive, she had said, in a breezy, beefy way. "How about dinner tomorrow night, if you're not tied up?"

She wasn't tied up, she said. Dinner tomorrow sounded fine to her.

You'd have thought, from the smile she gave him, that she could hardly wait.

Clyde's expression was even more fatuous. "That's a good kid," he informed Val solemnly, when the door had closed behind her. "A damn good kid. Good-looking, too. Hey, I wasn't stepping on your toes, was I, dating her up that way? No, of course not. Not according to what she said. Otherwise, it would have been strictly hands off with me. Because that's one thing about me, I never try to move in on another guy's—"

"Relax," said Val shortly. "I haven't staked out any claims on Hen. I like her. Period."

"Then that's squared away." Clyde sat down again and picked up his drink. But his attitude, now, was tense; he kept stealing nervous little glances at Val. "Look, Val, the fact is there's something else I've got to— That's the reason I've been stalling around, waiting for a chance to talk to you alone."

"Go ahead. Nobody's stopping you."

"Yeah. No sense beating around the bush, I guess." He took a gulp of his drink. Then he blurted it out. "It's about Doris. Doris and John Custer. I didn't let on tonight, especially not up there, with Monroe raising the roof. Or even in front of Hen. But the fact is— I guess it probably struck you funny, my trying to get hold of you first, even before Mother."

"I wondered about it, yes."

"John never contacted you, then?"

Val blinked. The mail box note. But let Clyde unload first; he had started this. "Why should he contact me? I didn't know there was such a guy, till he turned up dead."

"He knew there was such a guy as you, though. Because he wrote me this screwy letter, see. The last one I had from him, about a month ago. Said the next time I was in New York he wanted to see you and me together. I can't remember just how he put it. Something about for my sister's sake. My sister. That's Doris."

In case Val didn't know who Doris was. He already knew too, from the desperate way she had lashed out at Barbara, that Doris was playing some devious game. Then why should he feel such a sharp shock of distress at hearing it confirmed?

Clyde was going on doggedly. "Well. So you can imagine how it hit me, when I found out he'd been murdered. I figured, if Doris was mixed up in it, I'd better check with you first, and then when I found out from Hen that you were the ones that found him— Holy smoke, I didn't know whether I was coming or going. I kept trying to call you. And jittering more and more, until finally I decided to go up there and tackle Doris.

Only of course I never got a chance at either her or you alone, and with everybody there, Monroe putting her through the wringer— Hell, Val, she's my sister, she was in trouble enough without me opening my big mouth."

"She's in trouble, all right," said Val. And without Clyde ("She's my sister") and Monroe ("She's my wife, not yours") she would be in a lot worse trouble. "Listen, Clyde, didn't you even keep that letter from John Custer? Can't you remember exactly what he said?"

Clyde wrinkled his brow, like a puppy anxious to please. "I've told you as near as I can remember. 'Next time you're in New York I'd like to get together with you and Val Bryant. I'll tell you about it when I see you. It's for your sister's sake.' I should have kept it, I suppose. But how was I to know it was all that important? He just stuck it on the end of the letter, kind of a P.S. I wondered what was up, of course. But I didn't think too much about it till I hit Philadelphia and found out John was dead. And even then— According to what his sister told me, the police think it was just a routine mugging. They haven't turned up any leads that would make them think anything else."

"How about the sister?"

"She says what else could it be? Says nobody would have any reason for planning to kill John."

"It wasn't exactly planned. They just grabbed whatever was handy, his cane, and whacked him with it. Maybe they didn't even mean to kill him. And judging from what we heard tonight, I can think of several people that might get mad enough at him to whack him. Monroe, for one. Doris, for another, if she was trying to shuck him off and he wouldn't shuck. Even you ... How do I know you're not just handing me a line? Maybe you know more than you're telling. Maybe you decided to get him out of Doris' hair for her, and maybe she knew it, and that's why she was in such a sweat to catch you in Philadelphia."

"Why, you—" Clyde's glass thumped down on the end table. His face turned red. "Listen, bud, I can work this maybe deal on you, too, you know. How do I know you never saw John till he was dead? Maybe he did contact you. Maybe you knew all about him and Doris. Maybe you're still thataway about Doris yourself—"

"Okay. Simmer down. I don't really think you did it, Clyde. I was just pointing out the possibilities. To tell you the truth, I'm not sure John didn't contact me. I think he may have tried to the night he was killed." He took out his wallet and drew from it the note. Here was one angle at least that Clyde ought to be able to clear up. "Is that his handwriting? I didn't find it till Monday night. It must have slipped inside my mail box, out of sight."

Only partially pacified, Clyde peered at the scrap of paper. He read it several times in silence, then out loud, presumably for Val's benefit. "'… try again tomorrow morning.'" He looked up. "Did he? Try again, I mean?"

"If he had, do you think I'd be asking— What about it? The handwriting? Is it his?"

"Oh, that," said Clyde. "You've got me. He always typed his letters to me. Just scrawled his initials at the end. I wouldn't know his handwriting from a hole in the ground."

"You're a big help," said Val, and put the note under the ashtray on the end table. "If it's any satisfaction to you, I haven't showed this to anybody but Hen. So I've been keeping my little secrets, like everybody else. But I don't think I'm going to much longer. Not after tonight."

"Now wait. I mean … Wait." Clyde shifted anxiously. "I mean, like Monroe said, it's up to him. His business. His wife."

"Then he'd better do something about her. He'd better keep her from pushing Barbara around—"

"She fell. She said so herself."

"She didn't dare say anything else. Doris scared the daylights out of her."

There was a longish silence. Clyde stared at the floor. His face, ordinarily so cheerful and open, showed lines that Val had never noticed before. They made him seem, for the first time, complex; no longer the predictable, rather tiresome "good sport" who shed his troubles as easily as a duck does water. When at last he looked up, his eyes were hard and unsmiling. "So Hen was right," he said. "You and Barbara. Well. Maybe you can make her happy. I couldn't, and God knows I tried. Kept on trying, long after I should have seen it wasn't any use. Don't know when I'm licked, I guess." He got heavily to his feet. "I didn't even know she'd moved … Well, why should I? Only, I don't know, it's kind of hard to get out of the habit, when you're so used to looking out for somebody—"

"She just moved last week. She'd have let you know."

"Yeah? If you're thinking about the alimony, I send that to the bank."

"Oh," said Val inanely. He was thinking—not about the alimony—but about Barbara's unlisted telephone number, her complaint that she couldn't seem to brush people off in a nice way.

And after Clyde, having summoned up the ghost of his usual genial manner (he would "keep in touch"; "all this business" would straighten itself out), had taken his departure, Val was not greatly surprised to find that his mail box note was no longer where he had left it, under the ashtray on the end table.

TWENTY ONE

Friday morning. Eight o'clock.

Maudie roused from another light, fitful nap (she never slept straight through the night, the way she used to) and knew that this was the final nap, she was awake for the day. Those sanitation trucks, clattering and grinding. And then of course Barbara's couch, though it was really quite comfortable, considering, still it wasn't like her own bed. She raised herself on one elbow and cocked her head, listening. Oh dear, not a peep out of Barbara in the bedroom, and she would so like a cup of coffee. Maybe, if she was very quiet? She slipped into her blue chenille robe and crept over to the kitchenette. She would make a full pot of coffee so that when Barbara woke up it would be ready, and she would fix a breakfast tray for Barbara, a poached egg on toast would be nice, and after that she would call the doctor, that ought to take up quite a bit of the morning, and meantime she would sit by the window with her own cup, watching whatever there was to watch so as not to think. That was the thing. Never for a single minute to let herself think ...

In his hotel room Clyde suddenly reared up, yanked out of sleep by some obscure alarm. A nightmare? But no trace of it remained. There were no unusual sounds, either, to explain his pounding heart. The sad hiss and gasp of the elevator, a thump or two from the plumbing, the distant hum of traffic. All the sounds he was used to. Lord God, was he used to waking up in all the hotels in all the cities—Cleveland, Chicago, Pittsburgh, Philadelphia, New York. Wherever. And none of them was home. Since Barbara, none of them was home at all. In the dim light he stared at the two matching flower prints on the wall, the taupe carpeting, the valet service sign on the door, the figured drapes, his bag open on the rack. Forever and ever the same. His whole life a procession of indistinguishable rooms-with-bath. He lay back after a minute and closed his eyes against the desolation.

Monroe, too, woke in a hotel bedroom. He had stalked out of the apartment at midnight, away from Doris, away from what he could no longer bear to face. The lamp on the bedside table was still burning, a spiteful, yellow glare in his eyes. He did not feel as if he had slept at all. But he must have, and in his sleep he must have ... His hand moved up to the pillow under his head. It was wet with tears. At once he snapped off the light, though there was no one but himself to see. He turned the pillow over. Then he sat up, terror-stricken and stiff with shame.

On his living room couch Val stirred and groaned and finally opened one eye. Annabelle was squatting on the floor beside him, staring at him fixedly. "Hi, Val," she chirped, and it was as if with these two words she pulled the cork on a whole night's store of conversation, which now rushed out of her in a sprightly flood. She couldn't reach the toothpaste, and when she looked out of the window, what did Val think she had seen across the street? A black Eskimo dog, looking out of *his* window at *her!* Just like in the movie Gran took her to: it was way up in the Frozen Northland, blizzarding all the time, and the man had this dog team, and there was this other man, a bad one, that kept chasing him on account of the gold, and then there was this beautiful girl ... "Patience and fortitude," mumbled Val, and swung his legs to the floor.

In the apartment uptown, Doris slept on, heavily and dreamlessly.

And on the floor beneath Val and Annabelle (still mushing through the Frozen Northland in a wilderness of plot and counterplot) Hen's alarm clock trilled its brassy heart out. She groped for it. Found it. Bopped it on top of its head—just to teach it a lesson; it had already whirred into silence.

No, she thought. Oh no, oh no. Even if they fired her. Let them fire her. There were other jobs. She pulled the covers up around her ears and went back to sleep.

She woke again at ten, feeling like a new woman—though she produced quite a convincing croak when she called the office to explain about the awful cold she had sprouted overnight. (They didn't fire her. They were so sympathetic that Hen's conscience smote her. Momentarily.)

She was luxuriating in an extra cup of coffee when she heard a tentative tap at her door. Val tottered in, looking haggard.

"Please," he said. "Don't chirp at me. Don't say a word. Just a cup of coffee, please, and a moment of merciful silence. Why aren't you at work?"

"Same reason you're not, I assume."

"Oh no. There's only one Annabelle. I just delivered her at her school. Blessed be its name. But you. You're no doubt taking the day off to get ready for your heavy date tonight."

"It's an idea," said Hen. "Here's your coffee. How's Barbara this morning?"

"Pretty good, Maudie said. They were waiting for the doctor to show up. I'll go over later, when I get my strength back."

Yes indeed. Count on good old Hen to pitch in and build him up. He had to be kept in shape for Barbara. Okay, if what he wanted was merciful silence, he was going to get it. He got it, for quite a while.

"Well?" he ventured at last. "So where does last night leave us?"

And of course she couldn't resist him. Especially with all there was to say. She spilled out her impressions of the entire family group, and while she got her breath Val gave her the run-through on what he had gleaned from Clyde. Including the missing mail box note.

"He's just trying to protect Doris," said Hen. "He doesn't want you flashing that note around because if it should turn out to be John Custer's handwriting it would be one more link, and Doris is in deep enough, as it is."

"You sure take a kindly view of Clyde, don't you?"

"I wouldn't say that. But you can't blame a guy for sticking by his sister in her hour of need. I don't know what Doris has been up to. Maybe she even killed John Custer, but I doubt it."

"Why? You saw her last night. You saw how she gets when she really loses her temper."

"Oh, she could get mad enough, all right. But if she did it herself, she wouldn't be worrying about whether or not Monroe did it. And she was worrying, she was scared to death. Didn't you notice it? How relieved she was when Monroe said he'd never seen the guy?"

"That's so," said Val. "Of course, Monroe might have been lying ... Or maybe what scared Doris was not that he might have done it but that he might have seen her do it. Who knows where either of them went when they left the Russells' Saturday night? He could have waited outside for Doris, followed her to a rendezvous with John Custer, and seen her kill him in a fit of temper."

"It makes more sense the other way. That he made a date with John Custer for Saturday, not Sunday, got into a quarrel with him and killed him and then went quietly home."

"I suppose so." Val sighed. "I wonder if he and Doris got anything straightened out after we left last night. I wonder if they're still determined not to call in the police. She's sure to phone me at some point, to check on Annabelle."

She didn't, though. A couple of hours later Val stopped in again, on his way back from Barbara's. He didn't seem as gay as Hen would have expected: after all, he'd just had lunch with the girl of his dreams, whose ankle—according to the doctor—wasn't even badly sprained, another day or two and she'd be as fleet-footed as ever. (That gliding, graceful walk of Barbara's, thought Hen wistfully. Her fragile look.)

"I can't understand why nobody's heard from Doris," said Val. He balanced uneasily on the arm of the chair and frowned at Hen. "Maudie's tried to get her a couple of times, and so have I. No answer. I even tried the office, but of course she's not in today. I don't know whether she wants me to keep Annabelle down here tonight or not."

"What time does Annabelle get out of school?"

"Three thirty. It's within walking distance of the apartment, and Maudie picks her up usually. I'll do it today, unless Doris calls before three with some other arrangement."

"There's still plenty of time," said Hen. "She'll call."

"Oh, I'm sure she will. It's not a bit like her, to leave things up in the air where Annabelle's concerned. Whatever else you say about Doris, you've got to give her credit for being a good mother." He shot at Hen a glance of sudden disapproval. "What in the hell have you done to your hair?"

"Washed it. Set it." Hen patted her bobby pins defensively. "Any law against that?"

"Going all out for Clyde, aren't you? I hope you're planning to get those paper clips off your head before he shows up. Otherwise he's going to take one look and run. The end of a beautiful romance."

"Supposing you tend to your own beautiful romances and let me tend to mine. And may I assure you, I'm perfectly capable—"

"Oh, it's nothing to me. I don't get it, that's all. I should think Clyde would bore any sensible woman stiff. But don't mind me. You go right ahead and have just loads of fun."

"I intend to. And now if you'll excuse me—"

"You took the words right out of my mouth," said Val. He slammed the door behind him.

Of all the nerve, Hen said to herself. But to be quite honest—and Hen was, every once in a while—she wasn't angry. She was exhilarated. Not for more than a minute, though. That was the trouble with being honest: she couldn't side-step the possibility that Val might be jealous of Clyde not on her account, but on Barbara's. It was more than a possibility, more than a probability. It was the bleak truth, and she might as well face it. Barbara, Barbara all the way with Val; Hen was just somebody to tell his troubles to.

He had troubles to tell her, all right, when at three o'clock he tapped once more at her door. She knew it the minute she saw his pinched face and blankly staring eyes. "Hen," he said. "Hen."

"Tell me. What's happened?"

"It's Doris. Monroe just called me from the hospital. She tried to kill herself. That's why we couldn't get her all day ... An overdose of sleeping pills. They don't know whether she's going to come out of it or not."

Suicide. Doris. Then it all must have been true, thought Hen, and realized that she somehow hadn't believed it until now. Neither had Val, from the look of him. "Annabelle," she whispered in alarm.

"I'm going to get her now. Hen, would you call Maudie for me? Here's the number, Monroe didn't have it. And here's the hospital, I wrote it down. She'll want to go up there."

"Of course. Yes. I'll call. Clyde too, if I can get him. Bring Annabelle here, Val. I can take her off your hands if you want me to."

Some of the warmth came back into his eyes. He put his arms around her and hugged her before he hurried on down the stairs.

TWENTY TWO

It was confusing, the way they kept turning the lights on and off. Not with a sudden click, but with a gradual dimming. Like theatre lights. Doris couldn't seem to follow the action of the play, but the scenes were beautiful—strange, miniature landscapes that were shifted, with breathtaking skill, to interiors, equally strange and miniature and clear-cut. The dialogue, which went on all the time, was simply hopeless. Lots of characters, lots of talking; and all of it irrelevant—judging from the random snatches she was able to catch—irrelevant on a truly surrealistic scale. Even when the voices were familiar to her, and some of them were very familiar; she was just on the brink of recognizing ...

Someone said, "I think she's beginning to come out of it. Of course it's going to take time."

Someone else: "Keep talking to her. The doctor said ..."

"I know. It's a lovely day, Doris. Doris, the sun's shining, it's a lovely day ..." (Surely she knew this voice? Only it was too much effort, and they were turning off the lights again.)

Then a garble. She missed quite a long stretch, except for "Annabelle" and "downtown." That's nice, she thought. I know Annabelle. I know downtown.

"Doris darling, it's a lovely day. I'm here, Doris. I love you."

Scenes and scenes later she put a voice and a name together. A voice and a name and a face; she saw her mother—regular-size, not miniature like the landscapes and interiors—across the room and she heard her whispering: "I never knew it was against the law, to try to ... But the first thing this morning here came ... Of course I told them an accident ..." Poor Mother, she had been crying.

"She opened her eyes. There. She almost opened her eyes." She realized, with surprise, that they were talking about her. So I opened my eyes, she thought. This is a big deal? And why has everybody been crying?

But she had been crying too, way back there, a long time ago. They didn't trust her with Annabelle anymore. Monroe didn't believe her.

There was something else about Monroe that was the worst of all, too bad to bear. And the baby. A terrible fear clutched her. She was going to have a baby. Had been going to. She had lost the baby; that was why they were all crying.

She made a thick animal sound. It brought them fluttering around her. But she couldn't make them understand; her tongue wouldn't work.

"What is it, darling?" "What is she trying to say?" "She's asking something, she wants to know something."

At last the starchy woman exclaimed in triumph: "Oh! The baby! That's it, isn't it, dear? Now don't you worry. The baby's all right, and so are you. Going to be good as new in no time. You haven't got a thing to worry about. You've slept all your troubles away."

Just like that. "Slept all your troubles away." Was it possible? She had longed for sleep; after Monroe went away, she had felt that she would die if she didn't find some way to turn off the grinding mechanism of her mind. That was why she had gotten the little bottle of sleeping capsules out of the medicine cabinet. Respite. Escape. But was there a sleeping capsule that would work not only on her, but on her troubles themselves, dissolving them by some magic of chemistry? She pondered the miraculous possibility.

An arm slipped under her shoulders and lifted her; something hot trickled down her throat.

"I took ... Sleeping pill ..." she mumbled. Her tongue must be working better; it didn't take them so long to figure this one out.

"I'll say you did! And how! Scared the bejesus out of us all." She put together another name and voice and face. Clyde. Nice of Clyde to be here. Just when she needed him, on account of the letters. The letters. A premonition shot through her like a warning twinge of pain. Some of her troubles might be dissolved, but not all of them. Not the letters.

Tears kept running down Mother's face; she was saying, "Doris, dearie, why did you do it? I'd never have left if I'd had any idea ..."

"No, it was my fault," said Monroe. "No one to blame but me. I drove her to it." He put out his hand as if to touch her, and the hopeless, incurable, undissolved trouble rose in a sob that choked her. She turned her head away.

"Doris," he said, "I love you. I don't care what—"

But he didn't believe her. There was that to remember, and the echo of fear.

"Now, now," said the starchy woman, rustling like crazy. "Let's not get upset. Let's wait for all that, Mr. Ward, till we're all feeling better."

After that Monroe didn't come close to her or talk to her anymore. She knew he was still there, though, over by the window. Waiting for everybody to feel better, no doubt. Mother and the starchy woman kept pouring things down her throat, and Clyde kept telling stories. Clyde always had a new crop of stories. Without the tiny, vivid scenes—even when the lights dimmed, they no longer flashed before her eyes—she felt her mind beginning to work, like clumsy fingers trying to undo a hard knot. She wished it wouldn't, but there seemed no way of stopping the tedious, fumbling process.

She was glad when Dr. Fanning came in. She liked him; he had a nice, ugly face and no bedside manner, bless his heart. She had never known him to mince a word.

"Well," he said dryly, "have a good sleep? I hope you've got your wits about you by now." Mother and Clyde retreated to the window with Monroe. When he got through prodding and poking, Dr. Fanning sat down beside her. The three long strands of hair draped across his bald head were askew, as usual. He seemed irritated about something, but that was usual, too. It was Dr. Fanning's opinion that most patients didn't have a lick of sense.

"All right," he said. "I don't know what you thought you were doing, young woman, or where you got your hands on the stuff. Not through any prescription of mine. Be that as it may, we pulled you through. By the skin of your teeth. I trust you realize the trouble you've caused."

"Yes, sir." What a comfort the familiar pattern was—the doctor with his sham scolding, she with her sham meekness.

"Scared your husband and everybody else out of a year's growth. Disrupted my entire schedule. Tore up the pea patch in general. All because you had the bright idea of prescribing for yourself."

Her mind worked at the knot, slowly, clumsily. "I took—" she said.

"I know what you took. God knows I ought to. It wasn't the sleeping capsules I gave you, it was morphine, and if your husband hadn't found you when he did, it would have been goodbye for you. You know that, don't you? I only hope it's taught you a lesson."

They were all listening, over there at the window. ("Morphine!" Mother had gasped, and then clapped her hand over her mouth.) Doris pulled herself halfway up on one elbow. "Doctor," she said, so distinctly that she felt quite proud, "It was your sleeping pills. Two of them."

Behind his glasses his eyes sharpened. He did not speak for a moment. The whole room was very still. "Now, Mrs. Ward, no need for you to try to hide anything from me. I got you in here on an accidental overdose basis and there the matter is going to rest, as far as I'm concerned. But don't try to tell me that two of those capsules I prescribed could come within an ace of killing you, because I know better. Unless the druggist made some terrible mistake, and he couldn't have, because you've taken them before—"

She shook her head. "I don't mean that."

"Then what do you mean?" He was still watching her with that extra sharpness, and the others were still listening. "The only other explanation is that morphine capsules got into your bottle by mistake, and you took them without knowing it. And I don't see how anybody on earth, even you, could get as mixed up as all that. In the first place, why would you have morphine around the house?"

She steadied herself on her elbow; it was important that she make him—that she make them all—understand. "I have an enemy," she said laboriously. "A very—close enemy."

(The phrase reminded her of what Val had once said to her in the middle of a quarrel. One of their quarrels, there had been so many. "You're your own worst enemy, Doris." It had enraged her at the time.)

"Do you realize what you're saying?" asked Dr. Fanning.

She nodded.

"You're accusing somebody of trying to kill you. You think this 'close enemy' of yours switched capsules on you, not by accident, but on purpose, so that sooner or later you'd hit the morphine pills and die." He watched helplessly while she nodded again. "But look, Mrs. Ward, why would anybody want to ... Who is this enemy?"

"I don't know. I just know I have one." And as he turned, in agitation, to the group at the window, her voice thickened with bitterness. "Don't ask them. They'll say I did it myself. They don't believe me. They don't ever believe me." She sank back on the pillow and shut her eyes.

She did not open them until she heard Monroe's voice. Quite close; he must have crossed the room to stand beside her. Very queer and tense sounding. "I believe you, Doris." Her heart gave a leap of hope and relief. But then she saw his eyes, looking straight at her. Waiting for her answer. Daring her? "I believe you. Yes. Do you want me to call the police?"

TWENTY THREE

Morphine, thought Maudie. The police. Monroe's face when he asked it—"Do you want me to call the police?"—and Doris' face when she tried to answer and couldn't. That was when the terrified pounding had started inside Maudie. It was still going on, even now when she was safe in her own room, huddled in her own chintz-covered chair.

Safe? But was she really safe? Because Dr. Fanning had been there too. Morphine. The police. And Dr. Fanning's brisk voice: "If you seriously mean what you've been saying, Mrs. Ward, there's nothing to do but call the police. I'm certainly going to find out whether or not there's morphine in those pills I prescribed for you. You still insist that's what you took? You're absolutely positive?"

Doris couldn't answer him, either. Her face went whiter than ever; her thick tongue moved against her lips. But only a mumble came out.

"She's still too fuzzy to make any sense," Clyde burst out. "She doesn't even know what she's been saying. Anybody can see that. What probably happened, she doesn't know what she took, or how many, or ..."

"Maybe not," said Dr. Fanning. "You don't mind if I check, do you?"

"You can't." With difficulty, Doris turned the mumble into words. And she made a croaking sound, a sort of laugh. "It was the last two. Nothing to check."

She had told the truth about that, at least. Dr. Fanning said as much after he got through peering around Doris' bedroom in the apartment— oh, he came home with them, all right; made a bee line for the bottle on the bedside table. Sure enough, it was empty. He didn't stop there. He inspected every bottle on the dressing table, and after that every bottle in the bathroom medicine cabinet. "This the only bathroom?" he asked, and of course it wasn't, there was still Maudie's. So he looked there, too, and as he passed her closet door the pounding inside Maudie got so bad she thought they must surely all *hear* it ...

"Maybe she took the whole damn bottle at one fell swoop," Clyde offered, when they were back in the living room. "That would knock her out, wouldn't it?"

"It would knock her out, but it wouldn't turn those pills into morphine, no matter how many of them she took," snapped Dr. Fanning. "I keep telling you, it was morphine. The question is, where did it come from? And what about this 'enemy' business?" He looked around at the three of them, his ugly face puckered with doubt. "Could she possibly *have* such an enemy?"

"Of course not," said Clyde, with a tired sigh. "Listen, Doc, you know as well as we do what happened. You were decent enough to call it an accidental overdose at the hospital, but we all know it wasn't any accident. Doris wouldn't make a mistake like that. Let's not kid ourselves. She's been working in the drug line for years. This new account that she's been knocking herself out over—it's drugs, she's got all kinds of contacts with chemists, doctors, hospitals—"

"You mean she could have gotten the morphine herself," said Dr. Fanning. "Yes, I remember, she told me a good deal about her job. I suppose she might have ..." He left it hanging in mid air. Was it just by chance that his eyes came to rest on Maudie? Probably he expected her to say something, she was Doris' mother, any kind of a mother ought to be aware of her daughter's state of mind.

"She'd been working extra hard," Maudie faltered. "More pressure even than usual. And she's always been high-strung, apt to get upset, you know." (Oh dear, that might be a mistake.)

"Anything special upset her recently?"

"Well. As I say, overwork. And—and the baby, she'd just found out for sure that she was going to have the baby." Tears sprang into Maudie's eyes; she could see Doris so plainly, the way she had looked when she came home last Saturday—just a week ago today—so pretty, smiling at nothing, not cross with Maudie or anybody else. Happy, for once. Poor, prickly, difficult Doris; and if Maudie hadn't been too upset herself to understand— But she never had understood Doris.

"She seemed pleased about the baby," Dr. Fanning was saying. "When I saw her last week she seemed in good spirits."

"She was pleased. She was very happy until I—" Monroe spoke so suddenly and harshly that he startled them all. "Why mince words? I'm to blame, it's all my doing. I drove her to—whatever she's done. That's the plain truth, Dr. Fanning. No use trying to gloss it over. When I walked out of here Thursday night we'd been quarreling. She was distraught, and I knew it, and I walked out anyway. Thank God I had second thoughts and came back in time or I'd be—I'd be a murderer."

Dr. Fanning blinked. "But look here, Mr. Ward, if you think you drove her to suicide—attempted suicide—why did you say back there at the hospital that you believed her? About the enemy, I mean?"

"Don't you see that I had to? Don't you see that I can't let her down anymore, I've got to get it across to her that I trust her and believe in her and love her? I do. No matter what she says or does, I do."

After a minute Dr. Fanning said quietly, "Yes. I can see that." And after another minute: "Your theory, then, is that there isn't any real enemy, except in her mind, and the reason it's there is because you failed her somehow. Didn't trust her enough, didn't supply the assurance she needed or thought she needed."

Monroe nodded curtly.

"It's got to be that way, Doc," said Clyde. "I don't mean Monroe's to blame. Hell, how did he know she was going to— But I mean about it being in her mind. The enemy. She was scared to admit she'd taken those pills on purpose. You saw that. And she couldn't get by with saying it was an accident. She was fuzzy, but not fuzzy enough to try that. So she hit on the enemy business, just to get herself off the hook. You noticed how quick she backed off when Monroe mentioned the police."

There it was again. The police. And Dr. Fanning turning it over in his mind, soberly, carefully. "The police," he repeated. "No. She didn't seem a bit keen about having the police called in. I'm not at all sure myself that it's a matter for the police." He patted the top of his head. The result was an even more drastic disarrangement of his three strands of hair. "If we say it isn't, then what is it? No two ways about it—a matter for the psychiatrist. You can blame yourself all you want to, Mr. Ward, but the fact remains that suicide isn't normal behavior, even for a woman whose husband walks out on her in the middle of a quarrel. She's got to be what they call mentally disturbed in the first place."

"I realize that," said Monroe steadily. "I realize that Doris isn't as self-sufficient as I've always assumed. Otherwise she'd never have—"

"Exactly. She'd never have taken those morphine pills. If that's what she did. Or dream up this tale about an enemy who tried to kill her. She needs a different kind of treatment than I can give her." He paused for what seemed to Maudie the longest time. Then he apparently came to a decision. "Here, Mr. Ward. Here's the name of a psychiatrist. Better than most. I want you to call him right now and make an appointment for your wife for Tuesday. Tell him it can't wait. If he tries to put you off let me talk to him. I know how to handle these head shrinkers."

It wasn't necessary. Monroe's voice—they all listened while he made the call—had its old ring of authority. "Tuesday afternoon. Five o'clock. Right."

"Will she be well enough?" asked Maudie timidly. "She looked so pale today. So pale and sick."

"She'll be all right sooner than you think. She's got the physical constitution of a horse. Luckily." The doctor got to his feet and picked up his hat. He gave the three of them a last quizzical going-over before he said, as if to himself, "Well. There it is. If I'm guessing wrong on this deal, God forbid, I may turn out to be a murderer myself." A wave of his hand, and he was gone.

Clyde said, "What do you bet he goes right back to the hospital for another heart to heart with Doris? I wonder what she'll tell him this time. Poor kid, as if she hasn't got enough troubles, without us throwing her to the psychiatrists."

"At least he didn't call the police," Maudie blurted out. "I mean—"

"We all know what you mean," said Monroe wearily. "We none of us want the police. Doris least of all, apparently. Of course Dr. Fanning may still change his mind."

Clyde's answer, whatever it might be, was lost on Maudie. She fled to her own room, and here she huddled, in the chintz-covered chair that had always before seemed such a refuge. Not now. She wasn't safe, Dr. Fanning might still change his mind. Morphine. The police.

Gradually her thoughts steadied. She wasn't safe now. But she could be. What she had to do was very simple. She did it quickly and quietly, because she might never have a chance again. By standing on her dressing table stool she could reach the top shelf of the closet. Her fingers groped and found the box, the beribboned box that had once, long ago, held chocolates and now held an odd assortment of mementoes— Mama's thimble, her own school-day autograph album, a valentine Clyde had made for her in kindergarten, her husband's pocket knife. The raggle-taggle of an old woman's life. A silly old woman. Yes, here was the bottle, here in this clutter of harmless, sentimental other things was the bottle. She snatched it out. Replaced the lid on the box. Shoved it back on the top shelf. Hopped off the dressing table stool. All very quickly and quietly, because she might never have another chance.

There were still four or five tablets left, from the terrible days of her husband's last illness. She went into the bathroom and flushed them down the toilet. She scrubbed off the prescription label, watched it dissolve and go down the drain. Should she leave the bottle, empty, in her medicine chest? Better not. She put a few aspirins into it and tucked it into the bottom of her drawstring purse. It looked quite innocent. Just part of the paraphernalia you might find in anybody's handbag.

Now she was safe. Wasn't she? Well, safer than she had been.

When, a few minutes later, Clyde tapped at her door, she was able to call cheerily, "Come in."

"Let's go, Mud. Come on, I'll blow you to dinner. No use hanging around here. We can take in a show, or maybe you'd like to go downtown and see Annabelle and Val."

They asked Monroe to come along, but all he wanted, he said, was a shower and bed. Too tired to eat, even though none of them had bothered much about meals since yesterday afternoon.

But as Maudie told Clyde, he should have come; it was wonderful what a difference a good dinner made. And a couple of cocktails. Sitting in the big, luxurious restaurant with its glowing lights and muted sounds (Clyde always knew such lovely places, and what good company he was, so jolly) she felt almost like herself again. By mutual consent, they avoided talking about "it"—any of "it"—except for once, after a little silence, when Clyde said casually, "Morphine. Wasn't that what the doc kept saying?"

And Maudie, just as casually: "I think that was it. Something like that, anyway."

"Not that I know one drug from another. Never touch anything stronger than Bromo-Seltzer myself. It must pack quite a wallop, this morphine. Come to think of it, isn't that the stuff we had for Pop before he died?"

"Now that you mention it, yes, I think it was."

"Yeah. Morphine. Seems to me I remember you saying once that there was some left over, after he died, and you—"

"Why, mercy, Clyde, I threw the stuff out long ago!" Maudie fluffed her hair and airily straightened her collar. "You don't think I'm *that* kind of a silly old woman, to keep dangerous drugs lying around loose! What an idea! Of course I got rid of it!"

"Well, sure, I figured you had," said Clyde, but it seemed to her that he looked at her a little oddly. "Like you say, long ago. One other thing, Mother, and I'm dead serious about this. I'm going to keep my mouth shut about what Doris took, and how much, and why, and I hope to God you'll do the same. No point in telling Val or Barbara. Or anybody. I mean, if Doris and Monroe want to spread it around, okay, it's their business. Not ours. Right?"

"Right," said Maudie, from the bottom of her heart.

After that they relaxed again. Wound up having a brandy with their coffee. "Why not?" Clyde said, and he patted her hand, expansively, affectionately. "Might as well be drunk as the way we are."

TWENTY FOUR

Val supposed Hen was right: it was his duty to visit Doris in the hospital. For Annabelle's sake, if nothing else. But of all the things he would rather not do … "You don't have to stay long," Hen told him firmly. "Ten minutes. That's not going to shatter your dainty little nervous system. Take her a bunch of flowers and give her my hello—though on second thought I doubt if she remembers anything about me."

He paid his call on Sunday afternoon. Complete with a clump of violets that didn't look any too long for this world. (After he got out of the florist's he remembered Doris' favorite flowers: yellow roses.)

But it went off fairly well, after all. They had Annabelle to talk about. "I don't suppose she even misses me," said Doris. She spoke more slowly than usual, just as her gestures were not so quick or restless. She had a big-eyed look that—in spite of the way her features had sharpened—made her seem disconcertingly gentle. "They've promised to let me out of here tomorrow, and after that she can come home, can't she?" Val found the anxiety in her voice disconcerting, too.

"I don't know why not," he said. "If you feel up to it. It seemed simpler to keep her downtown this weekend, with Maudie and Monroe spending so much time here at the hospital." An obscure impulse made him stroke her cheek lightly, with the back of his hand. "You've done a good job on Annabelle, Doris."

Her mouth suddenly trembled. But she said, with a touch of her old flipness, "I'm glad to hear you testify. I think myself she's a nice little creature. Thank God she didn't inherit my shrewish disposition."

"Oh, now. I wouldn't go that far. Snappish, yes. Shrewish, no."

"Shrewish, and you know it. But the psychiatrist will fix all that. He's going to make a new woman of me. Isn't it wonderful? I'm not bad any more. I'm just sick, sick, sick. Did you know about the psychiatrist?"

"Maudie told me, yes." He eyed her cautiously. "Maybe it's a good idea, Doris. I mean, maybe he can help you ..."

"Help me," she repeated. Then her eyes switched to the door behind him, and she said, "Hello, Monroe."

Val's ten minutes were up, anyway. He could bow himself out with a clear conscience, and he promptly did so, But the sight of Monroe's face—ghastly, the man looked as if he hadn't eaten or slept for a month—set the whole business to churning again in Val's mind. The shock of Doris' brush with death had turned it off temporarily, had somehow kept it dormant through his little visit with Doris herself. He had thought of her, for these ten minutes, as Annabelle's mother; not as the desperate woman who might have shoved Barbara down the stairs and who had tried to kill herself because she was too deeply involved with John Custer, with infidelity, perhaps with murder.

One look at Monroe, and the honeymoon was over.

Just outside Doris' door he nearly collided with an ugly man who glanced at him sharply and said, "Who are you?"

Val told him. He was too taken aback to do anything else. But he added, with a sharp glance of his own, "And while we're on the subject, who are you?"

"Dr. Fanning. Mrs. Ward's doctor." He patted the strands of hair arranged across his bald head and assumed a sociable manner. "I don't think I've heard her mention you."

"No reason why she should. I'm her ex-husband."

"Oh, yes. Now I remember. She's told me about her little girl. Annabelle. Nice to meet you, Mr. Bryant. You're on friendly terms, I take it?" He nodded toward the closed door behind them.

"Friendly enough," said Val shortly. But after all, who was he to snap at Doris' doctor? The guy had pulled her through, from all reports; he had a right to snoop if he wanted to. "She was telling me she's going to see a psychiatrist. Prescribed by you, I expect?"

"It was either that or the police," said Dr. Fanning.

"The police!" Then Val remembered. "I keep forgetting, it's against the law to try to commit suicide."

The doctor lapsed into a thoughtful silence. At last he said, "Suicide. Yes. Not that the police are any more anxious than anybody else to press charges when some poor soul tries it. You don't think, then, that she could have taken the morphine by accident?"

"Morphine? Is that what she took? I thought it was just too many sleeping pills." Val paused, in confusion. Maybe morphine was what they used in sleeping pills. No. The expression on the doctor's face told him it wasn't. "It doesn't seem like Doris to make such a mistake. She knows a lot about drugs. And then— Well, she asked me to take Annabelle down to my place that night. Almost as if she wanted her out of the way. If I'd only had the sense to realize it at the time ..."

"She seemed upset? Depressed?"

"She was upset, all right. Look, Dr. Fanning, you don't think it was an accident, either, or you wouldn't be sending her to a psychiatrist. What does she say about it herself?"

"She says—"

But Maudie came trotting up, bubbling with conversation, as usual. "Val dearie, how nice to see you again. You and Dr. Fanning know each other? Yes, I can see you do ... How is she today, Doctor? Or maybe you haven't seen her since yesterday, either?"

"Oh, yes," said Dr. Fanning. "Matter of fact, I came back last night to have another look at her. And a little chat."

"Yes, of course. A little chat." Maudie suddenly stopped bubbling. Her hand, in its little white glove, moved to her throat and fidgeted with the fluffy bow on her blouse. Her eyes remained fastened on Dr. Fanning's face.

"I thought I'd sound her out about the psychiatrist. It seemed like a good idea to her, too. So that's all set. She said something that struck me as being very likely true. Said she'd always been her own worst enemy."

Maudie repeated it after him. "Her own worst enemy. Oh, it is true, you know. So true. I'm sure of it."

Val couldn't figure it out, the way they were beaming at each other over what seemed to him a fairly routine remark. What was so significant about Doris' saying she was her own worst enemy? It was true enough; he remembered that he had once pointed it out to her himself. He said his goodbyes and left them there—Maudie still smiling radiantly, the doctor patting his coiffure in a satisfied way.

It was nice that somebody was happy. Val himself felt depression moving in on him like a fog, even though he was headed for Barbara's where he had left Annabelle. (Not without considerable protest on Annabelle's part: "I want to go see Mommy too. Why can't I? She came to see me when I was in the hospital with my tonsils out." She had been only a hair's breadth away from tears when Val left.)

She still looked a little woebegone, he thought, when she came racing down the stairs in Barbara's house to meet him. "How's Val's girl?" She clung to him, all but hugging the breath out of him. But she didn't have much to say, and it seemed to him her cheeks weren't quite as rosy as usual. Well, of course the last couple of days hadn't been any ball for Annabelle, either—shunted from one place to another, and inevitably aware of the atmospheric disturbances around her.

"How'd you like to take your doll for a walk in the park?" he asked. "I brought your carriage down yesterday. And you know something else you can do? You can talk to Mommy on the telephone. She's waiting for you to call her right now."

At once Annabelle brightened. Val felt a lifting of his own heart: there was Barbara waiting at her apartment door. Annabelle darted past her, headed for the telephone in the bedroom, and Val seized the chance for a hasty kiss. (It was so long since they had been alone together, he and Barbara; so long since the night when, with Barbara his for the taking, he had fussed around over that damn ridiculous pot of coffee.) She crossed the room—hardly limping at all; her ankle was practically well—and waited at the living room window while he helped Annabelle negotiate her telephone call. Once that was underway, with Annabelle chattering not only to Doris but to Maudie and Monroe as well, he came back into the living room.

"How is she?" asked Barbara tonelessly, and it was only then that he realized how tactless he had been, he should have engineered the phone call from some other place, some other time. After all, the last encounter between Barbara and Doris hadn't been exactly sweetness and light.

"Much better," he said. "She's due to go home tomorrow."

"I love you too," piped Annabelle, in the bedroom. "Can I, honest and true? Oh boy! Bye. Bye, Gran ... Bye, Daddy."

When she came out she was hopping with excitement. "Val, Val! She's going home tomorrow, and she said I can too! Gran's going to come and get me at school like she always does, and we'll go home, and Mommy's going to be there in time for dinner!"

"Great, Annabelle, that's great. Listen, if you don't take a breath pretty soon you're going to bust, and then where'll you be? You'll be all over Aunt Barbara's rug, and we'll never get you home."

Annabelle (always his best audience) went off into a fit of giggles. But

Barbara's smile was forced, and he had trouble persuading her to come along on the doll-walking excursion.

"If it's your ankle you're worried about," he said, knowing very well that it wasn't, "then you're worrying about nothing. Because I'll carry you up and down the stairs. We won't walk far. Just to the park. The air will do you good. And if it isn't your ankle, then I'll never forgive myself. I'll brood. I'll go into a decline, and it will be all your fault."

A left-handed kind of apology, but he got by with it. Once they were out on the street, with Annabelle sedately wheeling her doll carriage a little way in front, Barbara's mood shifted to the muted gaiety that he found so charming.

"It's like playing house," she said. "Here we are, having our Sunday afternoon outing, like all the other family groups. It makes me feel so nice and average."

"Only, of course, we're way above average. You're beautiful, and I'm obviously a man of distinction, and anybody can see at a glance that Annabelle is a very exceptional child."

"And the sun's shining, and the wind's blowing through the grass, and the world's all rosy."

All the rosier, perhaps for the ominous shadows that they both knew were still there, lurking at the edges of their lives. Yes, thought Val, that was what made Barbara so poignant; her moments of happiness were plucked out of the wilderness that was her native land. Whereas a girl like Hen rambled through a pleasant, sun-dappled valley ...

Almost as if she sensed the drift of his mind, Barbara said, "Hen and Clyde seem quite taken with each other. Did you know they're having dinner together tonight?"

He hadn't known it; nobody bothered to tell him anything. "Good for them," he said. "How long is Clyde going to stick around, anyway?"

"I don't know. He'll probably stretch it out as long as he can." She sighed; then went on quickly. "Oh, I don't mean it bothers me, seeing him again. I couldn't have gone on avoiding him forever, anyway. But I'm glad he likes Hen. And that she likes him. Maybe they're just right for each other."

"That's ridiculous! Right for each other! Why, Clyde's nothing but a—" He stopped in time. However Barbara might feel about him now, she had once married the guy. Exactly: of all the objectionable things about Clyde, that might very well be the most objectionable. Val glanced uncomfortably at her; her eyes looked very wide and dark.

"Maybe you're jealous," she said. "Maybe you want Hen for yourself."

Oh Lord. Women. "Of course I don't want Hen for myself. Silly. If I'm jealous of Clyde, it's because he used to be married to you."

She gave a breathless laugh. "But he's not anymore ..."

"So there's nothing to be jealous about. So who said I was jealous of him in the first place? It's simply— Hey, Annabelle! Wait for us at the crossing!"

They sat on a park bench in the sun and watched the other Sunday saunterers—dog-walkers, pigeon-feeders, solemn babies in carriages and push carts, older babies staggering along, broad-bottomed in their snow suits, kids with balloons, with tricycles, with skipping ropes, giggling teen-agers, love-sick couples. Annabelle struck up a friendship with another little girl; they quickly abandoned their doll carriages for the swings and slides. Once or twice Barbara's eyes darkened as they rested on Annabelle, and Val knew that she was wondering—as he was—whether there would ever be another afternoon like this one. Because it was going to be many a dusty day before Doris forgot and forgave; Thursday night had blasted, along with several other things, Barbara out of her place as part of the family. Clyde and Maudie might hold no grudge (their manner toward Barbara had seemed friendly and easy enough last night, when they dropped in) but Doris was the pace setter. No, Barbara had most likely lost forever her forlorn, tenuous hold on her makeshift family. And it was all very well to say that she might be better off, being forced to make new attachments instead of clinging to the old. That might be true of other, tougher, luckier people. Barbara wasn't other people ...

Meanwhile, there was this afternoon, these few happy moments to be plucked out of the wilderness, while the shadows stayed—no matter how precariously—in the background.

Dusk was falling when they left the park for Val's apartment and supper. (He and Annabelle cooked it: ham and eggs and toast. It was a great success.) Later, while Val slicked up the dishes, Barbara got Annabelle ready for bed and read her to sleep. Barbara's idea: it touched his heart to see the yearning in her face, how much it meant to her to put Annabelle to bed one last time. And maybe Hen would be back and willing to keep an eye on Annabelle while he walked Barbara home. Or, if she and Clyde were still out on the town, he could ask Miss LaTour. He listened, with mingled pleasure and pity, to the murmur of Barbara's voice from the bedroom. Like playing house, she had said.

She was smiling tremulously when she came out and eased the door shut behind her. "Fast asleep," she whispered. "Oh Val, it's been such a lovely pink day."

She glided into his arms, and it was like the first time he kissed her, on the steps of that grimy rooming house, when he had felt himself and all the world brushed with magic.

"Barbara. Oh Barbara ..."

Steps on the stairs, a burst of laughter, a voice saying, "Sure he's home, I can see his light," a knock at the door. It was Clyde and Hen, radiating good fellowship. Not to mention a rich aroma of brandy.

"Coffee, anyone?" asked Hen, and from the way Clyde guffawed you'd have thought it was the world-beater of all witticisms. "Come on down. Let's have a kaffee-klatsch at my place."

"Can't leave Annabelle," said Val. "Pipe down, you drunk and disorderlies. She's asleep."

"Ssshhh," hissed Clyde. "You'll wake her up. Okay. Then let's have a kaffee-klatsch at your place. We're not fussy."

So in they came. "We're not really drunk and disorderly," Hen said to Val in an undertone. "Just a little mellow. Don't be such a crosspatch."

"Who, me? Why, I'm the jolliest fellow in town. Except, of course, for Clyde. How come you're home so early? I supposed you'd be out dancing till dawn."

"Oh, not tonight. We're going dancing tomorrow night." She switched across to the kitchen, where Clyde, who had proclaimed himself superintendent in charge of everything, was assembling the coffee pot. What was it that made her look so different tonight? High heels, spangly earrings, a black dress that showed off that posterior of hers to a fare-thee-well—could mere clothes work such a change? She seemed hardly at all like the Hen Val knew. It threw him off balance, somehow.

"So what's the good word?" asked Clyde, when the coffee was done and Hen had served it. His chair let out a creak of dismay as he relaxed. "I suppose you know Doris is doing okay and they're going to spring her tomorrow?"

"Yes," said Val. "I went up to see her this afternoon." They went on from there, chatting in an offhand way about Doris' recovery, being careful never to dip an inch below the surface. The three of them, that is; Barbara didn't say a word until Val—in all innocence—set off his conversational bombshell. "Just out of curiosity I'd like to know where she got hold of the stuff," he said. "Though I suppose, with her contacts, it wouldn't be hard to come by enough morphine to—"

"Morphine! It was morphine?" gasped Barbara, and he felt her stiffen and shudder beside him.

The word had a galvanizing effect on Clyde, too. He jerked out of his comfortable slump and fixed Val with an accusing eye. "Who told you it was morphine? Did Mother—"

"No, she didn't. It was Dr. Fanning. I ran into him in the hall. Who told you and Maudie? And where did you get the idea you had to be so hush-hush about it?" They had been, Val realized. Very hush-hush. Neither

Clyde nor Maudie had mentioned morphine when they dropped in last night, though they must have known it then, and though they had had plenty of opportunity.

"Who's being hush-hush? I mean, why bring up a lot of stuff that doesn't make any difference, anyway? I suppose Dr. Bigmouth Fanning unloaded everything else he happened to think of, too …"

Val stopped short, on the verge of a denial. He remembered the odd little interchange between Maudie and Dr. Fanning: "her own worst enemy," they had said, and had made it sound heavy with significance. And now here was Clyde, in an obvious dither … "We talked a while, yes," he said cautiously.

"Yeah. I can see you must have." Clyde took a gulp of coffee. But his eyes didn't swerve from Val's face. "Well, it's all a lot of bull! She didn't even know what she was saying. It was just a screwy story she made up. Why do you think they're sending her to a psychiatrist? Because she imagines things that aren't so, that's why!"

"I'm not so sure," said Val. (And a truer word was never spoken. At this point he was flying completely blind.)

"You're not so sure. If that's the way you feel about it, if you really believe she's got an enemy that tried to kill her, then why don't you go to the police?"

It knocked the wind out of Val. Out of Hen, too; her mouth was literally hanging open. Barbara made a sound like paper tearing. She sprang up wildly, her clenched fists raised halfway toward her face. "So that's it! Doris thinks somebody tried to kill her, it wasn't attempted suicide, it was—"

"It was not! I keep telling you, she imagined it. Please, Barbara honey, please don't go to pieces like this." Clyde was on his feet, too, trying to soothe her. But she pulled away from him.

"How do you know? How does anybody know? I've had a feeling all along, and now morphine … That proves it, Clyde! Morphine proves it! Because there was morphine in the house, Maudie had those pills, ever since your father—" She rushed on, heedless of Clyde's sputtered protest. "She did, and you know it, you were there the night Maudie mentioned them and Doris scolded her so, for not getting rid of them. Monroe too. He was there too."

"Barbara. She got rid of them. Long ago." But it seemed to Val that there was a hollow ring to Clyde's voice.

And Barbara had turned, now, to him; she was clutching frantically at his arm. "Val, Val! You mustn't send Annabelle back there! There's something terrible going on in that place! Don't you see it? I don't know what it is, but it's something terrible, and you mustn't let her go back there. You mustn't!"

"She's hysterical," said Clyde, and of course she was. Half-hysterical, at least. But mightn't she also be half-right? Val tried to stop the whirling in his head. Whatever was going on in Doris' household—attempted murder, attempted suicide—either way, it wasn't good. At best, it left Annabelle with an unstable mother who, to quote Clyde, imagined things that weren't so. Such as enemies bent on trying to kill her. Yes, and who then took it all back and called herself her own worst enemy. It didn't leave Annabelle alone with this poor, distracted mother. There was Maudie. But he wasn't sure he trusted even Maudie anymore. As for Monroe ...

"Promise me, Val," Barbara was imploring him. "Promise not to send her back. Not tomorrow, anyway. Not till you've had time to find out for yourself."

Tomorrow would give him time. Time for a showdown of some kind with Doris and Monroe and Maudie. And while he was at it, with Clyde, who had done several pretty peculiar things lately too. Time—why not?—for another talk with Dr. Fanning, who hadn't unloaded everything Clyde thought he had.

"All right." He drew Barbara down beside him and patted her tense, trembling shoulder. "I'll keep her down here another day or two. Please, Barbara, don't cry anymore. I'll look out for Annabelle. You know that. I promise not to send her home yet."

"Suit yourself. It's nothing to me. A lot of bushwah over nothing." Clyde shrugged and turned away.

But Hen saw it Val's way. He caught the barely perceptible dip of her head and felt a keen thrust of relief and assurance. If it seemed right to Hen, then that was good enough for him.

TWENTY FIVE

Oh oh, Annabelle on the warpath, thought Hen when she started out of her apartment door Monday morning, ready for work. She had been vaguely aware of a commotion above her while she was having breakfast coffee. Out here in the hall the sounds of woe were unmistakable—Annabelle's voice raised in bitter lamentation.

Hen paused, with her key in the lock. It wasn't her child or her problem. It was all Val's. Let him fend for himself. Or, if he needed the feminine touch, let him call on Barbara. So there.

Having argued the matter out thus sensibly, she went upstairs and tapped on Val's door. "Tantrum?" she inquired brightly when he appeared, wearing a pathetic, shrunken bathrobe and a harried expression.

"Oh Lord, what am I going to do with her?" he said, and drew Hen in as if she were the answer to his prayers.

Like him, Annabelle was only half-dressed. She had on a little round-necked slip, and she huddled, scarlet-faced and bellowing, in the corner of the easy chair. From the fragmentary phrases that roiled up like wreckage in the flood of her tears, Hen gathered that she wouldn't go to school, she wouldn't go to Aunt Barbara's, she wanted to go *home*: Not tomorrow, not the day after. Today. "You *promised*," she wailed at Val. Betrayal, heaped on all her other grief.

"But Annabelladonna … Look. I told you what Mommy said when I called her. She said it's better to wait. She's been sick, she's going to be tired tonight. This way it's going to be lots more fun for both of you." And at last, in desperation, "All right. Do you want to talk to her on the phone yourself? Only you've got to stop crying first, or you'll only make her feel bad too."

He was taking quite a chance, Hen thought, counting on Doris to back him up. Could he have told her his real reason for wanting to postpone Annabelle's homecoming? Hen whispered the question at him while Annabelle—calmed down except for an occasional hiccoughing sob—talked on the phone. "No," he whispered back, "but she's probably figured it out for herself. She took it all right. No argument. Said it might be better all around. And when I told her I wanted to talk to her again, that was all right too. She seemed—I don't know—kind of subdued. Not like herself."

Whatever her state of mind (and Hen didn't like to think of how troubled it must be) she had apparently preserved her firm motherly hand. Annabelle was doing more listening than talking. Doris even drew a shaky little laugh out of her at one point, and when she hung up she was clearly resigned to her fate. By no means the happiest child in town, but no longer the unmanageable rebel of half an hour ago.

"So now we get you dressed and ready for school. You're already 'way late," said Val—and here was where he met fresh resistance. With a difference: Annabelle, disillusioned by her venture at open mutiny, trembled her lip and looked forlorn beyond words. "Do I have to?" she quavered. (How early they learn, thought Hen; and what a pushover Val was.)

"I suppose I could leave you with Aunt Barbara. If I don't get into the office today I'm going to be out of a job— Now what?" he added, for the lip-trembling was still going on, full tilt. "What's wrong with Aunt Barbara?"

Annabelle wriggled. "She always wants to hug me," she said, and Val lapsed into helpless silence.

"That leaves you know who," said Hen. She made a face at Annabelle and laughed. "I guarantee not to hug you. If I get fired remember, you're going to have to support me. I'll call them up and tell them my cold's much worse. Come on, help me cook your breakfast, and we'll dream up something divine to do this afternoon. How about it?"

"All right," said Annabelle cautiously. But she gave a little bounce.

She had all her bounce back by mid-morning; bubbling away as if she had known Hen forever, her broken heart a thing of the remote past. Val, trailing a wake of half-hearted protests and whole-hearted thanks, had rushed off to work. Breakfast was over, and they had laid their plans for the day. They would clean house for Val (if an apartment ever needed it, his did; and Annabelle was enchanted with housekeeping) and after that they would go uptown for a festive lunch and the movies. Divine? Certainly, in Annabelle's dictionary. Well, and in Hen's; she was finding life with Annabelle highly entertaining.

She left her little charge blissfully "cleaning" the kitchen sink while she went downstairs after her vacuum cleaner. It took a little longer than she planned: she decided to dig out a dust cloth and some furniture polish while she was at it, because Val's cleaning equipment consisted of a broom and an ancient carpet sweeper. Period. And then the phone rang. One of the girls at the office, who felt like a dog calling Hen when she was home sick (what a piece of luck that she had chosen this particular moment to call!) but she simply couldn't find the Lake Stations file, Hen's boss was clamoring for it, and could Hen possibly tell her ...

Even so, it couldn't have been much more than ten minutes before she was back, with her load, at Val's door. She hadn't bothered to lock it; a shove of her shoulder and she was inside. And not much more than ten minutes was too much. Because Annabelle was gone.

At first Hen couldn't believe it. Annabelle must be playing a joke on her, hiding from her. There was a limited number of hiding places, and she covered them in short order, calling Annabelle's name—half-laughingly at first, then impatiently, at last with something like panic. No answer. No sound at all, except for the drip of soapsuds from the sponge Annabelle had left on the edge of the sink. And the thump of Hen's own heart. Her eyes skimmed the room, searching for some sign. There was one: Annabelle's plaid coat and hood were gone from the back of the chair. It sent Hen rushing to the window. She flung it open and leaned out, peering up and down the street.

Two things happened. The doorbell pealed, and simultaneously Hen caught sight of a little girl in a plaid coat trotting along hand in hand with a largish man. They were just emerging from the church yard down the block and were headed for a car—yes, with an Ohio license—parked across the street. (Only what in the world could Clyde and Annabelle have been doing in the church yard?)

The doorbell pealed again, and Hen ran to push the buzzer, in a fluster of puzzled relief. At least Annabelle was safe. But why had Clyde whisked her off like that, without leaving so much as a note? Was it his idea of a joke, to scare the wits out of Hen? It might be, and it would have been no particular problem for him to get in downstairs. Annabelle could reach the buzzer. Or the downstairs door might not have been locked; as often as not it wasn't. Still, what a weird thing to do, even for Clyde ...

"Val?" Hen recognized the timid voice, Barbara's, and felt a bubble of mischief rising in her as she opened the door. Here was something for Barbara to brood about—Hen busying herself with domestic chores in Val's apartment; Hen, not Barbara, left in charge of Annabelle. Not that it was getting Hen anywhere, but Barbara didn't need to know that. Let her brood about it.

She looked a bit taken aback, all right; and her pure madonna-face flushed slightly as she said, "But I'd have been so delighted to stay with Annabelle ... Where is she?"

The bubble of mischief went suddenly flat, while Hen did some quick deciding. No. She wasn't under any obligation to admit to Barbara that Annabelle had been spirited away while her back was turned. "Clyde picked her up a couple of minutes ago. He had some surprise planned for her, I don't know just what." (Surprise was right. And not for Annabelle. But surely he would phone. Any minute now. Because for all he knew Hen might be calling out the entire police force.)

"Clyde?" said Barbara. "That's odd. He didn't mention anything about it when he called me, a little while ago. I guess it's all right, only— Oh Hen, you don't suppose he's taken her up there, do you? To Doris'?" Her voice grew hushed and breathy; it was as if she spoke of a chamber of horrors.

"Of course not. Why would Clyde do that?" But Hen had to force her air of easy assurance. "Stop being such an alarmist, Barbara. You sound as if Annabelle had been kidnaped."

"I'm sorry. I just— They're a very close family, you know. Clyde and Doris. Maudie, too. They'd do anything for each other."

"Maybe. But I don't think for one minute that Doris has put Clyde up to— Excuse me, there's the phone."

She wasted no time getting to it, and the sound of Clyde's voice swamped her with relief, draining the strength out of her legs. "Don't worry, Hen. Annabelle's with me."

"I know," she began. "I saw you—"

"Okay." He seemed in a hurry, and abstracted. There were none of the prankster's guffaws that she had expected. Whatever Clyde was up to, it was no joke. "That can wait. I'll explain all that later. Listen, Hen, I don't know how to— Listen."

"I'm listening," she said coldly. "Not that it's done me any good so far. You're not by any chance taking Annabelle up to Doris', are you?"

"Where? Hell, no. Where'd you get that idea? From Barbara?"

"Well. It crossed my mind too."

"You ought to know better. I'm not built for skullduggery." His laugh rang, comfortingly, with some of its normal heartiness. "Annabelle's safe as houses with me, and you know it. I just want to— What's wrong with me giving the kid a little outing? The thing is, Hen, I want you to get ahold of Val for me. Yeah. He's the guy I've got to see. I haven't got his office number. Will you call him for me? Tell him to meet me later this afternoon. Say four thirty. That'll give me time."

Time for what? Hen didn't bother to ask; no doubt that was another explanation that could wait. "All right. I'll tell Val to meet you at four thirty. Where?"

"Yeah. Where ... I've got it. You know that place on Fifth Avenue where they've got the typewriter chained outside, on the street? So people can try it out? That's where. Tell him be sure to be there. Okay?"

"Okay. The chained typewriter place. Four thirty. I'll tell him."

"Thanks a lot. We'll be there, Annabelle and me. Thanks a lot, and Hen, take care ..." His voice faded.

"Have a good time," she said inanely, to the dead wire. After a minute she hung up. The whole thing was so peculiar, and she hadn't felt free to give Clyde a piece of her mind, with Barbara sitting here. The minute she left (and it couldn't be too soon to suit Hen) she would call Val and see what he made of it. Because Annabelle had been left in her charge; it was her negligence that had made this mysterious outing of Clyde's possible. She had a sudden, vivid mental image of Annabelle— the bright little face, the cinnamon-brown bangs—and the clutch at her heart got worse, an actual, physical pain.

"I'm afraid I'll have to ask you to excuse me," she told Barbara. "I just came up to get my vacuum cleaner, Val borrowed it, and I've got this luncheon date uptown, and—uh—"

Barbara was already on her feet. "I must go, anyway. I'm on my way to the grocery. When I got this far I thought I'd ring Val's bell and see if Annabelle—if everything was all right. And I'm sure it is, I'm sure you're right." Her shy, lovely smile blossomed. "You see? I've stopped being an alarmist. I know I am, sometimes. I haven't much common sense when it comes to Annabelle."

Or when it came to anything else, thought Hen as they went down the stairs—Barbara with only a slight limp in her graceful walk, as a memento of the other night's mishap; Hen encumbered with the vacuum cleaner. But then, with a face like Barbara's, who was going to quibble about a trifle like common sense?

Not Val. Hen made short work of her goodbye, dumped her clumsy load inside the door, and rushed headlong for the telephone.

TWENTY SIX

Maudie had a busy morning. She wanted dinner tonight to be special, in honor of Doris' homecoming. Chicken or a roast? Lemon sherbet or the apple pudding that had been Doris' favorite since childhood? It might be a little on the rich side ... Monroe was absolutely no help. Monosyllables. That was all she got out of him during breakfast, and a glum goodbye when he left for the office. She was glad to see him go; the man had missed his calling, with his disposition, he should have been an undertaker.

What with all the decisions she had to make, the marketing was going to take her longer than usual. And then the interruptions!

First of all, Clyde. He showed up before she even got to the marketing, and while he didn't look as much like a fugitive from a funeral as Monroe, he wasn't his usual cheerful self, either. Far from it. His face, normally so ruddy and good-humored, looked drawn, downright pale; and several times he all but snapped at her. She'd have been really hurt if she hadn't realized that of course it must be a hangover.

No, he didn't have time for a cup of coffee with her. And no, nothing was the matter, he wasn't coming down with a cold, he felt great great great. What he was after was—well, those letters that Monroe had gotten about Doris. Those poison pen letters. Did Maudie know where they were?

"Why, mercy, Clyde, I haven't thought a thing about them. Let me see ... Oh dear, there's the telephone. Now who can that be?"

It was Doris, with the news that they had decided it would be better for all concerned if Annabelle stayed with Val for another day or two. A disappointment, yes, but she had just talked to Annabelle on the phone and managed to get her straightened out. Doris sounded tired, but in answer to Maudie's anxious questions she said (like Clyde) that she was great, everything was fine, she'd see Maudie later.

"She just talked to Annabelle on the phone?" said Clyde, who had been standing over her, impatiently jingling the change in his pockets. "Didn't the kid go to school today?"

"Why, she didn't say. But I guess not. It's 'way past school time." Maudie was beginning to feel flustered and pecked at. "Most likely Barbara's keeping her for the day. I declare, Clyde, if you don't stop fidgeting! Now let me think a minute about those letters ... Why yes, I expect they're in Doris' briefcase. That's where they were the last I saw of them, she took them with her on that trip to Boston."

"Philadelphia," said Clyde. "So where's her briefcase? Hurry up, Mud. I haven't got all day."

Thank goodness she remembered where the briefcase was, on the book case, and thank goodness the letters were still in it; Clyde, after one quick look at them, shoved them in his coat pocket and headed for the door.

"Now you just wait a minute, Clyde! You just tell me what you're up to with those letters!"

"No time now, Mud. It's just an idea I've got. I'll tell you later. Look, try to keep your mouth shut about this. Will you?" A pat on her cheek; a wink that made him look, momentarily, like himself; and he was gone.

"Well!" said Maudie aloud, and all through her marketing she kept coming back to it, trying to puzzle out what Clyde could possibly want with the letters that awful man had written to Monroe. (Letters. Would she ever again be able to hear or say the word without feeling a cold prickle along her spine? And that other word too. Morphine. It was every bit as bad. Even though she was safe now, quite safe, on both counts.)

She was nicely started on the lemon sherbet when the phone rang again. It was Barbara this time, suggesting—of all things—that Maudie meet her for lunch. "Please, Maudie. I'd so love to see you. We haven't had one of our Schrafft lunches for the longest time."

"I shouldn't really," began Maudie. She was torn in at least three different directions. There was her loyalty to Doris, who was never going to forgive Barbara for what she had told last Thursday night. (Only Barbara hadn't wanted to tell; Doris herself had pried it out of her. Clyde didn't blame Barbara for it, and deep down inside Maudie didn't either.) And there was the old habit of pity for Barbara, who so seldom found the courage to make the smallest social advance. It wasn't like refusing anybody else. Now of all times, it would be a crushing blow to Barbara, conclusive evidence that she had lost Maudie along with Doris. There was also the fun—always hard for Maudie to resist—of an impromptu little fling. Oh dear, she thought, and cocked an eye at the kitchen clock. Quarter past eleven. "I've got this lemon sherbet started. I could stick it in the refrigerator, though, finish it when I get back. Well, mercy, why not ? Like I always say, all work and no play."

They arranged to meet between twelve and a quarter past, and Barbara's voice almost broke as she said, "Oh, thank you, Maudie. Oh, I'm so glad!"

So it was the strangest thing, Barbara's not showing up. Maudie was hardly late at all, and she didn't see how she could be mistaken about the time or place, though, on second thought, she had just taken it for granted that Barbara meant the Schrafft's where they had met on a few other occasions ...

She waited for a table that would give her a good view of the entrance, and then she waited some more, dawdling over a Daiquiri. (There was something so forlorn about having a drink all by yourself. But then surely Barbara would be coming in the door, any minute now.) She couldn't even try to phone because she didn't have the number, which was unlisted, with her. Not that it would have done any good, anyway. Oh dear, Barbara must be waiting, hurt and bewildered, at some other Schrafft's—which one Maudie had no idea. Finally, when the Daiquiri gave out, she ordered her lunch and ate it in solitude, still keeping an eye on the door, still hoping, just a little. Even the chocolate mocha cream pie didn't cheer her up.

Well, no help for it. All she could do was call Barbara, the minute she got home. But first, she decided, she would stop in at the hospital for a quick, final visit with Doris. Monroe was to pick her up at five thirty and bring her home, but in the meantime Doris' last few hours might be hanging heavy on her hands. Don't mention Barbara, Maudie kept cautioning herself on the way uptown; no use pressing on what was sure to be a sore point with Doris. Don't mention Clyde, either; "try to keep your mouth shut," he had said.

It was quite a strain. And poor Doris, though she was out of bed, sitting in the chair beside the window, seemed so strange and listless, with very little to say, and with her mind obviously way off somewhere, out of reach of Maudie's chit-chat. Her apathy lifted only a couple of times, and then Maudie wished it hadn't, because behind the apathy she caught a glimpse of something more frightening.

Once Doris said, "Val wants to come up tonight. He wants to talk to Monroe and me. He says there are some things we ought to—to settle." And suddenly she grabbed Maudie's hands. She didn't look like Doris at all; she looked like Annabelle herself, scared by a nightmare. "Oh Mud, they're not going to take Annabelle away from me, are they? Is that what they want to do?"

"Why, Doris honey, what an idea ..." But Maudie's throat tightened. She didn't try to go on, she just hung on to Doris for all she was worth.

It happened again, when she was about to leave. The sudden grab for her hands. The scared child look. "Mud, you'll be here tonight? Monroe isn't coming for me alone? You'll come with him?"

"Of course, if you want me to," said Maudie, who had planned nothing of the kind. "Now why don't you have a nice little nap, and before you know it you'll be home again, safe and sound." But she had the queerest feeling, all the way home. Try as she would, she couldn't keep it from springing up: the ugly, jack-in-the-box question. Is she afraid of Monroe? Is she afraid to come home?

When she opened the apartment door there was a small bang and a jar. Oh dear, she must have forgotten and left the door to the hall closet open again; the two doors were close enough together to produce this miniature collision. And she had tried so hard to train herself about the closet door, because it was one of the things that exasperated Doris most. Maudie would have sworn she had closed it when she left for lunch. But she couldn't have, and somehow it seemed like the last straw, proof of her own mental incompetence. Silly old woman. (Letters. Morphine.) Silly, stupid old woman who got mixed up about which Schrafft's and couldn't remember to close doors and didn't know how to help her own daughter. The one time in years and years when Doris—so capable, so self-sufficient—had turned to her, and Maudie had failed her, hadn't done one single thing for her but hold her hands tight.

I declare, thought Maudie, I'd just sit down and have a good cry if it wasn't for that lemon sherbet … Yes, and the living room would certainly have to be straightened up before Doris got home. It looked all out of order—chairs, even the sofa, a little bit askew. Like hell had struck with a meat axe, as Clyde would say. A funny expression; Maudie smiled dimly.

She might as well. There wasn't time for a good cry.

TWENTY SEVEN

Without lifting his head from the layout he was working on, Val reached for the buzzing phone, deftly avoiding the container of coffee and half-eaten sandwich at his elbow. His ordered-in lunch, still cooling its heels, though it must be nearly four by now. With Annabelle's tantrum as a starter, it had turned into one of those days for sure. His head ached, not only from the pressure of the work he should have done on Friday and hadn't, but from the tension of his other, private worries. He couldn't control them; they cropped up all over the place. Hen's call this morning hadn't helped, though he had assured her that of course Annabelle was safe with Clyde, of course he wasn't blaming Hen for anything ... If Clyde were up to any kind of dirty work he simply wouldn't have behaved as he had: calling Hen to tell her Annabelle was with him, making a date to meet Val in broad daylight in a public place.

"Hello," he said into the phone. Silence. As if he didn't have enough to contend with. Comedians who called him up and then wouldn't talk. "Yes? Who is it?" he said crossly.

The voice, when it came, brought his head up with a jerk. So far-away, so wispy, and yet he recognized it instantly as Barbara's. "Val. Oh Val, I'm so frightened. I don't know what to do. What shall I do? They— threatened me."

"Threatened you? Who did?"

He heard her breath catch. "I—I—" She began to sob.

"Barbara. Stop it." He couldn't suppress a surge of irritation at her helpless hysteria. "Where are you? Are you at home?"

"Oh, no. I couldn't stay there because they might—it might happen again." The sharpness of his tone had apparently had an effect; she was doing her best to swallow her sobs. "I'm in Grand Central. Oh Val, I'm so afraid ..."

"Listen, Barbara. You know where my office is, don't you? Come over here—it's only a block away—and I'll meet you downstairs in the lobby in ten minutes." He would have to leave soon, anyway, for his appointment with Clyde. He might as well take a few extra minutes. A threat, he thought. Real or imaginary? It didn't matter: Barbara's fear, at least, was real, and he could not leave her alone with it.

He saw her the moment he stepped out into the lobby; she was huddled in a corner near the street door, her face turned imploringly toward the bank of elevators. She had never looked lovelier, or more forsaken. With a little cry she ran toward him. He could feel her trembling in his arms.

"Now tell me what happened," he said. "What scared you?" He kept his arm around her as they went out onto the street.

A phone call, she said; someone had called her up and told her to keep her mouth shut. She didn't know who. Just a voice whispering, "Keep your mouth shut. You know what I mean."

"I was so happy, Val, Maudie and I were going to have lunch together, and then I—then it happened, and I didn't know what to do. I just ran out of the house, and I don't know where I went. I walked and walked, and finally I thought maybe if I called you, I couldn't think of anybody else—"

No one to turn to but Val, and he had seldom felt more inadequate.

"Was it a man or a woman? Could you tell from the voice?"

"It was just a whisper." She hesitated for a moment. "A man, I think. I'm sure, I'm almost sure—a man."

Not Doris, then. Monroe? Clyde? "Keep your mouth shut about what?" asked Val. "What do you know that they don't want you to tell?"

The tears welled up in her eyes. "Doris made me tell about John Custer, that day he came up to the apartment when I was with Annabelle."

"But why threaten you about that now? It's done, we all heard you, we already know about it. Besides, it wasn't Doris, you're almost sure it was a man."

"There's something else, Val." She gave a hunted little glance behind her. "The other night I said—about the morphine—"

"My God, Barbara!" They had been walking slowly toward Fifth Avenue. Val stopped now, staring at her in growing alarm. "If that's it, then it means that it was attempted murder, instead of attempted suicide. An enemy, like Doris said. Only she took it all back, afterwards, said she was her own worst enemy ... Why would she do that?" The answer was right in front of him: Barbara's terror-stricken face. Somebody could have scared Doris into silence, just as somebody was now scaring Barbara. "If Doris thinks it's Monroe— Yes. She must be afraid it's Monroe. Not sure. Because if she was sure she wouldn't keep still, no matter what. But from the very beginning she's been scared that it was Monroe who killed John Custer. He could have, you know he left the Russells' dinner party early, by himself. He had a reason. Those poison pen letters John had been writing about Doris. And then jealousy."

Barbara's lips quivered. "Val. It doesn't have to be Monroe. Clyde might have—"

"Clyde? Why, he wasn't even in town!"

"We don't know he wasn't. It's just his word."

"But they were friends, Barbara! Why would Clyde—"

"The same reason as Monroe. Jealousy. Oh, you don't know, Val! I've never told you, I've never told anybody—" Her eyes grew wide, and haunted. "Everybody thinks he's such a nice, normal, average guy—and he is, only not about me. He never was about me. Why do you think I never made any friends? I didn't dare to, he couldn't stand it if I so much as smiled at the grocery clerk. Even after we got the divorce— He kept calling me up, begging me to come back to him, accusing me of having affairs with everybody we'd ever known."

"Everybody you'd ever known. Did you know John Custer, Barbara? I mean, before he came up to Doris' that day?"

"Of course I didn't know him! I barely met him once, years ago, one day when I went into Clyde's office. John Custer was there, and he made the mistake of saying I had pretty eyes. That was all Clyde needed. He convinced himself that John Custer and I were seeing each other secretly, writing to each other, God knows what. He's been convinced of it ever since. He isn't *sane*, Val! He drives himself crazy with jealousy!"

"But I still don't understand," stammered Val. "John Custer, maybe. I suppose Clyde could sneak into town and kill him. But somebody tried to kill Doris, too. Monroe might have, out of jealousy or revenge, the same way he might have killed John Custer. But why would Clyde? Unless she had somehow found out—"

"She might have. That trip of hers to Philadelphia. She might have found out something then. And he knew about the morphine, I know that."

"Monroe probably knew about it, too. It just seems so fantastic to think of Clyde ..."

"You don't believe me!" cried Barbara, with such wild hopelessness that Val was shocked. "But you'll see! He's going to tell you all kinds of lies about John Custer. You don't believe me now, but you'll see!"

"Sh, darling. I didn't say I didn't believe you. I just said it seems fantastic, and it does. Right now the thing for me to do is meet Clyde and find out, if I can, what's on his mind. I can't do anything else, as long as he's got Annabelle."

"Oh Val, whatever you do, get Annabelle away from him! Don't let him keep her! Don't let Monroe take her! Whoever it is—Clyde or Monroe—they're planning to use Annabelle."

"Use her?" As a shield, perhaps, or as a weapon to enforce silence. Val felt suddenly cold, all through, to the marrow of his bones. "I've got to get over there."

"You're going to leave me?" whispered Barbara. "I don't know what to—"

But it wouldn't do, to take Barbara with him. And yet how could he leave her, at the mercy of her fears and of whoever was threatening her? "Look, Barbara, we'll grab a cab. You can wait in it while I talk to Clyde. Don't let him see you, keep out of sight, because if he's the one that threatened you it will tip him off. Just wait for me, and as soon as I've got Annabelle safe and sound, I'll be back with you. And after that we're going straight to the police. No matter what Clyde or anybody else has to say. I'm through fooling around. Okay?"

"Yes." It was hardly a word, more like a gasp or a sigh. "Anything, just so they don't take Annabelle ..."

He held her hand tight during the short cab ride. She spoke only once.

"Val," she said. "Val, I want to kiss you." And she really did want to; the difference between this kiss and all the others was the difference between a blaze of firelight and a paper match. She smiled fleetingly. Then, as the cab neared Clyde's meeting place—the typewriter chained to its graceful pedestal in front of the tall glass store front—she ducked down out of sight.

"Wait for me," Val told the cab driver as he got out. "I'll be back." That was for Barbara. A promise, a pledge. He let go of her hand and stepped out onto the street.

He saw only Clyde at first. He was inside the store (trust Clyde to improve each spare moment of waiting; he and the salesman he was talking to were no doubt exchanging pointers on merchandising, maybe even selling each other.) Only Clyde, not Annabelle, and again Val's bones turned cold. But the next minute she came racing out of the store to meet him. Rosy and cheerful as a robin. Uncle Clyde had taken her to the zoo, they had seen the monkeys, they had eaten hot dogs for lunch ...

And no one could have looked less sinister than Clyde, advancing with his hand outstretched, his hat pushed to the back of his head, topcoat open so that the full glory of his tie burst on the eye. "There you are, Val. So Hen got my message to you all right." But as he turned to the typewriter on its green-streaked pedestal, Val sensed a difference in him. Was it in his eyes? They looked darker, not so shallow or candid a blue. Or was it his manner? He seemed in the grip of an embarrassment so immense that it drove him to pecking nervously at the typewriter, complete with its sheet of paper, on which some uninspired passerby had typed over and over, "This is the day and this is the hour."

"Hey, this is some deal, isn't it?" he said. "Having this machine right out on the street where anybody can use it. Typewriters. That's my line too, you know. Typewriters and office machines. I was just saying to the guy inside, it's a damn smart idea ..." His eyes met Val's, and he fell into helpless silence.

"Okay," said Val. "What's this all about? You didn't get me over here just to tell me what a smart idea it is, having a typewriter out on the street."

"No. I— Well, no. Monroe ought to be here too. Any minute now. I want him to be in on this too."

"Oh, you do. Why? Quit stalling, Clyde, you can brief Monroe when he gets here. Meantime, you can brief me."

At last Clyde blurted it out: "I've found out about those poison pen letters to Monroe. John Custer told me. I got a letter from him this morning—"

"*What?* Listen, Clyde, the guy's been dead for a week!"

"I know it. My mail hasn't caught up with me for longer than that. Well, it did this morning. He wrote to me the day he was killed. I've got his letter right here, and I've got the poison pen ones to Monroe, and John's right, they were written on this machine."

"You mean this machine right here?" Val blinked down at the streamlined gray portable.

"Sure. Pretty slick. Pretty hard to trace. What I mean, a typewriter that's accessible to everybody in town ... But John was right. Take a look." He drew from his pocket a handful of letters, unfolded one and spread it out on top of the typewriter. "You don't have to be an expert to see it's the same. Look at the m's. Out of line. And the question mark slips, practically every time. Hell, what else can you expect? You take a machine like this, out on the street, everybody using it, it's hard on a machine, it's bound to—"

"Shut up," said Val. "Let me think." Of course John Custer would be right: who knew better than he what machine he had used for those letters to Monroe? But why had he told Clyde about it? Had he really told Clyde? Or was this part of what Barbara meant when she had said, "You'll see. He's going to tell you all kinds of lies about John Custer?"

He fastened his eyes on Clyde's beefy hand, spread out on the letter, and said, "I suppose you'll be telling me next that—that Barbara knew John Custer."

The hand clenched abruptly. Straightened out again, with an effect of cautious deliberation; Val thought of a lobster feeling its way toward some kind of safety. "So you already know," said Clyde. And then he went on, exactly as Barbara had foretold. "Of course she knew him. The guy was in love with her."

TWENTY EIGHT

Any minute now Hen expected to be picked up for loitering. She had been at it for almost half an hour, since a little past four. Loitering. Walking up and down this particular block on Fifth Avenue. Window-shopping. Especially at Brentano's, which was next door to the typewriter on the pedestal, and which provided a convenient niche for watching.

Her original intention had been simple and straightforward—to make sure that Clyde showed up for his mysterious appointment with Val, and that Annabelle, intact, showed up with him. Val had reassured her over the telephone. No cause for worry. But Hen found it a physical impossibility to sit at home with folded hands, not knowing what was going on. (And she could wither on the vine before anybody bothered to tell her. She knew that from past experience.)

So here she was, and here she continued to be, though her original intention had long since been carried out. Clyde and Annabelle had arrived early. Right on Hen's heels, in fact. From the shelter of Brentano's she had watched them, with so much relief that it was like pain. For Annabelle was capering along, hale and hearty, and Clyde seemed to have nothing more villainous on his mind than an inspection—quite a thorough one, Hen noticed—of the chained typewriter. She didn't know why she had stayed out of sight, instead of leaping forth with her questions about where and why. Hurt feelings, perhaps: Clyde hadn't invited her, any more than he had said one word about the dancing date they were supposed to have tonight. Or any more than Val had invited her.

She emerged from her hiding place enough to watch Clyde abandon the typewriter at last and enter the glass-fronted store, Annabelle holding onto his hand. Inside, he was soon deep in conversation with one of the salesmen. It looked to Hen like a very earnest, purposeful conversation, instead of what it undoubtedly was—the casual shop talk of two men in the same line. But salesmen were like that. Earnest. Purposeful.

On her next turn around the block she spotted Clyde's car parked in front of a stationery store on the downtown side street. One of his customers, no doubt; a delivery sign was stuck in the car window, in deference to the parking regulations. Then she was back at good old Brentano's, watching for Val. He would walk, she decided; his office was only a few blocks away. So she very nearly missed him when he fooled her by pulling up in the cab. He kept it waiting, oddly enough ... It was feminine instinct that gave her the answer. She didn't actually see Barbara. She just knew that Barbara was there, waiting in the cab.

Annabelle dashed out and was swept up in Val's arms. And here came Clyde; Hen craned her neck as far as she dared out of the doorway, trying to see what next. What next, struck her as an anti-climax, because all they did was go into a huddle over that dratted typewriter. She couldn't, of course, hear a word they were saying; Clyde seemed to have some papers in his hand, Val's head was bent over them too, how fine-grained he looked, beside Clyde's solid bulk ...

Annabelle, who had been hopping around the pedestal and the two men hunched over it, took a look up the street and let out a yip. "Daddy! Here comes Daddy!"

He did, indeed. Monroe, impeccable in homburg and well-tailored topcoat, approached from the uptown end of the block. It couldn't be chance; Clyde must have summoned him to the powwow too. He caught sight of Annabelle and waved, and she broke away from the pedestal and started, skipping, up the street to meet him.

Well, thought Hen, the gathering of the clan … And then it all happened very quick and frantic: the cab door flew open, a blurred streak darted out, snatched Annabelle's hand, and whipped on past Monroe to the uptown corner and into a cab, which turned smoothly into the stream of traffic down Fifth.

Hen stood frozen in her tracks, while Clyde yelled something and took off for the downtown end of the block, with Val a close second, and while Monroe, at his end of the street, veered off the sidewalk and, after an instant's hesitation, headed for the cab that had been left waiting, its door still open, its driver peering out in astonishment. Then Hen unfroze and began running as she hadn't run since childhood, panting after Clyde and Val. Clyde's car, of course. That was their goal, and Hen made it by a hair. They were both inside it and Clyde had the motor going when she jerked the door open and slammed in beside Val.

Their faces, blank as doorknobs, turned toward her briefly. Neither of them spoke to her. She couldn't think of anything suitable to say, either, even if she had had the breath to say it.

"Damn," said Clyde, as the light changed to red. "We'll lose them now, sure as shooting. They already had a block's start on us."

But Hen had spotted a familiar deadpan profile in the cab that had shot down Fifth while Clyde was maneuvering his car out of the parking space. "That was Monroe!" she gasped. "Monroe got the cab that was waiting, it's the green one up there, the one that just made the light …"

"Where? You sure? How do we know he hasn't lost them too?" Clyde raced the motor and fumed at the light. "Change, damn you, change."

They leaped forward. So did the green cab ahead of them. So, no doubt, had the other cab; farther ahead (a yellow one? Hen thought so, she was almost sure) that was carrying Annabelle and Barbara to wherever they were going.

She had her breath back by now, and she used it to ask questions. "Where would Barbara take her? It was Barbara, wasn't it? Why did she jump out and grab her like that? What was she doing there in the first place?"

Clyde didn't answer. He was too intent on the green cab, which wove in and out of traffic with reckless skill, to waste an ounce of energy on conversation.

Val's eyes were straining forward too, and he sounded as if he had swallowed his voice. But at least he said something. "She was waiting for me. Somebody scared her out of her wits, threatened her over the phone, and I was going to— She must have lost her head when she saw Monroe coming. She thinks he's after Annabelle, you see—"

"But I don't see. Of course he's after Annabelle. So are we. What else does she expect, snatching Annabelle like that? It doesn't make any sense!"

Clyde must have heard, he produced a kind of snort that might mean anything—or nothing. Val unglued his eyes from the green cab long enough to look at her with a belated flash of curiosity. "What were *you* doing there, Hen?"

"Loitering. I had to see if Annabelle was all right. And then I—" To her consternation, Hen realized that she was on the brink of nervous tears. "I don't know what's going *on!*" she cried, and beat her fists against her knees.

"You will," muttered Clyde. "Soon enough. I only hope to God you're right about Monroe being in that cab."

It was one of the few things she was sure about. The rest of her thoughts careened in a chase as crazy as the one that engaged Clyde's attention. But she felt better: Val had put his hand over hers. His felt cold, and he kept swallowing nervously. He doesn't know much more than I do, she thought, and found it comforting.

"She'd take her to her own place," he said, as they swerved around a corner, west off Fifth. "I can't think of anywhere else."

"Looks like it," said Clyde. They were headed downtown again, still on the trail of the green cab. The streets flicked by in a blur. Twenty-third. Fourteenth. Another turn west. "That's it, all right. Her own place. Unless Monroe's clear off the track."

He wasn't. They could see both cabs now—the yellow one slowing down, in front of Barbara's house a block away, the green one crowding close. Caught again by a red light and the law-abiding motorist ahead of them, the three of them leaned forward and to the right (Hen had rolled her window down) as if pulled by a magnet, concentrating with every nerve on the violent little scene. It was quickly over. Barbara, clutching Annabelle's hand, made a dash for the doorway; even at this distance Hen could sense the panic that possessed her. For Monroe was after her, cruel and purposeful as a bullet. His arm shot out, she struggled to wrench free and then seemed to collapse as he pulled her—still clutching Annabelle—back to the green cab.

"Oh God," whispered Val. "She didn't make it."

Clyde glanced at him, briefly, oddly. But all he said was, "Here we go again." Then he set his jaw and once more gave chase to the green cab.

Dusk was beginning to gather as they whipped back uptown. Here and there lights bloomed, and the streets swarmed with office workers headed for home. Deftly the green cab, with Clyde dogging its heels, threaded its way to Central Park. It turned into the park, already filled with shadows, swooped around curves, skimmed on and on; and Clyde never let go. His jaw remained grimly set. So did Val's; his eyes stared straight ahead, not swerving for an instant from the green cab with its precious cargo. The two people in the world that he loves most, thought Hen. And Monroe. She sat tense and silent, remembering the violent quality of that scene downtown, the ruthlessness of Monroe's arm, reaching out.

"He's taking them up to his place?" Val asked, in a low voice, and Hen knew he was thinking that that was what Barbara had dreaded most—the possibility of Annabelle's being taken "up there."

"Of course. Where else?" said Clyde. He was right; and when he had parked as close as he could get to the big new apartment house he did a queer thing. He put his head down on the steering wheel for a moment, as if he were weeping or praying. Hen wondered if Val had noticed. Probably not; he was stumbling over her in his rush to get out. They had already seen the green cab deposit its passengers—Monroe never relaxing his grip on either Barbara or Annabelle—and glide off about its business.

Then they were all hurrying along the street, into the building, into the elevator, out into the corridor. They found the apartment door unlocked, not even shut. Maudie fluttered toward them; she had her hat in her hand, and her face was puckered up, tearful with bewilderment.

"Clyde," she quavered. "Oh Clyde, it's so awful ... I don't know what's the matter. I thought it was just Monroe, coming to pick me up and go get Doris. But—"

"Where's Barbara? Where's Annabelle?"

"She simply flew past me into the bedroom, she's got Annabelle with her—"

They heard Monroe. His hand beating on the bedroom door. His voice, not loud but furious and insistent: "Barbara. Open the door. Open it or I'll break it down. Barbara. You wouldn't talk, all the way up here. But you're going to talk now. Do you hear me? Answer me, Barbara!"

A whimpering cry from Annabelle. Nothing else.

They broke down the door—Monroe and Clyde and Val. Barbara had flattened herself against the farthest wall and was clasping Annabelle (too scared to struggle) tightly to her. She would not let go until she saw Val. Then she flung her arms wide and cried out, "Val! Don't let them take her! Save her, Val! Help me!"

"Help you," said Monroe, in the same low, furious voice. "Why, you—"

"Don't, Barbara. It's no use." Clyde took a step toward her, stopped when he saw her shrink back. "It's no use," he repeated huskily. "John Custer wrote to me just before he was killed, so it's no use."

Hen blinked. But not Barbara. That luminous, calm gaze of hers, fixed with unwavering trust on Val! He must feel it, even though he was stooping beside Annabelle, soothing her. "I told you he'd lie about John Custer, Val," said Barbara. "I told you they threatened me. Clyde or Monroe. That's why I couldn't stand it when I saw him coming down the street. I knew one or the other of them would bring Annabelle up here, try to use her— Don't let them take her away from you! That's all I care about. Annabelle's the one that matters."

"You're telling the truth there," said Clyde. "For once. For a change. The rest has been lies. Nobody called you up and threatened you. What scared you was me mentioning the chained typewriter place. You realized that I was on to something. I haven't checked on this yet, but I'm willing to bet you were up here some time today, looking for those poison pen letters. Wasn't she, Mud?"

The question sent Maudie into more of a flutter than ever. "Oh no, Clyde, I didn't see her at all today. We had a date for lunch, only she didn't show up, I mean, I missed her and when I came back I ... Oh, my! I didn't forget about the closet door, then! And the living room, all torn up ... She— Somebody was here while I was gone ..."

"You're damn right somebody was." Clyde turned back to Barbara. "But I'd beaten you to it, I already had the letters. And when you saw Val and me at the typewriter place, comparing the typing, you knew the jig was up. No wonder you lost your head and tried to grab Annabelle. It was all you could think of to do. One last desperate—"

"You mean it was Barbara who wrote those letters? It wasn't John Custer?" said Monroe. He took off his homburg. Then he put it back on again.

"Of course it was Barbara. She's hated Doris for years. Ever since Doris had Annabelle and—and our baby died. Ever since then, she's wanted just one thing—to get Annabelle away from Doris. That's why she wrote the letters, to give Doris a black eye, make us all think she wasn't a fit mother. She got the idea from that poison pen article of John's. That's why she's been making this play for Val, because if she could work it right he'd get custody of Annabelle and she could—"

Val made a choked sound.

After a minute Clyde went on: "I didn't catch on to it any more than you did, Val. I guess you could say we were in the same boat. You and me and John. Poor bastard. He caught on to what she was up to, and it didn't make any difference, he was still in love with her, he thought he could cure her by loving her. Here. It's all here in his last letter." He fished it out of his pocket and handed it to Val. Then he gave a cracked laugh. "I told you it was no use, Barbara. John used to follow you, he watched you while you typed those letters. And here's what's funny, he wasn't the only one. That salesman I got to gabbing with this afternoon—he had a yen for you too, he noticed you because you came regularly, he described you down to the last eyelash—"

"I told you, Val," said Barbara, still with that air of calm assurance. "I told you he's insanely jealous."

"I'm sure you did," said Clyde wearily. "Another lie. Just like the one you dreamed up about John and Doris. Oh, you were slick about that one! And you damn near got away with it. We believed you."

"I believed her," said Monroe. "I believed her instead of Doris." He gave his shoulders a little shake and started for the door. "I've got to bring Doris home. I've got to tell her." An expression of dazed understanding crossed his face. "An enemy, she said, and she was afraid it was me. That's why. Oh God, that's why."

No one spoke until he was gone. Then Val handed John Custer's letter back to Clyde. His face was paper-white. "Annabelle," he said, "you go in your play room with Gran. Okay? You wait there for Mommy."

Annabelle's round, frightened eyes made a tour of their faces before she took Maudie's hand and trotted obediently off. Poor Annabelle, thought Hen. Poor Val. And even— Barbara's arms jerked forward convulsively and then flattened again against the wall—yes, even poor Barbara.

"What it says in the letter about Annabelle," Val began.

Clyde nodded. "It took a while, she's a loyal kid, and Barbara had worked hard on her. But I got it out of her this afternoon. She'd already let it slip to Doris that Barbara was with her the afternoon 'Cane' came up here. That's all she told, though. Doris didn't know the right questions to ask her, the way I did, after I read John's letter." He looked at Hen and tried to smile. "I had to nip off with her like I did this morning because I knew Barbara was on her way over there. Mother told me the kid wasn't at school, so I figured Barbara already had her. When I phoned her I found out I'd figured wrong, and then when I found Annabelle by herself—well, it was too good a chance to pass up. I got her out of there in nothing flat and we ducked into the church yard to avoid meeting Barbara. I'd seen her coming down the block, and someway I couldn't take it, meeting her when I knew ..." He let it trail off.

"What was it you got out of Annabelle?" Val asked dully.

"Just what John told me I would, in the letter. He was in a good humor that day, and he took a great notion to the kid. Told her all about how he was in love with Aunt Barbara and he was going to marry her and take her way off somewhere, but Annabelle could come and visit ..."

Hen felt the tears running down her face. She hadn't realized before that she was crying.

"She had to kill him, you see. He didn't just love her, like you and me. He loved her, but he knew her too. All the way through. The only thing he didn't know about her was the morphine pills, how she'd planted them in Doris' medicine bottle. She could have done that any time, you know, she had the run of the house. She pointed it out herself—we all knew Maudie had those pills."

"But Maudie said—" began Hen.

"I know. That she threw them out long ago. But I know Mud. I'll bet you anything you like she didn't throw them out till Dr. Fanning put the fear of the Lord into her. After they'd been used on Doris. It's exactly what Mud would do—go into a tizzy and throw them out when it was too late."

Val rubbed his hand across his eyes. "Barbara and John Custer," he said.

"Yes. When he phoned her that last Saturday and she told him off, he knew he had to do something to stop her, to—like he says in the letter—'go save her from herself.' Besides, he couldn't stand the idea of her marrying you or anybody except himself. He told her if she broke off with him he was going to get hold of you and me and Monroe and tell us exactly what she was up to. He tried to, all right. The date he made with Monroe for Sunday. The note he left in your mail box— I still didn't get it, even when you showed me that, I still thought it must be Doris he was mixed up with. I'm the only one he got through to, and by then it was too late. What did you do, Barbara, follow him down to Val's that Saturday night?"

She did not answer. Her eyes never left Val's face.

"It must have been that way. You didn't know about the note, but it dawned on you that he really meant business, he was really going to stop you unless you stopped him first. You had to do it, and so you did."

At last Barbara spoke to him. Scornfully. "You can't prove a word of this."

And it seemed to Hen that she might very well be right. Clyde, with John Custer's letter to guide him, had established Barbara as a dangerously neurotic woman, as a poison pen writer, as John Custer's ill-starred love—but there was still nothing to connect her with that fatal encounter on the church steps.

"Maybe not," said Clyde. He heaved a great sigh and added, rather absently, "I see you're still wearing your little chain, the one I gave you."

Instantly Barbara's hand leaped to her throat, to the fine gold chain. "Why not? It's mine. I have a right to it."

(It was only later, when she read John Custer's letter for herself, that Hen understood the significance of the chain. "One of the appalling things about love," he had written, "is that it drives you to such embarrassing, love-sick tricks ... Do you remember the gold chain you gave her, years ago? She's very fond of it, used to wear it all the time. The clasp broke, a couple of weeks ago, and I offered to have it mended for her. I immediately saw my chance ... Something of hers! Something that has lain in the warm hollow of her throat! Do you think I will ever part with such a prize? I keep putting her off, telling her the jeweler is slow, he hasn't gotten to it yet, when all the time I have it in my wallet, and intend to keep it there forever ...")

But at the moment Hen did not know. She did not understand the wary look that flashed over that flawless face, or Val's groan: "Oh, Barbara!" or Clyde's lunge across the room as Barbara, sensing—too late—that the chain had betrayed her, tried to tear it from her neck.

"Oh no, you don't," he muttered, holding her with one hand while he snatched the chain from her and thrust it into his pocket. "This is one thing the police are going to see ..."

She screamed. "Val! You believe me! Don't let him! Val! Val!"

"Believe you." He whispered the impossible words. "Barbara, I can't— I have to—"

She wrenched herself free and flew at him, clawing and shrieking, and for the rest of her life Hen remembered how Val looked at that moment. He made no move to ward her off. He swayed a little, bracing himself, and he closed his eyes against the sight of her haunting, demented face.

Clyde soon had her in his grip again, but it was no longer necessary: Barbara's blaze of rage had already spent itself. She neither resisted nor collapsed; she simply withdrew to some inner region so remote that she seemed no longer to hear or see or feel anything at all.

Clyde sat her down in a chair and lifted his haggard face to Val and Hen. "I'll call the police," he said.

"No," said Val. "I have to." He turned toward the living room, but as he brushed past Hen he stopped. His hand reached out and touched her cheek. "Don't cry, Hen," he said. "Dear little Hen. Please don't cry."

THE END

Jean Potts Bibliography
(1910-1999)

Mystery Novels:

Go, Lovely Rose (1954; winner Best First Novel Edgar Award)

Death of a Stray Cat (1955; reprinted in omnibus as Dark Destination, 1955)

The Diehard (1956)

The Man With the Cane (1957)

Lightning Strikes Twice (1958; reprinted in the UK as Blood Will Tell, 1959)

Home Is the Prisoner (1960)

The Evil Wish (1962; finalist Best Novel Edgar Award)

The Only Good Secretary (1965)

The Footsteps on the Stairs (1966)

The Trash Stealer (1968)

The Little Lie (1968)

An Affair of the Heart (1970)

The Troublemaker (1972)

My Brother's Killer (1975)

Mainstream Novel:

Someone to Remember (1943)

Short Stories:

The Lady Afraid (*Woman's Home Companion*, Feb 1942)

The Other Woman (*Collier's*, Aug 24, 1946)

Restless Redhead (*Liberty*, Feb 1948)

The Box of Apples (*McCall's*, March 1949)

A Family Affair (*McCall's*, Nov 1949)

The Bracelet (*McCall's*, Dec 1951)

The Heart Must See (*McCall's*, Apr 1952)

The Engagement Ring (*Thrilling Love*, Oct 1952)

Let's Start All Over Again (*American Magazine*, Apr 1953)

The Girl He Didn't Marry (*Woman's Day*, Jan 1954)

A Long Day's Journey (*Cosmopolitan*, July 1954)

The Ideal Gift (*Family Circle*, Oct 1956)

The Withered Heart (*Ellery Queen's Mystery Magazine*, Feb 1957)

Murderer # 2 (*Alfred Hitchcock's Mystery Magazine*, Jan 1961)

Just Like Jessica (*Redbook*, Feb 1963)

The Only Good Secretary (*Cosmopolitan*, July 1965)

The Inner Voices (*Ellery Queen's Mystery Magazine*, Apr 1966)

In the Absence of Proof (*Ellery Queen's Mystery Magazine*, July 1985)

Two on the Isle (*Ellery Queen's Mystery Magazine*, Jan 1987)

The Lady Macbeth Case (*Ellery Queen's Mystery Magazine*, Nov 1990)